I0822256

ENCHANTRESS RISING
BOOK 1

# OF GRYPHONS AND RUNES

E.A. BURNETT

www.eaburnett.com

Book Cover: Miblart, Blue Raven Book Covers (laminate hardback)

Map: Hanna Sandvig

Editors: Fiona McLaren, Devil in the Details

First Edition

ISBN: 979-8-9899716-3-3

CONTENT WARNING:
References to past domestic violence and child abuse; animal abuse; some violence.

STEAM LEVEL:
moderate, open-door

This novel is rated as New Adult (18+ years)

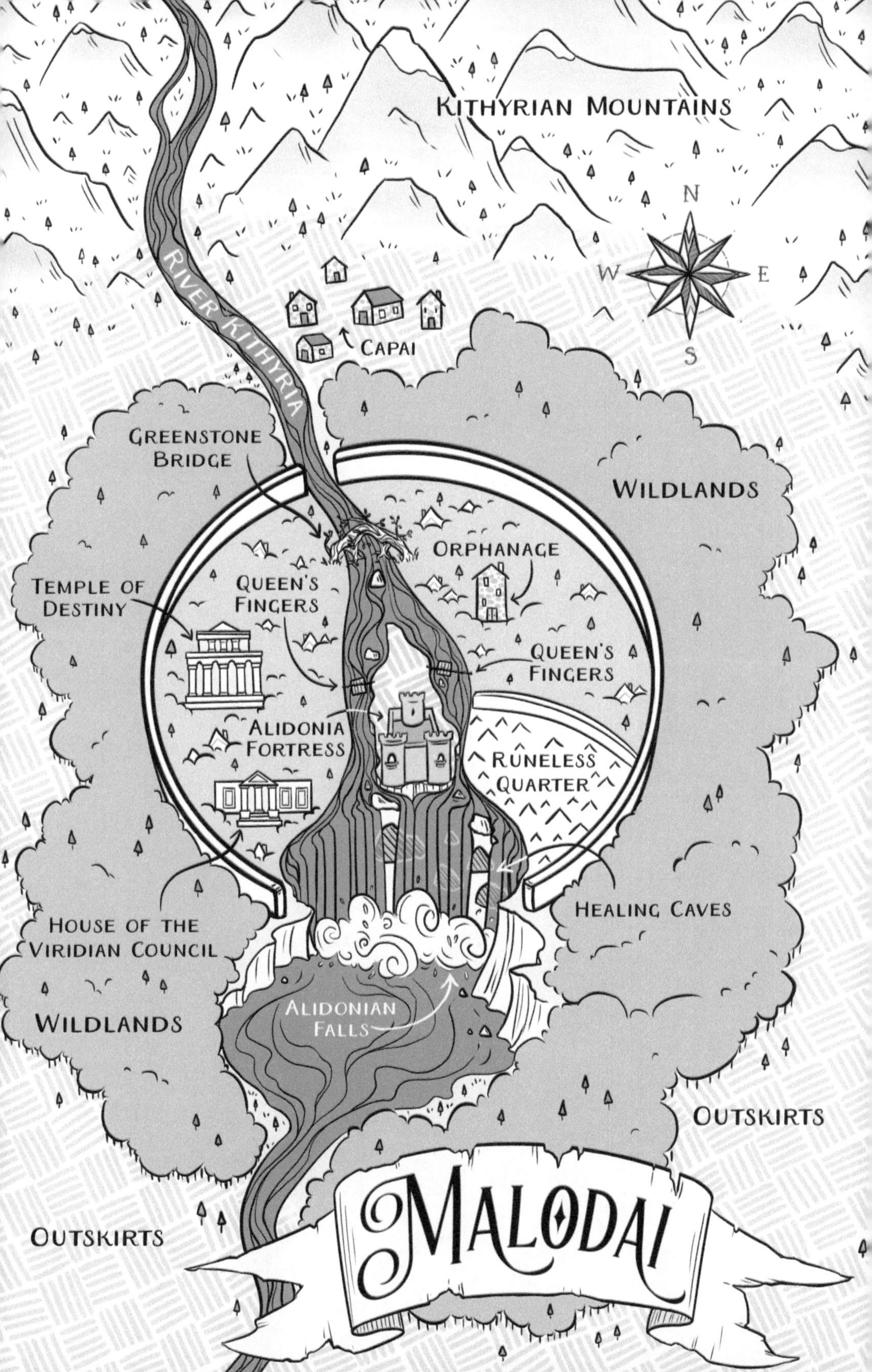
Kithyrian Mountains
N
W
E
S
River Kithyria
Capai
Greenstone Bridge
Wildlands
Orphanage
Temple of Destiny
Queen's Fingers
Queen's Fingers
Alidonia Fortress
Runeless Quarter
Healing Caves
House of the Viridian Council
Alidonian Falls
Wildlands
Outskirts
Malodai
Outskirts

## BY E.A. BURNETT

**SILVERGLEN WORLD**
Silverglen
Isle of Wings
The Sash-Maker and the Contradictory Queen*
Egg Thief* (prequel to Isle of Wings)

**ENCHANTRESS RISING WORLD**
Enchantress Rising Trilogy:
The Gryphon Key* (prequel novella)
Of Gryphons and Runes (Book One)

*Stories exclusive to E.A. Burnett's mailing list

For those who have lived with deep fear. For those who have overcome it, and for those who have yet to.

# PROLOGUE

FARREN BLACKBURN CLENCHED THE three hard-earned coins in her damp palm, grinning as beads of sweat trickled down her back. She had earned a few bruises in the fight too. However, she had still managed to win two rounds in a row—no easy feat considering both her opponents had been *Mustelids*, as feisty and aggressive as the weasels and badgers they runebonded with.

They had been nothing like Desmond though. From her vantage point atop a wooden fence, Farren scanned the crowds around the sparring rings for signs of her little brother. The village streets were packed; everyone had turned out for Demithya's Spring Festival, honoring the long-gone Enchantress with songs, dancing, and games.

When she saw no sign of her brother, she grit her teeth. *Stay right here*, she had told him before stepping into the circle. Of course, he had to wander off, probably curious about someone or something he had seen. Either that, or he was stuffing himself with honeyed puffbread and fried cheese balls.

She slid off the fence and edged around the sparring circles, moving through the cheering crowds drenched in colorful chitons. The smell of sweat mingled with the plump scent of bellhorn blossoms. Woodsmoke drifted in the air, as did the comforting musk of animal.

Farren maneuvered past stands selling treats and little wooden statues of the Enchantress Demithya embracing lambs and fox kits, through a small herd of children chasing a poor kid goat, and almost reached the trail leading to the woods when a slight figure dropped from a dewfall tree so close she felt the brush of his chiton.

Des landed nimbly on sandaled feet, a grin spreading from ear to ear as an impish coil of pale hair flopped into oak-brown eyes.

He was four years younger than her nineteen, but his slender frame towered over hers. The height difference—and her dark hair—were two painful reminders that Farren hadn't been born into their family.

"Gotcha," he said.

Farren crossed her arms as he held a hand up toward the lowest branch. A small black nose and two beady eyes peered down at her before the mink jumped off and landed on his hand.

"Why aren't you by the sparring circles?" she asked.

Two more minks plunked down from the tree, scurrying around his body before diving into pockets—of which there were no less than ten stitched into his worn knee-length chiton.

Des shrugged with his nonchalance. "I told you I wanted to watch the swim races."

"Des, we can go there after I finish sparring."

"And when will that be?"

"I'm going to try two more rounds. I might even earn enough to finish saving for my skin painting."

He moaned. "I'm missing everything interesting!"

"You're the only one here who thinks sparring isn't interesting."

"I've spent half my life watching you spar. It's all punches and kicks and grunting, and then you usually win. How is that interesting?"

Farren sighed. Although somewhat athletic himself, Desmond's true love involved anything about the world outside their village—be it found in books, people-watching, or picking a debate with an outsider. He could never understand why Farren chose to stay since she was old enough to work in the city of Malodai.

"I know you're tired of it. But you know what Mam said. She'll be furious with me if she finds out you went somewhere alone, and you know some nosy neighbor will tell her."

Des scoffed and shook his head. "I don't get what she's afraid of. Nothing ever happens in Capai."

"It doesn't matter. I'll try to make the sparring quick, but no promises. Now, please stay where I can see you."

"I heard there were folks from Malodai visiting for the festival," Desmond said as they headed back through the crowd. "Someone from the royal family, even."

Farren snorted. "Are you hoping to see a princess?"

Des' cheeks darkened to the shade of plumberries. "Don't be stupid. There aren't any princesses. Only princes." He waggled his brows at her.

"Well, I won't be paying any attention if they come around. I've got more earning to do." She flashed her coins at him.

His gaze lit. "Aw, three dremma? Mam only gave me one. What am I supposed to buy with that?"

"Get a statue of Demithya," Farren said. "And be glad she gave you coin at all."

His whining fizzled, and his gaze went soft. "Right, sorry."

"Don't do that, silly. No pity, remember?" She wasn't Mam's bloodchild, after all, and had been dealing with Mam's stiffness toward her since Da had brought her into their home at seven. "Now, come on, the next round is about to start. Don't you want to watch me kick some ass?"

"Fine, fine," Des sighed, pressing through the crowd with elbows out to protect his minks. "But only two rounds and then..." He sniffed loudly as a waft of roasted meat sang into the air. "Stewed goat...buttered flatbread...and spiced toma sauce."

His eyes widened as he searched for the source, and he practically drooled. They had just eaten before venturing into the streets a couple hours ago, but of course Des was hungry again. And a meal like that would cost more than a single dremma.

Farren sighed and held out her coins. "Take them."

He stared at her as if she were an Enchantress. "Really?"

"Really. Before I change my mind."

He squinted at her, though she could hear the minks chittering excitedly from the folds of his chiton. "I won't owe you anything later?"

"It'll be enough to not hear you complain about how hungry you are a thousand times before supper."

Des took the coins. "You're the best."

"I'm going back to the sparring rings," Farren said. "Get your food and come right back there. After, we'll go to the swim races."

"And hopefully, get a glimpse of these royals. I bet they're wearing silk chitons and smell of gold. Do you think they would talk to me?"

"They're people, Des, just like us."

"Just wealthier. And well-read. And more worldly. I've heard they even keep gryphons as pets."

"You listen to far too much gossip."

"We'll see about that." He sprinted toward the food stand, and Farren glimpsed the black nose and white chin of one of his minks peeking from a pocket as he disappeared into the crowd.

Farren had heard rumors about gryphons, too. She was never sure what to believe. But Da had told her the only surviving gryphons lived far to the east in the Blades—a cluster of knife-like mountains devoid of humans. Ancient gryphon remains had been found in the rolling mountains around their little village, but the massive bones were so old they crumbled to dust when touched. Because the beasts were half bird, half lion, it was said both *Avids* and *Felids* could runebond with them. *Avids*, like herself.

She shivered, then reached her mind up to one of the trees overhead, stretching her runeskill out until she sensed the small silver sphere of a golden sparrow's mind.

*Many creatures*, the sparrow said, a rudimentary phrase paired with a series of images that flashed through Farren's mind. People. Goats. Minks and beavers, dogs, turtles, snakes, and a purple cloud of silk moths.

*My brother*, Farren told the sparrow, sending him an image of Desmond's face. *Can you follow him?*

*Yes, yes, yes!* The sparrow chittered high up in the branches. Sparrows were always eager helpers; she hardly ever had to bribe them. The birds liked the attention, and the feeling of importance that went with helping humans.

*If he goes far, come get me.* The bird would be able to follow her mind, even if she had their runebond closed, which she certainly would have to do if she was to focus on sparring.

*Yes, come get you!*

Farren sent the sparrow a wave of pleasure and happiness, and the bird sang a lovely little tune before darting after her brother. Through the moving crowd, Farren could see him already scarfing down the food. At least that would buy her a minute or two.

When she entered the sparring circle, a rush of voices rose as bets were made, and she stretched her arms, waiting for her opponent to enter. She knew most in the crowd—villagers whom she had grown up with, who had witnessed her fighting skills improve over the years, both from Brin's advice and from her hard work. They had grown more confident in her abilities and now put their faith in her as they wagered coin. She owed them another win. Some of them had been watching her since the very beginning. Even the critical among them had softened to her, realized she might be more than they expected. Despite not being born there. Despite being an outsider.

With this sparring contest and the upcoming ones in midsummer, she might have enough coin to finally pay for a half-decent skin painting. Most received their first skin painting at the celebration of a rune rising—when a child's runeskill, known at birth, has matured enough to be used. Farren had already experienced her rune rising—although she couldn't remember it—before Brin had taken her in. She and Brin had been saving for her skin painting for years so that one day, she could wear proof of dedication to her runeskill like everyone else.

Beyond the bustling streets and cottages of the village, the forested mountains spread around them, trees alluring with the bright green of young leaves. She drank in the sight. The tall, dense forest and formidable mountains rising to the sky pressed their strength upon her. They lent her certainty. Familiarity. They were her first memories, after all. One breath of the mountain spring air was all it took to make her feel centered and focused.

"Let's get on with it, then," a voice said behind her.

Heat darted straight up to her cheeks. She dropped her arms and turned to face the young man who had stepped into the circle behind her, heart flit-fluttering like a wounded sparrow.

"Thestor."

"And you are...?"

Her fingers curled tight. "I'll let you think on it a while."

He stretched his arms, which rippled with muscle. "Have we sparred before?"

"More than sparred, I'm afraid." The crowd hushed a bit at that, and Farren bit her tongue.

Those muddy brown eyes hammered into her. "I guess I forgot."

Cursed *Avid*. She stalked up to him and dropped low into a fighting stance. "Let me help you remember," she said quietly, barely audible above the noise from the crowd. "It was only a few weeks ago. We sparred, and I won. Then we went to the olive grove."

The moon had shone that night through the olive trees, striking his dark eyes and turning his copper skin to gold. They had only drank a little honeyed mead, caressed each other while the scent of sweet olive blossoms kissed the air. It hadn't been her first time, thank the Enchanters. It would've been harder to bear what had come afterward.

Thestor's lips twitched as he angled himself for the fight. "I don't remember ever losing to a girl."

Farren nodded, playing along. "That's fair. Some boys have a hard time accepting it. But you can't deny rolling in the grove with me. I'll never forget how excited you were. How short and rigid—"

His face reddened, and he hissed at her, throwing a jab. Farren jerked to the right, glee spreading through her as he narrowly missed.

"Enchanters curse you, Farren Blackburn," he spat, jabbing again.

"I thought you might remember after that."

"Honestly, it's a bit of a blur." He did a double jab, which she parried smartly. "I've slept with lots of girls out there."

It was her turn to strike. Her pride still stung that she had gone with him. That she had actually thought he was interested in her and hadn't just been trying to get back at her for losing.

Her fist dug into the firm plane of his torso, and he grimaced.

"I mostly remember," he said, panting now, "that you were just like all the others. Destined to be some boring mam with too many kids running around."

His arm shot out, and his fist connected with the space just below her sternum. The air knocked out of her, but she still managed to raise her arm to block his next attack, aimed straight at her face.

"I do remember thinking how small you were though," he continued, backing away a step. "Pint-sized. I was surprised you could even fit around my—"

Farren didn't let him finish. She leapt and sent the powerful force of a front kick into his belly. He fell on the dirt, and she pinned his sweaty arm with a knee and flattened herself against his chest and neck so that he couldn't budge. Around them, the crowd hooted. Thestor ground his teeth and glared at her as he struggled.

"Size isn't everything," Farren told him. "You pretended to forget me after our little meeting. As if I didn't exist. You won't make that mistake again."

As the cheerful ring of the sparring bell signaled the winner, something darted in front of her. At first, she thought Thestor was breaking the rules by getting a bird to harass her, but it was the golden-winged sparrow she had spoken to earlier.

Farren released Thestor and connected with the bird, calming it enough to where it fluttered out from beneath her nose.

*He is going far! Going far!* The sparrow sent her a confused cascade of images: Desmond leaving the crowded sparring circles, a street filled with silken figures walking toward him, a giant beast towering above the people—a beast made of feather and fur.

Shouts resounded from out on the street. Farren lunged through the crowd and clambered onto the nearest wooden fence to scan the thoroughfare, searching for sign of—

Breath whooshed out of her.

A gryphon walked down the street among the silken figures flanked by orange-cloaked guards. The beast stood twice as large as a horse, with feathers painted red and gold and talons the length of a sword. Tawny fur rippled as it moved, and cold eyes glared above a beak that looked powerful enough to break stone. A thick chain attached to a metal collar that wrapped the beast's neck.

It was the most beautiful and terrifying creature Farren had ever seen.

A tremor swept through her. The people near the gryphon kept their distance from it, except for the one holding the chain. His expression was proud and distant.

A figure moved in from the side of the street and lifted a hand toward the gryphon's tawny shoulder.

A curious, gentle hand.

Desmond's hand.

The beast saw his hand in the same moment that Farren stretched her mind toward it, the molten sphere of its mind unfamiliar and too large and too complex, but she wrenched their runebond open. Anger ripped through her, and her fear flooded up into the connection, and she tried—she screamed—for the gryphon to leave her brother alone.

But her words drowned in a scouring wave of hatred. The gryphon's beak came down like an axe onto Desmond's head. The crowd jumped back from the beast, and a shrill cry resounded in the air as Desmond's head twisted.

Farren had already begun moving, surging through the crowd like a gossamer hawk in a dense forest. She would catch him. Shelter him from the monster. He would live because if he didn't—

Her brother crumpled to the ground.

*Too late, fool.* The voice from the runebond seared into her, and she yanked the connection closed.

Rivulets of blood ran down Desmond's face and neck. The crowd fell back as she knelt to pick him up, throat burning as she screamed for help. He was light, so light, and blood spilled everywhere—bright and warm and too slippery as she pressed on the gash along the side of his head.

Clutching him against her chest, she screeched at the crowd, the stupid crowd who remained still and watched as if the entire world wasn't shuddering. The royals watched, too, unmoving in their silk and brocade chitons. Why was no one helping? Were they all under a spell?

Desmond didn't open his eyes; he barely seemed to breathe. A strange tremor shook his limbs like brittle trees in a fall wind. When would the blood stop seeping?

"Here, child," a voice said, and Farren turned to a white-robed woman. A healer. "We'll take him to the infirmary."

"My brother's been bitten," Farren said, her voice high and thin.

Grateful. She was so grateful when the healer took her brother. The woman's capable hands worked rapidly to wrap a bandage tight around his head. Farren stood on uneasy legs. Desmond's trembling had ceased, but his eyes remained closed.

"What happened?" the healer asked.

Farren's tongue stuck to the roof of her mouth. "The gryphon... It attacked him."

Before the healer could respond, a man guffawed. "Attacked? He was *provoked*, girl. The boy made the beast feel threatened."

The man who had spoken was the one holding the gryphon's chain—a tall, dark-haired man with cruel eyes and a twisting mouth. He had lingered there, watching the proceeding with mild interest. The beast next to him glared down at them, breath bellowing from its bloodied beak and limbs quivering slightly. The chain keeping it captive was taut.

Farren didn't doubt that it wanted to do more harm.

"He was reaching to t-touch the beast," Farren got out. "He had no weapons. He's just a child—"

"And this one is an animal. What do you expect? The boy was a fool for getting so close to something that might harm him."

"He was just...curious. Is that so awful?" Farren's voice wobbled. Her entire body shook as she clenched her sticky-slick hands. "Do you have so little control over your beast?"

The man shrugged. "I could have stopped him. But I decided the boy needed a lesson."

She stepped toward him. "How dare you—"

A guard pressed a hand solidly into her chest, stopping her in her tracks.

"Try to threaten me," the man said, his mouth twisting savagely to the side. "Then I'll have a reason to put you in prison, which would be so unfortunate since you would miss your brother's funeral."

The guard pushed her back, and she stumbled. "Make way for Prince Anaxis," the guard ordered.

"Girl," the healer called, "are you coming?"

The healer and several others who had appeared had moved Desmond onto a litter dragged by a donkey. They had already started down the street. Farren propelled her unsteady legs to follow.

The scratch of talons on the flagstones sent a shiver coursing down her spine. She followed the healers and never took her eyes from Desmond's too-still face.

# ONE

THE SUMMER STORM RUINED Farren's plans. It shouldered into the midafternoon sky, darkening the world with growls and fire-lit cracks. The torrid rain turned the steep mountainsides into muddy rivulets.

When the storm swept away, the sun shone between the mountain peaks and warmed the rain-soaked forest until mist lifted off the emerald leaves and the air grew heavy with the scent of wet humus.

All around her, water plopped and splattered. The roar of the nearby flooded gorge made her skin prickle. After an unsuccessful hunting venture that morning, Farren had been keen to get out with her hawk again after they had rested. But with the gorge now flooded, her usual route over the river—a series of stones and a water-smoothed log—would be completely submerged beneath rising rapids. There was no other way to get across to her favorite hunting spot full of brush and rabbits, at least not one she could reach and hunt before dark.

She clutched the thin strip of her hawk's leather leash, trying to ground herself in the gentle pressure of her hawk's talons on her gloved fist. A closer area would have to suffice for hunting today, meaning less brush and fewer rabbits.

Farren sighed and stepped out from beneath the stony stoop of her cave and slipped in a patch of mud, catching herself before she could fall. Mellion flapped tawny wings in protest, and Farren caught a thread of disgruntlement through the narrowed channel of their runebond. She waited until Mellion steadied on her arm before widening the runebond enough for her hawk to speak with her, wincing as Mellion's frustration flushed through her.

*Sorry, lady*, Farren said.

*I would've warned you about that,* Mellion responded tartly, sending an impression with an image of the mud before Farren stepped in it.

*You know I prefer to only runebond fully while hunting.*

Mellion shook her head, bristling the feathers around her face and neck. *I liked it better before. It was fun and...* She felt Mellion struggle for the words, but some things were too complicated for the bird to put words to. Instead, a series of images flickered through the runebond—Mellion and Farren enjoying the sunrise together while sharing impressions of the colors; when Farren had her first taste of bitterwort tea and tried to explain to Mellion how terrible it tasted; and, in the spring, when Farren prepared to go to Demithya's Festival and attempted to convince Mellion that it was fun to spar with peers.

Farren's heart ached. They had discussed this too many times to count over the past few months. Each time felt more difficult than the last.

*I know you miss that,* she said. *But I can't do that all the time.*

*Does it hurt?*

No, Farren said, knowing Mellion was likely confused by the pain she could sense in Farren. She stepped carefully down the slick path that led away from her home and into the western woods.

Mellion hunched forward, peering from Farren to the forest around her. Torn between her friend and her dinner.

*I need practice,* Farren explained. *With the runeskill. With control. I can't be...lax with it any longer.*

*Lax?*

Farren chewed her cheek. *I need to be stronger. More skill.* To emphasize the point, she sent Mellion an impression of a young hawk trying to pin a rabbit. The rabbit wrestled itself away from the inexperienced bird.

*Stronger,* Mellion said, bobbing her head as if in understanding. *To kill the rabbit.*

*Strong enough not to lose it,* Farren gently corrected. Unbidden, the memory of the gryphon rose, and Farren quickly closed her runebond, not wanting the sudden rush of cold and heavy feelings to hit Mellion. She had shared enough of that day with Mellion during the weeks following the attack and didn't want to spoil their chances of a successful hunt now.

The soft ground mushed and churned beneath her leather sandals, and the wet shrubs soaked her leggings and shortened chiton. Farren veered northwest, where the woods thinned slightly and the slope rose to drier land.

Soon, it would be snow rather than mud they would have to worry about. And bitter cold nights. She had lots of planning to do. Like how she would get warm clothes and enough food to last the winter in the Kithyrian Mountains. Whether she should try to build herself and Mellion a real shelter so that they wouldn't have to sleep in a drafty cave. Being nineteen years old, Farren had spent many summers with her father in the Kithyrian Mountains and out in the Wildlands surrounding the city of Malodai, learning to live in the forests while they trapped young hawks to train. It was one of the reasons her father hadn't forbidden her from leaving home, as much as it had upset him. He knew she could take care of herself.

A field opened up before them, and Mellion shivered in anticipation. From the trees on the edge of the field, sparrows peered at them, their chatter growing agitated as they spotted her hawk.

Farren runebonded with Mellion once more and sent a memory—a series of impressions—so that Mellion would remember, too. Closer to their cave home, a flock of sparrows had chased her hawk, furious at her proximity to their nests. Mellion had played along for a bit, easily evading their reach, and then, at the last minute, had turned talons on them, sending them back into their shrubs. Mellion's smug satisfaction had made Farren laugh.

*You served them right, didn't you, lady?*

*It was only right with all their pecking and shrieking,* the hawk replied, making a guttural clucking noise Farren always took for laughter, her golden eyes gleaming as amusement rippled through their runebond.

Enchanters, she was lucky to have Mellion with her. Even though Farren kept their runebond narrowed most of the time, their bond was enough to ward off loneliness at night, enough that Mellion's fleeting impressions kept Farren sane in the quietude of the mountains. Farren still remembered keenly the moment she had first seen Mellion as a fat chick sitting up in her nest, screeching down her rage that someone was close by. It had taken weeks for Farren to break through that distrust and months still before she could fly Mellion on a creance. But once they had trusted each other—once Mellion stopped biting her glove and returned every time Farren called her—their bond had been unshakable.

Farren's stomach growled, startling them both. That midday supper of hazelnuts and dried plumberries hadn't lasted very long. She had given the rest of the rabbit to Mellion last night—as she had many of the nights since Mellion's molt began in late spring—to ensure that her new feathers grew healthy and strong. Farren had eaten whatever remained of the morsels of stale biscuit she had bought on her last trip to the village weeks ago.

She lifted her arm, and Mellion surged into the air, heading for a tall aspen from which she would keep watch for movement below. Farren grabbed a long stick and narrowed her runebond, leaving it open just enough that she could sense the honed edge of Mellion's eagerness.

Sweat gathered beneath her light linen chiton as she whipped at the grass, stalking back and forth to rouse any hiding rabbits. She didn't mind the sweat, the lazy hum of mosquitoes, or even the soft burn spreading through her thighs as she parted the grasses. It gave her succor and made her forget the clawing hunger in her belly. And for a time, curbed the ache in her heart that slept with her at night.

She had left home a few months ago when the healer told her family that Desmond's wounds had healed. But that hadn't been the truth because the gryphon who had attacked her brother had changed him forever, and there was nothing she could do about it. There was no going back to the way he was. She had been telling herself that since she had looked into Desmond's face and saw his confusion, the way he crumpled when there was too much noise, too much activity: the very opposite of how her life-loving, fifteen-year-old brother used to be.

And it was all her fault.

So she had fled to the Kithyrian Mountains north of Capai, knowing her brother would be better off if she was gone, ashamed that she couldn't bear to see the way he was now. It was best this way, with her parents keeping Desmond safe at home, helping him cope with his wounds. She had only returned to Capai a few times over the summer to get supplies and meet with her father at the village inn—but never returned to her old home. Da was always glad to see her, and she would ask about Des and how they were all doing. She would say whatever she could to soothe her father, to keep him from worry.

Something skittered just ahead. Farren glimpsed the brown fuzzy bottom of a mountain rabbit. Mellion's vision narrowed to a point. She took off and followed the rabbit as it darted from one grass clump to another to seek refuge. Farren chased it, flaying the sedges with her stick, pulse quickening every time she spotted fur through the viridian grass. It was a plump rabbit, and strong, too.

Mellion circled overhead and waited for the right moment while Farren prodded the rabbit uphill, not wanting it to head down to the heavy cover of thickets. Farren blinked, and the rabbit disappeared behind a cluster of boulders.

*Wait*, she told Mellion, proud when her hawk landed in a tree to watch her.

Farren scrambled up a boulder and hung over the edge to poke the shadowed fissures below. Nothing happened. She followed the great cracks between the stones, tapping the stick as far down as she could reach. The rabbit was likely laying low, knowing it was untouchable down there.

She was about to give up when Mellion's surge of excitement hit her. The rabbit burst from the boulders and sprinted for the thickets at the edge of the field, risking an open knoll with a single tree for cover. Without hesitation, Mellion dove. Farren jumped across the boulders, not needing to watch as she felt Mellion hit the rabbit with precision. Satisfaction washed through her runebond when the hawk's talons sank into the rabbit's chest. Powerful legs kicked, and the rabbit broke free from one of Mellion's talons.

Breathless, Farren reached the other side of the boulders, scratching her palms as she hung from the side and dropped down into a clump of shrubs.

Mellion half-hopped, half-flew as the rabbit thrust away until it finally wrenched out of her grasp and dove into the thickets beyond the knoll. Ripping through the shrubbery, Farren sent her hawk a wave of reassurance.

*You did your best*, she told Mellion. *We'll likely get another before sunset—*

A sharp jab of pain made Farren falter. Mellion's talon was caught and hurting, something burning up her small, feathered body. Pain seared Farren's mind, and she dropped to the ground, trying to see her hawk through the chaos of her runebond. Through jagged shrubs, Mellion's wings fluttered madly on the ground.

*Be calm*, Farren urged her, panic rising in her throat.

Mellion struggled in agony, but whatever had hold of her wouldn't let go. It dragged her down like a lead weight, impossibly heavy, and consumed her little by little.

Farren crawled forward, fingers bleeding as they dug into the hard ground. Mellion screamed and thrashed beneath the tree on the knoll. *Get up, get up!*

Mellion's fear fled like a sparrow's cry swept away in the furious blast of a gale. Emptiness replaced it; the runebond had been severed. Nothing moved on the grassy knoll, and the stillness caused bile to rise in Farren's throat. She stumbled to where Mellion stood on the ground, beak gaping and wings poised in the air, stiff as a wool-stuffed mount. Her talon touched a flower with bloodred petals.

Farren circled the hawk, trying to comprehend what her eyes were seeing. Mellion didn't move but looked as alive as ever. Her brown eyes shone, her slender tongue glistened, and the ruddy tint of her wings gleamed in the sun. Even the flower beneath her talon looked alive. Perfect. At any moment, it looked as if Mellion would twitch a muscle. Her wings would suddenly beat the air, she would race to Farren's arm just as she always had and give a soft *chirrup* of relief in her ear.

But she didn't.

Her hawk and the flower didn't so much as tremble in the wake of Farren's breath. Beneath the shadow of Mellion's talon, a bee nestled in a scarlet fold of petals. It didn't move, either. Buttery pollen dusted its body. Farren reached out and touched it.

A rush of heat pulled at her, penetrated past skin and bones, and hunted down and down to the very runes that made her. It wanted to spread like wildfire, to leave only emptiness in its path. For a breath of a moment, something shifted inside Farren—a twitch so deep it seemed to come from beneath her rune-made soul.

She jerked away, gasping at the tingling pain in her arm, and scrambled back from the bird-flower statue. A statue like ice, but hot rather than cold. Emptiness where there should be rune-filled life.

A strange, impossible disease. Farren racked her mind, thinking of all the diseases she knew of that affected birds, but nothing came close to this.

Maybe she had felt it wrong. Or misunderstood it somehow. Her runebond had been drowning in Mellion's fear, so she might have missed something. It wouldn't be the first time her bond with birds prevented her from thinking clearly.

Farren dug her fingers against the ground, oblivious to the sharp stones cutting through the thin soil. Mellion blurred for a moment, lost beneath a sudden tide Farren couldn't quite catch hold of. She pressed her fingers deeper into the soil, using the pain to focus her mind. If her father were there, what would he say?

*Look for signs of dehydration, disease, stress. Check her keel, make sure she's not underweight. Has everything been normal—the mutes, breathing, and eating?*

But it all checked out. Farren had even given Mellion the larger share of caught food to support her emerging feathers post-molt. The only possibility was a sudden fit of apoplexy, which could kill a bird in minutes.

She might figure out more if she brought Mellion back to the cave and inspected her, just as her father would do at home. But the thought of touching Mellion again made her want to vomit.

Shaking, she forced herself to her feet, limbs loose twigs stranded together by thread. Mellion was her closest, most trustworthy hawk; Farren owed her more than abandonment. She needed to see her father. He was the only one who would know what had killed—or frozen—Mellion. And he would be willing to let her take one of the other hawks she trained so that she might have a chance of surviving the winter in the mountains.

Farren reached again for the connection with her hawk. Barrenness greeted her. A shiver slid down her back. No more of Mellion's amused chittering, no more breathtaking impressions of the hunt or those moments afterward when Mellion was vibrant with exultation at her kill. And worst of all, Farren would no longer find the warm embrace of Mellion's mind when she awoke.

She stood a moment more, memorizing Mellion's form, wanting to look away but unable to.

*I'm sorry I couldn't help you,* she told her hawk, speaking to the emptiness where their runebond had hummed between them. *Or give you a proper burial so that your runes can be released.*

Farren picked a nodding clump of daisies nearby, and as she crouched to lay them near Mellion's body, one of Mellion's golden feathers—broken loose by Mellion's panicked wing-flapping and caught in the grasses—twitched in the mountain breeze, almost as vivid as gold itself. Farren touched the feather, warmth flushing through her when all she felt were the soft, normal bristles of a feather. She picked it up and brushed it over her cheek, remembering all the moments when Mellion's wingtips had caressed her just so. Then she tucked the feather into a small pouch inside her satchel, where it would be safe and close.

Trembling, she turned from her hunting hawk and made her way back to their small camp, alone. Her stomach clenched. She was no longer hungry, and she didn't think she'd be able to eat again until she had answers.

She entered the small cave where she and Mellion had lived for the summer on their own and spent the remainder of the day packing their things. Beneath Mellion's perch, she swept up stray molted feathers and took them outside the cave. Next to a sturdy pika sapling, she dug a hole in the muddy ground and placed the feathers inside.

*May your runes be released and free to bless another*, Farren prayed, wondering whether Mellion's runes would release from her frozen body or if the disease had frozen her runes as well. Her father should know, but if he didn't...only the Enchanters who created their world would. And they were long, long gone, if they had ever existed at all.

Farren wiped her eyes and finished tidying the cave, thinking distantly that she would be back again with a new hawk and supplies to last through the winter. She just needed to focus on the future, the routine, on survival. And make sure she never took a hawk to that knoll again. Then she curled up on her bedroll with Mellion's golden feather clutched to her chest and let the grief roll through her. In the distance, owls shrieked at the forlorn night.

# TWO

Farren shifted her packs and winced at the ache in her shoulders. At least she had finally made it to the main road heading into the Outskirts of Malodai. The trek down from the Kithyrian Mountains had taken a whole day—long enough for her tears over Mellion to run out. Her hawk's death still rolled over and over in her mind, confusing shards of memories and impressions that refused to make sense.

The sight of her village nestled in the foothills calmed her nerves. Her village was one of many in the Outskirts—a fringe of land with farming villages that formed a near-perfect ring around the Wildlands of the great city of Malodai—but she had never seen a village as beautiful as Capai. Quaint homes made of stone and thatch sprawled along ambling dirt roads, cushioned by green-gold fields of crops and grazing pasture. Glittering rivers—the headwaters to the great River Kithyria—wandered between the hills like the seams of her patched leggings.

Her chest tightened at the sight of her home on the edge of the village, attached to a long mew outbuilding. So many of her childhood days had been spent in those mew stalls and out in the yard, flying a lure on a rope or watching the hawks bathe in shallow basins of water. She would hide in the tall grasses outside the weathering yard, basking in the sun while they stood on their posts with wings braced wide, drops of water falling like glass beads from their feather tips.

Through some spare trees, she saw her mother hanging laundry on the line. Her faithful badger—a creature Farren had always despised for its awful stench and tempestuous demeanor—lay close to her feet.

Her father would be in the mews, cleaning up from the day's trainings. Like Farren, her father was an *Avid*, holding a runeskill with birds since birth. A lucky thing, her father always said, since he had found Farren wandering in the woods alone as a young child. If it hadn't been for Farren's delight at the mews, he was certain she would've wandered off to be taken in by a different family. Farren hadn't believed him, of course. Meeting Brin had been the luckiest moment of her existence—when her real life had truly begun. What hungry, lost child who had no memories of her own parents could've refused the patient love and quietude that Brin had shown her?

Familiar laughter caused Farren to stop short. From behind the house, her brother ran full-tilt, flying a little paper kite. Three ink-black minks bounded after it.

Farren struggled to breathe. It was as if the accident had never happened. As if he were the same fifteen-year-old boy he had been before—energetic and full of questions about the world.

Her mother watched him, a hand covering her grin as if she could hold it in and never let it escape. Because it could take only a moment before Desmond's mood shifted. Still, Farren wondered if her mother had ever looked at her that way, with joy. She could only remember a persistent, chilled distance, which had soured into resentment after the accident.

Farren veered away and headed into the center of the village. She would visit her friend Keira first before sending word to her father to meet her. Keira might know something about the disease that attacked Mellion since she was a skilled *Planteri* and had more knowledge about plants than anyone Farren knew.

Keira's home was a compact stone building tucked between a bakery and a chandlery. A garden plot framed the doorway to the front—the entrance to her shop—and emerald cinnaferns spiced the air as Farren went inside. Cluttered shelves lined the walls, and bundles of herbs hung from the rafters. Every window ledge brimmed with potted plants.

In the far corner of the room, Keira's slender form bent over a potted, dark-leaved tree. Finger-length spines ran along its spindly trunk. She stared intently at it, seeming oblivious to the noises of children coming from the back of the house. She had heard the door, however, as Farren shut it.

"Be with you in just a minute," she said, not taking her eyes from the plant.

In moments, buds formed among the leaves. They grew heavy and fat, then peeled open to reveal dazzling blue petals the size of Farren's palms. A delicate sapphire scent touched Farren's nose and reached into her, lifting her mind and body.

"Just beautiful," Keira murmured, and the petals seemed to brighten under her gaze.

With thick brown hair, rosy-gold skin, and a pretty smile, Keira was as beautiful as the flowers she bloomed. She had used her runeskill as a *Planteri* to build her livelihood, supporting her family with the little apothecary. Although she was nearly eight years older than Farren, it had always felt as though they were just a few years apart and as close as blood sisters. Being separated from Keira hadn't hurt any less than being apart from her family.

Farren forced down the sudden knot in her throat. "What is that one called, then?"

Keira whipped around, eyes warm and bright as she grinned. "Farren! I thought you were a wraith for a moment. You look famished. Shall I call Benny to fetch you something? He and the children are playing a game of seek-and-find."

"No, don't. Let them play." Farren set her packs on the floor, and Keira pulled her into a tight embrace. The spice of cinnafern was a salve to Farren's grief over Mellion. She studied Keira's dark hair, twisted into a bun, and the finely detailed fern frond imprinted all the way around her neck.

"This is beautiful," Farren said, touching the dark green markings, wondering how painful it must've been. Wishing she had been there with Keira as her skin was needled with colors, as a good friend would've been. "When did you get it?"

"Weeks ago. It was a gift from Benny. He saved up during his two years of Servitude at Alidonia so that he could pay a traveling skin painter." Keira pulled back, smiling at her. "Weren't you saving up for your own? Did you ever get it?"

"I used the money to pay Desmond's healer for the surgery."

"Oh," Keira said, squeezing her arms. "I'm so sorry."

"I don't regret it," Farren said. Her father had been hesitant to spend it after years of saving with her, saying he could pay the healer on his own. Farren had pushed it on him anyways. She would take bare skin for a lifetime if it meant keeping Desmond alive.

"Of course not," Keira said easily. "Enchanted skies, it's been forever since I've seen you. So much has happened."

Although Farren returned to Capai every few weeks, she had only stopped at the local inn to meet with her father and hadn't seen Keira since she left her home in the spring. With the shop and all the children, Keira had her hands full, and Farren hadn't wanted to bother her.

She assessed Farren through slitted eyes, her smile faltering. "You look like you've been crying. What's the matter?"

Farren brushed at her cheeks, brittle with dried tears. "It's Mellion. She died yesterday."

"I'm so sorry, Farren. I know you loved that bird."

"That's actually part of the reason why I came," Farren said, her throat working.

Keira studied her a moment, lips pursed. "Here, come sit." She motioned to the sturdy wooden counter and pulled out a stool from behind it. Then she went to the shop door and flipped the sign to tell customers it was closed.

"Oh, you don't need to do that, Keira—"

"Nonsense. You rest, and we will chat. I'm doing well enough that I can be closed for a bit today." She bustled back behind the counter, where a wood stove was already hot with a pot of something steaming. She pulled out another pot and filled it with water from a clay pitcher, set it on the stove, and sprinkled some herbs inside. "Tell me what happened, Farren. Was it another animal that hurt Mellion?"

Despite the warmth emanating from the wood stove, Farren's skin prickled. "It-it was some sort of disease I've never seen before. Do you know of a flower that can freeze things? Make them...like ice?"

"No," Keira said, frowning as she stirred one of the pots. "That doesn't sound possible."

"Mellion touched the flower. I tried touching it, too, and it was as if everything I am, all of my runes, were being pulled out of me."

"Enchanted skies," Keira breathed. "Are you sure it was a flower? Not something else, something to do with the bird?"

"I'm going to see if my father knows anything about it. Maybe it's a disease, or..." Farren shook her head, at a loss.

"You were...runebonded with her when she passed?"

Farren nodded, not wanting to recall the awful sensation of fire and terror clawing its way through Mellion.

"That must've been difficult." Keira went to her tree and plucked three of the sapphire petals, then dropped them in the pot of simmering water. She sat quietly with Farren while the herbs steeped, then poured them both a hot cup of it.

Farren picked up the clay cup, the liquid inside as blue as an afternoon sky. "This won't force me to feel happy, will it?" Farren teased, knowing Keira always had the best intentions at heart.

Her friend chuckled. "Something to ease the pain, that's all. Did you want anything else? I have a cheer-balm, or a healing salve with infused calm, a sleeping tincture, a lover's lotion—"

"What in the Enchanters' Realms would I need that for, Keira?"

Keira laughed, and Farren swore every plant in the shop leaned toward the jingle of it. "Just in case you met someone while you were away."

"Someone I needed desperately to fall in love with me?"

"It's not for love, silly," Keira said. "It's for *lust*."

"Oh, right. I'll definitely need that."

"Well, you are a little bony. I'd like to feed you."

Farren couldn't stop her laughter. "Why not just give me a hunger potion? Then I would actually want to eat."

For a moment, Keira's mirth flickered, and she motioned for Farren to drink the tea. They sipped in unison. The liquid tingled over her tongue before traveling down and down, all the way to her toes. Warming them...lifting them.

"You missed Capilion's Sun Festival," Keira said.

Even though the Enchanters were gone—to sleep in the Kithyrian Mountains, some said, or dead, if they hadn't abandoned humans altogether for a better land—everyone celebrated them with festivals and temple offerings. At the end of those long, celebratory nights in her village, Keira's aged grandmother would sit up in the dark, playing a sad melody on her flute so that it floated high over the fields and into the feet of the mountains. The old woman believed the Enchanters could hear her songs and that the music would one day draw them back.

"How was it?" Farren asked. Even her throat felt softer somehow, her voice floating like a feather.

"Good. There were the usual peddlers with citron fruits from Ibezia—that's where I got the *zifulsa* tree from," she said, nodding to the prickly tree full of blue flowers. "A beauty, in and out, and completely worth the cost. Let's see...there were the horse sellers, the traveling minstrels and performers, all the usual things. It was busier than Demithya's spring festival, but the fighting matches weren't nearly as interesting without you."

"Yeah?" Farren chuckled, her cheeks heating. "I do miss throwing six-foot boys on their bums." That exquisite look of surprise mingled with shame and begrudging respect.

Farren had quickly fallen in love with sparring after her father had begun teaching her years ago. She loved the challenge of it, the thrill of what her body could do, and the way she felt after, covered in sweat and her muscles burning with sweet heat. And there was something else, too, that she missed: the intimacy of it. Wrestling had taught her all about boys' bodies, particular weaknesses or strengths they had, and how their patterns of thought were revealed by the smallest of movements.

Farren took a few more sips of tea and felt the clouds in her chest breaking apart, drifting away. "I'm sure there were other girls there to remind the boys what we're capable of."

"None of them had quite your tenacity," Keira replied. "Anyways, we had a good deal of city folk and all their trappings. Benny recognized the royals from his Years of Servitude to the crown—the eldest prince came to visit."

Farren nearly choked on her drink. "The eldest prince? Do you mean Prince Anaxis?" The very name filled her heart with hate.

"Of course, you've been isolated so you wouldn't have heard," Keira said hesitantly. "While you were away...the king and Prince Anaxis died."

Farren's heart thundered. "What? How?"

"The rumors say the king fell down a set of stairs. And the prince... It's said that he was killed by his own gryphons. I'm sure it's not true—"

"I believe it," Farren said, gripping her cup as she fought a sudden trembling in her hands. Anaxis, the man whose gryphon had nearly killed Desmond. Dead.

After the attack, Farren had just wanted to hurt him. But a guard had caught her before she got too close to the man, and after he put her down, some of the anger had left her. Some of it turned inward. Knowing the man was gone now and his haughty carelessness with him made her eyes burn. She closed them and sipped her tea, silently thanking the Enchanters—if indeed they were still alive and could hear her.

Keira's warm touch on her arm startled her. "How are you feeling?"

Farren gave her friend a wobbly smile. "I don't know. Relieved? Glad? Guilty that I'm relieved."

Keira rubbed her arm. "Drink some more tea."

Farren obliged, letting the warmth pool in her belly, allowing it to lift the tension from her shoulders.

"Anyways," Keira said after a moment of silence, giving Farren a tentative glance. "The prince that came to visit is a son of Queen Aurelia. We heard he went up into the mountains while he was visiting Capai. Who knows if it's true."

"Aren't the views at Alidonia nice enough?"

Keira's eyes gleamed. "Apparently, they can't see the Kithyrian Mountains as well from there. The prince is a skilled painter, it's said."

"Hmm." Farren sipped more tea. Her limbs had begun to feel weightless, her mind high and light and clear.

The door behind Keira creaked open, and noise from the back of the house rushed in as several little heads emerged in the opening.

"Auntie Farren!"

No less than two little boys and three girls tangled themselves around Farren's legs, squeezing her tight with their sticky hands.

Farren grinned and hugged each back in turn. "Hope you've been staying out of trouble? Being good for your Auntie Keira?"

They nodded happily and clamored for her attention, faces smeared with dirt and cracker crumbs. Between their feet, a rabbit, puppy, and frog hopped up and down, exuberant with the children's excitement.

Although Keira wasn't their blood mother, she was mother to them in every other sense of the word. Keira, after years of trying, hadn't been able to have children of her own, and had jumped at the chance to help out her ailing sister, who lived nearby.

The eldest girl, Ivie, tugged on her arm, cheeks like ruddy plums. "Did you see the prince in the mountains?"

"I didn't see any prince in the mountains," Farren said.

Ivie's blond brows floated high on her brow. "We saw gryphons at the festival, too!"

Farren froze, her cup halfway to her mouth. The clouds that had receded from her insides came swooping back in.

"Ivie!" Keira scolded, causing the girl's copper cheeks to darken further.

"But I-I thought... Anaxis was...?"

Keira gave Farren a look she knew too well: wariness and pity. Farren dragged in an uneven breath. Anaxis' death had meant nothing, then. The new queen was no different than him, allowing gryphons on the streets. Nothing had changed.

She tried to focus on Ivie. "How many gryphons?"

"I saw three different ones. One with purple feathers, one with red feathers, and another with feathers like gold. But we didn't go near them," Ivie added, glancing nervously at her aunt, which told Farren they *had* gone near them. "We know they are dangerous."

The room suddenly felt too hot. "That's right," Farren said, frowning down at Ivie. "You should never go near them. They are unpredictable, capable of killing with no more than a twitch of beak or claw. Even if they are walking beside a royal—no matter how handsome he is."

Ivie couldn't meet Farren's gaze. She softened her tone, and touched the girl's shoulder. "You're eleven, Ivie, and smart enough to know how dangerous gryphons are. Some think they can train a gryphon into submission, but it isn't possible to have them under full control." And, Farren thought to herself, if those haughty aristocrats had brought three gryphons to the festival this year, they had grown even more foolish.

She swallowed and smoothed her hands down her lap. "What else did you see at the festival?"

While she let the girl tell her stories, her heart galloped. Every time she looked into one of the children's faces, she saw how small and fragile they were. So she kept her eyes on her tea, and only pulled them away when Keira's husband called for the children to return to the back side of the house.

"You know I would never do anything to endanger them," Keira said softly. "You know what they mean to me."

Enchanters, how she knew. Farren had been there each time Keira had miscarried. She had held Keira while she raved with jealousy and bitterness, and finally grief, at each successful birth her sister had. And she had rejoiced with Keira as the years went by and gifted Keira with nieces and nephews, as she grew into the motherly figure Farren had always known her friend could be.

"I know," Farren said, her eyes burning suddenly. "It's just that after everything with Desmond—"

Keira wrapped Farren in her arms, smothering her words. "I remember everything you've told me. Everything that we've seen. I can't forget it." Keira set her at arm's length. "And I know you won't, either. How much longer will you be in the mountains?"

Farren sniffed and blinked the dew from her eyes. "As long as I can be."

"The winter?"

"Yes."

Keira shook her head and waved around her house. "Come live here, Farren. You'll be warm and fed. The children would love it."

For a moment, Farren considered saying yes. But with five children already sleeping there much of the time, Farren knew she would take too much of the precious space. Keira had always been generous, no matter how little she had.

Farren shook her head. "How would you deal with my nagging about the children?"

Despite herself, Keira smiled. "I would tell you to knock it off." She lifted her brows. "Well?"

Farren bit her lip. "I can't, but thank you."

"What will you eat when everything is frozen?"

Farren shrugged. "I'll have stores. I should be going now." She would fetch a little bird from outside to fly to her father, tell him to meet her at their usual spot at the inn.

"Wait." Keira rummaged in a cabinet and pulled out two bars of soap wrapped in leather. "They're scented with cinnafern and sweet bellhorn. You could use the nice fragrance," she said with a sniff.

"How practical of you," Farren teased, tucking the bundle against her chest.

"And here, just a few more things. You have room in your satchel?"

Keira didn't wait for an answer before diving into the shelves all along the walls of the store. "Without my apothecary, you'll need some things over the winter. Spice rub to keep the cold at bay—especially on your feet. A balm for chapped lips and cheeks. A healing salve for cuts and burns. Would you like a sleeping tincture? You look like you haven't been sleeping." Jars and clay pots clinked as she gathered them up in her arms. "Oh, and I have a mind-sharp draught to help with hunting." She flashed Farren a sudden, wicked grin. "And I've made a new sweet. I'm calling it silly chewtack."

Farren made a face. "Why does that make me think of a cow's cud?"

"It's a chewing sweet—not for swallowing, mind—that helps the laughter come out. It's a blend from a few different plants of mine."

"I'm not sure how useful that will be in the mountains."

Keira quirked a brow at her. "When was the last time you laughed?" At Farren's silence, Keira gave a brisk nod. "Precisely what I thought. Laughter is medicine, Farren."

Keira gingerly placed the jars and pots in Farren's satchel, cushioning them with a length of blanket. The satchel bulged.

"How about food?" Keira asked.

"I'll grab something from the inn."

Keira's mouth set with unease. "You know, one day, you'll have to forgive yourself. You can't live up there forever, away from all your friends and family."

The burning started in Farren's eyes again, and she turned away, pulling the packs over her shoulders. "I need to see my father about getting another hawk. I can't make it in the mountains without one."

A furrow deepened between Keira's strong brows. "I've heard that your father is selling his hawks. He might not have any left."

Farren had started tightening the straps on her pack, but her hands paused at Keira's words. "What?"

"I'm not sure why, but he came to my husband asking around for potential buyers."

Her father would never sell his hawks. Her family depended on the falconry business he ran, which had a reputation good enough to draw buyers all the way from Malodai. And with Desmond's special needs—the tincture their mother used to calm him—plus the fees they still owed the surgeon who had mended his wounds, he couldn't risk giving up his business. It would ruin them.

"I have to go," Farren said.

"Be careful."

"I will." She kissed her friend on the cheek and, knowing she had to see for herself if what Keira said was true, left for her father's house.

*For home*, she thought stubbornly. No matter how long she lived in the mountains or how difficult it was to return to, it would always be that. She refused to let it go.

# THREE

KEIRA WAS RIGHT. THE mews outbuilding, normally full with twenty hawks and falcons, had only three. Sensing them with her runeskill as she reached her family's cottage, Farren forcibly tamped down a rush of worry. She knew her father. Brin would have a perfectly logical explanation for selling them, as she had never known him to do anything without considerable thought. But she couldn't think of a single reason for him to sell the hawks they relied on to make a living.

Farren entered the mews first, hoping to settle her unease. Everything was tidy and neat, just the way she and her father always kept it before she had left for the Kithyrian Mountains. Other than the dearth of hawks, nothing appeared unusual.

Gnawing the inside of her cheek, she opened a runebond with one of the hawks, a burnished female hunched in the slanting light of her barred window, and immediately caught a wave of nervous restlessness. Something wasn't right, but the hawk was so glad to feel Farren that she started to forget whatever was bothering her.

*Where is Mellion?* the hawk asked, flashing her an image of Mellion.

Farren held tight to her memory of Mellion, frozen on the flower, knowing the image and emotions tied to it would upset the hawk greatly. Instead, she sent a thread of her grief to the hawk and closed her runebond as the hawk lifted its wings and keened in sorrow. Farren's eyes burned as her own grief welled just under the surface. She left the hawk to mourn.

She pulled out her father's logs and skimmed through the last day's pages. A line caught her eye.

*1 gold-winged hawk sold to P. Fausa for 964 dremma.*

Her eyes leapt to the previous page, finding a similar line. Flipping back in time revealed a record of each of the sales her father had made, jotted in his unadorned pen-strokes. She snapped the book shut.

She couldn't be angry at her father for not telling her since she was the one who had chosen to live far away in the mountains. But he could've at least sent a message with a bird.

Farren passed the vegetable garden and lingered by the window, breath fogging the glass as she tried to see past the curtain. Should she just walk in? Knock?

The last time she had been inside the cottage was the day she left home. Her mother, Ena, had remained silent while her father pleaded with Farren—barely audible between Desmond's screams—not to leave. Then her mother pulled out the tincture to calm Desmond, who beat at her arms as she pressed the tinctured cloth to Desmond's mouth and nose. The sudden flash of his anger had faded the way light did from a dying rabbit's eyes, and in its place was a resigned quietude. The sight of it had made her stomach turn.

It hadn't been the last time Farren had seen them, though. Every few weeks, when Farren returned to the village inn for supplies and to speak with her father, she had watched Desmond on her way from a distance, knowing it was best for all of them if she stayed away, but hating it nonetheless. She had begun to question how much she knew her brother now and whether he missed her.

The rotten scent of the badger's home drifted down from the hill where it lived in a burrow just outside the cottage. Her mother used to let that nasty thing inside, but after it bit Farren, her father demanded it out. Her father, normally a soft-spoken man, had surprised them both, and her mother removed it, commenting that it was adding a *particular odor* to the cottage anyways.

When Farren entered, an empty kitchen greeted her. She stepped in and closed the door quietly, ears straining. A half-tended fire dwindled in the hearth. Her parents argued behind the closed door of their room—not a full-blown argument like they used to have, Ena yelling and Brin responding in a quiet voice—but one of those fights with tightly restrained whispers so as not to upset Desmond.

Desmond's door was open, the room beyond it blackened with silent shadows. He was likely sleeping now, and she didn't want to disturb him. He didn't need to know she was there, anyways. She would quietly speak to her father and be gone, and he would never know she was there. Farren set her packs gingerly on the floor, wincing as Keira's jars clacked together, announcing her presence.

Something rustled in one of the wide chairs near the hearth, and Farren turned to see Desmond poking his head out over the armrest.

His strained voice called out, "Farren, is that you?"

"It's me."

The floor creaked as she approached. Glazed eyes peered at her from a slack face—signs her mother had recently given him the tincture.

He curled deeper into the chair, knees bent as he tucked his arms around the two minks nestled on his stomach. A third mink slept on his feet, its soft belly rising and falling with its breath.

Seeing him like that, folded like a small child in the chair, made her long to hug him close. But who was she to hug him? It wouldn't be fair if she acted like nothing had happened, as if their relationship hadn't been swallowed whole by a gryphon, by her lack of control over her runeskill. So she curled her fingers into her palms and sat in the chair opposite him. "How are you, Des?"

"I'm okay," he mumbled. "They're arguing again." He closed his eyes for a moment, seeming to fight back weariness. A long, deep scar ran down the side of his head and curved behind his ear. It looked better than when she had left.

She waited for a moment, expecting him to open his eyes and yell at her for leaving in the spring. But the tincture must've drowned that pain.

"What are they arguing about?" she asked.

"I wanted to help Da with the birds. Mam didn't want it, but he let me." The words came out as slow, knobby things, a side-effect of the tincture. "But one bit me, and I..." Desmond rubbed a hand over his knee, his knuckles turning white. "I couldn't help it. So I took the tea Mam made." He motioned to the empty cup on the side table.

Despite the heat from the fireplace, cold crept over Farren's back. She knew asking Desmond more about it would only agitate him further, so she made her tone light and said, "She makes a tea now?" At least that was better than her mother smothering him with a tinctured cloth so that he was forced to breathe the calming vapors. Did that mean he was less violent now? Better able to control his temper?

Desmond shifted, frowning at her. "Are you staying here?"

She clenched her hands together, hoping he would be asleep by the time she left. "Why don't I tuck you into bed?"

"I'm not five anymore," he mumbled. "I think I'll sleep here tonight."

"You'll get cold."

"Then I'll get a blanket."

Farren sighed hopelessly. He closed his eyes, and she thought he had fallen asleep until he said, "Where did you go when you left?"

She listened for the sound of betrayal and was surprised when she didn't find it. The tea, most likely. The healer had told them the tincture would deaden his feelings and make them more tolerable—or rather, *him* more tolerable—and it was likely the tea did the same.

Farren rose and grabbed a heavy iron poker to stir the fire. "I went into the mountains."

She glanced back at her brother and saw his brow lift. The slight movement reminded her sharply of how he used to be: eager and curious and brimming with pesky questions. *Why do you like fighting with boys so much? How did the Enchanters disappear? Will we ever visit the city of Malodai? Do you think you'll ever remember where you came from?* Her chest ached for those times. Maybe he was still the same old Des deep down beneath the restless, explosive temper he had wielded since his injury.

"Did you make yourself a new house?" he asked.

"Hardly."

"Where did you sleep?"

Farren prodded the fire, then knelt by her brother, stroking the mink that slept in a ball on his foot. "In a cave."

His eyes opened and he gave her a quizzical look. "And you're worried about *me* getting cold?"

Farren smiled. She knew what he really wanted to know; it was important to tell him before she left again. "I just needed to be alone, Des. I didn't want to leave you, but I had to get away and face things by myself."

"Face things?" he repeated sleepily.

She wanted to reach up and smooth the sandy waves of his hair, but he would hate that. "And I thought about you all the time," she told him. "I hope you aren't—"

The floor creaked, and she looked up to see her father's wide, quiet eyes. "You're back," he said. His tone held a hint of alarm.

Behind him, Ena pushed forward, face like the knotted bough of a pine tree. Badger claws inked into either side of her neck glinted long and sharp in the firelight.

"What do you want?" Ena asked.

As if this weren't the home Farren grew up in or the place where her family lived. Farren looked more closely at her father. He seemed guarded and her mother exhausted. What had they really been arguing about?

"I came to speak with Da...and to see Desmond," she added, not wanting her mother to think worse of her.

Ena's lips twisted. "After months of forgetting him?" She shook her head, then shoved between Farren and Desmond, reaching out a hand to him. "Come on, sweetheart. Let's get you into bed."

Desmond swatted her hand away, but he got up, causing the minks to titter as their warm bed moved. He wobbled to his room, their mother hovered in his wake, and the door shut behind them.

Something inside Farren tightened. She grabbed Desmond's empty cup from the side table and plopped it into the wash basin in the kitchen, scrubbing as if it had poison inside. While her hands kept busy, her mind began to feel a bit clearer. She was aware of the way her father walked into the kitchen, slowly but not as if he were injured or sick.

If not injury or illness, what other reason could he have to sell his birds?

His warm hand landed on her shoulder. "It's good to see you again. What has it been, five weeks? Four?"

"Three weeks and two days, Da."

"Seems so long ago, now." She heard the sad lilt in his voice but knew he wouldn't pressure her to stay. He had learned to accept it, had learned there was little he could do besides offer support to Farren whenever she needed it. She loved that about her father; when trying to reason with her had failed, he didn't give up on her or shame her but only said *I'm here for you when you need me.*

"Are you hungry?" he asked.

"No." Farren mopped the table off with a rag. "What happened with Des today? He said you let him handle a bird. Has he been getting more gentle?"

Her father sighed, the sound like heavy rain gusting through the forest canopy. "I know what you're thinking, but... Des had been watching me with the birds for some time, and I swore it was helping him. So I asked if he wanted to put on a glove, and he said yes. It was fine at first, but I think it was too much for him. When Esper bit him, it set something off, and Desmond flung her away. I called Esper to me, but Des went after her. He nearly stomped on her when she was on the floor."

Warmth drained from her, and she reminded herself Esper was safe and sound in the mews. "You stopped him," she prompted her father.

"I..." Her father's voice cracked, and he shook his head. "I pushed him to the ground and held him there until your mother came out with the tincture."

She set her rag down and reached for her father's warm, calloused hand. "You did the right thing, Da." All she had to do was remember how Desmond's anger ignited to fury with a lash of a fist that didn't care who or what it hit. Her mother, her father, or an animal—but never his minks. Thankfully, his mind hadn't been damaged to that extent.

"It didn't feel very right," her father replied.

"I know." Leaving home hadn't felt right either, but she had known it was the right thing to do—for everyone. "Did he seem... remorseful? Afterward?"

Her father's eyes remained dark as he sank into a chair. "Only because he knew what it would've meant to the business had he succeeded."

Farren sighed, not wanting to think about all the ways her brother had changed since the accident. "How's the business going?"

Her father grunted and reached for the clay bottle of birch water. "As good as can be expected."

She sat and laid a board of cheese between them. The musky odor of it filled the silence while her father sipped water. Farren studied the familiar, tiny feathers imprinted on each of his fingers: the only indication of his runeskill beyond the runemark on his inner wrist. Her father wasn't one for elaborate displays.

"Da, I heard that you've been selling hawks. I checked the mews. Why are there only three left?"

"I sold the others. Figured it was time for a change."

"A change for what?" Farren glanced around the cottage, suddenly wondering if they were planning to move. Where would they go? To the city? "Wasn't the business doing well before?"

He nudged the board of cheese toward her. "You should eat something. Has Mellion been successful up in the mountains? Are you getting enough?"

To pacify her father, she took a small bite of cheese and poured herself some birch water. "I need to talk to you about that. I was hoping you'd be willing to give me another hawk. I can stay for a few days, help out around the mews if you'd like."

"Mellion isn't getting you enough food then."

"It's not that, Da..." Farren swallowed, her fingers tightening around her cup. "She died yesterday." Her father wouldn't be as hurt by it as she had been since Farren had been the one to bond with Mellion and train her, but he would understand what kind of loss that was.

His eyes glistened, and he blinked rapidly. "She was a good hunter. Young, though." He sniffed, brow furrowed. "What did her in?"

Farren studied the round of cheese, the small crescent formed by the sharp blades of her teeth. "It was some sort of disease. Do you know of something that spreads by touch? It's fast, once it touches you." The hair along Farren's arms rose as she remembered. She rubbed her fingers together. "It froze Mellion somehow. I don't know how it worked."

Her father's brows creased deeper, and he scratched his dark beard as he considered. "Any discoloration? Odors? How was her behavior?"

"She was trying to get away. She was terrified, like the disease was consuming her."

He went very still and looked like he might be sick. "That doesn't sound like any disease I know. Did you bring her back? I could take a look."

"There was another strange thing. Her talon had touched a flower that seemed to be affected by the same disease. When I touched it, I could feel the disease...or whatever it was, trying to affect me." Farren crossed her arms, chilled. "I had to leave her there, Da. It was awful."

Her father reached out and squeezed her arm. "I can ask around, see if anyone has seen something similar."

Farren nodded, hesitating for a moment before she turned her mind to other important tasks—things she wished could wait, but with winter coming, there was little time to lose. "Will you be able to give me one of your last hawks?"

Warily, he pulled his hand away. "What do you think about staying here, helping me out with the business? You've been gone long enough, Farren. You can't stay up there during the winter months."

"It will be hard," she agreed. "But not impossible." Well, the frigid cold might kill her, but more likely, starvation. Deep snow made hunting difficult, and she didn't know if she could store enough before then to last the long winter months. Worst of all, she wouldn't be able to come down from the mountain should she run out of food. Deep snow and blizzards would trap her.

"The truth is," her father said, "I need your help in the mews. And taking care of Des—"

"Mam won't let me care for him," she said, pushing away from the table. She busied herself with putting the cheese beneath its cloche. "And why do you need help if you only have three hawks left? And *why* didn't you send word if things were so dire you had to start selling them?"

"I sent three birds."

Farren's hand froze on the cloche.

"Three times I sent birds your way," her father repeated. "When you didn't answer, I thought maybe you wouldn't come back. That I would never see you again."

She returned to the table. "Da... I would never ignore a message from you. What birds did you send?"

"A sparrow. A kestrel. Then a bright bunting. Maybe they couldn't find you."

Farren's throat clamped. The birds *had* found her. She had been busy hunting, or skinning a rabbit, or collecting water. Their fluttering attempts to get her to open a runebond hadn't worked; she had used them to continue practicing control over her runeskill, keeping the runebond closed tight as a fist.

"You didn't runebond with them," her father said softly. He could read her too well. "You were doing it before you left, after Desmond's injury... The hawks told me you wouldn't runebond with them much. Narrow and brief connections, they said." He studied her for a moment. "I know it's been difficult after what happened with the gryphon. But Farren, you're an *Avid*. You must let yourself be vulnerable with your rune animals. Strength comes from those deep bonds, and they will nourish you."

A tremor had begun somewhere at the base of her spine and grew when her father clasped her hands. "Were you at least...bo nded to Mellion when she passed? She didn't die alone?"

"Of course not, Da. It was the closest I had been to her since leaving."

Just then, her mother came out of Desmond's room, looking bristled. "Keep your voice down," she whispered fiercely, eyes like shards of ice as they closed in on her.

An old, familiar dread settled on Farren's chest. Her body began tensing as if it could protect her from Ena's harsh words, as if it could ward off the cold distance that had hardened to ice since the accident.

In a burst of irritation at her body's uncontrollable response, Farren faced her mother. "Why is Da selling his hawks?"

She scowled. "It's not any business of yours. Hasn't been since you left us. If Brin doesn't want to tell you, then..." A new thought seemed to cross her mind, and she stalked to the table, setting her hands on it as if she were a captain steering a ship. She pinioned Brin with a glare. "Tell me you're not thinking she'll take over what's left of the business for you? That she can take care of *us*, too, eh?" Her mother shook her head in disbelief.

"What is she talking about, Da?" Farren's voice rose, and Desmond's door creaked open. He looked out blearily, but it seemed to Farren his tea was beginning to wear off. Her mother didn't seem to notice as she stalked off into her bedroom.

"What else can I do?" her father asked, and the weariness there, the hopelessness, drew Farren to the chair next to him.

She grabbed his large, calloused hand. "Da, please tell me what's going on. Is the business failing? Are you ill?" Not for the first time, she wished she had a runeskill with other people. But that was only a legend, something told in children's tales. How convenient it would be to know her father's thoughts, avoid all this circular chatter.

His eyes gleamed. "If you don't stay, Farren, I'll have to sell the other hawks. Promise me that you'll stay, no matter what—"

Her mother came back from the room and threw something onto the table. A folded letter with a broken seal: orange wax stamped with a gryphon claw. The royal emblem meant the letter had arrived from Alidonia, the fortress heart of Malodai.

"It came weeks ago," her mother announced.

Farren, barely daring to breathe, opened the letter and read. "You're being called to fulfill your Years of Servitude to the crown." Her voice sounded strange, as if it came from someone else. "They are calling for more *Avids* to work in the royal mews."

"We know what it says," her mother snapped.

The call to serve the crown was expected among those with the most useful runeskills—with predatory, intelligent, or beautiful animals as well as medicinal or edible plants and fungi. When a child was born, a Rune Seer would sort through all of the child's runes—hundreds of them, but only visible to the Seers—until the one binding the child to another life form was found. The Seer recorded the rune for the crown and imprinted the rune on the inner wrist of the babe so that he or she would never forget. With that record and the queen's watching spies, anyone could be taken to benefit the royal family.

Farren clutched the letter in her hand. "I'm sorry, Da. I should've realized you had sent word. I—I wish I hadn't—"

Her father's hand found hers and wrapped it in warmth. "I didn't want to ask you to come back. I didn't want to put you in that position. But you are here now. Will you stay?"

Her mother snorted, but her father and Desmond stared at her wide-eyed.

"I-I don't know," she managed to say. "I'm not sure I can take care of—"

Rapid banging resounded on the cottage door, making them all jump.

Her mother fell back, her hand flying to her throat. "Who would be here at this hour—"

BANG! BANG! BANG!

Desmond came fully out of his room. "Da?"

Their father had turned to ashen stone, eyes locked on the door. "It must be them. I've waited too long—"

BANG-BANG-BANG!

The door rattled on its hinges, and a voice boomed through it. "On the order of Queen Aurelia and King Linius of Alidonia, you must open this door!"

# FOUR

TWO THOUGHTS ENTERED FARREN'S mind as she crossed the room to the door. The first was, *Is this a nightmare?* The second, *I won't let them take him*, indicated that she wasn't thinking clearly. She was weak and exhausted, in no condition for a fight.

Oh, and there was this little thing called a dungeon, which she might be thrown into if she rebelled against the queen's orders.

The moment her hand turned the doorknob, two guards burst in with hands gripped to the pommels of sheathed swords at their hips. Beneath the brilliant orange of their royal cloaks, black leather armor was pocked with scrapes and nicks. A pair of burnished coyotes slunk in behind them with ears that twitched around the cottage.

Farren didn't move back as one of the guards rolled past her; she *swore* he looked familiar. His smug expression reminded her of some of the boys she had happily put down during the festival fighting matches. Desmond's quickening breath prodded her shoulder.

"Are you Brin Blackburn?" the other guard, a woman, asked her father. She was tall for a woman, with broad shoulders that left no doubt about her physical strength.

Her father stood, shoulders pressed back and chin lifted. "I am."

"You received a letter calling you to your Years of Servitude to the crown. Because you haven't brought yourself to the fortress, we've had to come fetch you. The queen is very disappointed."

Brin's bristly cheeks darkened. "I have a business to run. I needed time to—"

"The queen doesn't care about your business. She ordered you to arrive at the fortress within a week of receiving the letter. You're required to work in the royal mews. Would you like to see her decree?" The guard pulled a short roll of parchment from a chest pocket.

"I would like to read it," Farren said, snatching the paper from the guard's hand. She skimmed the words, taking in every little detail. They wanted him working in the royal mews, as the letter had said, and the Servitude would be...

Farren gripped the page. Not one or two years as was customary, but *ten whole years*. A ridiculous, impossible number. Ten years away from his business, away from them. It felt like a lifetime.

"This can't be correct." Farren was unable to drag her eyes from the clearly marked number. "Ten years is...unheard of. Why is it for so long?"

The male guard snorted. "Can you believe this, Iana? The girl thinks it's acceptable to question the queen's business." He tapped a finger on his sword hilt thoughtfully. "What do you think, Iana? Would the queen give him fifteen years instead? Maybe twenty?"

Heat rose to her cheeks at the guard's outrageous threat, but she bit her tongue as her father edged out from behind the table, his face ruddy with unease.

"That won't be necessary," Brin said. "Let it be, Farren."

Desmond pushed forward, and his three minks scurried between his feet. "Da, you can't go!"

"Who will take care of us?" her mother asked. "I cannot keep up the business, Brin."

Their father looked different in the weak firelight, exhausted in a way she had not seen him before. "Farren will stay."

"Absolutely not!" Her mother planted hands on her hips. "Look at her! She's only nineteen, and she can hardly take care of herself."

Farren glared at Ena, all too aware of how thin her own body had become. And she needed a bath.

Next to her, Desmond crossed and uncrossed his arms, eyes darting between the guard and their father. The minks scrambled around his feet as if they, too, couldn't decide what to do.

"And we all know what happened the last time she looked after Desmond," Ena said. "So distracted by flirting with those boys, she let that gryphon attack our son!"

"Fighting, not flirting," Farren corrected. Not that it made any difference to what her mother thought had happened.

Desmond picked up one of the minks and clutched it in his arm. "It's not her fault, Mam!"

*Oh, Des, if only you knew.*

Ena huffed. "If she hadn't been flirting with those boys..."

Farren stopped listening because her thoughts whirled inside her head as they always did, berating her with the truth: if she hadn't been fighting at the festival, if she had cared less about earning coin and more about watching over her brother, she could've kept him from reaching out to touch the gryphon. And if she had had more control over her runeskill, she wouldn't have gotten lost in the gryphon's mind, stunned by its blaze of anger. Then she might've stopped the vicious beast from biting her brother.

Her father held up a hand, cutting through Farren's thoughts and her mother's condemning words. "Now is not the time for this—"

"Now is exactly the time!" Her mother's voice rose to a caterwaul pitch. "Our family is hanging by a frayed thread, and you want to hand it all over to her! She left us, Brin. Remember that?"

"There's no room for argument," said Iana, her figure as solid and unmoving as a mountain. "You've had plenty of time to get your affairs in order."

Then the male guard grabbed her father by the arm. "Let's get a move on with this night. Do we need to shackle you, old man?"

"Don't hurt him!" Desmond barreled forward, too quick for Farren or her father to stop him, and flung a fist at the guard's face.

Farren leapt after her brother, knowing he would need saving from the guard who seemed all too eager to use force to get what he wanted. The guard released their father and ducked to avoid Desmond's fist, then pulled him into a tight, twisted hold.

Her father stood with clenched hands, holding himself back, always a model of restraint—something he tried vainly to teach Farren. But when Desmond cried out in pain, Farren couldn't stop herself. In one motion, she pulled the guard's fingers off her brother, bending them back painfully, and whacked the heel of her other hand into the guard's nose. Her brother staggered free, cradling his arm into his belly, and the guard reeled into the wall behind him.

"That's enough!" Iana shouted, taking Farren roughly by the arms so that she couldn't do any more damage.

"Farren, you must let them take me—" her father started, but suddenly Desmond's minks raced around them. Iana released Farren, crying out as the little balls of fur became tooth and claw, biting up her legs.

Farren cursed; there was little she could do about animals with which she had no runeskill.

The coyotes snarled and pressed forward, one chasing a mink as it scampered away. Desmond pulled his hair as he screamed in panic, and her parents urged him to calm down, but the male guard leapt at Desmond and pulled him up against the wall, one fist balled in the neck of Desmond's chiton, and the other hand reaching for his sword.

Before Farren could react, something dark and fat scurried across the floor. The stink of it followed not far behind. Her mother's badger went right up to the male guard and bit his ankle.

The guard yelped and dropped his hold on Desmond but not on his sword. The blade glinted as it started to slide from its sheath.

*No you don't.* Farren yanked the male guard back, locking his head in a tight hold. Well, as tight as she could manage; she had never felt so weak in her life, despite the fire surging in her blood. Her forearm pressed against his windpipe, and she knew if she held it there for long enough, eventually he would pass out. He seemed to know it too, and beat her arm. Grimacing, she held on just long enough for Desmond to get to the other side of the room, where her mother pulled him into a corner.

The moment Farren released the guard, he staggered away. She turned to see where Iana had gone, and a fist slammed into her cheek.

The punch sent her sprawling. Dazed, she peered up at the white fangs of a snarling coyote. Its hot, meaty breath touched her cheek. Black whiskers rose high from its curled lip, poised to bite. Farren barely dared breathe.

Iana had apparently scared off the minks and loomed over her with a scowl. "I said that's enough."

The coyote ceased its growling and backed away just enough for Farren to move out of easy reach. She got to her feet and swayed as she shook her head. "Not until that ass stops touching my brother."

The male guard sneered. "I should have you imprisoned for this little rebellion. But, since you're so far removed from civilization, I'll forgive your stupidity this time."

Iana held the pommel of her sword, her face a mask of stone. "We will take what we came for without more fighting."

The badger waddled over to her mother, and the minks tangled between Desmond's feet. Her mother stood in front of him, shielding him from the guards as she tried to calm him in whispered tones. He looked furious still but was following her instructions to take deep breaths. Her father went to them, and his calm voice seemed to soothe Desmond further.

"Take me instead."

Her father's soft eyes turned toward her, but she kept her focus on the guards.

The male guard wiped a bit of blood from his nose. "Maybe she can't read," he stated to Iana, grinning.

"By orders, we are to take Brin," Iana explained, slowly as if Farren was having trouble understanding.

Farren rubbed her throbbing cheek, wondering how big a bruise it would make. It wouldn't be the worst she'd had. "I can read, actually. And the decree says that there are exceptions to the order. You could take someone who has the same runeskill. I can get the work done just as well as my father."

"Farren, no," her father said. "I can't let you—"

"You can," Farren told him. She pulled her mouth into a smile, willing him to understand that she had to do this for him and for Desmond.

The male guard grabbed Farren's hand and tugged it toward him to check her inner wrist. While he studied the runemark imprinted there, proving that she was an *Avid*, she thought of how satisfying it had been to hit him in the nose. She hoped it healed crooked.

Iana glanced at Farren's wrist. "Just because you have the same runemark doesn't mean you have the same level of skill."

Brin shook his head, his expression gaunt with worry. Desmond held one of the minks to his cheek, watching her with wide, hurt eyes.

"My runeskill is strong." She straightened her back. "I've been raising and training hawks with my father since I was a child. I have trained three of them all on my own," she added, although she wasn't sure the guards would understand the significance of that. How much her father trusted her, and how much trust it took in herself and her skills to accomplish it. "You won't likely find someone like that among the general populace of the city."

The bloody-nosed guard finally released her wrist, sneering. "You'd be surprised by how many people train pigeons on the streets."

Farren bristled and checked to see what her father thought of the man's insult, but his mouth was pressed tight as a tomb.

"I am younger than my father," Farren pressed on. "I can get more work done."

"That's true," the male guard said, eying her in a way that made her skin prickle. "Your father might be a doddering, feeble old man toward the end of his Servitude. Not much use for the queen."

Farren's fingernails bit into her palms. She wouldn't lash out at him. She would stay composed, as her father was. She flicked Brin a glance and met his shining eyes across the room.

"Everything aside," Iana said to her companion, "the queen is keen on fighting skills and might be willing to forgive this transgression. She would make a good addition to the new guard." She gave Farren a stern look. "But know that if you don't do well in your Servitude, you will likely be imprisoned, and your father will be forced to take your place."

Farren repressed a shudder at the sudden coldness winging up her spine. "I understand."

Farren was determined to leave with her dignity. She would *not* be shackled and dragged to the fortress for all the city folk to see and pity. She had chosen this—had wanted it. She would hold her head high and be brave.

When she said goodbye, her father's tears disappeared into his beard. "I'll miss you so much, my girl." He held her tight as if he never wanted to let go. She breathed in his familiar smell—musty like birds but spiced and warm from his beard oil—and allowed herself a moment to feel the safety and security she always felt when he hugged her. A sweet, childish thing that made her eyes burn.

"When I come back, I'll help with the falconry business. I promise, Da."

He pulled back. "For now, just promise that you'll stay out of trouble. And that you won't forget all that I've taught you. Take care of yourself. Don't forget who you are, what your runeskill means."

She gave him a wobbly smile. "I'll do my best."

Then she turned wordlessly to Desmond. His eyes were angry, but he pulled her close. "Don't go, Farren. Not again." Mink fur pressed against her neck, and she worried for a moment that the mink would turn and bite her, then was immediately ashamed by the thought.

"I have to go, Des. It's different this time."

"How? You still won't visit, and Mam won't let me go see you at the fortress."

Farren cast a sidelong look at her mother, who wore a closed, resolute expression. Would she ever let Desmond leave home? "I'll write letters. I promise."

"You had better."

"Let's hurry it up, girl," the male guard said by the door. "We don't have all night."

Despite herself, Farren felt a small burst of gratitude toward the guard for giving her an excuse to breeze through saying goodbye to her mother. The woman stayed as stiff as ever and didn't even try to hug her. "Do your duty," was all she said. As if it had been Farren, and not her father, who had been called away.

Then Farren left and mounted the extra horse the guards had brought. They had secured her bags to the saddle, eager to get on their way. The empty road stretched ahead, a wide rocky path bathed in yellow moonglow. The guards flanked her on either side, and the coyotes trotted behind them, eyes glittering in the growing shadows.

"We'll ride through the night," Iana said. "If we travel without stopping, we'll get there by nightfall tomorrow."

Farren shifted in her saddle. "You don't intend to rest?"

"And get sliced open by bear or boar in the Wildlands?" The male guard sneered. "You must be mistaking us for fools. Besides, didn't we tell you how eager the queen was for help? She's growing her guard and needs people like you."

"People who can fight?" Farren asked, a tremor stirring in her belly.

He rested a hand on the saddle pommel and leaned back with a smug, relaxed posture. "*Avids*. Outskirts scum or not. She's forming her very own gryphon guard."

She must've heard wrong. "Did you say gryphons?"

The guard gave her a sidelong look. "Aye. The big feathered beasts. Half eagle, half mountain lion. Maybe you've never seen one up here in the Outskirts."

"Of course I have," she snapped. Why was her heart beating so hard? "I thought I would be working in the royal mews?"

He wore that stupid sneer again. "The royal *gryphon* mews. You're not scared of gryphons, are you?"

Farren fought the urge to look back at her family's cottage. It was too late to turn back now. Besides, did she really want her father to take her place?

She gripped the reins with trembling hands. It would be fine. She would get to the fortress and speak to whoever was in charge of her servitude. And hopefully, convince them that it was in everyone's best interest that she not work with the beasts.

# FIVE

By the time they passed through the dense forests of the Wildlands and the city of Malodai was in view, Farren was amazed she hadn't fallen off her horse from exhaustion. And that she had managed—several times—to stop herself from punching the smug male guard, Scipio. He seemed to relish prodding her as if she would put on some sort of display when poked enough.

"Bet you've never seen a city, eh?" he asked as they steered their horses downhill along one of the well-traveled thoroughfares cutting through the Wildlands to Malodai. "It's always a shock for country bumpkins such as yourself."

Farren held tight to the reigns as her mount picked its way over the rough trail. The ground was hard and pocked from oxen and carts from the farmers who brought their goods to the city. The city of Malodai wore the Wildlands like armor. But its protection was solely for the animals in and around the city rather than for the people.

Ahead of the guards, tall stone pillars marked the edge of the Wildlands, and beyond that, the forest thinned until it met the high wall surrounding the city of Malodai. Farren's heart beat faster at the sight of where she would be spending the next ten long years of her life.

It was true that she had never been to Malodai before; she had never had reason to leave her village. Now, the chaotic city below would be her prison. Cluttered homes, shops, and tall windowed buildings made of oakwood abruptly gave way to stretches of green that ran from one cluster to another—tall grasses with walking paths, patches of trees hung with lichen, and stands of reeds broken only by maze-like boardwalks. The thick band of the River Kithyria split the city into two halves, and Farren could just make out the dark smudge of the fortress, erected long ago on the river island of Alidonia by the Enchanters themselves. A massive stone wall rose along its border, reining the entire city in.

"What is the wall for?" Farren asked.

"It helps keep dangerous animals out," Iana explained, her wide shoulders straight with pride as she surveyed the city. "Bears and mountain lions, mostly. Anything trying to get in would be swept away by the Kithyria."

"Gryphons?" asked Farren, innocently.

Iana lifted a brow. "The city has a Watch to take care of dangerous flying animals."

"But the fortress doesn't?"

Located on its island between the halves of Malodai, the fortress of Alidonia was part of the city but apparently had different rules if the queen had decided to keep gryphons there.

"That's up to the queen," Iana said. She pulled some dried meat from her saddlebag and tossed it to the coyotes behind them. The food barely hit the ground before it was gobbled up. "At the moment," the guard continued, "the law says that gryphons are to be kept caged. Unfortunately, before Queen Aurelia's rule, royal gryphons were sold in secret to certain families." Iana glanced warily at Scipio, and Farren didn't miss the way his teeth suddenly clenched. "It can be very difficult to assure that all owners are following the laws."

Farren dug her nails into the reins. She knew from first-hand experience that even royal gryphons weren't kept caged all the time. Like when the royal family came gallivanting into Capai with only a leash to keep their beasts in control.

"Tell me, little Outskirts flotsam," Scipio said, pulling his horse in close, cruel eyes flashing in the sunlight. "Do you know anything at all about Malodai or the fortress?"

*Hopefully, they aren't full of people like you*, she wanted to retort, but just then, she noticed a second wall inside the city, far to the south, where the greenery came to an abrupt stop. Inside that portion of the city, paved walkways smoothed the way between sturdy, orderly buildings. The sight of it sent a shiver coursing down her spine. "Why is that part of the city cut off from the rest?"

"That is the Runeless Quarter," Iana said, nudging her mount to pick up the pace. "The Runeless Sect lives there. A safe place, but one without animals and with few plants."

Farren had heard about the Runeless Sect. They apparently lived in denial of their runeskills. They actively removed their runemarks from their wrists—something that made Farren's stomach turn—and believed that runeskills enslaved humans to a primitive lifestyle.

Farren urged her mare to a trot, catching up with Iana as they rounded a small clearing in the forest. "Is it true that they don't let Seers read their children's runes at birth?"

"Aye," Iana said. "They think the runes are a curse, that to be in favor with the Enchanters, they have to be purged of the runes that bind them to the earth. They are trying to prove they belong among the Enchanters, high above other animals."

Scipio wedged his horse between them so abruptly that his mount's shoulder nearly bruised her leg. "Stupid thinking since they can't actually remove their runeskills. They'll all die of runelack madness, anyways."

Iana gave Scipio an appraising look. "And yet I haven't seen a single one of them with runelack madness."

Scipio scowled. "Which Runeless have you actually seen? The ones who pretend to be leaders under the queen's watchful eye?" He snorted. "No, you'd have to venture past the fortress walls to see the truth of it. The madness is in them, and they clog the streets like dung. Why do you think they're building that strange tower?"

"I've heard it's called a water clock," Iana said. "It's a contraption that keeps tally of the time..."

Farren stopped listening to their idle talk as an errant breeze swept through the forest, carrying the strange scent of the city—woodsmoke, river water, and cold stone. She shivered and shifted in her saddle, wincing at how numb her bottom had become.

Runelack madness or no, the idea of a child not knowing his or her runeskill made her inexplicably sad. How would she know her true strengths? How would he learn what it felt like to be close to a rune animal, to know its instincts—so similar to his own—or its freedom on ground, water, or in sky? To not know her runeskill, to live in denial of it, would make her feel...ungrounded, like a kite snipped from its string.

When they reached the tall arched gate, Scipio cantered ahead, muttering something about a hot bath and meal. Iana kept on at a steady pace, leading Farren through winding cobbled streets.

Farren grimaced at the strength required to stay upright. The saddle seemed made of stone rather than goat-hide. She hoped for a bath and a meal as well, but what she wanted most of all was sleep.

The city of Malodai glittered.

It wasn't due to the lanterns, which were few and far between, but to the hundreds of fireflies sparking in the cloak of night. Farren stared at them, mesmerized, through the bedroom window of the inn.

The moment she had stepped foot inside the city, the wildness of it hit her. It wasn't merely the grassy roads, vine-covered buildings, or animals prowling in the deep vegetation. Those things existed all around her village, too, in a tame sort of way. Rather, it was the way the city pulled the wilderness around itself, and Farren wasn't sure where wilderness ended and civilization began. Despite the wall surrounding the city, the interior felt boundless. Rows of songbirds flocked over house eaves, keeping beady eyes on the grass-ways below. The ancient Greenstone Bridge, painted with moss and dripping with tendrils, arched high over the river, a graceful path safe from the rapid waters below. Through the tall, nodding grasses surrounding the inn, a child giggled and played merrily with fox kits.

If her Servitude had been in the city, she might have come to enjoy it in time. Would the fortress be very different?

The fireflies were a welcome distraction to the gnawing ache in her belly. She had forced herself to eat a few bites of Iana's dried meat. She even splashed her face in the inn's bathhouse fountain under Iana's watchful eye, but when she had laid down to sleep, her mind kept circling.

How would she tolerate being around gryphons? She had seen what one could do with a single, vicious bite. Every time she thought of a gryphon, the things she felt from the accident flooded right back in, and it was difficult to breathe. Nearly worse than that was the stretch of time spanning before her, a temporal prison she had no chance of escaping. Even though she had been living in the mountains, she had at least been free to visit her village. She might've worked her way up to visiting with Des again, and maybe after a few years, would've tried returning to live at home with her family. Now, all of that was impossible. By the time she finished her Servitude, Des would be an adult and Farren would be old enough to be considered a spinster. All of Keira's children would be grown, and she would have missed everything. She had no idea if she would see them again before the ten years were up, and the realization caused a terrible knot to form in her throat.

Farren closed heavy-lidded eyes and rubbed her aching shoulders. The din from the lower floor of the inn didn't help; she was accustomed to the natural sounds of the mountains—frogs croaking, owls shrieking, and the occasional scream of a fox or lion. Not exactly relaxing, but it was noise she had grown used to.

She glanced into the shadows where Iana slept. The large mound of her body hardly moved as she softly snored. Before they reached the city, Iana had let her coyotes go their ways. Scipio hadn't returned so she assumed Iana would be the only one seeing her to the fortress of Alidonia tomorrow. Before Iana went to bed, she told Farren that she wouldn't watch her but that if she woke in the morning to find Farren gone, she would return to Capai and take her father to the fortress instead.

She had said nothing about staying in the room all night.

Farren tiptoed to the door and slipped out, then made her way down the stairs. A mug of ale would help her sleep. She just needed something to dull the chatter of her mind, then she could get a bit of rest before they left in the morning. They would have to travel on one of the Queen's Fingers, the East Tow—a raft dragged by rope and pulley across the raging Kithyria to the island of Alidonia, where the fortress stood. A way best taken during daylight hours, Iana informed her, to make sure the ropes were in good condition, and to have the best chance of rescuing anyone who might fall into the water.

The lower floor of the inn was bustling, and no one noticed as she came down and sat at an empty table tucked at the back. A grease-stained royal notice hung on the wall, threatening three years in the fortress prison for anyone who threatened the life of a gryphon. Another notice, looking crisp and new, declared that all gryphons kept within Malodai rightfully belonged to the royal family and as such, must be returned to them due haste to avoid steep fines.

Farren recalled what Iana had told her about someone from the royal family selling gryphons in secret, and wondered just how many gryphons really existed inside the city walls. The queen must've been desperate to create her gryphon guard if she risked angering families allied with the crown.

It should've reassured Farren that there might be fewer gryphons stalking the streets. Instead, it only made the cold dread in her belly grow heavier.

Turning her back on the notices, she took a seat against the wall and ordered a cup of ale from the barkeep, noting which customers were drunk and which were nearly drunk. Two tables to her left were crowded with raucous men and women playing a game of snake bones. A third table close to the door held one lone, burly man who tore into his hunk of bread like a bear. Two ladies wearing gold-embroidered chitons at the table next to him watched the room as warily as Farren, a younger man sitting with them looking bored.

The door of the inn jostled open, letting in a stream of humid night air. A stooped man hobbled inside, clutching a torn cloak to his body.

"Close the bloody door. Letting all the bugs in," the bear-like man said through a mouthful of bread, turning his wide, muscled back on the cloaked figure.

The cloaked man bared yellowing teeth and nudged the door closed with a dusty shoe. He peered out from the hood with eyes that bulged from sallow skin, his wet gaze sliding from table to table, head cocked like a listening wren. Despite his stooped back and frail appearance, he had the face of a younger man. He seemed to be muttering to himself, although Farren couldn't make out the words from where she sat.

She sipped her watery ale. An odd pair sat at a table to her right. A woman hunched forward, dabbing tears with a cloth, while a man sketched rapidly on a piece of paper. The man leaned back, apparently finished. The woman looked over his work before nodding and emitting a quiet sob. Then he stood and went to peg it to a wall, which Farren had seen but didn't understand. Numerous sketches of faces stared back at her, and the drawing the man added now was of a boy who couldn't be much younger than Desmond.

The sobbing woman thanked him and left, hugging herself. Farren studied the pictures a moment more. There were thirty-two of them in total—young children, adults, a few elderlies. When a server came to see if she needed anything, Farren pointed to them.

"Who are they?" she asked.

He looked at the collection of faces. "The missing."

Farren waited for the server to elaborate, but when he didn't, she asked, "Is someone looking for them?"

"Only the ones who've lost 'em. That's why we keep 'em here on the wall. In case anyone has seen 'em. Probably an animal got to 'em, maybe a bear. Sometimes, people go outside the city wall into the Wildlands. Sometimes, the Kithyria sweeps them away." He shrugged as if it was to be expected.

"The queen doesn't search for them?"

The man's jagged teeth shone as he laughed, drawing attention toward her table. "The queen?" He guffawed again, then looked her up and down, taking in her dusty clothes and weary demeanor. "You must be from the Outskirts." When she didn't reply, he squinted at her and tried again. "Weldonia? They've a particular short stature like yourself, although you don't speak like one..."

Heat rushed to her face, but she ignored his probing question. "Why wouldn't the queen help?"

"The queen is too busy to look for a handful of missing folks." He squinted around, then added in a lower tone, "Too worried about her precious gryphons and all them rich folks who've been keeping 'em hidden. That new law"—he cocked his head at the notice on the wall behind her—"caused quite a stir, probably got her chiton all in a twist. The prince, now, might have tried to find the missing folks. It's said he saved a young girl from a rotten home, took her in as his ward. Guess his generosity only extends to one of us though, eh?"

Farren pursed her lips, wishing she had paid more attention to rumors from the city. The little things she could remember hearing about the fortress—the two princes whose names she forgot, the supposed Enchantments that existed there, and the fact that the king was a heavy napper—were useless knowledge to her.

"Isn't there a City Watch?" She was sure the guard had mentioned one.

"Aye, but they're not much use. Besides, that's just the way it is here. You gotta look out for yourself. Don't go outside the walls, especially not with folks who have runeskills with bears or lions. You might just get eaten!" He cracked up again, and Farren watched him leave, feeling sicker than when she had come down.

She should be glad that Desmond wouldn't be able to visit her, after all.

A voice rose above the din. "You'll all be sorry when they come!"

It was the stooped man in the tattered cloak who loitered by the door, nodding and waggling a finger as he spoke to the room. "The Enchanters will see how base you are, how little you've tried to raise yourself above the primitive urges of your animal sides. They won't help you—"

"Shut your face, old stick," the bear-like man said over his shoulder. "No one wants to hear what the Runeless have to say."

The stooped man grinned. "Yes, yes, I am Runeless. See the very mark I've been freed of!" Stepping into the light of the nearest candles, the man wrenched up his sleeve and exposed an inner wrist mottled white and pink. "Burned away by fire, and it purified me!"

Ale stuck in Farren's throat, acidic and biting. He had willingly seared his runemark, obliterating it. Being freed of a runemark didn't rid one of a runeskill, as runes couldn't be changed...at least not by anyone other than an Enchanter if the legends were true. Was the so-called purification what all Runeless believed, or did he suffer from runelack madness, going for so long without using his runeskill that he grew mad? Farren clutched her mug as the noise in the inn quieted.

"Put your ugly scars away, Faustus," a red-faced woman said from one of the tables where they played sow-seeds on a pitted wooden slab. "We've all heard your story enough to tell it ourselves."

"Aye," a man piped up from the same table, holding his greasy mug out to the room. "The Enchanters will come and kill us all, after they've pissed on us and our animals."

"But they'll hold the Runeless in high esteem," a third said. "So high, in fact, that they'll mate with them all and have bastard half-Enchanter children!"

Chuckles rolled around the room, and Faustus scowled down at them, his drooping cheeks flushing dark.

"It's no wonder they haven't returned," Faustus spat. "You animals are worse than pigs, stuffing your faces and braying like donkeys. If we are lucky enough for the Enchanters to return, it will only be because they've seen the potential of *our* community. You've no idea what we're working on, what sorts of brilliant thinking goes on in our Quarter—"

"Save your words for those who care, wastrel!" someone called out.

"Is it that little tower you're speaking of?" another said. "Is it a tower of water or some sort of phallic symbol? I'm surprised your kind will deny a runeskill but not the use of an equally important tool—"

A burst of laughter erupted with a few jeers, and as the clamor in the inn rose, the innkeeper motioned to the door with a damp towel. "Faustus, now, I think it's best time for you to go—"

Faustus threw back his hood, revealing a severely balding head, and glared around the room. Spittle flung from his lips as he spoke. "The Enchanters will smite you, but perhaps not before the Runeless get a chance at it!"

A chair scraped the floor as the bear-like man pushed from the table, and before Farren could blink, a thick fist lashed out. The frail man flew back onto a table, his arm twisting oddly as he tried to catch himself. Mugs clattered to the floor, and customers leapt from their seats, backing away as the bear man took another step toward Faustus. The Runeless man lifted his head. Strained breath puffed from thin lips, and a gash seeped below his eye.

Farren clutched her mug, willing the foolish man to turn and walk out the door. He looked sickly and frail and would likely get seriously injured—if not killed—if he chose to persist in his challenge. Runeless or not, Farren couldn't stomach watching the man be beaten horribly in an unfair fight.

The big man paused, apparently satisfied that he had taught Faustus a lesson. Then Faustus grinned.

Farren cursed as Bear Man lurched toward Faustus and grabbed him by the collar, yanking him upright. In half a breath, Farren tore out of her seat and hurled her mug across the short space of the inn.

The sweet crack of pottery on Bear Man's shoulder resounded in the room. He paused just long enough for Farren to dive between the men. She shoved an elbow into Bear Man's ample stomach, and his grip on Faustus' cloak loosened.

Farren plucked the frail man away and whisked him toward the door. She had just flung it open and shoved Faustus through—reaching her mind out into the dark shadows of switchgrass and fireflies—when something snatched her hair.

"What are you up to, little snake?" the bear said as he hauled her down to the floor, a greasy lip curling into his bushy beard.

"More like a bird, actually," she said. He gripped her plaited hair, exposing the claw-like lines of a bear runemark imprinted on his meaty inner wrist. Figured. He *was* an *Ursid*, after all.

Through the door, Faustus hobbled away, rubbing what was surely a bruised arm. Did they have healers in the Runeless Quarter?

The *Ursid* pulled her up by her worn chiton so that it tightened around her throat. "Why did you let him go? He was asking for a beating."

"I agree with you there, Bear," Farren wheezed. "But you already busted his cheek and probably dislocated his shoulder. Any more might've killed the man."

His shoulders were nearly twice as wide as hers, and his chest heaved like a bellows. Fighting him would be futile—not only because of his size but because he would only get angrier at being challenged. *Ursids* were much more likely to go all-in on a fight than to back down with a little less pride. Besides that, she had come downstairs from her room for a drink, not a life-or-death match.

Her runeskill found what she was looking for. *Wake up, little birdie!* The sunsparrow roused quickly from slumber with a juicy image of a pipmelon, which she promised to bring the next morning.

The *Ursid* growled low at her, and she scrambled to think of a way to calm him. She opened a runebond with a second sunsparrow and a third—annoyed at the lack of efficiency at only being able to connect with one at a time—and hoped they would fly together.

"I saved you the trouble of killing him," Farren rambled, spots gathering in her vision as his grip tightened. "So now you can get back to your stew. It smells delicious, doesn't it?"

Food had to be a good bet for an *Ursid*. Her vision cleared as his fist slackened on her chiton, and her feet sank blissfully to the floor as he glanced back at his table.

The *Ursid* roared and seized her once more. "He stole my food! He's a thief!" His face purpled as he shook Farren like a rattle. "You let him get away!"

Well, that Faustus was a sneaky son of a vixen.

Just as Farren was starting to regret ever leaving her room, tiny yellow birds darted overhead, berating the *Ursid* with wings and chirps. Farren wrenched away from him and slipped around the tables. Customers cried out at the little flock, and the innkeeper hollered for the door to be closed.

Farren thanked the sunsparrows profusely and turned toward the staircase, head down as she fled the chaos behind her. She didn't want the *Ursid* to see her leave, in case he got it into his large head to come after her. Luckily, she was fairly confident that Iana would protect her from him, given that Farren was now the queen's servant.

A figure slid from the shadows, and Farren's momentary gratitude died.

Apparently, Scipio had stuck around to spy on her. A sneer hung on his face as he placed a hand on the cold iron railing of the stairs. "Did you enjoy poking the bear?"

She didn't respond but put her foot on the stairs resolutely.

His rough hand moved to cover hers, anchoring it in place. "Or perhaps you agree with the Runeless man, and that's why you saved him."

Farren's stomach tightened. "He was clearly suffering from madness."

"Why not let the Bear put him out of his misery, then?"

"By beating him to death? He was unarmed and sick. He needed a healer."

Scipio chuckled low in his throat. "Silly bumpkin, bringing your soft country morals to a place like this. Malodai is sharp-toothed and vicious, which you'll no doubt learn quickly. And you should know that there is no cure for Runelack madness...only slow, agonizing death."

Farren tried to pull her hand out from under his, but his fingers tightened to a bruising force.

"You don't recognize me, do you?"

"You mean from before I broke your nose? No, your face isn't particularly memorable."

"I wasn't positive before, but after that little scene..." He flicked a finger toward the room behind them. "It just confirms that you're the one who fought at Demithya's Festival in Capai. The same girl that I heard was a strong fighter was the girl I saw weak and weeping over a dying boy."

Farren froze, heart pounding as she looked Scipio over more closely. He had looked familiar to her before. But she would never forget Anaxis, and besides, that man was dead.

"You're not him," she said.

He cracked a smile. "Of course not. But I was there. I saw it all go down." He squinted at her and his smile twisted. "Is that why you wanted to leave home so badly? To get a shot at revenge? You tried it before, and that didn't work out too well."

Enchanter's foul dreams. Now she remembered. When she had finally mustered the courage to confront the gryphon owner about the attack on Desmond, a young man close to her age had laid her flat with a swift uppercut to her chin. He had told her to bugger off and spat on her for good measure. She hadn't realized it then, but he had the same dark curls as the gryphon owner, the same strong nose and pitiless mouth.

"Anaxis was your father?" she asked in a flat tone, trying to hide the way her blood pumped hotter. "He's already dead, so there's no revenge to be had."

Scipio smiled, and the tiny white daggers of his teeth were too similar to his coyote's. "You wouldn't have gotten close enough to my father to try. But I meant the gryphon. The one who almost killed your brother...and who *did* kill my father."

Cold shuddered into her, and she clutched the rail with a sweat-slicked hand. Knowing that the gryphon was alive—and likely at the fortress—sparked something in her she had thought long dead. Mind reeling, Farren moved around the guard, forcing her legs up the stairs as her stomach churned.

His hand snaked out, catching her by the arm. "Let's be clear, Outskirts wastrel. I've seen what you can do, and I know a little about where your heart lies. If you try anything like that spat you had"—he motioned to the room behind her—"on the queen or her gryphons, I'll have no trouble wedging a dagger into your heart."

Farren fought to keep her face and breathing steady, but cold dread spread in the pit of her belly.

She forced a smile. "So you are Anaxis' son. And yet, you aren't on the throne. Are you part of the royal family, or just...a simple guard?"

Scipio constricted her arm. "The only simple one here is you, bumpkin. You'd better have some care with your words and maybe try to learn something about the royal family. Otherwise, they might eat you up."

Farren yanked from his grasp and marched up the remaining stairs, his words ringing in her ears. When she finally curled into bed, she stared sleeplessly at the door.

# SIX

THE INNKEEPER SEEMED GLAD to see them go, and Farren couldn't blame him. He would likely spend a good part of the day cleaning bird droppings off the tables and chairs.

They ate a quick breakfast, and Farren used the last of her coin to buy a few plump pipmelons for the sunsparrows. The birds chattered blithely, and she basked for a moment in their joy, feeling a little less alone. Their shallow, fleeting impressions were nothing like the keen way of hawks, who lived by the strength of their talons and hunting intellect. And they were far different from the stunning, roiling mind of the gryphon who had hurt Desmond.

Farren sucked in a breath and banished all thoughts of gryphons. She refused to think about them again until she spoke with whoever was in charge of her Servitude.

The guards led her down the river harbor to the East Tow, where a wide, flat-bottomed raft waited to be pulled across the River Kithyria to the island of Alidonia. A shroud of mist—spewed from the thunderous Alidonian Falls—clouded the bright sky and obscured the river downstream. Far out in the middle of the wide expanse of river, Alidonia was crowned by a dark wall and three round towers. The air shuddered from the power of the falls. Did the fortress stone tremble the way her bones did?

"You aren't scared, are you?" Scipio's voice slid into her ear. "Because if you're not, you probably should be. The Alidonian Falls are four times the length of those distant towers. Fatal. Try not to slip."

The craft was made of sturdy wood, but beneath it, the water barreled downstream, tugging at the craft as if it were little more than a branch waiting to fly off the edge of the falls and plummet down and down and—

Farren took a shuddering breath and held tight to the rail. She eyed the ropes that pulled them, relieved they seemed in good condition.

"Why don't they just build a bridge like the Greenstone Bridge upriver?" Farren asked, and the guards stared at her over the steaming mugs of tea the rivermaster had offered them.

"The queen prefers it this way," Iana explained, "as it makes the fortress harder to breach."

Scipio leaned against the railing of the raft, dangling an arm over the side as he drained his cup. "Plus, it helps keep the servants from trying to run off."

Farren scowled, resenting the suggestion and their nonchalance about the crossing, and forced herself to sit and focus on their destination.

With each skin-prickling pull of the raft, the fortress grew more visible. Black river stone glittered along its wall and around the sheer sides of its towers, swaths of it obscured by a green skin of moss. Would she ever be allowed to see the horizon again once she stepped foot inside those walls? What was the difference between a fortress and a prison if you had no freedom and could barely see the sky?

A flat-topped keep rose above the wall, and next to it curved an iron grate, its rounded belly bulging toward the sky. Scipio leaned over her shoulder, his breath fogging in the cool river air. A sharp nudge from her elbow only made him give a *Canid* grin.

"See that iron cage?" he asked. "It's for the gryphons. That's where you will train for the guard."

Farren suppressed a shiver. The crash of the waterfall echoed off the fortress walls. Two of the towers stood at the front end of the island, with wide balconies that jutted from them like great shelves hovering high over the precipice.

When they finally reached Alidonia, the hard, packed earth beneath her soles was a relief. She sucked in a deep breath, and the smell of wet stone clung to her insides. The guards led her through the shadow of the gatehouse, and Farren expected to see more stone walls inside the fortress. Instead, they emerged into a small courtyard framed by lush gardens of trellised vines and tidy walkways. Beyond the gardens, the massive domed gryphon cage swelled upward, a lattice of ironwork that expanded to the height of the keep next to it.

Iana paused just inside the gate. "It is time for me to leave you," she said to Farren. "I expect you to become accustomed to your new duties. I don't want any more trouble from you. Is that clear?"

Farren gave a brief nod, tight-lipped. The guard turned to Scipio with a hard expression. "Take her to the bathhouse to begin her official induction."

Scipio turned to Farren. "Right this way, little—"

"And Scipio," Iana cut in. "Behave."

Scipio flashed blade-like teeth. "Like a prince." His words dripped irony, and when Iana frowned at him, Scipio placed a hand over his heart and gave her a slight bow. "Commander."

With that, Iana whirled away, her orange cloak rippling as she headed to the keep. Scipio reached for Farren's arm, but she flinched away. He smirked and pointed down a narrow path to her right, which disappeared into the garden. "That way."

The bathhouse was a squat stone building bustling with servants. Scipio passed her to a burly female.

"She's from the Outskirts, so be sure she gets a good scrubbing," Scipio said.

"Did you hear that, Dehlia?" the servant's voice rose above the bathhouse din. "We've got another from the Outskirts here! You want to wager on the smell again?"

"Give her here. I'm sure she's as ripe as the last." Dehlia was tall and thin as a rail-bird and stuck her big nose right into Farren's neck. The servant made a strangled sound, and Farren flinched away. "Aye, she'll need a thorough scrubbing. I told you," she said to the burly servant over her shoulder as she pulled Farren away. "They only bathe once every full moon."

The burly woman cackled with laughter. Farren didn't bother explaining that when she wasn't living in the mountains, she had bathed nearly every day, meticulously checking for lice and ticks. Those last few days in the mountains had been more difficult, as she had spent much of her time hunting and preparing food.

Cheeks burning, she threw a glare over her shoulder at the guard. Scipio wore his coyote grin, one that didn't reach his eyes.

The servants whisked Farren away. With no decorum, they took her to a private chamber, stripped her of clothes, then dragged her to the large interior of the bathhouse where the walls held stone fountains shaped into giant gryphon heads. Water gushed from a gryphon maw, dousing her in frigid water. The servants scrubbed at her body with brushes, scouring her like a dirty dish, and the cold shock of it made it impossible for Farren to speak. By the time they whirled her out of the water and dried her, she realized she wasn't the only servant being treated in such a manner. All ages of men and women took their cleanings silently, looking frozen and grim.

A different servant handed her a bundle of clothes—a worn blue chiton, a cloth for her loins, strips of padding for her monthly bleeding, an unadorned headscarf, and frayed rope sandals. A woman began barking at them while they tugged on their clothes, and after a moment, Farren realized she was telling them the rules of the fortress: *Do not enter the keep unless expressly invited. Do not leave your place of assignment without verbal permission. Bathe yourself daily. If you are sick, you must stay in your bedchamber and avoid contact with others. Do not look upon any of the direct royal family unless permitted. Bow before the Crown. Stealing shall be met with ten lashes; harm to another with twenty lashes; attempts at escape with thirty lashes and forfeiture of a month's worth of stipends. Persistent failure to obey your orders will result in fifty lashes and a possible extension of your Servitude and is at the discretion of your master.*

The chiton had five holes in all, and the bottom hem was tattered. When she tried to ask for a pair of leggings—best for fighting—they shushed her.

Dressed and raw-skinned, Farren was pulled back to the bathhouse entryway, where Scipio stood watching the proceedings with mild amusement. Had he seen everything? The beady-eyed, trailing look he gave her made her insides clam up. Other new servants like herself joined them, and Scipio led the way down another pathway to a smithy. The pungent smell of hot metal burned her nostrils as the thick-fingered smith measured her wrist. Moments later, he shoved a bronze shackle over her hand, scraping her fingers bloody as he pushed it on. The thick bronze band was cold and heavy.

Different guards led the other servants away. None of them, apparently, were to work alongside her. She was alone with Scipio.

"This way, bumpkin," Scipio said, leading her down another path. "Hope the bangle doesn't chafe too much."

Damp river air clung to her skin, and she tucked her cold fingers beneath her arms. The path curved as they walked around the gryphon cage. The hair on her neck rose when a feather-like rustle sounded close by, but her view of the cage was obscured by tall gardens.

The next bend in the path revealed a long stone building that reminded her of her father's mew. Was that where the gryphons were kept?

A girl suddenly walked out from behind some shrubbery, a fat pigeon clutched in her hands, and ran right into Farren. The pigeon burst free of the girl's grasp and flew straight into Farren's face, its wings beating her cheeks before it took off.

"Oh, I'm so sorry!" the girl exclaimed. Her pale, round face flushed the shade of a currant. "The dratted pigeon was to feed one of the little gryphons!" Despite her words, she seemed a little relieved as she watched the bird winging away.

The girl had skin like clouds and eyes as blue and clear as a mountain river. Even her hair, pulled back into many small braids, reminded Farren of the goldengrass that filled the seams between the Outskirts farmlands in the height of summer. Her appearance was similar to others she had met from the flat western country of Weldonia. Everything about her was bright—even her butter-yellow chiton that draped down to her sandals—except for the shadows smudged beneath her eyes.

"Did he hurt you?" the girl asked suddenly, peering close at Farren's face, where there was a loud bruise from where Iana had punched her. "Their wings can be brutally strong..."

"I've been hurt by worse. No need to worry." Farren meant for it to be funny, but the girl's eyes sharpened on Farren's bruised cheek before darting to Scipio.

"Don't you have work to get back to, servant?" Scipio drawled, eying the girl in a way that made Farren's skin crawl.

The girl tossed her braids, ignoring him. "My name is Camilla," she told Farren. "I'm an *assistant* here."

"I'm here to deliver this country bumpkin to the mews. She's to join the recruits for the gryphon guard, so I need to take her straight to the Lord Falconer whenever you are done with your idle chatter."

Farren glared at him, then softened her gaze on Camilla. "My name is Farren, and I would like to speak with the Lord Falconer as soon as possible."

Camilla smiled. "Of course, but he's away at the moment, probably with the queen." She turned her gaze to the guard. "You may go. I can take care of her from here."

"I'll stay," Scipio said, looking pointedly at Farren. "She's a bit feisty."

Farren bristled. "I'm not going to hurt a child." She bit her tongue to stop herself from saying more. Despite the rules of the fortress, Farren had no respect for the queen's guards. She had learned how awful they could be when her brother lay bleeding in her arms and they stood doing nothing to help. And Scipio...he was even worse than them.

"I am capable of taking care of her," Camilla said again. "And I will shout if anything goes amiss."

"I am to take her to the Lord Falconer," Scipio repeated. "Those are my orders. I'll not leave until I've filled them."

Camilla sighed, then took Farren by the arm and pulled her along the path. Scipio followed, keeping only a few paces behind. "I'm not a child, you know."

"You're certainly younger than me."

"I'm fourteen, and I'm able to bear children. That makes me a woman."

"I still wouldn't fight you like I did him."

Camilla touched Farren's bloodied hand and tutted. "We will need to see the healer about these scrapes."

"I have salve in my bags. Though I don't know where they are..."

"Oh, Iana brought them to your room earlier. I'm sure everything is in order."

"Do you know when the Lord Falconer will return?"

"No. He doesn't keep a strict schedule. Thankfully, he has us to keep things in order. I was told to give new servants a tour of the gryphon mews and yard."

"Oh... Would it be possible to wait to do the tour?" Farren let her voice drop so that Scipio couldn't hear. "I really would like to speak to the Lord Falconer because I-I'm hoping to work only with the hawks."

Camilla chuckled, but sobered when she realized Farren wasn't joking. "I'm sure the Lord Falconer would like to discuss that with you. I'll take you to your room first. We all sleep behind the mews so we can be close in case of emergencies."

"Like a gryphon attack?"

The girl gave her a curious look. "More like illnesses, a birth, or a fight between gryphons. We have a few animedics that live here too."

"And healers?" Incidents between humans and gryphons must've happened often.

Camilla ran a hand over the ends of her braids. "There are a few in Alidonia, and they come around to the mews sometimes."

The mews was a surprisingly tidy and lofty building full of wooden doors strengthened by iron frames and bolts. It smelled similar to her father's mews: musty, feathery, with a faint undertone of the prey they ate, which never bothered Farren much. And then she caught the acrid whiff of feline.

Farren shuddered. Was it the feline part of the gryphon that made them so changeable and unpredictable? It wasn't the eagle part, she knew, because eagles were consistent and reasonable; they wouldn't attack unless provoked. But felines lashed out if you merely deigned to glance at them.

She relaxed a little when they reached a corridor with normal doors. Camilla pushed one open. "This is to be your room."

Besides the bare floor and walls, there was a small window with a view of the garden, and a blanketed bed, which sank down and hugged her when she sat on its edge. She would sleep better imprisoned than she did when she was free. A small chest at the end of her bed held her bags.

"Breakfast is at dawn," Camilla said as Farren checked her things. "All meals will be eaten in the kitchen hall, which is attached to this building. There's also the servants' bathhouse, which you already visited. The queen values good hygiene."

Three meals a day provided for her *and* regular baths? It almost warmed the leaden weight in her belly. She stood from the bed and made to look out the window, then cleared her throat. "Are there any other luxuries I'll get as an indentured servant?"

From the doorway, Scipio snorted. "You don't know what real luxuries are, bumpkin. These are just basic necessities. Still, you should be groveling at the queen's feet for her generosity."

Farren gripped the window ledge. She was starting to despise Scipio, but she couldn't completely disagree with him. She wasn't entitled to any of this, servant or not. She should still be in the Kithyrian Mountains, struggling to survive and sleeping on a cave floor. It was the least she deserved for what happened to Desmond.

"Ignore him, Farren," Camilla said softly. "All the servants have access to food and the baths, plus get weekly wages at the end of each week. Mind, it's not much, and if the work isn't done well, the Lord Falconer has a right to withhold them."

Farren plastered on a smile and turned back to Camilla. "Will you show me the rest of the grounds?"

The girl showed her through the vast kitchens, past the keep where the royal family lived, around the royal stables and barracks where the royal guard slept, and across a tidy row of shops erected along the fortress wall.

Then there was the gryphon yard. Scipio hung back from the gate and crossed his arms as he watched them. Well-oiled hinges made no sound as Camilla's delicate hands unbolted the metal gate and swung it open.

Wide walkways nearly drowned in waves of frilled-petaled irises, and the high tinkle of sparkling fountains filled the air. The woven iron dome mantling the yard cast crisscrossed shadows that checkered the ground with sun and shadow. And the gryphons...

Her chest squeezed tight. Long beasts of golden fur and feathers draped over large boulders, drank from fountains, and slept in the shade of a tree bent with the weight of amethyst flowers. Each talon curved as long as a sword, and their beaks looked strong enough to split stone.

A swing of a head, a twitch of a claw, a cruel nip from a beak, and she would be maimed, or worse.

"As you may have heard, it was the queen's brother, Prince Anaxis, who first owned the gryphons," Camilla said quietly as she ambled inside, oblivious to the fact that Farren had stopped just inside the entry gate. "He went east to the Blades to catch them. He always talked about how gryphons and humans were meant to live together, but he mistreated them awfully. It was likely that his abuse caused his own death."

Camilla walked along one of the paths, raising her voice. "When he died and Queen Aurelia took the throne, she saw it differently. She believes they will cooperate if they are treated well. This main courtyard was converted to a gryphon yard when she began her program several months ago. They spend most of their time out here. The gryphon mews is actually an old stable, which the queen expanded..." Camilla glanced back and gave her a reassuring smile. "It's alright. They are accustomed to people. If you runebond to one, you can feel how calm it is."

"I-I'll stay right here." Farren kept her runeskill closed tight as she wiped sweaty palms down her chiton.

Looking at her sidelong, Camilla led her back out. Her breath came a bit easier as the girl slid the gate bolts home.

"Have you seen gryphons before?" Camilla asked.

"Yes. They had...colored feathers." Like ornaments, rather than the beasts they were.

"Anaxis often did that when out in public. Now it's a bit of a tradition while on public outings. She's been doing less of those lately since the new training has started."

Camilla dragged Farren into the mews, and the stale, dusty air was punctuated by the tang of feline musk. Thirteen gryphons lived there in the chambers, including a litter from the nursery where they were breeding even more of the beasts.

Far more gryphons than she had imagined. All of it was part of the queen's plans for building a gryphon guard. She thought to train them into submission. To get them to follow orders by runeskill alone.

Sweat poured from her as she silently tailed Camilla. Chains rattled behind a door—a recruit leashing a gryphon, Camilla explained. Down another hall, a massive door shuddered and groaned against the hinges as the gryphon inside scraped its talons. Splintered wood gathered in the gap at the base of the door. Five steps later, a raptorial shriek set her heart thudding like a drum.

"This is the way to the viewing tower," Camilla said, leading her down another hall with a steep stone stairway. Farren had long ago lost track of where they were in the mews. "This is where we watch to be sure a specially selected pair has mated."

A few more doors lined the hallway, and she edged down it, hoping Camilla would just move on. Scipio followed them, eyes darting to another gryphon door that rattled and thumped.

Camilla didn't move. "Do you want to go up and see it?"

"No." Her mouth felt stiff. "I would really like to speak to the Lord Falconer." She had to tell him that she simply wouldn't—*couldn't*—

"It's a beautiful view. Cato selects breeding pairs himself, based on their types of magic. The queen prefers ones with—"

"Magic?" It couldn't be true.

Camilla spoke gently, as if to a frightened kitten. "Some gryphons have magic, though not all. It's a well-kept secret, for now, but I'm sure Cato will explain everything once you meet him."

The old tales of her childhood told of gryphons with magic, how they had once been close to the Enchanters who made the world. But they were just stories. Before gryphons began to be taken by humans, the beasts had remained hidden in the depths of the Blades, so no one had known much about them, and rumors could be dismissed.

Farren turned abruptly from Camilla and forced herself down the cloistered, narrow hall, her mind spinning. How would anyone in Malodai be safe with a queen who thought to walk the streets with gryphons—*magic* gryphons! No matter how strong their runeskill, no one could *control* another animal—only persuade them.

How long would it be before someone got hurt like her brother did? Or maybe, Farren thought with a jolt, some already *had* been injured by gryphons. It would explain all those missing people in the city.

Farren walked faster, struck by the horror of it. Were gryphons snatching people away? How had no one noticed or cared?

"Wait," the girl called.

"I'll get her," Scipio muttered, cursing under his breath.

Farren almost felt bad, but any stray remorse evaporated when she saw that one of the doors was labeled with a sign, *Lord Falconer*, and that someone was speaking inside. The Lord Falconer was in, after all.

Without waiting, she reached for the handle.

Camilla's voice squeaked. "Farren, please just—"

Her body trembled as she threw open the door. In a fraction of a moment, she took in the scene before her: a slender young man lounged in a chair at a desk, drawling on to no one in particular, and a quill scribbled words over a sheet, all by itself.

As she burst into the room, the quill startled, veered for the inkwell and crashed into it, spilling ink all over the desk.

The young man leapt up from the chair. "Quill, dammit, look what you've done! Why do you always have to be so jumpy?" He grabbed the now-saturated paper by an untouched corner and held it up for the ink to drip off. The quill, apparently ashamed, stuck its head into the now-empty inkwell.

Farren stared, unsure of what she had just seen. The man glanced at her. "The quill frightens easily. Did you see the sign?" He indicated the door with a tilt of his head.

Beneath the sign reading *Lord Falconer* was a smaller one written in fine script. *Please knock before entering*. Well. Farren likely wouldn't have paid it any attention, even if she *had* seen it.

"Or maybe you can't read?"

The man spoke innocently, but Farren still wanted to bite his head off.

"I can read just fine," she retorted. But he didn't notice her tone because he was still trying to save his dratted page, blowing on it as if that would miraculously stop the ink from spreading. It rather seemed to be making things worse.

Scipio shoved into the room behind her and bumped into Farren's shoulder. "What in the Enchanted realms are you doing?" he asked Farren. "You can't just barge into the—"

"It's fine, Scipio," the Lord Falconer said. "I can see that she's new."

"I was just going to speak to the Lord Falconer *alone*, if you don't mind." She glared at the guard. A fine tremor had worked its way into her body, and she clenched her arms against it.

Scipio frowned. "But he's not—"

"She can stay." The Lord Falconer nodded at Farren to get on with it, his light eyes calm and insistent.

The quill trembled like a scolded pup in the inkwell, refusing to lift its head.

"It's Enchanted, like many things in this dreadful place," the Lord Falconer said. "A relic from the time of the Enchanters."

The time of the Enchanters was one of the legends she had grown up hearing. Long ago, the Enchanters discovered a beautiful world—full of vivid colors and creatures—but nothing had lived. An Emptiness ruled the land and held the beauty in an unmoving embrace. The Enchanters eventually grew tired of the sameness and created the very first runes to imbue the world with power and growth. Runes allowed the world to shift—for beauty to live, die, and be reborn in another form. Thus, runes could never be created or destroyed, except by Enchanters. Runes made the world breathe.

Out of all the runes making up living things, the Enchanters created one special rune that bound human to animal, so humans would never forget their close ties to the earth. After imbuing the world with runes, the Enchanters were satisfied with the beautiful place they had made. Some said that they put themselves to sleep deep in the Kithyrian Mountains, while others believed they died off. A few stories claimed that the Enchanters were immortal and that they chose to live among humans, disguising themselves as they built the fortress of Alidonia.

While a young girl, Farren fantasized about immortal Enchanters roaming the earth, but now that she was older and more mature, she had accepted that they were probably dead, if they had ever existed at all. Seeing the Enchanted quill made her feel off-balance, as if something in her world had shifted. Apparently, the Enchanters had given runes to a few nonliving things as well.

Camilla came up behind her, out of breath. "I'm so sorry, Cato."

"Don't worry, it'll be fine," he said, eyes warming at the sight of the girl. He set down the page and wiped his hands on an ink-stained cloth. "As long as the quill calms itself down before our next writing session. And no one intrudes." He shot Farren a meaningful glance.

As he moved, she was struck by how young he looked—only a year or two older than herself. How had someone so young become Lord Falconer? She studied his hands, but they were too covered in ink to see scars, and she couldn't catch sight of the small runemark on his inner wrist.

Farren took a shaky breath. "I would like to discuss with you my duties during my Servitude."

Cato smiled. "Oh?" He set the cloth down and came to rest against the side of the desk, crossing his arms. An exquisite skin painting of feathers spread like wings from somewhere beneath the luxurious folds of his sleeves all the way to his hands. The dark ink gleamed as richly as the waves of his hair, which fell loose to his shoulders. The silk of his chiton was fine as well, not the sturdier linen she would expect a Lord Falconer to wear.

"This is Farren Blackburn," Camilla explained. "She is taking her father's place and has agreed to ten years of Servitude in the royal mews."

Scipio's breath pooled on Farren's nape, and she inched forward. "I would like to request that I w-work with the hawks, sir."

"Of course you can work with hawks," Cato said, sounding relieved. "When you are done with your other duties."

"I mean, only with the hawks, sir."

"Only the hawks?" He scrubbed at the stubble on his chin. "The Servitude is for the entire royal mews. That includes the gryphon mews."

"I would prefer to work only with the hawks." Farren's back began to cramp. "I am not comfortable around gryphons."

He gave a considering nod, and Farren tried to calm the sudden hope that leaped in her chest. "Have you worked with them before?"

"No."

His brows lifted, and he turned to the desk, shuffling the papers there. "Do you have the order with you?"

"It's here," Scipio said, pulling the parchment from his vest and handing it to him.

He read the queen's order, the crease in his brow digging deeper. "This can't be right. You shouldn't replace your father if you haven't had any experience with gryphons." He threw Farren a questioning glance.

"Neither of us worked with gryphons, sir." She was beginning to feel relieved at his consternation. Maybe this would work out after all.

Cato folded the parchment and tossed it on the desk. "You have no experience working with gryphons, and you aren't comfortable around gryphons." He snorted. "I should've known she wouldn't listen to what I told her." He shook his head and rubbed a hand over his mouth, then straightened his shoulders decisively. "The order says you must, and I know the queen won't budge on this. Take it from me that she's just... She's far too desperate..."

His words died off, and he seemed to go deep into thought as he stared hard at the desk. Farren glanced at Camilla, wondering if this was normal. The girl looked pained as if she worried about whatever Cato was thinking.

"Is it possible that I might speak with the queen," Farren asked, "or write her a request?"

Cato's eyes flashed to hers, startled, and then he broke into laughter. "You won't be able to convince her of anything. She's pretty stubborn. She'll want you in the gryphon guard, no doubt. Did Scipio tell you about it?"

Her breath puffed quick and shallow. "Yes, but I—"

Cato sighed. "The queen wants *Avids* and *Felids* who can train to fight beside gryphons. The Runeless Sect has been inching their way into powerful positions, and she feels that a gryphon guard would quickly put down any...threats...that might occur."

"But—that's not what the order was for. It said working in the royal mews, nothing about fighting alongside g-gryphons."

"Listen, I don't want you doing it either if you've never worked with gryphons and clearly don't like them."

"I don't. And I'm not a-a fighter."

Scipio gave a loud snort. "That's a lie. She fought an *Ursid* alone."

Farren kept her attention on Cato, knowing she needed to convince him. "I had help from some songbirds. I wasn't alone."

"She gave a guard a bloody nose," Scipio continued. "And nearly broke his fingers."

This time she did set her scowl on Scipio, long and hard.

"Well," Cato said dryly, "it sounds like you'll make a fine addition to the queen's gryphon guard, then."

Spots appeared in her vision, and her voice rose several notches. "I c-can't be part of the gryphon guard. I would like to request an audience with the queen or—" Her voice broke, and she dug nails into her palms, scrambling to think of a way out. "Gryphons are wild beasts, and I will not be subjected to standing beside them while they injure and kill people!"

Cato's expression darkened, but Farren had little time to think of what else she would say because someone gripped her shoulder.

She thought it was Scipio, but the guard had moved back. Instead, a short, bearded man stood there, and his hand was puckered with old nicks and bite marks. One long, dark scar drove down the center of his forehead, marking a permanent scowl there, and his voice growled low in her ear. "You better have a damn good reason, girl, for yelling at Prince Cato in such a manner."

# SEVEN

THE OLD MAN, SCIPIO, and Camilla looked at her like she had just yelled at an Enchanter and that they expected her to grovel. She looked at the prince again, wildly searching for a clue of his title. He neither looked nor sounded like one and was even now carefully avoiding all of them, pretending to pore over a letter from the desk.

"He didn't tell me he was... I didn't know—" Her face flamed. "I assumed he was the Lord Falconer."

"And you would speak to *me* in this way?" the gruff man asked, his face difficult to read.

She recognized the scars on his hand left from where a beak had torn into skin or a talon scratched deep, and he had far too many to be a novice. She swallowed. "No. It is clear you have more experience, sir."

"Experience isn't the only merit demanding respect. You aren't the first Outskirts servant to come here, nor the first I'll have to teach harshly. Rules of conduct are different here. You'll take your first week without pay for your impertinence and be glad it's not a lashing."

She could hardly meet his eyes. "Yes, Lord Falconer."

Scipio chuckled low in his throat, and she ground her teeth.

The Lord Falconer's lips quirked then, tiredly, and his hand dropped. "Call me Horat." He shuffled toward the desk, and it seemed that he took special care in lifting his legs one in front of the other as if it pained him to do it. "And you should know that the prince often uses my study while I'm away." He turned a keen eye back to Farren. "You owe him an apology."

Farren wished her face wasn't burning so hotly as she forced out the words. "Your Highness, I'm sorry I—"

"That's not necessary," Prince Cato said shortly, waving a hand of dismissal.

"Continue," Horat ordered, as if the prince hadn't spoken.

Farren balled her hands. "I'm sorry that I yelled, Your Highness."

The prince said nothing, only remained tight-lipped while Horat scanned the queen's order.

Horat grunted. "So, you are filling in for your father?"

"Yes, sir."

He eyed her beneath bushy brows. "We'll have to write up a contract and have you sign it." He tossed the parchment on the desk. "Now, what is it you were yelling about?"

The prince spoke up before Farren could. "She has no interest in working with gryphons."

Farren forced her shoulders to ease back despite the tension coiled there. "I was simply asking if I could only work with hawks and falcons, as I'm uncomfortable around gryphons. I'm very skilled at all things falconry. Daily trainings, feedings, cleaning, and gutting prey items to prepare for cooking. I can do whatever is difficult or unpleasant for others to do."

"Your father taught you?" Horat asked.

"He's a very knowledgeable falconer, and buyers come all the way from Malodai and the other villages to purchase his birds."

"Yes, I've bought a hawk or two from Brin before. He certainly knows what he's doing." Horat eyed her. "I expect he taught you well. Any skills you've learned with falconry will come in handy for gryphon training." Horat rubbed at the scar on his forehead, then sank slowly into the chair. "Unfortunately, the queen's orders are final. She's keen on this gryphon guard. She's commanded that the *Avids* like yourself be trained and ready to work by the Festival of the Forging in six weeks."

A wretched weight pressed on her chest. "But surely I can request to speak with her, o-or one of her Councilors—"

"And tell her what? That you are afraid of gryphons?" Horat's voice turned sharp. "Queen Aurelia would never respect such an excuse. And I happen to agree that just because you are afraid of something doesn't mean you should avoid it altogether. In fact, your experience with birds will make you a valuable asset to the gryphon program."

Farren swayed as she stared at him. How foolish she had been to think they would listen to her—to think they would be reasonable. She would be trapped here, would be forced to get close to an animal who might rip off her arm, snap her neck—

She lifted a trembling hand to her chest, where her heart thundered like horses' hooves. They would never understand the thing that tried to strangle her, the thing that filled her with dread every time someone uttered the word *gryphon*. Flecks of black formed in her vision.

*Breathe, dammit, breathe.*

A hand wrapped her arm, and she flinched. Camilla had stepped up beside her.

"Did you hear Horat, Farren? He said Cato and I will help you. You won't be alone."

"But she doesn't want to learn," Cato exclaimed. "How am I supposed to teach someone who despises gryphons?"

Horat turned to his desk, clearly done with their discussion. "It will be a good challenge for you. And if she becomes too difficult to work with, you might remind her that her contract can be voided, and her father will be brought here to take her place. Now leave me. I've work to do."

Cato brushed past her, his mouth tight and shoulders hunched like a hawk about to take flight. Camilla gently tugged her out of the study, and Farren followed on unsteady feet. Her hands were so cold and the world had gone wobbly—

"I'm sorry I didn't tell you he was the prince," Camilla was saying in a hushed voice. "He is more like a brother to me. And he would have had my head if he heard me utter his title."

Farren struggled to sort the girl's words as her breath gusted in and out. Her lips had begun to tingle.

"Are you alright?" Camilla's summer-blue eyes peered at her, bright and worried. A moment later, the girl's face receded, dragging farther away until she seemed a pinprick swimming in a shuddering sea of shadow.

*Tap, tap, tap. Tap, tap, tap.*

Something tapped the side of her hand. A rhythm.

*Breathe, dammit, breathe! Breathe, breathe, breathe.*

"Slower, Farren. That's it. Come back to my fingers. Feel this?" The tapping continued, pulling Camilla closer.

She could see the girl's face again, but it was all swirly-wet. Farren wiped her eyes and blew air through pursed lips.

"Keep going," Camilla said. "Follow my fingers."

*Tap-tap-tap. Breathe. Tap-tap-tap. Breathe.*

Like a ragged feather dragged through a beak, her thoughts slowed. Began to sort themselves. Her heart returned to a normal pace, and the tingling faded.

"Thank you," Farren whispered. "I don't know...what just happened."

"Healer Selena calls them attacks. I get them sometimes, too. It helps to tap yourself like this. And to breathe slowly."

"Why do you...?"

Camilla pulled her hands away. "The same reason you just did. We both have a ghost that haunts us. Not a real ghost, I mean, but something like it."

Farren wiped her face dry with her chiton. The weight that had forced itself on her had diminished somewhat, but something hard and cold had settled in her belly.

"Come, let's go to the kitchens," Camilla said, standing. "We'll get you a warm cup of tea."

She didn't know what she had done to deserve Camilla, but she went with the girl gladly.

Camilla showed her the kitchen, where the cooks laid out tea, dried figs, olives, and bread spread with a thick herbed cheese. It was the most food she had seen in months. She didn't even mind the kitchen staff who eyed her approvingly as she ate a few bites, nor the *slick-slap* of the massive kitchen frog that sat next to the refuse pail as it caught bugs.

There were far more animals in the kitchen than Farren would've thought appropriate, but each had a function. Besides the frogs that snatched at flies, cats herded mice and other vermin out the doors, and an otter helped scrub dishes in a large basin of soapy water. Long-limbed dogs carried the refuse pail out to the refuse heap, where a hoard of raccoons eagerly waited to eat it. Each of the kitchen staff directed their rune animals to help out.

Other things, too, made Farren stare while she ate. A broom that swept by itself—a temperamental tripping hazard, the cook told her, unless one knew its route around the kitchen—and a knife that chopped on command. Farren hoped it preferred to cut only food.

After they ate, Camilla took her to the hawk mews, telling her they would start with the gryphons first thing in the morning. When they entered the hawk mews, tension eased from her shoulders at the familiar, orderly interior. She made a mental list of what she would do in the coming days. Read over the logs, familiarize herself with each hawk and falcon, their medical histories, diets, and where they were with their trainings. Scanning the logs, she noticed that the prince's initials were missing from the entries and felt relieved. Perhaps he only worked with gryphons, and she wouldn't have to worry about running into him at the hawk mews.

"What's a prince doing working in the gryphon mews, anyways?" Farren asked Camilla, who had gone to the closest stall to check on a young hawk. "Shouldn't he be preoccupied with princely duties?"

Camilla spoke softly so as not to startle the bird. "He never was much for princely duties. His brother does most of it, so he is able to focus on the gryphons."

A brass plate on the stall displayed the hawk's name: Tayra. Her leather hood—worn over the eyes to keep her calm—was made with oiled leather, fine golden thread, and scarlet-dyed feathers, far fancier than others Farren had seen and used. Not that the hawks cared. Mellion had always felt the same about the hood, regardless of what it looked like; the hood was something Mellion had resented yet submitted to. It had made her feel safe.

Farren runebonded to Tayra, and curiosity sparked down their connection. Mellion had always welcomed her with a similar flush of interest. Farren closed her eyes, recalling the last time she had seen Mellion's ruddy feathers and knifing gaze, frozen and clear as icicles in the dead of winter. Their connection, sundered.

She closed the runebond with Tayra. "The queen and king don't mind the prince working with gryphons instead?"

"Not now, since the queen has realized how gryphons can help her cause," Camilla said, stroking Tayra's creamy, feathered chest. "And Cato is the perfect person to lead the training for the gryphon guard, as he's been working with gryphons since he was a little boy. His uncle always kept some, trapped when they were kits, and Cato spent much of his childhood bonding with them."

Farren was starting to understand. "Was it the prince who started the breeding program?"

Camilla hesitated, tugging at her long bundle of golden braids. "His uncle had begun breeding them before his death. The first litter was born this past spring, and shortly after, the queen came to Cato with her request for the gryphon guard. *That* was her idea, though."

"But one that the prince agreed with?"

The girl seemed to realize that she wasn't helping Farren to see Cato in a better light. "He didn't have much choice. You'll understand once you meet the queen."

Farren would likely never understand the royal family. But one thing was certain: gryphons had no place among the streets of Malodai—whether they were part of a trained guard or not. And now that she was here, in Malodai, she could try to prevent it from happening.

Six weeks, Horat had said, before the gryphon guard would be functional. Would she be able to stop it before then? What could she even do without risking the little she had left? Farren pressed her hand over the leather cover of the ledger, the embossed ridges of the royal sigil—a gryphon claw—curving beneath her fingers. The other option was to do nothing. To commence with training, to work with gryphons. To fight with them. She would not only witness slaughter but be the reason for it.

That was a fate she couldn't stomach. Besides, didn't she owe it to Desmond to do something?

Farren chewed on her lip. If she failed, her father would be forced to take her place at the fortress. But her father, more than anyone, would understand why she would try. Just like Farren, he had been deeply affected by Desmond's accident, and he would never agree to the way gryphons were being used at the fortress, knowing how unpredictable and violent they could be. He had always taught her to choose her fights carefully, to be sure that her instincts aligned with what she knew to be right. She could hear his voice as distinctly as if he spoke right beside her, and the words rang in her heart.

*If you know you must fight, then fight without hesitation.*

# EIGHT

FARREN WOKE EARLY THE next morning when something poked her cheek. Wincing, she pushed up on her elbows and stared at the little golden feather with its tiny prodding quill. It still carried Mellion's warm, musty scent. She tucked it under her pillow and rolled off the cover of a book that lay half-open beneath her.

*Diseases of Plants, Animals, and Humans*. Right. She'd been searching for any hints about what had happened to Mellion. Another tome lay down by her feet, tossed there when she realized *Adventures of an Animedic* referred to the excursions of a lascivious animedic in the bedroom—and inn, and storehouse, and on a boat—rather than his experiences treating animals with illnesses.

She marked her place in the open book and stowed both on her desk. Horat had given her permission to borrow a few books at a time from his study, noting aloud that she clearly had some things to learn. Unfortunately, she hadn't found anything worth noting, although she *had* learned a lot about diseases. And prurient adventures.

Out her window, a whisper of dawn lightened the sky—and from the quietude outside her door, she knew the servants must still be asleep. Dressing hurriedly, she tried to gather her wits in the darkness. Little sleep had left her foggy-headed, but now she needed to see everything and consider it all carefully.

In the hall, candles flickered sleepily in their sconces, casting dazed shadows on the stone floor of the mews. Farren didn't waste a moment lingering. She walked the corridors at a brisk pace, only hesitating when she entered a hall lined by the giant, double-paneled oakwood doors of the gryphon chambers. No guards stood sentry there. That was good.

The doors were bolted closed, but none locked. From the tour Camilla had given her, she knew there were thirteen gryphons in all—including the litter, which apparently didn't get use of the yard. Did each gryphon have their own chamber? Farren counted six doorways, then turned breathlessly down the next hall, ears pricking at the sound of what could only be talons against stone. To distract herself, she whispered the numbers aloud.

"Seven, eight, nine"—*scuff, scuff, scuff*—"ten, eleven, twelve. There must be more down the next hall—"

She nearly screamed as she ran headlong into something—some*one* who was warm and tall and smelled faintly of mint.

Farren jerked her head up, trying vainly to look calm and collected. A pristine velvet sash draped from the shoulder of a slim man, and the white of the silk chiton beneath it had a smudge of what looked like charcoal. A large leather satchel hung from his other shoulder. However well-dressed he was, there was no mistaking the dart of his eyes down the corridor behind her. A moment later, he looked at her fully and his mouth quirked.

"You're not sneaking around, are you?" the man asked. "Cato would be quite displeased."

"No, I was making my way to the hawk mews. I'm new here, and I'm afraid I'm a bit lost." She glanced around, feigning confusion.

"Right, I wasn't sneaking either." He grinned at her. "Actually, I'm trying to avoid Cato. He'd be livid if he caught me here."

"Yet you don't look very afraid." Far from it, in fact. He seemed to be studying her with some intensity. Heat rose to her cheeks. When had a man last looked at her like that? Probably Thestor, although Thestor had never managed to look quite so...perceptive.

The man shrugged. "Cato's easier to deal with when I keep my distance."

His eyes, mottled brown and green, reminded her of the mountains in springtime. His skin was the same coppery shade as Prince Cato's, with a similar pretentious tilt to his brows. Cato's brother, but she couldn't recall his name.

"So why are you here?" she asked.

"To sketch the gryphons. This is where they live, by the way." Irony dripped from his words.

"I'll keep that in mind." Farren was just about to step around him to continue her task when she hesitated. "You said you sketched the gryphons? Can you tell me anything about them?"

The young man chuckled and lifted his hand to rest on the strap of his satchel, inadvertently exposing his inner wrist. Where a runemark should've been etched in ink, a scar formed an uneven circle of whitened and warped skin.

He saw where her attention was and carefully dropped his hand, his smile diminishing. "You could ask me about gryphons, but Cato would know much more than I."

"Perhaps..." Farren chewed her lip. "You might know other things though. Like why the Crown needs a gryphon guard."

He gave her a peculiar look, and she tried to hold steady beneath his burning stare. "It is very likely that you and I know the same things. The queen is building a strong guard to protect against threats."

Cryptic. Vague. And utterly unhelpful. "What about the king? Does he have any part in it? Does he agree with—"

*Ki—ki—ki!!*

Farren whipped toward the noise—a shriek so loud it threatened to split her skull—and her body fell into a fighting stance, facing the door from where the noise had risen. Blood roared in her ears as she grappled with her panic, leashing it with every stroke of breath she took.

The door remained closed, and the gryphon behind it quieted. The roaring in her ears faded, and she crossed shaky arms over her chest.

"I take it you don't much like the gryphons?"

"No, I uh..." She cleared her throat and flicked the prince a wary glance. "Much like you and your brother, the gryphons and I will get along better if there is distance between us."

His lingering smile seemed to freeze for just a moment. "Sometimes it's better to face our fears."

"Then I suppose I should tell Prince Cato that you were here. You can face your fear and hash out your differences."

The man held up his hands, bowing his head in acquiescence. He hadn't stopped smiling. "I didn't mean any disrespect. But why all the questions?"

"As I said, I'm new here. And"—she held up her wrist, shackled by the bronze bangle—"I'm stuck here for a while. I'd like to better understand the people I work for."

"And you don't think my brother would answer your questions?"

The way he watched her, really *looked* at her, was leagues away from Prince Cato's aloofness. "I have a feeling you understand people far better than he."

He stepped closer, an arm-length away, and the minty smell of him shivered in the air. "Well, I am happy to answer your questions...if you agree to one thing."

Farren studied his firm jawline, tracing it to his smooth, tilted lips. "What?"

"By letting me paint you."

"I'm not amused."

"I'm completely serious."

His eyes flickered over her face as if he could see something beyond her skin and hair. When she lifted her chin, his gaze drifted down her throat, caressing it. Warmth flushed into her.

"I have a lot of work to do," she said.

The prince smiled, nodding appreciatively. That threw her. "You're welcome to work while I paint. Actually, I'd prefer it. It's the birds I'm really after, anyways. You mentioned working with hawks, so I assume that you actually like them."

"I'm a falconer," Farren stated. "It's what I do."

"Then you are the perfect candidate. I'll arrange it all, no need to worry."

"I haven't said yes yet."

The prince paused and looked at her sidelong. "But you want to. It makes too much sense to say no." He didn't give her time to refute it. "Bring a hawk or two with you."

"With me where?"

"I have a well-lit chamber I use for painting in the keep."

"You want me to go to a chamber in the keep with a complete stranger." Farren lifted a brow at him.

"I'm well-known around here. I've painted many people, so you wouldn't be the first." With perfect ease, he reached into his satchel, pulled out a pink apple and bit into it.

"You may want to discuss it with your brother first. He might not be too happy you're taking me away from training." Or he would be thrilled since he hadn't wanted to train her anyways. "And the Lord Falconer," Farren added, doubting very much that he would get approval from both.

He winked at her. "Leave it to me."

"I don't even know your name."

He looked pleasantly surprised. "My apologies. I tend to forget my princely manners when sneaking around." He held out a hand, and when she gave him hers, he pulled her a bit closer. "Prince Isander. Lovely to meet you...?"

"Farren."

"Farren," he repeated, then he bent and brushed his lips over the back of her hand. "I'll be seeing you soon."

He spun on his heel, suddenly moving with alacrity. She watched him go, breathless with the lingering warmth of him on her hand. Even the scent of him remained in the hall, like a cool drink in the heat of summer.

But rather than quenching her thirst, it only made her want more.

The Lord Falconer entrusted the care of the hawks to several of the servants, and one of them had met her and Camilla in the mews the evening prior to review the schedules and duties. Farren would assist with Tayra and some of the other hawks, and the servant seemed to have no qualms about giving small tasks over to her after hearing about Farren's experience with her father's mews.

Farren used the few remaining moments of dawn to check on Tayra and feed her. Tayra would need to be put on the glove habitually in order to get used to Farren. An easy task and one she loved because of what it meant. She would learn to trust Tayra, and Tayra would learn to trust her—and every moment of it would build the foundation of their future hunting partnership.

When Farren headed back into the gryphon mews, she ran into Camilla emerging from one of the gryphon chambers. A huge golden eye and the gleam of a beak filled the doorway as she closed and bolted it. Farren clenched her hands and fought to keep her breathing even. The bolt was no thicker than a stick and might snap if—

"Farren?"

She flinched. "Yes?"

"Is it another attack?"

She loosened her claws. "No. I'm...fine. Thank you."

"Promise to tell me if you need something? Anything at all?"

Farren gave her a tight smile. "That's kind of you, but right now, all I have are questions. Like why Prince Isander paints servants."

"Oh, you met him? He paints whatever takes his fancy in the moment. He's a very respected artist, held in high regard by the king and queen. When he isn't engaged in princely duties, he spends all his time painting."

"Has he painted you?"

The girl shook her head and petted her braids. "I've not spoken to him before. Cato prefers I stay away from him."

Farren found this very interesting despite knowing she should not get involved with the royal family. Too late for that. "Well, he seems a bit arrogant, so consider yourself lucky." Camilla began walking down the hall with her, and her stomach flipped. "Are we going to see Cato? To start the training?"

Camilla smiled up at her. "The Lord Falconer has requested that you spend the morning cleaning to get familiar with the layout of the mews. I'll show you where the supplies are kept."

Despite herself, Farren grinned. Cleaning. Good. She could do cleaning and do it damn well.

Farren listened and watched while she cleaned. She would need to familiarize herself with the other servants and their habits and try to learn as much about gryphons as she could—without getting too close.

But the gryphons themselves made it difficult for her to concentrate. Every time she glimpsed one out of the corner of her eye or heard talons rasping against the stone floor, her whole body clenched tight as a claw on a mountain rabbit.

A similar tension sprang up whenever Prince Cato passed her, which was often. He was always empty-handed, always lost in thought. He barely noticed her, which she wouldn't mind except for the fact that there was so much to do, and he seemed to be doing, well...nothing. Other servants scuttled around the mews—many of them recruits like herself—tidying the chambers, oiling the iron chains and collars, hauling water and meat to the chambers, or bringing platters of tidbits and drink to the study, where the prince returned between ambles.

Cleaning harder seemed to help with her growing irritation. She scrubbed the dingy windows, wiped cobwebs from far-flung corners, and mopped and mopped. The mop was excellent; it left the stone floor spotless, even when the bucket water grew thick with grime. She closed some of the windows so the dust wouldn't stir around too much, but the one in the entryway seemed broken, as it had opened again. She pulled it closed once more and latched it just to be sure.

She passed through a corridor she had already mopped, noticing a clump of dirt and feathers in the corner. She set the bucket down, dipped the mop, and scrubbed again. Despite cleaning the rest of the floor perfectly, the dratted mop didn't seem to be able to get all the way into the corner, no matter how she angled it or how hard she pushed.

Muffling a cry of exasperation, she decided she would just have to scrub the corners with a bristle brush. She grabbed the bucket of dirty water and heaved it down the corridor, then paused as a draft flew over her.

The window she had latched was open. Again.

Farren glanced around the corridors, wondering if someone was playing a trick on her, but the others had gone to move the gryphons to the yard, leaving her alone to clean.

The bucket of water grew heavier in her hands. Sighing, she abandoned the window and trudged to the end of the corridor, walking straight into Prince Cato as she rounded the corner.

Water sloshed onto the floor, wetting his fine rope sandals. He looked up, surprised, then stiffened when he saw who it was. "Excuse me," he said, his voice as flat as his expression.

So, he had already decided to dislike her. Farren wasted little time with politeness, making her tone equal to his. "Excuse me, Your Highness. What exactly do you do here?"

"Me?"

Farren glanced around. "You seem a bit aimless...Your Highness."

He bristled. "I'm not aimless. I'm thinking."

How was it that Horat put someone like Prince Cato in charge while he was gone? Farren wondered if being a prince was his only qualification.

"And stop calling me that," the prince continued, "It isn't... You don't need to."

"And why is that, Your Highness?"

His lip began to curl, although he seemed to be making a decent effort at smothering his irritation. "Because I said it's not necessary. You can just call me Cato. The same as everyone else here."

"Well, maybe you could help mop up the west corridor. Or fix the window in the entryway. Unless"—she lowered her eyes, pretending deference—"you feel these things are beneath your status."

"My status—?" Confusion, then exasperation, leapt over his face. "I can certainly help. Which window is broken?"

When Farren brought him to the window in the entryway, he laughed.

"It's not broken," he said, "just Enchanted."

Farren shivered in the cold river breeze rushing through it. "Why would someone want a window that constantly opens itself?"

The prince shrugged as if it was completely normal. "It's Enchanted to open whenever it senses the need for fresh air."

"So, all the time."

He chuckled. "I wouldn't worry about the window. But there are some other Enchanted objects around you might want to know about, if Camilla didn't tell you during your tour."

"I did tell her; she just wasn't listening," Camilla said as she came down the hallway. She hauled a bucket of what looked to be animal organs and her delicate nose crumpled at the smell. "There's the window here, plus the mop that avoids corners—"

"What is the purpose of a mop that avoids corners?" Farren asked, scowling as she adjusted her hold on her heavy bucket of water.

Camilla gave a wan smile. "Not all of the Enchantments seem to have a purpose. But that mop does clean better than the others—with the exception of corners—so I believe it was Enchanted for that. It's just that sometimes they also have...quirks."

"Quirks?"

"Perhaps it was an apprentice Enchantress who did the work, and she did it poorly. Or maybe the Enchanters had a weird sense of humor," said Camilla.

"We can only speculate," the prince told Farren, "since most written records of the Enchantments have been lost."

"It's not dangerous—usually," Camilla said. "You'll just have to watch out for the kitchen fire, as it tends to get a bit hungry, and there's a pair of darning needles one of the servants uses, which get into fights, and you don't want to get in between the two, and oh, there's a broom that sweeps by itself, and if you try to stop it, you might get hit in the head. Better to leave that one in the closet."

"As long as you stay away from the keep, you should be fine," the prince said. "There are far more dangerous things there. It's easy to get lost, and there remain some relics that even my family won't touch."

Farren felt herself nodding as if this was completely acceptable, then said, without thinking, "And here I thought the gryphons would be the ones to kill me."

The prince's face shuttered closed. "The gryphons are far less dangerous than Enchantments," he said tightly. "Camilla, I'll have Farren help you with feedings today. She needs to get used to being around them."

Cold flushed through Farren. She wasn't ready to be around them, not yet—

"It's alright," Camilla said. "I'll show you exactly what to do."

"I need to empty this." Farren indicated her bucket of dirty water. She just needed a moment alone to get some fresh air—

The prince reached for the handle. "I'll take care of it."

Farren held on tight. "I'm perfectly capable of doing it on my own."

The prince tugged, tumbling water down the sides. "I'm sure you are. But you need to go with Camilla. You can't spend all your time cleaning."

"I probably could." She glared at him.

His pull on the bucket handle was unrelenting. "Listen, I don't want you to be involved with the gryphons, either. But Horat—and my mother—command that you work with them. It'll be far easier if you just accept that"—he tugged hard on the bucket, drenching her shoes—"and get over your fear of them."

Farren grit her teeth and released her hold, causing the bucket to tilt wildly toward the prince's torso. Grimy water flew out and soaked his extravagant silk chiton. Camilla gasped, and the prince stared open-mouthed at his dripping clothes.

A light tread of footsteps approached from down the hall. "Oh, there you are!" a servant—named Livigena, Farren remembered—called out when she saw Farren. The silvery beads in her dark hair flashed as she handed a missive to Farren and eyed the prince as he tried to wring the water from his clothes without damaging the silk. She turned her attention to Camilla, rubbing her chest with one hand. "Camilla dear, can you swing by once you're done with...whatever it is you're doing with that meat? My chest is just aching from the way Aktin spoke with me last night. I could hardly close my eyes! I'm sure he is done with me, and it just makes all of my insides..."

Farren ignored the woman. The note was from the elder prince, Isander, calling her to his art chamber. He had cleared the matter with Horat, as well, and urged her not to worry. Farren repressed a smile as she shoved the missive at Cato. "Looks like you won't have to deal with me after all. Prince Isander requests my presence."

Everyone froze and Cato stared at the letter. His expression hardened as he read. He gave a wordless look to Camilla, then he turned on his heel, taking the sloshing bucket with him.

# NINE

FARREN MOMENTARILY FORGOT PRINCE Cato's warning about the keep as a guard led her and Tayra through the immense wooden doors of the keep. A short, tiled corridor opened up to a grand atrium. Columns surrounded a rain pool that mirrored the dusky sky from the rectangular opening in the roof overhead. Potted plants fringed the pool, dotted the walls, and hung from baskets and pointed clay containers that dangled by long chains from the ceiling. Like Keira's apothecary back home, the air was lush and green, but beneath that lingered the pervasive scent of ancient stone.

Past the rain pool, two thrones stood empty on a dais, and behind that—

Farren halted as a massive gryphon walked idly behind the thrones, separated from them by what appeared to be a transparent glass wall dividing the chamber from the gryphon yard. Every hand-span of the gryphon declared strength and confidence, from its pointed beak to its well-muscled limbs rippling with golden fur.

Tayra twitched, sensing her sudden fear. *It's alright*, she told Ta yra...or maybe herself. The gryphon peered through the glass and saw Farren. It was as if she met the gaze of a human: inquisitive, intelligent, and all-seeing. It would take only a mere opening of her mind for Farren to runebond with it. But what was there to know besides the ferocious wildness she had felt of a gryphon before?

So *much*, that gaze said. The gryphon had a sharp face and keen eyes, feathers fringing them like a mane. Wide, tall ears opened to her as if the gryphon could hear her through the wall. Or perhaps the gryphon *wanted* to hear her.

"This way," the guard said, and Farren took a breath.

The gryphon moved away, and Farren followed the guard, keeping her fist steady so Tayra wouldn't get frightened. They passed from the large atrium into a wide corridor with brilliant yellow walls, which turned toward a sort of sitting chamber. From there, Farren lost track of where they went. Halls of different colors led to stairwells and even more corridors, all becoming less vivid the deeper into the keep they went. The light, too, seemed to diminish, and Farren wondered where all the windows were. After climbing yet another flight of steps, they finally arrived at a narrow door.

"I'll wait outside until you and Prince Isander are finished, then lead you back," the guard told her, giving the door three solid knocks.

Farren relaxed minutely, knowing she would never make it back on her own, and thanked the guard. How much of what Prince Cato had said was true? She hadn't seen anything odd-looking around the keep. And yet, her skin prickled with the sensation of immense vastness and something else—a slight pressure to the air, as one would feel standing next to another person.

The door swung open. Sunlight poured around Prince Isander, streaming in from the tall, wide windows behind him. Farren squinted in the sudden brightness and realized that she stared directly at the prince's chest. He wore a loose—*very* loose—Weldonian shirt with a deep cut down the front. Averting her gaze down, she realized there was even more to see, outlined by his well-fitted leggings.

"Farren. A delight to see you. Do come in. Make yourself comfortable."

The room was cluttered but tidy. Clean jars, rags, and brushes were stacked in piles on a table, and blank canvases were propped against the wall. Covered easels stood silent in shadowed corners, and a cushioned chaise sat across from the window.

"Where would you like me to stand?"

The prince strode right up to her, and she swayed at his sudden proximity. He peered into her eyes, then glanced around her face, nodding to himself. He took her free hand and pulled her to the windows, which had a clear view of a portion of Malodai and the wide blue Kithyria. From here, she could see smoke billowing from chimneys, carts weaving in and out of grassy lanes, and a flock of red-bellied swallows chasing a hawk until it fled beyond the stone wall marking the city's boundary.

"The light is wonderful today, isn't it?" The prince spoke quickly, each word carefully formed and light. His hand was soft but firm, directing her as if he had done so a thousand times before. "And here, I think." He placed a hand on her shoulder and turned her gently toward the light. His eyes brightened. "Yes, that will work. Stay right there. Are you comfortable? Do you need a refreshment before we begin?"

"No...but will I be able to speak while you work?"

"Of course. You can ask your questions after I begin, though I might not be able to answer you the way you'd like." At her puzzled look, he added, "The work is my focus, and that is where my mind will be. If it's something more complicated, we can talk more after I'm finished. Does that sound agreeable?"

"Yes, but—"

"One more thing. I'm limiting you to three questions with each painting session."

"Each? How many times will you—?"

"As many sessions as it takes. So, think carefully before you ask."

"That's not what we agreed," Farren said, heat rising to her cheeks. Was he trying to play games with her?

"I'm putting a condition on our agreement because I respect your time and mine. If I spent all my energy answering your questions, I would have little left for my artwork, and that isn't fair to me. Because it would take me longer to paint, it also isn't fair to you. Don't you agree?"

Farren bit her lip. Fine. She would think of three questions. Careful questions that would somehow help her disrupt the gryphon program.

"Miss Blackburn?" He waited for her answer.

"I agree."

"Very good."

He got to work, pulling over the blank easel, gathering his paints and jars. He sketched with a slim piece of charcoal first, quietly marking the canvas as his strong brows drew down, eyes leaping from her to the easel, never slowing. Every once in a while, he would drink from a clay cup, and the fresh whiff of mint swirled between them.

Farren recognized his intensity. It was the same way she felt when she got pulled into a fight. The world shrank to a pinpoint, and intuition took over, guided by the sound of breath and rustling clothes, the glimpse of a muscle twitching or weight shifting, and the feel of air gliding over her skin as she dodged the pernicious lunge of a *Mustelid.*

Tayra shifted, and Farren pulled her eyes away from the prince's sleek form.

The gryphon feeding and yard schedules were the same every day, so easy to learn, but disrupting those would only irritate the queen, not shut down the program. The other things—the mating pairs, the magic, the training—had far more potential. But as of yet, she knew nothing about those particulars and doubted Isander would. No, the best things she could learn from him would be about the royal family itself. She already knew the question she *wanted* to ask: What would stop the queen from putting the gryphons in the streets? But that would be far too suspicious.

"You told me that the queen wants the gryphon guard to protect against threats," she said. "I heard that the threats are from the Runeless Sect. Is that true?"

"Yes. My mother is concerned that their numbers are growing, and so too their influence on the streets and in Alidonia."

Farren thought of the frail man, Faustus, from the inn that had babbled on about purging runeskills and removing runemarks from wrists. His words had been half-crazed, but the man himself hadn't seemed much of a threat.

"Why isn't the queen's royal guard enough? Or is it more about appearances for her? That sounds like something Anaxis would do—" she cut herself off, realizing he might be offended by the mention of his uncle.

His hands paused. "You know those are two questions. Unlucky for you, it's one answer." He continued sketching. "The Runeless Sect are inventors. They put all of their resources into building, creating, and thinking. Sometimes, they share their creations with us. A bow that shoots arrows twice as far; a system of pumps that helps move water from a cistern up to a bedchamber; a toothed knife that can slice through bone like parchment. Many of their creations they do not share with us. That is what the queen fears."

Farren chewed on her cheek. She had already asked her three questions, but the answers had only given her more to ask.

"I haven't heard of the Runeless Sect actually harming anyone," Farren stated.

"It's the possibility of a real threat that the queen worries over. The politics of Alidonia require careful planning, foresight, and posturing. If they attacked suddenly, it would be too late for her to do anything."

"But—" She puffed a breath out, wishing she could just ask a question. "I fail to see why they would attack Alidonia."

The prince's mouth twitched. "I see what you're doing, Farren. Questions that aren't questions." He *tisked*. "And the answer to that one would take too much of my attention. Anyways, I am surprised you don't know more. Where are you from?"

She gave him a wan smile, knowing he had probably never heard of her home. "A small village called Capai. It's—"

"In the Outskirts to the north? Yes, I had the pleasure of visiting there some weeks ago."

She blinked at him. Hadn't Keira mentioned something about a prince visiting to paint the mountain scenery? "I hope you enjoyed your visit."

"Very much. You're lucky to have grown up surrounded by so much beauty. The fields and mountains were utterly captivating." He wasn't looking at his work anymore but at *her*. The afternoon sun beamed over his handsome brow, gilding it like a crown. "You must miss it terribly."

Farren cleared her throat. "I do."

"What is your favorite thing about it?"

"The simplicity of it," Farren said. She stroked her fingers down Tayra's chest and sent the hawk little waves of calm. The hawk needed to learn that human touch wasn't a bad thing and that it could even be good. "It's a predictable place, most of the time, and I know everyone there, and they know me."

"I know how that feels," the prince said, grinning.

"Of course, everyone knows you. But you can't possibly know everyone here."

"You're right," he amended, taking a sip from his cup. "But I know more of them than you might think."

Perhaps he did through a distant, princely view. He likely pitied those he saw, seeing how little they had compared to him. Was that why he had wanted to paint her?

The prince drew more lines with quick, precise movements. "Did you hunt with hawks often?"

"All the time."

"A skilled huntress, then." It wasn't a question, and the way he said it—like it was an important and respectful thing to be—made heat rush through her.

"Most of the time," she said.

In the mountains, Mellion hadn't been enough to keep them both fed, and it had been unfair of Farren to put that pressure on them. Farren saw it now and wished she had returned to Capai more often. Perhaps Mellion would still be with her, not frozen on a mountain.

The light from the window burned gold along the stone floor as late afternoon turned to evening. Her arm was beginning to ache from Tayra's weight, and she shifted. The prince noticed the tiny movement and immediately set down his charcoal.

"I'm done for today. I'm sure you and the hawk are tired." He came forward, warmth in his expression. "Would you be able to come again tomorrow?"

"Tomorrow?" She could smell him—a not unpleasant twining of earthy minerals and mint. *Mostly mint*, she thought, breathing deeper. Oh, Keira would have appreciated that scent. "Well, I'll have to speak with Horat—"

"Leave it to me. He'll understand. I'm sure it won't be an issue."

Farren chewed her lip. "And I will get three more questions next time?"

The prince drew closer and reached to take her hand, but she pulled back. He had held her hand once before, and that had pressed at some boundary between them. Some boundary that she hadn't let any man pass in months after that cursed Thestor. Besides, she didn't need more distractions during her time at Alidonia. That would only lead to trouble.

"Three questions every time, for as many sessions as it takes," the prince said, his hands curling as he remained where he was. "And you can bring your hawk with you again. I'll have a perch brought so you can rest your arm. Come after you're finished for the day if you'd like. I have some duties in the city at midday but will be back before supper."

"What sort of duties?"

Prince Isander gave her a sidelong look. "Your limit for questions is up, remember? But since we're still getting to know each other... I take baskets of food to the orphanage once a week. The children are particularly fond of sweet-cake, which can be tricky to transport, but I always promise them one and they would be livid if I forgot."

The image arose clear and bright in her mind. Isander, hauling a basket loaded with food as a hoard of hungry children clamored for his attention and love. Would he sit with them, tell them stories as he handed them bread or figs? Would he let the little ones sit in his lap, laugh with them, or cry if they needed to?

"Do you—" Her voice cracked, and she cleared her throat. "Do you enjoy it?"

"To be honest, I think they enjoy it more than I. But the world is a better place with less misery, don't you think?"

Something in his gaze was dark. Searching.

"Of course," she heard herself say, unable to look away.

The guard outside the door coughed, and she flinched. She dragged herself to the doorway, and Isander opened it for her, his smile easy once more. She followed the guard down the twisted steps, feeling the prince's eyes on her back as she descended.

BANG! BANG! BANG!

Farren jerked upright in her bed, dreams scattering as the reverberation of the pounding door rang through her skull.

In moments, she leapt out of bed and pulled on a chiton and a pair of leggings Camilla had given her. The banging didn't let up. Unnerved, Farren threw open the door, ready to yell at whoever was making such a racket.

The guard, Scipio, filled the narrow doorway. He leaned against the jam with one hand while the other fist lifted to pound once more.

"Finally," he said. "I was about to charge in."

"That wouldn't have gone well for you," Farren said, voice scratchy with sleep.

"What, you would set some sparrows on me?" He snorted. "Let's go. The prince wants me to get your bum to the gryphon yard."

Farren pressed her lips in a thin line. It was time for their training to begin. "I haven't had breakfast—"

"I don't give a damn whether you've eaten, bumpkin. Maybe you laze about in the Outskirts, but here at Alidonia, we keep a strict schedule. If you don't think that agrees with you, then maybe you'd prefer the lick of my lashings instead?"

Heat drained from her face. She had slept too late after her long day yesterday cleaning and working with Isander.

"No, I uh—I just need my sandals."

Scipio watched her wordlessly as she strapped on her sandals and swigged water from a cup at the desk. By the time she left her room, her palms were sweaty and her breath puffed in shallow bursts.

At the curving iron gate of the gryphon yard, her feet planted themselves into the ground.

"Come on," Scipio said through clenched teeth as he swung open the gate.

Her pulse pounded in her ears. There were no gryphons in the yard. Yet.

Scipio huffed, grabbed the back of her neck, and shoved her through the gate. Farren nearly stumbled but caught her balance and sent a glare back at the guard. He was too busy closing the gate to see it, so she turned her back on him and forced herself to walk deeper into the yard.

She wiped her hands on her chiton, eying the ten other recruits who gathered there, waiting for Prince Cato to bring out the beasts. Each recruit wore ruffled chitons and spoke in a smooth Malodai accent that reminded her of water rippling over stones in a brook. *Avid* and *Felid* runeskills were apparent in their elaborate skin paintings of feathers, furrowed raptor eyes, claws, and even a curled whiskered maw of fangs—a skin painting that must have cost a fortune for the recruit. The oldest recruit was close to her father's age, and Farren herself seemed to be the youngest. One of the younger ones, tall with springy dark hair held back by a leather band, sidled over to her.

"You new?" He spoke around something in his mouth. "I'm Alexon. Day five."

"Farren. You've a bit of time left to your Servitude."

He flashed her a smile brimming with yellowed teeth, then proffered a tiny leather sack. "Honey drop? They're my greatest weakness."

She took one of the hard amber candies from the sack and popped it into her mouth, grateful for the distraction from her pounding heart. "Thanks. Have you...learned anything about gryphons yet?"

Alexon folded lanky arms and frowned. "Well, the bonding is a bit tricky. Gryphons like gifts, but only certain kinds of gifts, and they can be put off by smells, or sounds, or thoughts. But...hopefully, today goes better. They aren't as frightening as they look, at least."

Farren made a skeptical noise, but before Alexon could respond, the gate to the yard opened. Prince Cato came in, leading three gryphons—without chains, leashes, or anything to contain them. Camilla—short and slight next to the beasts—followed behind them. The girl was not technically part of the guard—as she was too young to join—but she insisted on helping Cato despite the danger it put her in.

The gryphons ambled to the center of the yard, where the gardens gave way to a wide expanse of flagstones. Farren crossed her arms. No amount of courage could've prepared her for the sight and proximity of the royal gryphons. Immense and tawny, their muscled limbs bulged as they walked, and their ears twitched as they gazed at the recruits. Blade-like talons grated on stone.

"This is Phynx, Grit, and Naronimus," the prince told them, pointing to each gryphon with an ink-stained finger.

Farren thought she recognized Phynx as the one she saw behind the glass wall in the keep. Grit barely looked at the recruits before sauntering to a large, flat rock to lounge. As soon as the gate closed, Naronimus began pacing the perimeter of the yard, ears flexing back and forth. He was far less sleek than the others. Where they had shiny fur and feathers, his were dull and pocked with patches of skin. Either he had some sort of skin disease...or they were scars.

"Your first task today," the prince continued, "is to convince a gryphon to come to you without laying a hand on them."

Farren stifled a gasp, but not before the prince heard it. He glanced at her with a frown. His gaze slid to the other recruits. "Take your time. Remember to ease into the runebond, keep things positive. Treat the gryphons as you would any other person, and introduce yourself."

The hair on her neck rose at the sound of talons behind her, and she whipped around. It was Naronimus, striding along the cage wall behind her. She kept an eye on him as she put distance between them.

The other recruits dispersed, silently working with their runebonds. Grit perked up and stared down at Alexon from the rock where he lay. The gryphon's ears swiveled, and he leapt off the rock in one smooth motion, making Farren's heart skip a beat. The recruit winced at the nearness of the gryphon, but calmed when Grit came to sit directly in front of him, tail twitching like a rope along the ground. How could Alexon look so placid with the great beast a mere arm-span away?

Phynx took an interest in two of the female recruits, her sharp eyes locking with first one and then the other as if they all conversed with each other.

"You could at least pretend to try," the prince said quietly as he neared her. "They don't bite."

Farren wished she could hurt him with her scowl. "Really? I know someone who would say differently. Your Highness."

The prince frowned. "They only bite if provoked."

"By what, a glance?"

He rubbed his cheek, considering. "They might if there's a physical threat. Or unrestrained anger and fear."

Farren swallowed, remembering the fear that had consumed her when she saw that gryphon standing so close to Desmond, its head high above him. She had always assumed the attack had been partly her fault—that her fear had encouraged the gryphon to act—and now the prince's words confirmed it.

"Just take a deep breath and ease into it," the prince told her. "Try to see them as something to be understood, not something to be feared."

Shadows edged her vision, and she belatedly remembered Camilla's tapping. "I—I'm not sure I can—"

"What do you plan on telling Horat then, when he checks on your progress?"

Farren clenched her jaw, forcing evenness with each breath. She tapped a quick rhythm on the side of her hand with trembling fingers. If she could just calm her body enough to think clearly, she might be able to make a decision about which gryphon to choose—

The prince ran a hand through his hair. "Why don't you try connecting with Naronimus?"

Naronimus had upped his pacing to a canter as if going faster would get him out of the enclosure. Farren fought the inane urge to laugh. "You're right; an injury would be a perfect way to get out of this."

"You might have more in common than you think," he said. "Naronimus is impatient and restless. Headstrong, too."

Just as Farren opened her mouth to say something, she caught Camilla's soft gaze. The girl looked at her imploringly from where she stood by the gate.

Farren's mouth snapped closed. She sucked in a fortifying breath of air and took one step closer to Naronimus's approaching form. Through her runeskill, she sensed the silvery spheres of the three gryphon minds—glowing balls of energy emanating warmth and something else: a deep toll like a great bell, so strong that the vibrations shivered into her.

Naronimus came to an abrupt halt as she touched his mind. His hard, sharp eyes veered toward her, and she felt a strange tug as he accepted her connection. Unlike the relatively simple runebonds she shared with hawks and small birds, she could sense the power of Naronimus's mind, the depth and complexity too deep for her to ever reach the bottom.

A tremor ran through her, but she widened the connection so that she could sense him more clearly. He felt thorny and trapped. Resentful of the humans who kept him.

*My name is Farren*, she told him.

He didn't care, and he turned away to continue pacing.

The prince made a noise of frustration.

Farren shot him a glare. "He hates it here."

"I know that."

"Then why not let him go?"

"You know I can't do that."

Farren frowned. "Because the queen says so, Your Highness?"

The prince's shoulders tensed, and his expression turned wooden. "Would you stop calling me that?"

"Why don't you like being called by your title?"

"Because. I just don't. Not that it's any of your business," he said, tight-lipped.

"You're right. I overstepped my place. I shouldn't be speaking to you as an equal."

"Are you always this sarcastic?"

She smiled a little. "Only when I'm annoyed."

He shook his head. "Naronimus is important to the success of the program. Each gryphon has something valuable to offer."

"Magic?"

"That, and their size and strength. The queen sees what a positive addition they would make to the guard." The prince stepped away from her abruptly and addressed the other recruits. "Spend some more time speaking with the gryphons. They need to runebond with us in order to understand us."

Seeing that the prince was done with her, she refocused on Naronimus. He came around the perimeter again, wings half-raised so that one wingtip brushed the iron lattice.

She opened the runebond once more, and he barely glanced her way. He didn't care for small chat; luckily, neither did she.

*Where would you go?* she asked him.

His trotting slowed. *Why do you care?* The question came through as a vibrant impression tinged with annoyance.

*Because I, too, am forced to be here.*

He looked at her then, and she felt the connection between them dilate. Panicked, she tried to regain control of it, not wanting the gryphon to sense the negative thoughts she was having, but it was as if the runebond was being pried open by sharp, careless talons.

Farren's throat tightened as Naronimus approached. Each step seemed to pull the runebond further, stretching until it gaped between them. She couldn't stop her fear from pouring through, and hatred rose beside it, two swords pointing inevitably at the gryphon. Memories of the accident swirled around her mind, and the gryphon saw them. He tasted her fear, her fury, and smelled the scent of blood from her brother's wound. Instead of understanding, she felt his resentment grow. He stepped closer, his head towering above hers.

*What an impudent brother you had.*

*He is still alive*, she said, sending him a recent memory of Desmond standing tall and strong with his minks.

*He's lucky, then. He should've died for trying to touch a gryphon without permission.*

Farren bit back her shock and struggled to narrow their connection. *Why is your pride more important than the life of a human?*

The connection gave a little, and she reigned it in, using all her focus to keep it small, allowing only tiny impressions through.

Naronimus's tail flicked back and forth. *Because gryphons are better than humans. You are weak, and stupid, and afraid. It is we who should be ruling you.*

*You are a monster*, she said, not holding back her disgust, then she forced the runebond closed.

In a flash, Naronimus's head lunged and he snapped his beak inches from her face. Farren reeled back, throwing her arms up to protect herself, and fell hard.

"Naronimus!" The arrow of Prince Cato's voice cut across the yard, and Naronimus sauntered away. The prince came to her side and offered her a hand. "Are you alright?"

"Yes." She batted his hand away, swallowing back bile. Every part of her body shook as she stood and lurched toward the gate, brushing past Camilla without a word.

# TEN

FARREN FOUND THE FRESH basin of water in her room and splashed handfuls of cold water over her face. Trembling, she clenched the basin and sucked in slow breaths. Panic whirled in her, a scouring wind that tore through her chest and mind. After a moment, she peeled her hands from the basin and tapped a quick rhythm along the side of her hand.

*Tap-tap-tap-tap-tap...*

The gale diminished to a breeze. Rather than scattering her thoughts, it moved around them.

How was she going to work with gryphons when she could barely stand being close to them? She couldn't even keep control over her runeskill—despite having worked extra hard at it while in the mountains—so how would she ever be able to protect her feelings and prevent a gryphon from becoming aggressive again?

She scrounged for a towel and dried her face.

More importantly, how was she ever going to disrupt the gryphon program if she couldn't get close to the gryphons? She needed to be like the other recruits, obedient and calm.

She would focus and come up with a plan. Pretend to get close to the others so she could learn more about the program. Pretend she didn't mind the gryphons. Brush off the incident.

And her brother's attack?

Something in her heart shuttered closed. The horrible memories would never be forgotten, but she couldn't let the attack prevent her from stopping the gryphon program. She was doing it for Desmond *because* of the attack. Knowing her reason for it would make it easier to keep the memories at bay. Already, it helped her mind clear and sharpen.

The Festival of the Forging was less than six weeks away, at the start of the seasonal turn. The winds would be coming soon—harsh and full of thunder and lightning—and the Rain Days would follow, soaking the world to a dull grey. The festival itself celebrated the day—one hundred years ago now—that Queen Myrtilla united the two warring sides of the city and built the Greenstone Bridge. The bridge was a symbol of their unity, and the people of Malodai celebrated every year by parading from one end of the city and crossed the bridge to the other side. In Capai, they didn't celebrate the occasion, but news of it always reached their village. The Festival of the Forging was by far the biggest event of the year, which meant the streets would be flooded with revelers.

To have gryphons walking among them would be disastrous.

Farren rubbed her forehead. She could learn a lot in the coming weeks and find ways to stop the gryphons from ever walking the streets among innocent people.

She took a few more moments to gather herself, retied her hair into a knot she liked for sparring, then returned to the gryphon yard.

Camilla and the gryphons were gone, likely back in the mews, and the prince yammered on at the recruits.

"...and direct eye contact can indicate a willingness to connect. It's important to consider behavior before opening a runebond..."

Farren noticed a figure standing just behind the prince and groaned inwardly. Scipio. The prince turned and set a hand on his cousin's shoulder.

"This is Scipio," Prince Cato said. "He is one of the queen's personal guards, dedicated to protecting the throne. He'll be training you in hand-to-hand combat during your entire Servitude."

Scipio stepped forward, lifting his chin so he looked down his nose at them. "We'll break off into pairs first. The aim is to get your opponent to the ground."

Farren closed her eyes. Somehow, she had thought it couldn't get any worse—

"I'll pair with *Farn* to start with."

Her eyes flashed open. Scipio sneered at her, and her disappointment soured.

"It's Farren," she said loudly. "And I'll gladly put you on your rear end."

Scipio's face darkened at several muffled chuckles, and Prince Cato gave a disapproving shake of his head. Farren ignored him as Scipio stalked toward her. She widened her stance and lowered into a slight crouch, ready to take whatever he threw at her. Even angry, Scipio still swaggered. She marveled at it while he approached, her breath quickening. Oh, she needed this.

Scipio paused before tackling her. "It'll be nice to have a clod-hopper in training. Someone to make me look good every time. Take care now; it might get a little dangerous."

"Like it did last time?" Farren asked, recalling that she had his windpipe pressed beneath her arm.

He took a swing at her, and thoughts flew from her mind. Her skin buzzed as she fell into old habits, patterns of fighting she had learned from years of practice. Her whole body tightened around her movements as she ducked, spun, and lashed out with feet and fists. She tracked Scipio's every twitch, kept up with each attack, parrying the blows as he attempted to land them.

Sweat tracked down her back, and the sunlight filling the court-yard blazed heat around them. She could smell Scipio's sweaty feet and heard the strong rush of his breath, which told her he wasn't tiring. Her own body sang, tired though it was. She wouldn't be able to keep him off much longer.

She avoided a blow to her stomach and sent a kick to his side. Fast as a hawk's talon, he grabbed her leg and twisted, sending her body spiraling into the air. Pain lanced through her hip and shoulder as she landed, gasping. She sat up gingerly and noticed that some of the other recruits watched them. The pain eased as she stood and rolled her shoulders.

Scipio brushed his clothes off, although there was no dust on them. "That wasn't terrible, bumpkin," he said, clearly pleased with himself. "You have a strong will, but you lack technique. And your stamina seems a bit...off."

"I'm out of practice," she said, shrugging. Besides being out of practice, she had weakened considerably while living in the mountains. But she knew what her father would tell her. He would be leaning against the yard fence watching her practice with a padded wooden post, a hawk on his fist and a half-smile beneath his beard, eyes bright as he would say in his simple, straightfor-ward manner, *You need to get stronger. Eat well, practice more.*

*What about my height*, she used to ask. *They are all so tall!*

*Pay no attention to that,* he would say with a slight shake of his head. *It's quickness of body and mind that matter more. Good food will feed both, and practice will teach you to channel that energy.*

What with the dearth of food in the mountains, she had some work to do. Still, the fighting made her feel better than she had in a long time.

"Lucky for you, we'll be practicing often," Scipio said. "That gives you lots of opportunity to demonstrate to the others what *not* to do." He chuckled, amused at his joke.

"You assume that I won't get better," Farren pointed out, knowing she needed to improve. Her father had taught her how to fight at first, but in the end, she was largely self-taught, a far cry from the fighters in the queen's guard.

Scipio stepped close, and his breath flicked at her ear as he spoke. "You might get better, but you will continue to lose. You know why? Because I'm making it my personal business to make your time here miserable. It's the least you deserve for that little fit you threw back at your village."

"Oh, was it that bad? I hope your nose doesn't heal too crooked."

He drew back, a furious grin on his face. "You think you're funny, don't you? But I'm sure that humor will fade once you start working with gryphons." He watched her closely, his grin reaching his eyes. Farren fought to keep her expression composed, but it had been so long since she'd been around people that her effort did little. "That's right," he crowed. "And there won't be any running back to your safe little village."

Farren fought the urge to look away and pretended she didn't hear his words. She squinted at his nose, assessing it from a couple angles. "I think it *is* healing a bit crooked, actually."

Before he could throw another punitive comment at her, she spun on her heel and joined the other recruits, who had already finished their practice and were gathered around one of the many lavish fountains in the gryphon yard. She looked forward to practicing with someone else—*anyone* else—and getting back to cleaning or hawk training. If it weren't for the gryphons, and Scipio, her ten years of Servitude might not be so terrible.

Something made her look over to the glass wall of the gryphon yard. Behind it, Prince Isander was leaning forward, casually watching them.

Their eyes locked. He had seen her fight, and his intense expression made her belly flutter. The prince held her gaze, and heat spiraled into her.

A movement behind him caught her eye, and the heat dissipated. A short, delicately-boned woman stood watching the recruits as well, with a face of impassive stone. Her chiton was sumptuous, dipping low in the front and leaving her arms exposed. Even from where Farren stood, she could see the vibrant red and ocher of an exquisite skin painting that mantled the woman's neck, shoulders, and arms. On the woman's head glinted a slight, jeweled crown. She had to be Queen Aurelia.

Farren averted her gaze and turned away from the wall to hide her expression. If the queen was watching them practice, she'd have to be very careful. She should avoid Scipio and hold back while practicing with him if she wanted to blend in with the other recruits. She certainly didn't want the queen's attention. Nor Scipio's. Being the queen's personal guard and nephew, he might as well be her spy.

She crossed her arms, disappointed that she would have to hold back while fighting Scipio. It was too bad, really, because she might've been able to set that arrogant nose of his even more crooked. But she couldn't compromise herself or her goal; she owed it to Desmond and to every other person who might get hurt by a gryphon walking the streets.

# ELEVEN

AFTER AN INTERMINABLE DAY in the mews, Farren prepared to go to Prince Isander's art chamber. No less than four hawks would do—that ought to keep her quite busy. Farren set them up on two carrying perches—long, T-shaped staffs—and gathered the other things she'd be taking: her best pair of hawking gloves, a few pigeon breasts in her hawking bag, plus an extra leash in case one broke. While she worked, Camilla brought her a wedge of flatbread, knowing she had missed supper.

Farren brushed off a tuft of feathers stuck to one end of the bread, lifting a questioning brow at the girl as she did so.

"I was in the dovecot," Camilla told her sheepishly.

"Feeding the pigeons bread?" Craters pocked the bread where some had been pulled out.

"I know it's not good for them...but they love it, and I only give a little." Camilla picked tiny, mottled gray feathers from her braids, letting them whirl to the floor like ashen snow. "Do you want to talk about what happened earlier?"

"No," Farren said quickly.

"Oh." Camilla's cheeks tinged. "You just seemed really upset."

"I was." The girl was looking at her with all the hesitation of a scolded pup. Farren swallowed. "You should know that before this, I was living alone...for months. I've, uh, been having trouble dealing with some things. If I sound cold, it's not because I'm trying to be...mean or rude or—it's just that I'm used to being alone." She cursed silently at her muddled words.

"Well... I'm here if you ever need to talk."

"You've already done enough, teaching me to tap."

The girl's eyes shone. "Is it helping?"

"I think so." Farren hesitated, remembering that she had mentioned her own troubling attacks. "You told me earlier—"

A boy barged into the mews and handed Farren a parcel.

"From Prince Isander," he said. Then he was gone.

Camilla sidled up to her as Farren took it to the only desk in the mews and unwrapped it, startled at the feel of silk that greeted her. Atop the bundle of fine fabric was a note written in long, elegant ink:

*Farren, for our session tonight, please wear this dress. It will match the style of the portrait, and it will serve you well.*

With a sense of dread, Farren pulled out the dress. Layers of soft, teal silk and damask slid between her fingers. Fabrics she had never worn in her life because firstly, they were far too expensive. Secondly, they weren't appropriate to wear for anything she loved to do.

The clothes were certainly not who she was or ever would be. What had the prince been thinking? That she would *pretend* to be this person?

"How lovely!" Camilla said, stroking the fabric.

Farren balled the dress up and shoved it back into its wrapping. It was clear that he didn't want to paint her, but some mirage that he apparently found more appealing. She was willing to stand being painted if it meant getting questions answered...but this was too far.

"That's quite generous of him," Camilla said warily, watching Farren crumple the note. "Does he mean to paint you in it?"

"He does," Farren snapped. "But he won't. I'll be back shortly."

She took the parcel and marched her way to the keep. The guard at the door took her at once to the prince's art chamber, put off by her clipped tone and scowl. They passed through a corridor painted bruise-purple and another as red as a fresh cut.

"Come in," the prince called when the guard knocked.

The guard pushed open the door. Prince Isander had exchanged his royal outfit for the more casual Weldonian clothes and regarded a collection of paintings leaning against the wall. A servant wearing a bronze bangle sat at his desk, quill poised over a piece of parchment.

Farren tried to ignore the servant as she strode into the room. Copper skin gleamed in the opening of Prince Isander's shirt. It made a good target as she thrust the parcel at him.

"I've come to tell you that I will no longer have time for being painted." She turned on her heel, ready to walk out, but the prince snagged her elbow.

"It didn't fit? I was sure I had the right—"

"I didn't try it on. I'm not interested in wearing it."

"Did you get my note?"

"It's ridiculous that you'd expect me to want to wear such extravagant clothes."

He shrugged. "They're just clothes, Farren, nothing more."

"You know that isn't true."

The prince pursed his lips and turned to his servant. "Darius, that is all for now. I trust your judgment. Choose the best five to take to the Temple of Destiny and arrange for them to be delivered tomorrow. Be sure they know the gift is from the Crown, not myself."

"Yes, Your Highness," the servant said, bowing with hand held to his chest. He swept out with a sidelong glance at her.

The prince set the dress on a nearby table, then came close, peering out the expanse of window to the wide band of the Kithyria and the city beyond it. Farren glanced at the closed door.

"It's funny how much power we give to fabric," he said thoughtfully. "You can tell a pauper on the street by his rags and a merchant by his pointed shoes. Everyone wearing what they should so that we can see who to trust or distrust, who to fear, who to ignore. We've boxed ourselves in with fabrics. We've defined ourselves with them, but in so doing, limit ourselves as well." His gaze returned to her, unwavering. "Don't limit yourself, Farren."

"I'm not—" Farren lifted a hand, then dropped it. "The dress isn't *me*. I don't want to pretend to be someone I'm not."

"And who are you, exactly?"

Farren studied the way his dark hair tumbled in perfect, loose rings down to his shoulders. "I'm a hawker. A woman hawker."

"Is that all?"

Farren's cheeks burned. "I'm a servant, and..." A *sister*, she wanted to say, but her teeth closed over the words.

The prince rubbed at his inner wrist, where the skin was rippled from a burn scar. "That's not what I see."

"You don't know me."

His dark brows lifted, but he didn't disagree with her. "Alright. Come here. Look out at the city with me."

Farren, still stiff, edged closer. The prince's breath was soft and minty, the scent of him warm and clean.

"What am I looking for?" she asked.

"If you could be anyone out there, who would you be?"

"I don't know. Someone who could have food, a place to sleep."

"And a hawk?"

Farren smiled, giving in a little. "A hawk would be nice."

"A dozen hawks?"

"An entire mews would be the most I could wish for."

He looked at her sidelong. "A gryphon?"

She flinched. "No. I much prefer hawks."

He didn't press her. "Then maybe a home of your own. An estate. Someplace to fly your hawks and train them. Maybe a horse or two. A husband, children?"

Her chest ached suddenly. "I don't know about all that."

He nodded. "What about fighting?"

"Fighting?"

He gave her a knowing smile. "I know you enjoy it. Would you still fight?"

"I suppose I would like that. Someone to spar with."

"You could spar with someone. Or maybe you could be in the guard. Or maybe you could lead your own as a captain."

She stared at him, wondering what sort of fantasy he was living in. What was the point of dreaming of things that could never be? Of things she didn't even know whether she wanted?

Quick as a shrike, he took her hand and flipped it over, exposing the *Avid* runemark on her inner wrist. "Farren, this marking is just a hint of your potential. There is so much you could do and be. That is what I see. The possibilities."

The way he looked down at her suggested that he could see her very rune-made soul. She wanted him to hold her, suddenly, to keep her steady in the wildness of his words.

His voice softened. "You don't have to wear the dress if you don't want to. I'll paint you as you are. But it might be fun to try on someone else for a little while."

*I'm not here for fun. I'm here to work*, she thought, and the moment she did so, she felt a flash of disappointment. When had she become such a stick-in-the-mud? The last time she had fun was... She swallowed, remembering the game she had played with Desmond in the river when they raced with the minks to see who could swim the fastest. That had been the morning before the gryphon attack. A lifetime ago.

Wearing a fancy dress wasn't exactly her idea of fun, but she didn't want the prince to think she was as stodgy as she was beginning to feel. "Fine, I'll wear the dress. But I am still going to work with the hawks. And I get to ask four questions this time."

The prince's gaze glimmered. "That's fair."

"I need to send a note to the mews." She felt herself loosen, minutely, as the prince went to the table to mix his paints.

"There's parchment and a quill there on the desk. You can change in the corner," he said, indicating a small dressing area hidden by an amber curtain.

The prince's desk, much like the rest of his art chamber, was neat and tidy. The quill, before she dipped it, was spotless. She jotted a quick note to Camilla, then blew on the ink to dry it. A row of books lined the left side of the desk like foot soldiers, perfectly even and ordered by size. Most of the books were about painting, but one had runes, rather than words, imprinted on its leather binding.

She glanced over at the collection of paintings the prince had been surveying and tried not to stare. There were eight of them in total—not enormous portraits but large enough to hold substantial detail. One depicted a young and handsome man with skin of gold, his hand set on a fine white stallion while the sun rose brilliant above him. That had to be the Enchanter Calipion. Another beheld the Enchantress Rhealia in a vision of watery blues—shades Farren never would've noticed if not for the way Isander had rippled them across the canvas. A third portrait boasted the Enchanter Tyrili, laughing cheeks ruddy as he filled his belly from gleaming platters of food.

"What do you think?" Isander asked.

Farren gave a soft exhale, searching for the words. "They are remarkable. Why are you giving them to the Temple of Destiny?" She had heard of the Temple before—a sacred place in Malodai where the Rune Seers kept all knowledge of the Enchanters and runes.

"The Temple will appreciate them. The queen owes the Rune Seers a great deal, and sending them gifts is one way to keep our agreement with them...smooth."

Of course, that's how the queen knew who had which runes. She had access to the Rune Seer's records of runemarks determined at birth.

Farren abandoned the paintings and sent the note with the guard, then took the dress into the changing area. Did he often have women—or men—change there? Farren grew hot as she shucked her short chiton and leggings. The sound of the prince mixing and tapping things on the table reassured her that he was preoccupied.

She pulled on the silk chiton. The unnaturally vibrant teal slid with remarkable softness between her fingers. It fit like a second skin.

"Do you like the color?" the prince asked from the table where he worked.

"I've never seen anything quite like it."

"The dye is made from a type of clamshell found at the bottom of Alidonian Falls. They reside in great numbers near the Healing Caves."

Farren had heard of the caves, vast chambers at the base of the cliffs that formed behind the falls, said to cure any ailment.

"Have you been there?" she asked.

"Once."

Farren eased out from behind the curtain and went quietly to the window where the prince had her standing last time he painted. The silk chiton rippled around her legs like water. The teal cloak, made of heavy velvet, settled over her shoulders and caressed her neck with luxurious folds.

"And did it help with whatever illness you had?" Farren asked.

He turned, realizing she was out. His eyes lit when he saw her, and he seemed to forget whatever it was he was grinding with mortar and pestle. "I wish it had," he murmured. "Exquisite."

Farren clenched her hands in front of her, wishing she didn't feel so uncomfortable.

He sucked in a breath as if drawing his attention back inside. "I'm nearly finished."

He mixed the powder into a small bowl. Several similar bowls filled the table, along with jars of different things—pieces of what looked like rocks in shades of beige, black, and red; dried leaves of plants; dried flowers that ranged from pale white to deep violet; and some other items Farren didn't recognize. Another bowl held eggs.

Whereas before the table had been neat, the prince didn't seem to mind making a mess as he mixed egg yolk with his powders. Under his steady hands, beautiful colors formed. Would watching him paint the canvas be just as magical?

A knock on the door made her jump. Camilla came in, followed by Iana, the queen's guard. They brought the hawks with them, and Farren busied herself with placing them around the chamber on the perches the prince had installed earlier. Camilla's eyes brightened when she saw Farren, but the girl said nothing aloud.

When the prince asked Camilla and Iana to leave, Camilla tugged Farren close. "Will you be alright here...by yourself?"

The girl's concern for her was sweet and gave her a little rush of shame. After all, shouldn't it be Farren who looked out for Camilla? *She has Prince Cato to look out for her*, she told herself. "Yes, I think I can take him down on my own if need be."

Camilla's plump cheeks—blushing to the shade of a summer sunset—swelled as she smiled. "I bet you could."

"I'll send for you when I've finished," Farren said.

Camilla glanced surreptitiously at the prince, then left with the guard.

Was it odd that she was there alone? Was it inappropriate?

Farren forced her gaze out the window, not sure how much it mattered. Unless people started to talk. She bit her lip as she thought of her conversation with the prince, the way he held her hand as he looked at her runemark.

"That little interrogation earlier," she said, now that they were alone. "Do you do that with all the people you want to paint?"

The prince had poured his paints onto a wooden palette and brought it to the canvas. "Only with the ones who don't care to be painted." He pulled out a paintbrush and dipped it, his eye tracing from the canvas to her dress.

"I don't mind being painted," Farren said. "I just don't understand why you want to do it."

His eyes slid to hers. "I think you know why."

"Because you see potential." Farren fought to slow her heart, which thrummed like the wings of a honeybird. "You see something I'm not."

"Because I see you, who you are, who you could be, and I want to capture it. It's a compulsion, really. It helps me." Before she could ask what it helped him with, he said, "Now tell me about your village."

"You still owe me answers to four questions."

His sensual lips quirked. "Two, actually."

Farren cursed silently. She had hoped he hadn't noticed the first two she asked, given how busy he had been with the paints. At least she had already come up with a few questions that were hopefully less suspicious than the ones she really wanted to ask.

"How is it that your cousin, Scipio, isn't King? I would've thought him next in line after your uncle."

The prince took a sip of his warm tea, the minty scent of it so sharp she could almost taste it. "You truly are far removed from the city, aren't you?"

"It has never been an issue before," Farren said, busying herself with pulling on a thick handling glove and urging a hawk onto it.

"My cousin joined the royal guard and, by doing so, waived his right to the throne."

Farren opened her mouth to ask why he would do such a thing but thought better of it. Only one question remained, and she wasn't sure knowing more about Scipio would help her stop the gryphon program. Although he *had* told Farren he would make her life miserable.

"He seems to have it out for me," she said.

"Hmm, I always thought he was a nice young man." For a moment, he looked serious, but when he looked at her, a grin broke out.

Serious, he was handsome. Happy and grinning...she couldn't take her eyes from him. That charming look was so warm that it stole her breath.

"He can't very well be nice as the queen's guard," Isander continued, his focus already slipping back to the canvas. "Besides that, his father wasn't exactly a decent person."

"Anaxis," Farren said, filling the word with hate.

"Ah, so you've met him."

Farren returned the hawk to its perch, unwilling—unable—to say more.

"I wouldn't underestimate Scipio," Isander added, almost under his breath. "He is capable of more than he seems."

Something in his words caused her skin to prickle. If Scipio was anything like his father, he may well have hurt someone...or worse. Whatever he had done, the guard wasn't the type of person to let something go. He would gnaw on it until every morsel of meat was eaten, until the bone had fractured into fragments of its former self.

Farren shuddered. The best way to deal with such a *Canid* was to let him win, to let him look good. He would get bored with her soon enough.

"Do you wish to stop?" Isander asked, pulling away from the canvas.

"I still have one more question."

"Why don't you save it for a bit. You are starting to scowl. Tell me about your village."

Despite Prince Isander's focus on his painting, he seemed to hear every word she said about the village. He laughed at her stories of village fights she had settled and seemed absorbed by her description of the snow-bright winter days full of sled rides, icicles, and owls hunting for rabbits beneath the crust of snow. She told him of growing up as a falconer's daughter, of what it was like to see the mountains change with the seasons.

"You love it there," he stated when she had run out of things to say.

"Of course," Farren said, hefting another hawk on her wrist. "It's my home. Don't you feel that way about this place?"

"I find it...engaging," the prince said.

In the light from the window, the hard edge of his jawline and fine chin were softened by the gleam of burnished copper. The sleek feel of it on her neck would—

"Especially the parts that are forbidden," he added, glancing at her over his canvas.

Warmth crept into her. "I didn't realize that parts of the fortress would be forbidden to a prince."

"The queen commands it of everyone. But she doesn't know who goes deep into the keep. She doesn't wish to waste guards, and I don't wish to waste a good adventure."

"Why is it forbidden?" Farren recalled the wariness of Prince Cato when he told her of the Enchanted items kept there. "Is it dangerous?"

"There are old relic Enchantments that are harmless enough. A few portraits that go on monologues about the past. Doors that don't open, no matter how much force you put behind them or which key you use. But it's the doors that do open you need to be careful of." He set his paintbrush down and wiped his hands on a cloth. "They sometimes change where they go. And some of the corridors change too. One time, you might step through a red door that opens into a sitting room, and the next time you step through that same door, you end up in an old musty library."

"That doesn't seem too bad."

Prince Isander's brows lifted. "It's easy to get lost. I once spent an entire day and night going from door to door. There aren't many windows, and it's dark and dank. I thought I'd never find my way out."

"Why would they make things so confusing?"

"Likely to protect secrets they didn't wish discovered."

Farren swallowed. She set the hawk back on the perch, her arm aching from the weight. The prince's paintbrush rustled as it stroked the canvas. "Can I see the painting?"

"When it's finished. Perhaps in a few days. You are well past your four-question limit, by the way."

"What? But I didn't ask—" She bit her tongue.

"You did ask. Many different questions."

She stared at him, hard. She had learned nothing—other than a warning about Scipio and the keep, which did her little good. The other questions hadn't been her intended ones, but it was too difficult choosing them when she literally knew nothing about Alidonia. How was she to know what information could help her end the gryphon program?

She cursed silently, wishing she could ask him what she really needed to.

"I'm not sure this is working for me," Farren said, her tone clipped. How many precious hours had she wasted already when the queen would have the gryphons on the streets in a matter of weeks?

The prince's brows lifted, and he gave her his full attention. "We can't stop now, Farren."

"Of course we can."

He waved his brush at the canvas she couldn't see. "It's halfway finished. I told you I need—"

"You'll have to offer more."

He set his brush down and wiped his hands, then came to stand before her, bringing that tantalizing scent of mint with him. "More what?"

Why did he have to be so handsome? To stand so close to her, just within reach? And why in the Enchanted realms did her body have to ache for him to reach out and *grab* her—

"I want more questions answered," Farren said, crossing her arms.

"Is that all?"

"Six questions each session."

"Five. I need to be able to focus on the painting, remember?"

"Six."

The prince sighed, a light smile catching on his lips. "Six it is."

# TWELVE

SHE SENT A MESSAGE to retrieve Camilla, then changed hurriedly. By the time she emerged from the changing area, Camilla had arrived and held her perch with two hawks. Farren bunched the dress and cloak between her arms, carrying the other perch with the garments tucked under her elbow.

The prince still worked at the canvas, so she left the chamber without a word.

"How was it?" Camilla asked the moment the door closed, puffing as she hefted her perch. "What did he say to you?"

Farren picked her way carefully down the stairs. Ahead of them, Iana trotted lightly down the steps, probably eager to be somewhere more interesting.

"It's been a bit frustrating, actually. He won't let me see the painting. And he doesn't like it if I talk too much."

"I've never had much chance to speak more than a few words with him. Cato doesn't like me being around him, although I don't know why, as he seems perfectly charming." The words tumbled out of Camilla in a rush.

Well, Prince Cato certainly wasn't helping his cause by keeping the girl away from his brother.

"He doesn't talk much about himself," Farren said. "So I really don't know any more than you."

"What did you talk about, then?"

The sound of sandals snapping against the stone floor drew near. Farren adjusted the hawk perch and winced as the dress slipped from under her arm. She slowed, watching with dismay as it tumbled to the floor.

"Camilla," she started to say, but suddenly, the sandaled woman was on them, and Farren's heart nearly stopped when she saw who it was. Iana bowed.

"Your Majesty." Camilla rested the bottom of her perch on the floor as she dipped into a low curtsy. When Farren didn't move, Camilla elbowed Farren's side.

"Your Majesty," Farren echoed, her chest inexplicably tight.

In her brief glimpse of the queen, she was startled by how short the woman was—just about the same height as Farren—and how regal she looked despite that. When the queen stooped to take up the dress on the floor, Farren's stomach flipped.

"Oh, please let me—" Farren started, her voice catching when she grabbed the dress at the same time as the queen.

The queen straightened, gently tugging the dress until Farren let it go.

"I'm not afraid of a little work," the queen said in a voice like honey. "Are you, Farren Blackburn?"

Her cheeks flamed, and she tried not to show alarm that the queen knew her by name. "No, Your Highness."

The queen caressed the fabric with fingers wreathed by gemmed rings. "What's the meaning of this?"

Farren tried to stand tall beneath the queen's questioning, expansive gaze. "It's a dress, Your Highness."

Iana made a frustrated noise, and Camilla spoke up. "Excuse her, Your Highness. She's been working hard all day. The dress was a gift from Prince Isander—"

"It's a costume," Farren rushed in.

She didn't dare meet the queen's gaze again but instead stared at the skin painting that mantled the woman's neck and shoulders. Inked flowers adorned her—each linked to one another by exquisite, unfurled vines. The blossoms spread down until they reached her chest, where a single blood-red iris bloomed within a cluster of gryphon feathers. A glittering silver necklace rested over the skin painting, and from it dangled a clear, plain gem.

Camilla cleared her throat emphatically.

"I-It is for his painting project, Your Highness," Farren added.

The queen shook out the chiton and folded it neatly. "This is no costume fabric. It's certainly far too rich to be dropped on the floor. I hope you aren't this reckless with my hawks and gryphons."

The heat in her face intensified. "No, Your Highness, I am very careful with the animals."

"It would behoove you not to forget that the animals are your priority here. Not my son. Camilla, perhaps you could remind her of that next time she decides to visit the prince. The servants need to stay in line, even if they are your friends."

Farren opened her mouth to tell the queen that *he* had invited *her*, but Camilla rushed to speak first.

"Of course, Your Highness." Camilla dipped into another swift curtsy.

"Oh, and you should both know that the son of one of our former gryphon buyers will be visiting tomorrow. He is interested in joining the new guard. His family is not content with my edict about all gryphons being returned to Alidonia, so it is imperative that he has a good experience while here. If all goes well, he'll join the recruits. I've sent a note to Prince Cato, but...you know him."

Camilla bowed her head. "We will do our best, Your Highness."

The queen handed the dress back to Farren. "And do take care of this dress."

Farren clutched it as she fought to keep her composure.

"And Iana," the queen said. "Once you're done escorting these two out, I need you to relay to the other guards that guests are no longer allowed to bring weapons inside the keep. That wretched Diocleto thought it amusing to display a dagger at the last Viridian Council meeting—brandishing it not three arm-lengths from me as if expecting us all to drool over it. I decided not to cut his tongue out but gave a sound verbal lashing. Be sure to search him thoroughly whenever he sets foot inside this building."

Iana dipped her head. "Yes, Your Highness."

The queen left them, sandals clapping along the stone floor. The guard gestured for them to move on. When they were alone and out of the keep, Farren whispered to Camilla.

"Why does the queen know my name?"

"She knows all of the servants in her employ. Cato tells me she keeps records of each one, with a little sketch of them with it. I would expect she knows all about you and your family."

"Why would she need that much information? We are just servants."

"I imagine it helps her feel better somehow, knowing about the people working for her."

Farren adjusted her grip on the perch, her palms slick. "I think I'll have to say *no* to Prince Isander next time he invites me."

"She just wanted to make sure that you weren't overstepping your place. Prince Isander tends to do whatever he wants, and it's well-known that he tends to mingle with servants."

Fire swept up Farren's face. "There's nothing between us!" The hawks above Farren rustled, and she lowered her voice. "And what did she mean about keeping servants in line? She made it sound like you aren't one of us."

"I'm not," Camilla said simply. "I'm Cato's ward."

Farren pursed her lips. This changed things. Could she trust Camilla, knowing she was close to the royal family? The girl was already close to Prince Cato. If Camilla suspected her of sabotaging the gryphon program, would she report it to the queen or just to the prince?

"I don't like to mention it," Camilla said, looking at Farren sidelong, "because people treat me differently when they know."

Farren did her best to hide her speculation.

"Maybe they worry that you're spying for the queen," Farren suggested.

Camilla laughed, her braids falling back in golden cascades as she tilted her head. "Trust me," Camilla said, "that is the furthest from the truth. The queen despises me."

She cast the girl an incredulous look. "She doesn't."

"She really does. She hates that I'm Prince Cato's project."

"Because she wants him to focus on the gryphons?"

Camilla smiled. "See, you're already understanding how things work around here. Now we just have to work on that curtsy."

"What was wrong with my curtsy?"

"Well, I guess there's nothing wrong with looking like a newborn goat..."

She gave the girl a playful smile. "You'll have to teach me how to not look like a goat, then."

"Deal."

After the hawks were tucked away, Farren spent a few moments alone in the mews tidying up. It wasn't until she was leaving that she remembered what the queen said about a visitor coming and how he needed to have a good experience.

*We'll see about that*, she thought, shutting the door of the mews with a firm tug.

# THIRTEEN

THE GRYPHON BUYER'S SON, whom the queen had mentioned, arrived the following morning. It was up to Horat to convince the young man, Virilus, to become a recruit for the new gryphon guard. Horat decided that the best way to convince Virilus to join was to have him bond with one of the royal gryphons—preferably Elya, the most easy-going of them all.

Everything had to go well, Horat told them. Virilus would be an excellent addition to the guard, and tensions between his family and the crown would be smoothed over. Horat charged Prince Cato with giving Virilus tips and making sure the young man had a good idea of what to expect, emphasizing that he didn't want any surprises. Camilla would gather the other recruits to come and observe. To Farren, he tasked the menial chore of fetching the gryphon food from the kitchens...to which she quietly acquiesced.

A simple enough chore, and one he said he didn't think she could muddle.

As she stepped onto the smooth kitchen tiles, a giant frog tongue darted out in front of her, catching a fly in midair. His tongue slid wetly back into his mouth, and his vocal sac bulged as he croaked at her from the floor.

"Don't mind him," a female voice drawled. At the wide kitchen table where the servants usually supped, a woman Farren recognized hunched over the table, a bowl of pea pods sitting idly in front of her. It was Livigena, the servant who had a particular fondness for Camilla. Her head—black hair swooped up by a sash and adorned with silvery-blue beads—rested on folded hands. Livigena gave a great sigh as Farren looked at her. Then, with an effort, she lifted her head and propped it with a hand. "I hope you aren't here for food. All the cook left out is bread and these peas. Nothing will be ready until midday. I would offer to make you something, but I have a splitting headache."

"There's no need," Farren said, caught by the flashes of yellow and red covering Livigena's hands, arms, and every other exposed part of her body. The woman immediately noticed where she looked and sat up straight, rolling her sleeves back to reveal more colors.

"Do you like my fish? I have the blue riddle fish, the yellow-bellied gup, the demure nightfish, and, of course, our lovely mistfish," she rattled off, pointing each in turn. Vibrant blue waves churned between each sleek, scaled form. Only the wealthiest in society could afford such a quantity of permanent skin paintings. The woman gave a sly grin. "It was all because of sweet Penor. He doted on me so much, and he was a skin-painter's apprentice, so of course I asked him for a favor...or rather, several favors. It was the least he could do for all the time he wanted to tussle in bed, or in the straw, or on the flour sacks, or in a hidden corner of the gardens..."

She trailed off, and Farren glanced around. "I just came in to pick up the meat for the gryphons."

Livigena pursed her lips and nodded. "Of course. The cook mentioned something about that. I told her that I had such a headache—no doubt caused by that selfish groom Aktis, who I *swore* loved me, but then, just yesterday, I caught him eying some young maidservant who happened to stroll into the stables looking for a fine gelding—but the cook insisted on leaving me here all by myself anyways, with only that dratted broom for company!" The woman motioned to the broom, which was coming around from the far corner, sweeping on its own. "You'll have to watch out for that one. It's in a foul mood this morning and doesn't seem to understand that I cannot move every single time it wishes to sweep beneath the table." Livigena put a hand to her forehead and turned away to trudge deeper into the kitchen, talking all the while. "Camilla may have told you, but I suffer frequently from ailments. She's the only one who understands my pain, and she's seen me through the roughest spots without complaint or judgment. She's like the daughter I was always meant to have..."

Livigena disappeared into the back. She emerged a few moments later with a wooden bucket.

"Is this everything?" Farren took the bucket and glanced around the kitchen as if it held an answer to how she could disrupt the bonding attempt between Elya and Virilus.

Livigena sniffed. "Were you expecting more?"

"No, uh..." Farren peered into the bucket. "Is it enough? What about..." She made a show of examining the chunks of meat in the bucket. "These look a bit fatty. Horat was wanting something lean for the special bonding that's taking place today."

"Special bonding?"

"You didn't know?" Farren filled her voice with astonishment. "It's a *very* important client, and the queen wants everything to go as smoothly as possible. Only your best piece of meat will do. Prince Cato has requested it." At the servant's look of dismay, Farren quickly added, "And you know how much he means to Camilla."

Livigena's nostrils flared. "I do. That poor sap is always living in his brother's shadow. No doubt he aims to impress his mother." She rolled her eyes. "I really don't understand why Camilla clings to him so, but I don't have the heart to disappoint her. I'll see what the cook has in the larder."

The moment she left, Farren set down the bucket and searched the cupboards and shelves. What if she added something to the meat? Salt? Spiced peppers? What if they had bitterwort tea? Her mother used to drink the stuff to clear her mind, and the stench of it had been strong enough to send away her mother's dratted badger.

The *swish-swish* of the broom grew closer, and Farren closed another cupboard, empty-handed. Where did they keep the seasonings?

She cast an eye over the counters and glimpsed a clay pot labeled *pickled garlic bulbs* on the counter near the door where she had left the bucket of meat.

Livigena's footsteps approached, only a moment away. Farren lunged toward the bucket just as the broom decided to turn toward her. With barely a thought, Farren lashed out at it, sending the broom spinning as she dove away. Racing across the kitchen, she grabbed the pot of garlic and poured a bit of the liquid over the meat—careful not to let any of the garlic cloves out—hoping that gryphons abhorred vinegar.

Behind her, Livigena shrieked. The broom, furious at being handled, swung its wooden handle sideways, connecting with Livigena's head.

"Bloody cursed Enchantments!" Livigena wailed, stooping as she clutched a bleeding nose with one hand and covered her head protectively with the other. The broom spun and whacked her on the back, knocking pots and pans from the counter in the process.

Farren grimaced and returned the jar to its location, then vaulted back to the poor servant.

The broom handle took a swing at Farren as she reached for it, but Farren was faster. Bristles jabbed her legs as the broom tried to whirl out of her grasp. Livigena tried to help her, but it whipped out and sent the woman tumbling backward. Farren threw herself onto the broom, squeezing her arms and legs around it while it bucked like a mad stallion.

"Are y—you alr—right?" she shouted at Livigena, her voice jolting with every bruising thrust of the broom.

"Get it in the closet!" the servant squealed, pointing to a slim door next to the pantry.

Farren grappled the jerky broom to the closet door. It tried one last time to bop her in the nose, but Farren swiveled her head out of the way just in time. The miss caused the bottom to swing forward, and Farren used the momentum to shove it into the closet.

She rammed the door closed and pressed her back flat against it. The broom thrashed against it, and Farren cringed at the racket it made. "Does it always get this angry when touched?"

Livigena had gotten herself off the floor, her head scarf trailing loose over one shoulder, and sent Farren an exasperated glance as she held a cloth to her bleeding nose. "You touched it?"

"I think I accidentally bumped it." *Liar.* She swallowed. It was for a good cause...if it worked.

"That cursed broom does more harm than good. It'll need a good week in the closet before it cools down again." Livigena found the piece of meat she had brought and tossed it into the bucket. She sniffed the air, her brow wrinkling.

"Why not burn it?"

"I'd rather not suffer the consequences," Livigena said. At Farren's confused look, she said, "You've never heard of what happened to the royal family? The queen was but a child."

Farren locked the closet with two heavy bolts, then dusted off her hands. "What happened?"

Livigena, seeming to forget the smell of garlic and vinegar that lingered in the air, went to scrub her hands in the wash basin. "A necklace. The story goes that it had been gifted to her mother, the former queen, by her father. He had found the necklace deep in the fortress, and it was so old and forgotten that it was tarnished and covered in dust. Now, he didn't know of the Enchantment at the time, and when he placed it on the queen's neck, the necklace squeezed and squeezed until the queen's face turned purple. Queen Aurelia was just a child and watched in horror as her mother was nearly strangled to death. The king, fast and strong as a lion, tore the necklace off and ordered it destroyed."

Farren had picked up the bucket but found herself frozen by the story. "But it wasn't destroyed?"

Livigena dried her hands on a towel and shook her head. "They tried flame. They tried hammers and cudgels. Then, finally, the blacksmith's forge. None of it worked. It was as if the necklace was made of something...other. Not of this earth. So they put it away, burying it deep in the keep so that no one should ever find it again. And one by one, those who were ordered to destroy it fell ill. All of them were dead within two weeks."

"But it's just a rumor?"

"The cook told me that story. Her mother had been there to see it herself and had known the people who died. It's no rumor." Livigena took a deep breath and straightened her apron. "That's why the queen forbids anyone to go into the northern portion of the keep. She doesn't want anyone else getting hurt."

Did the queen know that Isander went there? Farren shook her head, dismissing the thought.

"Well, I should be getting back. Sorry about the broom. I'll try to be more careful next time."

"Please do. I didn't think my body could handle any more pain." Livigena winced as she pulled the cloth away from her face and stared at the clotted blood. She turned suddenly and headed back to the table, a hand on her belly as if she might be sick. "Can you tell Camilla to come see me when she's done? I need her company."

The woman sounded on the verge of tears, so Farren hummed acknowledgment and bolted out the door. As she lugged the bucket to the gryphon yard, she stopped a young servant boy dashing through the hall to fetch a healer to the kitchens.

The recruits gathered in the yard with several gryphons. But Prince Cato and Virilus stood apart from the rest, speaking quietly near a fountain with twisting rivulets that slithered from one level of chiseled stone to another. Camilla stood close to the pair, hovering at a respectful distance. Farren set her bucket far enough away that none of them would smell the vinegar.

"I was starting to get worried," Camilla said when Farren joined her.

"Sorry. There was an incident with the broom."

Camilla blanched. "Are you alright?"

"Just a few bruises. Might have to check on Livigena later, though."

"What happened? Is she alright?"

"I've sent a healer to her," Farren reassured the girl. "There was just a little bit of blood."

Camilla's eyes widened to twin moons, darkened by the shadows stroked beneath them. She looked like she hadn't slept well in days. "I'll pop over there after this exercise."

"She was asking for you, but I do think she'll be fine," Farren said gently as the girl began to fiddle with her braids.

"There's Elya," Prince Cato said to Virilus as he pointed toward the gryphons. "You'll want to take a piece of meat, open your runeskill to her, and let her feel how glad you are to see her. Then, offer the meat by tossing it on the ground."

Virilus nodded his head of blond curls, a grin on his well-cut face. As he went to the bucket, the prince glanced at Farren and frowned. Probably noticing the wrinkles on her chiton, Enchanters forbid it.

The other recruits watched as Virilus stood by the fountain, blood dripping from the meat in his hand. Elya approached, her tawny fur glossy in the sunlight as she stalked the flagstones, and Farren's breath went still.

"She's very gentle," Camilla told her quietly. "Less dominant than the other gryphons. See that cut on her ear?" One of the gryphon's wide, triangular ears had a piece missing. "That's from a fight with Naronimus. They don't get along well. I think Naronimus takes advantage of her subservience."

Despite what Camilla said, nothing about the gryphon appeared submissive to Farren. She walked boldly, her eyes cutting into Virilus with a sharpness that all gryphons held. The hot air of her breath steamed in gray threads from her beak, beading along the sharp curve as it met chill air. Her ears twitched toward Virilus when he tossed the meat between them.

She stepped closer to inspect it, then reared her head and gave a sharp cry of disapproval. A gust of wind cut through the yard, whipping dust and plant debris around the fountains. Some of the recruits called out in alarm, and Farren squinted through the grainy air at Camilla.

"It's Elya," Camilla told her, wiping dust from her eyes. "She has air magic."

Virilus held out an imploring hand to the gryphon, but Elya backed up, sending little tunnels of dust twisting toward his feet.

*Perfect.*

The prince was at his side in a moment, muttering into his ear. Virilus nodded, reached into his pocket, and pulled something out. He stepped forward and placed it carefully on the ground. Elya's ears perked, the wind dropped, and she immediately went to it. The object was small and metal.

"Can you see what it is?" Farren asked, chewing her lip.

"Oh, I think it's a bell. Cato made sure Virilus brought something interesting for the gryphon just in case he had difficulty."

"Why would a gryphon want a bell?"

Camilla gave her a startled look. "I forget that you don't know much about gryphons," she said, then shook her head apologetically. "You'll learn. Elya is particularly fond of things that make noise with wind—especially if it's musical."

Elya grabbed the circular handle of the bell with her thick beak and twitched her head. A bright, cheery note chimed across the courtyard. Elya's wings half-opened as she bobbed her head, releasing a rhythmic ringing that caused the other two gryphons to emit little whinnies. Finally, Elya approached Virilus and offered the bell back to him.

Then Farren saw the strangest thing. Virilus spoke to her aloud, explaining the bell as he swung it back and forth in differing rhythms. Elya's eyes swiveled from Virilus to the bell in his hands like an astute child engaged in some lesson about arithmetic.

Farren snapped out of her awe when Prince Cato turned with a frown toward the bucket. Farren had no time to react before he lifted it to examine the contents inside. His face turned to stone. He set the bucket down and stalked to where Farren stood with Camilla.

"I think it's going well, Cato," Camilla said, the brightness in her voice wavering as she saw his daunting expression.

Prince Cato gave Camilla a tight nod as he passed her, then set his glare on Farren. Shoulders hitched high, he looked ready to fight, and he didn't stop walking until he stood inches from her. The sudden proximity of him made blood rush to her cheeks. The scent of sour vinegar twined between them as he bent to speak quietly in her ear.

"I know what you did." He pulled his head back, his expression one of controlled fury. His breath was hot on her face. "Horat *will* hear about this. You can expect to go without your pay for another week. And that's the least you deserve."

Farren grit her teeth. By the look in Cato's eyes, she knew he would see through any pretense of ignorance, and in a moment of panic, Farren said the first words that popped into her head. "I didn't know princes had tattle-tongues."

As soon as the words left her mouth, she heard how spiteful and childish she sounded. Foolish, to goad a prince so. Reckless. But hadn't she trained herself to lash out when cornered?

Cato's lip curled. Farren was saved by Camilla's gentle voice. "Is everything alright?"

Something shifted minutely in Cato—a slight softening, a sudden twitch to his shoulders that seemed to show an awareness of how close he stood to Farren. He took a step back and turned to Camilla. Farren's heart pounded as she studied the stubble on his cheeks, and she wondered for the first time if she had underestimated him. "You take over for recruit bonding. No meat though. Farren will be removing that."

Without looking again at Farren, he spun away.

# FOURTEEN

Horat called her to the study just after dawn the next morning. She shoved on a wrinkled chiton and light-woven leggings, fighting the tiredness from a long night of thinking rather than sleeping.

She regretted her behavior—and words—with Prince Cato. The problem was that she was a trained fighter who didn't like giving in to the other side. Submission, that was the word. Her father had known it, and had cautioned her on it once when a fighter much larger and more skilled than herself had nearly knocked her unconscious. *Just as you must know when to fight,* he had said while her head spun, *you must also know when to cease fighting. Accept the loss as a lesson learned, and step back with graciousness.*

Graciousness. She wasn't sure she could ever have *that*, but she would try. She couldn't let herself slip like that again. Tainting the gryphon's food had been too obvious, and she had wracked her mind for other ideas. She tussled with the worry that it was too selfish to try dismantling the queen's program. After all, her family would be the ones who suffered for it if she was caught.

But Farren would never be able to forget the way that gryphon attacked her brother, and there was no way she would allow that to happen to another person. Gryphons were not meant to be kept like pets among people and would never make good service animals. Unlike horses, they couldn't be broken.

She tugged a comb through her unruly hair, tangled from a night of tossing and turning, then confronted herself in the mirror. Determined eyes greeted her. A strong, slightly curved nose dove down to a quirky mouth and a button-like chin.

She was irritated that she didn't know the gryphons well enough. That she hadn't foreseen the trick with the bell. She needed to be more careful next time. Do something more subtle, something that couldn't be pinned on her. Farren had considered every impossible, outrageous mode of sabotage. Ruining every training she could. Burning down the mews. Killing the gryphons. Somehow stopping the queen. Yet each of those held the most risk and were things she knew she couldn't compel herself to attempt.

Only five weeks remained before the queen's new guard would be stalking the streets during the Festival of the Forging. It wasn't much time to learn the weaknesses of the gryphon program, nor the weaknesses of gryphons themselves. Her mistake with the food proved how little she knew the beasts. She could read every book about gryphons in Horat's study, but that would take too much time.

She stared into the umber rings of her eyes. The only way to learn about gryphons—and to have a chance at dismantling the queen's gryphon program—was to do the one thing she feared the most: runebond with them.

When Farren arrived at the study, she found Horat dressed in sturdy cotton riding clothes and in a strangely pleasant mood. He spoke idly with Prince Cato, who rummaged through the bookshelves in the study.

"Morning," Horat said when she came in, not moving from his desk chair. "I'll be in the fields north of the fortress with the queen today. She's requested to take some of the hawks hunting."

Farren flicked a glance at Prince Cato. He scowled into a book, turning the pages faster than his eyes could possibly read them. Farren held her breath.

"I'd like you to work with Camilla today," Horat continued, and Farren released a small breath. "She'll be tending to the gryphons in the nursery."

Her heart sank, but she tried to hide her disappointment from Horat. "Of course," she said, keeping her tone neutral. "Anything else you'd like me to do? Scrub the fountains? Feed the gryphons?"

Prince Cato's head shot up so quickly she thought it might pop off his neck. Skeptical eyes dug into her, but Farren kept her gaze steady on Horat so that the Lord Falconer knew she was serious. Horat's expression was one of marble, difficult to read, and made even more confusing by the mean scar cutting a ragged line down his forehead. He tapped thoughtfully on the desk. "You may help

Camilla with any other tasks today. I'll let her decide what you're ready for."

With a grimace, he pushed himself out of the chair and walked to the door in his jilting gait. He paused when he reached her, huffing a little. "And listen to Cato if he offers you any advice. He has a keen instinct with the gryphons. He might just be able to help you become more comfortable with them."

He left, and Farren's gaze slid to the prince's. He was watching them and gave Farren a scathing look. He snapped the book closed and pretended to look for another.

When she was certain Horat was out of earshot, she said, "You didn't tell him."

The prince's fingers skimmed the book bindings as if his hands might find something his eyes could not among the musty leather-bound tomes. "I decided against it. But let's be clear here." He tugged another book out and blew the dust off with a quick burst of air. "Your work with Camilla today is your punishment for tainting the food."

Farren crossed her arms. "So I have you to thank for that."

"Maybe I should have had your father brought here instead. He's probably more pleasant to work with."

Her stomach tightened at the thought of her father being taken from his home and business...and from Desmond. "He would hate it just as much as I do."

The prince grabbed another book and brought the stack to the desk. "At least he wouldn't be fool enough to try what you did."

"You're right. He would probably do something a lot smarter."

When she didn't elaborate, he looked at her suspiciously. "Whatever you're trying to do, just don't."

"I'm doing what I was brought here to do. Work with gryphons. Train to be a guard."

"Well, your efforts against Virilus were a waste. The bonding was a success."

She wandered to the books, fishing for a way to distract him from the topic. He would never believe her innocence, not after she tainted the food.

"What exactly do you do in here all day? Besides talk to the quill, I mean?" She studied the titles on the shelves, which she had already gone over a dozen times while looking for answers to Mellion's death. *The Animal Mind. Runeskills. The Elusive Gryphon. How Animals Mate.*

"It's...personal." The prince plucked blank sheets of paper from a drawer and laid them on the desk. Other pages, brimming with writing, formed a stack to the side. "Are you enjoying the books you stole from me?"

"It's very kind of you to share the great knowledge of the mews. I'm particularly fond of one title," she paused, searching her memory for the book about the lascivious animedic. "*Adventures of an Animedic.*"

She bit her lip, trying not to laugh when the prince's cheeks flushed two shades darker. "I don't care for that one."

Farren eased closer to the desk, trying to read what was written on the pages there. She wanted to poke at him more, but her curiosity got the best of her.

"Do you write about gryphons? Their behavior?" She caught a few words on a page before the prince covered it with one hand, the skin-painted feathers on his arm rippling as he pushed his palm down and stared at her.

"Do you really want to know? Or are you fishing for something cruel to say?"

Her lips quirked. "I want to know if you really think you can tame gryphons. If you really believe it's acceptable for them to be walking the streets, and if you've ever thought once about those who have been hurt by them."

He glanced over her. "Have you been hurt by one?"

"Just because you can't see it doesn't mean it hasn't happened. There's an entire city out there and villages beyond it. You can't know everyone's story."

"You didn't answer my question," said the prince, an edge sharpening his tone.

"Did you know that people go missing in Malodai? Women, men, and children?"

The prince's brows creased. "Why do you think that?"

"There's an inn full of sketches of the missing. No one seems to care."

"I didn't know." The prince rubbed the stubble along his jaw. "But there's no way a gryphon is the cause. They are locked in the mews or in the gryphon yard. We haven't had any escape."

"Are you sure? Aren't they smart? Maybe they figured out how to open your doors and escaped, and then returned the next morning. And what about the gryphons kept by other families?"

"All of the gryphons have been returned to Alidonia. The City Watch is there to protect the people *if* a gryphon ever happened to escape."

"Well, the missing people weren't protected. And no one, including the queen, is doing anything about it."

The prince looked solemn. "I can speak with her about it. But she..." he seemed to sink into his thoughts and withdrew from the desk, forgetting her completely.

*What an awful habit he has*, Farren thought. She doubted he would actually *do* anything about the missing people. Talking to the queen wouldn't get him anywhere, not if the woman cared more about her gryphon program than her people.

Farren headed for the door.

"You never answered my question," the prince said. "About whether a gryphon has hurt you."

"I have work to do," Farren tossed over her shoulder before swinging the door shut behind her.

Farren avoided the kitchen, not wanting to relive the broom incident, and waited for Camilla in the hall. Her stomach rumbled loudly, and she moved away from the study, too aware of how quiet it was since she had closed the door.

Since arriving at the fortress, she had grown accustomed to eating three square meals a day, and that, along with each day's abundant physical activity—and a *very* comfortable bed—had made her feel stronger and more energized than she had been in months. She had even taken up stretches and a little routine each morning to help her body remember how to fight. The more she practiced, the faster she became, and the less she had to think before her body responded.

Glancing around to be sure she was alone, she did some stretches in the hall. Her stomach pinched, and so did several muscles along her back. She bent at the waist, easing into the stretch, and her stomach snarled.

A giggle sounded behind her, and Farren peered through her legs at the blond girl.

"You missed breakfast," Camilla said, grinning. "I could hear your stomach all the way from the kitchen."

Farren straightened, embarrassed, and saw that Camilla held out a wedge of buttered flatbread.

"Oh, may the Enchanters bless you," she said, savoring the chewy goodness. "I could kiss you right now."

"I would let you, except that your lips are covered in butter," Camilla said happily. "I checked on Livigena. She's doing better, and the broom is still locked away."

They walked down the hall, and Camilla glanced at her sidelong. "I told the cook about Elya refusing the meat. I wondered if she had prepared it differently, but she hadn't. Livigena told me that she thought she smelled garlic before you left."

Farren forced down her last lump of bread. "The broom did hit her head pretty hard."

"Did you...do something to the food?"

"The prince didn't tell you, then?"

"Tell me what?" Camilla asked.

"That I made a foolish choice. He's seen fit to punish me. He's making me help you in the nursery today."

Despite her concern, Camilla smiled. "A punishment? Maybe for you, but I love it there."

"I guess the prince is finally understanding me, then."

Camilla's smile seemed to grow secretive and knowing, and Farren frowned. They picked up brooms, the mop, a shovel, a bucket of water, and some scrub brushes, then headed down a wide corridor that led to the nursery chamber.

Encased in stone walls, the nursery felt more like a damp, dank prison to Farren than a place where baby gryphons should be born and raised. Narrow barred windows lined the top of the room, but the air threading through them wasn't enough to freshen the fetid smell of gryphon dung. Straw scattered across the floor, dirty and clumping in spots. Crates lined one wall, each laying on its side so the gryphons had their own beds. Camilla explained that they liked to use the crates to stash trinkets or bits of food for later. The walls were flat and grey as rain, bland except for a large tapestry of a wild landscape: rolling hills that rose suddenly to sharp-edged mountains, so tall and strange and out of place in the otherwise dismal chamber.

"Those are the Blades," Camilla said, noticing her stare at the tapestry. "It was the only thing Delphi requested from Prince Cato when she was moved here."

"They're..."

"I find them too hostile. Formidable, even." Camilla shivered and touched her braids lightly.

Camilla was right. The sharp mountains, which were far southeast of Malodai, cast sharp, deep shadows. Fog gathered at their base, cloaking any sight of the ground. Farren pulled her gaze from it.

In the far corner of the chamber, Delphi sprawled with slumped wings, peering at them through exhausted eyes while four gryphons, each slightly larger than Farren's forearm, pounced around her.

"Here you are, little ones," Camilla murmured to them and pulled something out of her pocket: a smooth wooden ball. She placed it on the floor and rolled it across the chamber. It bounced and clattered over the straw, and four pairs of wide eyes tracked the ball until it bumped gently against Delphi's belly.

Camilla chuckled when they tried pouncing on it, most tumbling clumsily over their mother's thick side. "I bring it every time, but they still act like it's something novel. They're just like little kittens."

Farren made an uncertain noise in her throat.

"If you try to connect with Delphi, it's like a gentle hum. She knows we don't mean harm. I'm not sure if this will help you, but...she has no magic of her own."

Delphi watched her calmly. If she opened a runebond, the beast would catch hint of her fear; magic or no, just being around gryphons made Farren's pulse quicken. To distract herself, Farren set to work.

Her father would've been appalled by the filth inside the chamber. She would start with sweeping up the straw and droppings. When she inquired how often it was cleaned, Camilla admitted she didn't know and mentioned that Cato was in charge of assigning cleaning duties to the servants.

Perhaps they didn't do their chores thoroughly. Perhaps the prince didn't realize that he might need to teach the servants how to properly clean the chambers. Or perhaps he was too distracted by his writings and musings to realize he needed to be doing more important things. Farren thrust the broom across the floor and formed a dense, stinky pile of straw. She thought she saw fish bones in there, too.

"Maybe Horat should be in charge of it?" she suggested. The gryphons squawked as two got into a tussle over the ball.

"It does seem to have been a while since it's been cleaned. I can check with Cato. Horat allows him to take charge of the breeding and training since Cato knows the most about it."

Knowing and doing were completely different things, and Cato was clearly lacking in the latter.

Farren dug the broom head into a corner, then worked her way slowly around the gryphons, careful to keep several feet between herself and Delphi. Although the large gryphon remained lying down, Farren tensed with each twitch of her ear or swish of her tail. She clutched the broom handle, forcing her breathing to remain steady.

"He seems distracted by whatever project he works on in the study," Farren said after a few moments.

A cloud of dust formed around them, and Camilla sneezed. "His book," she said, sniffing. "He's collecting information about gryphon behavior and magic. He has some interesting theories."

Farren was about to ask her what sort of theories he had when one of the little gryphons pounced on her broom. Farren froze, and the gryphon jumped off, wide ears splayed as he sat, waiting for the broom to move again. His tail twitched. Farren swept again, slowly, and the gryphon leapt on the broom, biting down and ripping into the stalks with his tiny beak.

"I call that one Torch," Camilla said, watching fondly as he destroyed the perfectly innocent broom.

"Why? Does it have to do with his magic?"

Camilla shoveled the pile of refuse into a bucket. "His magic hasn't risen yet and might not for another year or two. Some gryphons never manifest it, like Delphi. Either way, Torch has a fire in him."

Farren shuddered and pulled the broom away from Torch, setting it high up across the window ledge that spanned one chamber wall. Torch sat, looking startled and disappointed. She kept an eye on him as she set to scrubbing the floor by hand, watching as he attempted to jump up to the ledge. Luckily, he was too small to jump that high, and his little wings weren't strong enough yet to carry him there.

As Camilla went on talking around her, Farren took solace in the *shush-shush* of the scrub brush against the stone. Besides feces and straw, she found what appeared to be fish entrails hardened there. Bile rose in her throat, and she scrubbed harder, transforming the muck into creamy bubbles.

"One of Cato's theories is about their magic and where it comes from," Camilla was saying. "Legend says that they got their magic from the ancient Enchanted stones that formed The Blades, but Cato thinks the magic is passed down from parent gryphons."

Farren's arm began to burn as she scrubbed. "If only he applied as much thought to the cleaning schedule," she ground out, blaming every stuck fish scale on the prince's laziness.

"You should really give him a chance, Farren. He cares about the gryphons more than anyone."

Wood scraping along the stone floor drew their attention to the windows. Torch pushed his head against a crate, moving it closer to the wall, and then looked up at the broom. He wiggled his furry bum as he readied to pounce, then leapt onto the crate, talons scrabbling for purchase. Claws hooked deep into the wood, and he pulled himself up, taking only a moment to assess his target before he opened his wings and jumped up to the narrow window ledge. He latched onto the broom and dragged it down with him as he fell to the floor.

Clever. Maybe her suggestion to the prince about gryphons letting themselves out of the mews wasn't so far-fetched after all. She didn't bother taking the broom from him this time, as he had already removed half the bristles within moments of getting it.

Camilla rolled the ball for the three other gryphon kits, and they chased after it, beating their tiny wings in an effort to move faster. Limbs splayed as they fell over the ball and sprawled atop one another.

"When I first met Cato, I didn't know who he was. I was with my father." Camilla's words grew strained, tightening on the word *father*. "I was so hungry, and a stall at the market had a basket of apples out, so close to the street that I didn't think anyone would notice. Cato happened to be walking behind me and saw me take one. I don't think he would've cared about the stealing, but my father did. He noticed the bulge in my pocket and hit me."

Camilla finished sweeping and heaped the rest of the refuse into the bucket. "It was normal for me, but Cato didn't like it, so he kept an eye on us as we went through the market. My father had put a mouse in my pocket after that and made me keep my hand in there with it. Cato noticed me crying, then noticed the blood dripping from the pocket."

Farren stared at Camilla's hands. "Your father made the mouse bite you?"

She took a shaky breath, holding out a hand for Farren to see. Scars mangled the skin of her fingers. "It was the way he punished me when he couldn't hit me much, when we were around other people."

"What about your mother? Didn't she notice?"

Camilla looked solemnly resolute. "No." She picked up the bucket of refuse. "But Cato did, and he interceded. He ripped my pocket open and killed the mouse with his boot. He wrapped my hand with a piece of his shirt and asked how I'd like to come live in the fortress, far away from my family. I didn't believe him, not until my father shoved him, and royal guards materialized from the streets to surround us."

Farren had a hard time picturing the prince doing such a thing.

"He offered to take me in as a ward of the crown," Camilla continued, "a place usually reserved for well-to-do orphaned children. So I said yes, and Cato proclaimed it. And now I have a better family than I could ever ask for," she said, indicating the mews around them.

Farren eased back on the scrubbing as Camilla took the bucket out of the chamber. She begrudgingly admitted that the prince had done well to protect Camilla, but that didn't mean he was the same person now as he was then.

Feathers flashed in the corner of her eye, and Farren snatched her hand away just before Torch pounced. He landed on her scrub brush, right where her hand had been, and dug into the wood with a sharp beak.

Swallowing back a scream, Farren snapped open her runebond and thrust her anger at the gryphon. *Don't you attack me! I am not food, and neither is my scrub brush!*

Torch scrambled away, ears flattened as shame and fear rippled back through the runebond. He dove behind his mother, chastised.

Farren's body trembled. She wiped sweaty palms on her leggings and rubbed her forehead, tapping a quick rhythm there until her trembling receded. He hadn't hurt her, so she had no reason to be upset. He had just startled her.

The fear coming through their connection spiked again as he looked at her over his mother's shoulder.

*It's alright*, Farren told him, grinding her teeth. *You just need to be calmer. And stop attacking things that move. You are far stronger than you think, and you could hurt someone.* Testing, she sent him a little bit of her own fear.

He eased out from behind his mother, curious. He sent her an impression of being pounced on by his brother and the fear he remembered feeling.

*That's right. Fear*, she encouraged him. *It's not a good feeling.*

Camilla came around behind Farren and dropped down to her knees to help scrub. Torch's curiosity grew, and he stepped closer.

*Remember, stay calm. We are not food*, she told him.

*Play?* he asked, using an impression of tussling with his brothers and sisters.

No, *we cannot play with you. You would hurt us.* She sent him a sensation of pain and felt Torch's distress. *Your beak is sharp, and your claws.* She showed him the damage gryphons could do, not from her dark, bloody memories but from tame imaginings: a cut finger, scratched arms, a deep bite to the wrist.

Afraid to move, Torch sat and watched her while she scrubbed. His gaze tracked her brush, but every once in a while, he would gaze at her face and send her a questioning wave.

*I'm cleaning the floor because it's dirty*, she tried to explain.

He sent an impression of the floor, that it was always that way.

*It's dirty, not healthy. You could get sick.*

He had never been sick before, but he seemed to understand the impression she sent of not feeling well. Behind him, his siblings tussled, and he twitched an ear toward them.

*Go play*, she suggested, but the gryphon hesitated.

*Angry?* He sent her an impression of her outraged face, and Farren made an effort to smooth her features.

*Not anymore. But have care around humans.*

He understood and sent her a bolt of happiness. Then he darted away, tail swishing and wings half-open in excitement as he joined his sibling's fray.

"He seems to like you," Camilla said.

"He tried to pounce on my hand, and I may have been a little harsh in response."

As they cleaned, Torch occasionally circled back to Farren and asked what she was doing and why. Communicating with the gryphon felt almost like speaking to a small child. And Farren found that she didn't mind his little feathered head popping in. She kept their runebond open, at first narrowly, only allowing a droplet of feeling in. Gradually, she widened it, pulling their minds closer so that the runebond encompassed more of their thoughts and feelings. His rowdy excitement toward his siblings reminded her of playing games with Desmond. His deep bond with his mother, too, was akin to her feelings towards her father, whom she missed more than anything.

After the kits wore themselves out playing, Torch and his siblings encircled their mother, sprawling across her or tucking themselves into spaces that should be too small. Delphi lay half-asleep in the sun coming through the window. Golden dust motes spun in the light as she lifted her head to Torch, and Farren had the uncanny sensation that they spoke with one another. She almost thought she could feel their conversation, like a distant whispering over a lake dense with fog.

Settling between his mother's talons, Torch sent Farren a strand of impressions laced with feelings. A fly buzzing in the window, its veined wings shimmering in the light. Feathers drifting to the floor as he preened, spinning lazily as if they danced to a different tempo of time. The *swish-swish* of his tail against the stone floor that sounded so different from her scrub brush. With every beautiful, curious impression he shared with her, something warm blossomed in her chest.

By the time she left the nursery, she realized she had runebonded with the little gryphon longer than any animal since Desmond's attack. That's what Mellion had been missing all summer in the mountains...and Farren had missed it, too.

# FIFTEEN

When Farren returned to her chamber that evening, she found a note at her door.

*Please come to my art chamber at your earliest convenience. Would you mind wearing the dress again?*

Prince Isander was likely itching to paint, but he would just have to wait. After all the cleaning she had done, nothing could come between her and a bath. At the servants' bathhouse, Farren scrubbed the feces and grime from her body with Keira's blessed cinnafern soap.

The spicy-sweet scent of Keira's soap brought her right back to her friend's house, brimming with warmth and children and beautiful plants. Her chest ached at the memories. In the letter she had gotten from Keira just days ago, her friend had reassured her that the children were well. A huntress from the village had gone up into the mountains and never returned, and others were readying to search for the missing woman.

Farren pressed her eyes closed. At least she didn't have to worry about Desmond going up there. Despite what he might want, her mother would never allow him to leave. She used to hate her mother for restricting him after his accident, when all he had ever known before then was swimming in the river and running with Farren through the village in search of trouble. Now, she was grateful for her mother's decision.

After she bathed and dressed, she gathered Tayra in the hawk mews, knowing she would be too tired to handle more, and headed to the fortress keep. By now, the sky had darkened to a velvety shade of plum, and the sultry air hung inside the fortress walls like Lidellian syrup—thick and sweet, with a lingering heat that made her limbs loosen.

Torchlight rimmed the tall keep doors, dazzling her as she approached. Nightfall had not softened the oiled planes of the oak doors or diminished the gleam of the black iron reinforcing the wood. Bloodred irises had been painted on each of them, and their color flared with the bold flicker of torchlight. Farren swallowed. Despite the danger of being in the gryphon mews, that building felt far more comfortable to her than the keep, where she knew no one other than the prince and where her presence was questionable, if not entirely unwelcome.

Farren took a fortifying breath and approached the guard she was familiar with, Iana. The broad-shouldered woman checked Farren's note with a stony expression and lifted a brow.

"If I remember correctly, the queen said you should be prioritizing her animals. Not the prince," Iana said.

"I've spent all day with animals," Farren said. "And I'll continue doing so until I return this hawk to the mews."

"You know the queen will hear of this."

"From you? I would suspect as much." Farren chewed her lip, knowing she should have declined the prince's request. "I'm sure it won't last much longer, anyways."

"That isn't the point," Iana said, settling a hand on the hilt of her sword.

"Nothing is happening between us. He just paints me. A-And the hawk."

"Do you think I'm a dolt?"

Humid air clung to the insides of her mouth. "I d-don't think that..." Farren licked her lips. "I'm surprised that you think the prince would do such things...and that you'd discuss them openly."

A smile cut the hard lines of Iana's face. "I don't think, recruit. I know. But we're not speaking of the same things. The prince isn't rakish. But him painting you...isn't just him painting you. Is it?"

Heat fanned up Farren's throat. "I don't know what you mean."

Iana stepped close to her and spoke in an undertone. "The prince can see things that others cannot. It can be helpful sometimes... He convinced me I had the strength and intelligence to become one of the queen's captains, and here I am. But he also told me that I could be other things, that I could do more than—" She cut herself off with a quick shake of her head. "I always put loyalty to the Crown first. That's what mattered. But if you get close to him, if he ever tries to convince you to act outside of your duties—"

"He hasn't," Farren said too quickly.

Iana's mouth set. "Very well. You can't say I didn't warn you."

The guard crumpled the note in her hand, then motioned for Farren to follow her into the keep. When they arrived at the prince's art chamber, Iana closed the door briskly behind her, leaving Farren alone with the prince.

"I was beginning to think you might not come," he said as Farren moved Tayra to a standing perch.

He already had his paints made and wore the same easy cotton shirt and snug leggings, although the casual Weldonian clothes didn't make him look any less regal. The front of his hair was pulled back into a knot, leaving the rest to fall to his shoulders.

Farren pulled her gaze away. *Just a painting session*, she reminded herself firmly, then said with levity, "It was a long day of cleaning a particularly filthy gryphon chamber."

Prince Isander hummed curiously and retrieved a box from his desk. "This is a gift for you. For your time," he said, "and for the inconvenience of wearing a dress you do not like." He gave her a knowing smile.

"I *do* like the dress," Farren corrected him, taking the box and opening the lid. "It's just not something I'd ever wear if..."

Inside the box, cushioned in velvet, sat a yellow-dyed falconry hood with a plume of red feathers. The rich scent of leather floated up to her as she reached in to examine it. It had been expertly crafted, the stitching even and leather well-cut. The royal emblem—a gryphon claw—was embossed on both sides, and a set of slender silver beads threaded the base of the plume.

"It's beautiful. And far too lovely for a hawk head," she joked.

"The hood isn't for a hawk head. It's for a *royal* hawk head."

"It's wonderful, Your Highness, but..."

"What is it?"

"A hawk needs to be measured first, so it fits properly—"

"Yes, of course. The hoodmaker told me. I know you have a fondness for Tayra, so I had it made for her."

"Oh, I see." Farren hoped her cheeks weren't as red as they felt. "This is very generous of you."

She brought the hood to Tayra. *Hood*, she told the bird, and Tayra sent back resigned acceptance, knowing that a hood would make her feel safe, even if it meant she couldn't see.

She slipped the hood over Tayra's head and tightened it, then stepped back. Like the dress the prince made her wear, it transformed Tayra from hawk into something different. A creature who was more than an animal. A statement, perhaps. Was that how the prince saw her when she wore the dress?

The smell of mint curled around her. Prince Isander hovered a small distance behind her. "Shall I put the dress on?" she asked him without turning.

"Of course."

For a moment, he didn't move and neither did she. Her nape prickled with the sensation of his gaze, with the yearning for touch. Enchanters, she needed to take care of herself before the night was over. Otherwise, she was bound to do something foolish.

She headed for the changing area and shucked her linen chiton for the fine silk. It slid over her body like water, gliding over her hips until the hem nearly reached the floor.

"Has my mother bothered you yet?" the prince asked.

"She didn't seem too pleased to see me after I left our last session."

The prince gave a soft snort. "Don't mind her. She does that to everyone I paint. It doesn't amount to anything. I will speak to her if you'd like. She knows how important painting is to me. I've managed to convince her that pursuing art is the most important thing I could be doing. Other than my dull princely duties, that is."

Farren emerged feeling lighter. The dress was starting to feel familiar to her, like an embrace from a warm, very wealthy friend. She thought that the dress might be making her look taller, making her feel more...regal.

The prince gazed at her from the window. He had thrown a clean cloth over one shoulder and twirled a paintbrush between his fingers as he waited. What else would those long, strong fingers be capable of?

"It's fitting on you."

Farren pulled on her falconry glove. "It does fit rather well."

"You know what I mean. You can feel it. Like you're a different person...but also, *you*."

She nudged Tayra's legs to signal that she should step onto the glove. "Is that what you tell all the women you paint?"

The soft jingle of Tayra's bells filled the shrinking space between her and the prince.

He gave a lopsided smile, a look that made him seem far less princely. "That is what some of them have told *me*."

"How many women have you painted, exactly?" Farren teased.

"Are you sure you want to waste one of your questions with that one?"

Farren pursed her lips, considering. "Yes."

"Fine. I've painted too many to count. But all of them unique."

"That sounds rehearsed."

The prince stepped closer until he was less than an arm-length away. The scent of mint filled her lungs once more, pulling warmth down to her belly.

"I mean it, Farren. You are different from the others."

She could make out the green and brown flecks in his eyes. Had this been what Iana warned her of?

"I don't believe you, Isander." His name popped out unbidden. Heat coiled up her cheeks, and she clamped her teeth together. He would be offended at the lack of title, the assumption that she could be personal with him.

But he wasn't. His ember gaze flared. He lifted his paintbrush handle to her chin, tilting it upward and toward the window. His breath was soft and shallow, nearly matching hers. He ran the brush handle down her jaw, smoothing across the plane of her cheek. "I will show you," he said softly.

He leapt into movement, directing her to a place by the window. Every time he touched her, even the slightest graze, her skin tingled. She grew hot in the dress, and it took some time for her heart to return to its normal rhythm and her thoughts to steady.

Once he appeared engrossed by painting, she cleared her throat.

"The gryphon guard will be patrolling the streets soon. What do you think will happen if someone gets hurt?"

A slight frown, but he didn't lift his eyes from the canvas. "We have healers in Alidonia if a guard is hurt."

"I meant if a bystander is hurt."

"Hm. Well, if the bystander was threatening the guard and is hurt because of it, they can be taken to an infirmary."

Farren pursed her lips. "If a bystander *wasn't* threatening the guard. If a gryphon attacked them without cause."

"I don't think the queen would put the gryphons on the streets if they couldn't be controlled."

Her pulse flickered in her throat. "Didn't Anaxis think they could be controlled, too?"

His paintbrush stilled. "My uncle was...deranged. He believed he could beat them to the point of control. The queen is taking a different approach."

Already, she had used up half her questions. Farren sighed quietly through her nose. If the prince insisted on answering her questions with one or two sentences, she would learn nothing.

"And if the queen finds that her...approach...isn't working, what then?"

"Then she'll likely find a different one."

"You don't seem very concerned about it all."

"I'm trying to paint, Farren."

"What of your people—the orphans, the—" She waved her hand wordlessly at the window, where the dark city sprawled. "Don't you ever think about them?"

His entire body leaned toward the canvas, eyes riveted to the strokes he made with deft flicks of the brush.

"Incessantly."

"Isander—"

With a sharp intake of breath, he pulled away from the canvas and walked to her, brush still in hand. Black paint gleamed along the tip. "I think about them all the time, probably more than what is natural for a prince." The squint he gave her over the strong curve of his nose—as if he tried to read her thoughts—made her heart patter. "You are like a fox, digging and digging. What is it you're searching for?"

She lifted her chin minutely. "I simply want to know what you think about the gryphon program."

"Ah, is that all?" He took a step, bending close as he said quietly, "Well, the queen tends to do whatever she wants, regardless of what her children think about it. Using the gryphons to her advantage might be smart. As far as being safe for the people...I'm not sure. I'm afraid that entirely depends on those who will be training with the gryphons."

Farren's voice rasped. "And if we can't guarantee safety?"

"Then Malodai will become a more dangerous place."

"And you think that's acceptable?"

"You don't seem to think it is." He leaned nearer, his lips almost brushing her cheek. Warm, steady breath caressed her nape. "Then everything must change, don't you think?"

A shiver rippled down her spine and spun into molten copper in the pit of her belly. "What are you saying?"

He made a noise low in his throat as he pulled away from her. "No more questions, Farren. I've let you go over your quota again."

"You didn't *let* me—"

He made another noise, and this time his finger found her lips. He rested it there—soft and gently pressing—for just a moment, and then it was gone.

Her mouth tingled.

She posed for nearly an hour, trying to untangle the prince's words—and harder yet, to forget how close he had been...as if him being a prince and her being a servant mattered little. And how her body filled with heady feelings she hadn't had since...well, since Thestor. Enchanters, she wished she could forget that one.

The prince remained silent while he painted, entirely focused on the canvas. When she started to grow weary, he set his paints aside and had trays of refreshments brought up. Another servant came in to clean up the paints. After the servants had gone, Farren returned Tayra to her perch and glanced at the prince as he scrubbed his hands in a basin of water. He was intent on the task, just as he had been intent on painting. His focus was a bit disconcerting, and had a way of making her feel invisible when it wasn't on her, and then much too close when it *was* on her.

What sort of painting would such intensity create? If the painting of her was anything like those of the Enchanters... She crept toward the abandoned canvas, curiosity pulling her like a starving hawk to a meaty rabbit. A couple feet away, Isander's arm flashed out, blocking her.

"It's not ready yet," he said.

Her cheeks warmed. She stepped back, tilting her head up so she could meet his gaze as squarely as she could. "When can I see it?"

"Soon." He motioned to the trays of fruit, nuts, and cheeses. "Are you hungry?"

Her stomach pinched. Despite eating more than she had every day since being in the mountains, her hunger hadn't diminished. For food or...other things.

It was odd, being in a chamber and eating with a man she hardly knew anything about. He had an unfair advantage over her, and she hated that imbalance—royalty or no.

She reached for the bowl of plums, but when she saw his hand reaching for the tray of cheese, she suddenly took his arm and drew it toward her. He nearly snatched it back in alarm, and Farren almost let go, knowing she was crossing some sort of line. He gave her a sharp look and seemed to decide that whatever she was about to do was acceptable.

Farren flipped his hand palm-up and inspected the scar on his inner wrist where his runemark should've been, much as he had done to her during one of their first sessions. The scar had a circular sort of shape, as if the skin had been burned by something round. It had been purposeful, not an accident.

"When are you going to tell me that your true runeskill is with those giant frogs in the kitchens?"

He laughed a little at that, and pulled his arm back, rubbing the scar that had destroyed his birth-given runemark. "Maybe when we know each other a bit better. When you trust me not to attack you with frogs."

"Attack me!" she said, mocking offense. "Why would you attack me?"

She grabbed the plum and bit in, leaning against the table so that she could face the prince. She was enjoying his company far too much, and didn't want to let it go. It almost made her feel the way she did before Desmond's attack: carefree, playful, and a little reckless.

*He's a prince, I'm a servant*, she told herself sternly. She would do well not to forget that.

Isander brushed her arm as he reached for a few sweetnuts. "Because what else would you think when you discovered my small army of frogs?"

She nearly choked on her plum as she imagined it, then said in a stately announcement, "Prince Isander, leader of the Great Frog Brigade. You're right, it sounds positively threatening."

Isander chuckled, and she could feel his gaze lingering on her while she finished her plum. She should move away, create some distance between them. Her bum felt rooted to the table, frozen by the need to pull away and the need to stay close to Isander's warmth and the foolish possibility of his touch.

As Isander sipped from a cup, the scent of mint floated over her, sharp and sweet.

"What is that?" she asked.

"Lidellian *birali*. It's a tea made of various mints and spices. It helps with focusing the mind. Would you like to try some?"

He held out his cup, and she sniffed. Definitely potent. She tipped the cup to her lips, acutely aware that his lips had already touched it. Was he thinking the same thing as he watched her? The drink slid down into her like ice, frigid and burning all at once.

"It's refreshing." Farren handed the cup back to him.

"I rely on it more than I care to admit," Isander said.

Although she was curious about why he had burned his rune-mark away, she didn't want to press him. With an effort, she pushed away from the table. "I'll go change."

Isander placed a hand on her elbow, stopping her. His face was inches from hers. "Wait, Farren. I—"

The door to the room opened, and Farren tugged away from him, putting distance between them as someone came in. It was Iana, and when the guard saw them, her brow drew down almost imperceptibly, noting the dress with a quick flick of her eyes. "The queen requests your presence," she told the prince.

"Of course, I will be right there," Isander said.

As soon as Iana left, Farren changed swiftly back into her clothes.

"Don't worry about my mother," Isander's voice came floating through the curtain, distant as if he stood by the window. "I will make sure she understands what this is."

Farren emerged from the changing area, and saw that Isander studied the painting. "And what is it, exactly?"

"Me painting a servant. The same as always." He looked up, and then winked.

Farren turned from him as she gathered Tayra to her glove, hiding the way her cheeks burned. What in all of the rune-made world did that wink mean?

She made for the door with her things, avoiding the prince's eyes. Why did she suddenly feel as awkward as a featherless bird?

"Thank you for your time," he said as she passed.

She hummed acknowledgment—apparently she also had lost her ability to speak like a human—and spared a single glance at his perfect, sensual lips, where an amused smile still lingered.

# SIXTEEN

FARREN DREAMED OF ISANDER'S gentle, capable arms around her. His slender fingers stroking her the way his brush stroked the canvas. When she woke, she felt alive and buzzing, like a sewing bird on its way to a favorite thatch of foxglove blossoms.

A servant knocked on the door and delivered a breakfast tray with a cup of steaming *birali*, a dainty round of barley bread, and a dish of figs. A small sketch sat on the tray too: a tiny portrait of Tayra made in clean, sweeping lines.

"From a special admirer," was all the servant said, winking at her before scampering away.

It was all Farren could do not to moan in pleasure over the spiced *birali* and sweet figs. She continued thinking of Isander as she dressed, and still a breath of him remained in her mind nearly an hour later, when she pulled into a fighting stance across from Scipio.

The other recruits shuffled and grunted around her in the dawn-lit gryphon yard. Scipio's unsmiling eyes watched her. "You're distracted," he said. "Got something on your mind, Outskirts drift?" He sneered. "Or maybe *someone*?"

Farren was getting tired of seeing his conceited coyote smile. She lunged at him, but her aim was a little off and he darted out of the way, grinning.

"You look tired," he taunted. "Word spreads quickly in the fortress. I heard about your romantic night with the prince. The queen's not at all pleased."

She grit her teeth and attacked again, this time aiming right, but he blocked it with ease. He didn't bother attacking her, but rocked back and forth from foot to foot, as if he were itching to dance. He shot a glance toward the splashing fountain, where Camilla sat and watched the recruits, her pale face lit by the reflection of sunlight off the water. Something in Scipio's gaze made Farren's stomach seize.

Taking advantage of his lapse in tension, Farren lashed out again, catching Scipio on the cheek. He growled, then made an actual effort to fight her.

*Good, this is good*, she thought, even as his fist connected with her ribs and he brought her quickly to the ground. She was letting him win, just like she had wanted. He would get bored and leave her alone, if she could take a few more hits.

She groaned, half-miserable, half-breathless with happiness at being able to fight. Scipio stood over her, dusted his clothes, and cast another glance at Camilla.

Ugh. Farren sent her leg darting out and kicked Scipio behind the knees. His ass hit the ground with a satisfying thump. That would be the best part of her day.

"That wasn't fair, bumpkin," Scipio said, cringing as he pulled himself up. "I know you country wastrels like to play dirty, but here in the royal guard, we keep things civil."

Farren repressed a snort. "Just because you land me on the ground doesn't mean we're finished."

"Actually, it does." Scipio headed for the fountain where Camilla sat.

Farren cast a glance around for Prince Cato, wondering what he would think if he saw Scipio trying to flirt with his young ward. But the prince was nowhere to be seen.

Camilla spoke shyly to Scipio while he leaned close to her. When she tried to edge away from him, he blocked her by resting an arm on the fountain statue. She went to move the other way, and he reached up to stroke one of her braids. The girl's cheeks darkened to cherries and her gaze stumbled around the courtyard, seeking help.

Farren reached her mind out for the little sunsparrows in the trees and shrubs around the courtyard, and asked each one for a favor. Two responded, eager from her promise of sweetmeat tidbits later in the day. Tiny rufous wings flashed like miniature spears as they darted at Scipio's head. He swatted at them, cursing furiously as Camilla covered her mouth with a hand, trying not to smile. Scipio glared at Camilla and muttered something under his breath, but Camilla responded with a shake of her head, suddenly looking worried.

*It's me, you fool.* Farren waited for him to figure it out. Finally, through the flash of wings he saw Farren watching. His expression darkened. A hand snapped out and caught one of the birds mid-dive. Farren gasped as he squeezed, feeling the sudden terror of the struggling bird wash into her runebond.

Camilla turned pale as parchment, eyes widening in horror. The second bird made to dive for Scipio's face, but Farren called it off—rapidly closing her runebond with the squeezed bird so she could open a runebond with the other—not wanting another to fall victim to his violence.

Farren glared at him as he continued squishing the life from the sunsparrow. Farren reached out to it once more, breath hitching as they runebonded. Within a few moments, the bird's fright succumbed to numbness, the reluctant surrender to death.

Next to Scipio, Camilla balled her fists. "Let the bird go!"

The guard winced as though he had forgotten about Camilla, and his grip slackened on the sunsparrow. He glanced around, his sneer wavering as the other recruits looked on with disgust. *Canids* had no place threatening *Avids*—especially not when there were so many of them watching; such behavior could result in a flock of birds coming down on him, no different than a mobbing of a coyote in the wild.

His eyes slid back to Farren, dark and cruel. The only way to save the bird was to drop her challenge. Camilla gave her a tiny nod.

Farren scowled one last time at the repugnant guard, then turned on her heel, pretending to look for another fighting partner. She sagged in relief when she felt the sunsparrow's sudden release. It was in shock, and sent wave after wave of trepidation toward her. She widened her runebond with it incrementally, reassuring it with safety, comfort, and detailed impressions of the sweetmeats to come. She remained connected to the bird until it returned to a familiar tree, waiting even until it became occupied with searching for bugs along the branch before she allowed herself to sink into the bliss of hand-to-hand combat.

It wasn't until later, when her skin shone with sweat and dirt and a few purpling bruises, that she realized she hadn't thought once of Isander since she had begun fighting.

Once combat practice concluded, Farren went to Horat to sort the cleaning schedule. He agreed that she could clean Torch's nursery daily, as long as she stuck to her training schedule with the other recruits. She also vowed to herself that she would try to runebond with gryphons each day. Perhaps, if she got over her fear, she could find out more about them and learn some of their weaknesses.

Torch was the perfect gryphon to start with. Farren lugged a bucket of water, scrub brushes, and a broom to the mews nursery. Musty feline air greeted her as she pushed through the doorway and set down the bucket of sloshing water.

Something small darted past her. Talons scrabbled on the stone, and Torch's rope-like tail zipped through the door's opening.

A cry erupted from Torch's mother, Delphi, and the gryphon rose to her feet, wings half-opened in panic.

Without thinking, Farren opened a runebond with Delphi. *I will get him.*

*Hurry!* Delphi replied, her voice like thunder in Farren's skull.

Farren closed the runebond with Delphi as she rushed out of the chamber, and stretched her mind to the little gryphon careening down the hall.

*Torch, stop!*

His ears twitched back, but he didn't slow. Instead of responding with words, he sent an impression that crashed into her. She floated above a massive fall of water surrounded by a plume of mist lit white and gold by the sun. The water plummeted down to a pool far below, where lacy-winged fish darted between rifts within the cascading falls. Farren nearly tripped as the impression faded, returning her unsteadily to the mews hall. The image was beautiful, but treacherous.

*You can't go there, Torch!*

*Mother showed it to me, and I have to go! It's so close I can smell the water—*

*It's too dangerous.* Farren puffed as her legs pumped beneath her.

Torch darted around a corner, and a moment later a crash of clattering wood resounded down the hall. Farren cringed and rounded the corner. Torch had somehow run straight into a stack of empty crates stored in an alcove, and struggled to get out of them.

*Torch, we need to go back to your mother. Now come with me.*

Instead of approaching her, Torch weaseled out from the mess of crates and loped down the hall.

*Mother said the falls aren't dangerous for us because we have wings. She said I have to wait until I'm bigger, but I can fly already.* See?

With those words, Torch opened his wings and beat them while he ran. He took another turn, and Farren swore aloud. How was it that the little beast could move so fast? She chased him down the hall leading to the door of the mews—which was always locked—when she caught the baked whiff of late summer air. Not twenty paces ahead, the Enchanted window was wide open. Certainly wide enough for his little body to wriggle through.

*Torch, you're going to get hurt!* Farren shot him an image of plummeting down the falls to his death. He only beat his wings faster, lifting himself enough that his talons and claws inched off the floor. Farren barreled toward him, throat constricting as he rose to the window ledge.

"No!" She threw herself the last length and grabbed Torch around the torso before he could launch from the window. She clutched him to her stomach as she fell on her side and rolled to protect him, grimacing as his beak dug into her bracing arms.

*Let me go! I just want to see it!*

Farren lay on the floor, panting. Blood beaded her arms, and she struggled to stay calm. *You're too little, Torch. Your mother said no, and you should listen to her.*

Farren cursed roundly as Torch's nipping beak hit her wrist bone. *Stop biting me! I won't let you go until we are safely back in the nursery.*

*I'm tired of the nursery. It's dark and musty and dirty.*

He stopped biting, and Farren nearly sagged in relief. *That's why I'm trying to clean it.*

*And it's boring;* he said. *Everything is the same every day.*

Farren almost smiled. Torch's complaints sounded like Desmond's after the attack, when their mother never let him leave the house.

*Who is that?* Torch asked.

Farren startled, and narrowed their runebond. She hadn't sent her memory to Torch, so how was he able to see it?

*No one*, she told him.

Carefully holding him, she pulled herself up. Blood dripped down her arms while she repositioned the kit, wrapping her hands around his front legs so he couldn't grab her.

*You like him a lot*, Torch said, growing oblivious to the way she held him as his curiosity grew. He looked up at her with glittering eyes. A tuft of feathers stuck up from just beside his left ear, and his tail flicked eagerly against her. He was a little cute, she had to admit.

*It's called love*, Farren told him. *I love him.*

*Why?* Torch inquired.

*He's my brother*, Farren explained. Torch sent her an image of his siblings. *That's right*, she told him. *You have a brother and sisters that you love, too.*

He emitted a warbling cry and shared an image of his brother pouncing on him, biting his neck.

*They can be annoying sometimes*, she agreed. As she walked back down the hall, she picked a clear, brief memory, showing him a time when Desmond had playfully dunked her head under the water while they swam in the river.

Torch immediately perked up. *What's that?*

Unsure, she sent him a picture of the river once more—a slight dancing ribbon compared to the River Kithyria—and another wave of curiosity shot through their connection.

*It's a river*, Farren said.

*Can I go there?*

Farren sighed, veering down a stuffy hall. *It's too far away.*

*But I can fly!* Torch struggled against her, and Farren mustered a beam of tranquility, letting it pool down their runebond. The gryphon settled, but not without resentment. *Where are you taking me?*

*To the animedic.*

*Why?*

*Because you crashed into those crates. I want to make sure you didn't hurt yourself.*

*You're the one with blood*, Torch remarked. *I don't like him. His breath smells.*

His legs were tensing, so Farren breathed more calm down the connection. The door to the animedic's study was open, and Farren peered inside. Dressing the small chamber were shelves lined with books, scales, and a variety of glass jars. Other tools cluttered a table, where a barrel-bellied man wearing trousers and a short chiton stood examining what appeared to be brown excrements beneath a glass scope. Farren stepped in, and he looked up.

"Little cat-bird," the man said, exposing yellowed teeth in a practiced smile. On his forehead twisted the long, looping sigil of an animedic, and small rabbit foot prints marked the skin beneath his eyes. He held his hands out for Torch. "What's the matter here? Ach, do you have to bite every time I touch you? Cursed sharp beaks you all have."

"He nearly escaped the mews," Farren said, "and I'm worried he hurt himself in his haste."

The animedic hummed in his throat as he set Torch on the table. He spent a few moments prodding the gryphon before declaring that Torch had nothing wrong with him.

Farren gathered Torch back in her arms, relieved when he didn't try to bite her. Instead, he stuck his beak beneath her arm and buried his head there. Farren closed their runebond, giving him privacy to sulk alone. She hesitated at the door.

"Can I ask you a question?" she said.

The animedic lifted his brows. "Call me Muta."

"Do you know much about animal diseases, Muta?"

The animedic lifted his brows. "I know all diseases. I've had this," he tapped on the animedic skin painting on his forehead, "for thirty years. Nothing I haven't seen."

"Do you know of a disease that turns things to ice? That can travel from plant to animal?"

Muta's mouth hung open slightly as he studied her. His belly expanded with every breath he took, and he had wiped the blood from the bite wound on his hand in a long smear over the apron covering his chiton.

"I was hunting with my hawk recently," Farren explained, "and it landed on this strange flower, which seemed frozen, like ice—"

"Are you feeling alright?" Muta stood, cocking his head at her. "You have a large bruise on the side of your head."

Farren repressed the urge to touch it, knowing it was from a fall while sparring earlier. "I'm fine."

Instead of looking relieved, Muta continued his assessment of her as if she hadn't spoken.

Farren clenched her teeth. "My hawk touched this flower, and it completely froze her. We were connected, and I could feel it killing her. It was like a fire that wanted to consume every part of her."

While she spoke, Muta shuffled close and nodded as he listened. "You say a flower killed your hawk? A flower that was possibly diseased, and the disease spread to your bird?" With large hands, he tilted her head this way and that, and his breath washed over her—stale and acrid with the stench of pickled fish.

"Yes, that's right." Her stomach churned, and she wasn't sure if it was from his breath or from the memories of Mellion's death.

"Doesn't sound familiar," he said. "Have you had times where you've lost consciousness? Have you felt dizzy or nauseous? Confused?"

Farren took a step back. "No. I'm just trying to find out what happened to my hawk."

"Are you sure this flower was diseased? That it wasn't something already in your hawk?"

Farren paused, thinking. "I don't think so. She seemed perfectly healthy. And the flower didn't look...normal." She would never forget the faultless form of scarlet petals, the bee unmoving in its center. "What sort of diseases move from plants to animals?"

Muta huffed. "There are none."

"But...I know I saw something odd—"

"And I know all diseases," he said, shaking his head. "This is no disease. I think maybe you bumped your head very hard."

"But—"

"Get some rest," Muta said, turning back to his table. "Wash and wrap those wounds on your arms so they don't fester. And try to stop worrying over your..." He waved a hand as if searching for the right words. "Fragmented memories."

# SEVENTEEN

As she left the nursery, Mellion's death turned over and over in her mind. It remained an exasperating, unsolvable puzzle. She stopped by her room to dress the wounds Torch had inflicted on her arms, using the materials Keira had stuffed into her bag. The healing salve smelled of sage and rosemary and bright Lidellian *limoni*. The scent brought her instantly back home.

Home. The low stone mews chill with the cold of the mountain winter. Fur-lined leathers bracing her legs, a cup of hot tea to warm her hands, and anticipation for the coming hunt to brighten the day. Feathers rustling in the early morning light. Setting off with her father and two hawks in the brisk snow. She could almost feel the ache in her legs from hiking in the brush, the icy lash of the breeze on her cheeks, and the steadying, revitalizing pressure of a hawk's talons gripping her fist. Nothing was quite akin to the trust of a hawk, to the bond shared when hunting together. Each moment through her hawk's eyes, a blessing. Then they would return to the house, and...

Before the attack, her mother's tight smile would be waiting with a simple supper. Desmond would be gone, out sledding or shoeing in the snow with friends, and he would come home past dark and play snake bones with her by the crackling fireplace.

After the attack...

Farren's mind couldn't envision what Desmond would be doing. Not the Desmond she knew now, for she didn't really know him at all. Would he be changed even more in ten years?

Her eyes burned, and she forced the thought away. She quit her chamber and went out to the gryphon yard, cringing as the gate announced her arrival with a squeal.

A gryphon named Grit stood with Prince Cato in the middle of the yard where the other recruits flocked uncertainly, some sitting idly along the fountain walls and others standing with crossed arms and grim looks. Alexon stood sucking his usual honeyed candy and gave her a nod when he saw her. By the largest basking rock, Camilla released a second gryphon from her leash, a sight that sent another bolt of worry through her.

Fighting the urge to go shadow the girl, Farren cast her attention around the perimeter of the yard. It appeared that only Grit and Thella would be training with them today. No Naronimus in sight, thank the Enchanters. She didn't think she could connect with him again.

Farren eased toward Alexon and tensed as one of the grim-looking recruits nudged her. "Farren, is it?" the woman asked, looking at her from beneath thick brows. "Couldn't help but notice you've got a bit of fight in you."

Unlike many of the other recruits who had apparently only packed fancier embroidered chitons for their Servitudes, this woman was dressed in a plain chiton with leggings, her unruly hair snatched back in a careless braid. She was taller and older than Farren, with thick arms protruding as she placed her hands on her hips. Farren was reminded keenly of her village's carpenter, a stern woman who had once given Farren a little carved statue of a falcon.

"Maybe you could teach me a few tricks," the woman said, "so I look less fool than I feel? Don't want that Scipio crawling up my bum about being a woman and all that."

Farren couldn't stop her smile. "I can teach you a little, but not too much. We don't want him to feel threatened."

The woman sniggered. "Right you are. My name's Anisha. Came all the way from little Torion," she said, naming a village that Farren recalled was in the western portion of the Outskirts. So Farren wasn't the only recruit from outside the city's walls. "Left behind my five children and a small herd of housecats for this cursed Servitude," Anisha continued. "It's immoral to pull a mother from her family."

Farren couldn't disagree. At least she had left Desmond in the care of her parents. "Is your husband taking care of them alone?"

"He passed last year. An accident on the farm."

"Oh, I'm sorry to hear that."

Anisha sniffed and nodded. "It's probably for the better. He'd have turned purple as a beet if he'd been there when the guards arrived. Would've driven a scythe into their bellies to stop me from being taken from the children." The woman rubbed her arms as if taken by a chill. "They're being looked after now by my brother and his wife."

"Do you write to them?"

"I would if I could, but I never learned to write." She scratched her nose, and Farren caught sight of the sharp curves in her inner wrist that delineated a feline runemark. An odd tremor of unease swept through Farren. It wasn't Anisha, but rather the reminder that gryphons tied two different runeskills to one another. What other animal had that capacity? None that Farren knew of. It only added to the strangeness of gryphons, to Farren's discomfort with them.

"Well, I can help you write to them," Farren offered after a moment.

Anisha's face lit up. "Would you? But then I would owe you double—once for fighting tips and again for the writing."

Farren shrugged. "I'm sure we can work something out."

"Good." Anisha perked up. "Ah, finally, the prince is telling us what in Tyrili's name we're doing here."

Reluctantly, Farren turned her attention to the prince, who had come close enough to the group that Farren could make out the ink smear on his chin.

"We have only a handful of weeks to prepare you and the gryphons for your duty to the Crown. It will be a difficult task, and you will likely make mistakes. I'm here to help you, but most of the work rests on your shoulders. Today," he said, sounding tired but resolute, "we'll start with the simplest of tasks. You must figure out what magical ability each gryphon in the yard has." He waited expectantly, but no one moved.

"Is that it?" Anisha asked, her lips pursing.

Prince Cato's brow quirked. "It's not as easy as you might think. Gryphons don't like to reveal their greatest strengths, not until they have learned to trust you." The prince's gaze skimmed over Farren's, narrowing for a breath of a moment before moving on. "But we have a young gryphon today, Thella, who recently discovered her magic." He motioned to the gryphon that Camilla had brought in. "We thought she wouldn't have magic at all but were proved wrong. The tardiness of her magical rising has been eclipsed by the strength of her magic. She may be more eager to show it than the others."

Farren flinched as Camilla's hand reached out to stroke Thella's shoulder. *Just breathe*, she told herself, finding it easier when Thella sat, elegant and poised beneath Camilla's touch. The recruits spread out, and Farren started toward Thella, hoping to get the task over with quickly, but several other recruits headed that way.

Sweat formed on her upper lip as she stalked across the sun-drenched courtyard to the massive rock where Grit lay. She opened a narrow runebond with him, and he accepted and widened it. Farren's stomach clenched as some of her control slipped. But instead of being flooded with anger or curiosity, a strange warmth came through the runebond: contentedness. A great sigh bellowed out of Grit, who lay on his side with talons draped over the rock edge.

*My name is Farren*, she said. The same steady stream of warmth came through the connection. *Are you sleeping?*

No, he replied, sending her a sharp, brilliant impression of the hot sun on his feathers.

*Basking*, she said. How well could gryphons understand their language? With Torch, it seemed somewhat rudimentary, but with an adult gryphon...

Prince Cato would probably know. Self-consciously, she shot a glance around and found him hovering near Thella and the recruits who worked with her. Camilla was laughing at something he said, and it was such an odd thing to think that the prince could say anything funny that Farren stared. As if he could feel her staring, Prince Cato met her gaze across the yard, frowning. She turned back to Grit.

*Do you have magic?*

A talon twitched and scraped a piece of stone loose, and it clacked to the ground. Farren fought the urge to pick up the stone and toss it at him.

*Do you know what magic is*, she prodded, sending him an impression of a gryphon creating fire and another of a gryphon moving air.

Finally, Grit's head lifted, and he gazed at her long enough that she grew certain he thought her stupid.

*Yes, I do.*

Farren grimaced as he twitched his talon again. A large piece of stone broke away and landed with a *thud*, only a few hand-spans from her foot.

*You can manipulate stone?*

*Stone and earth*, Grit said.

Well. So much for Prince Cato's advice about the gryphons needing their trust.

*I see no reason not to trust you*, Grit replied, and Farren pulled back, reflexively tightening their runebond. She hadn't meant for that to slip out.

*Thank you for making it easy*, Farren said, privately wondering whether this gryphon was always so trusting. Perhaps she could use that to her advantage.

But before Farren could communicate further, he sent her a wave of tiredness and lay his head back down. *Is there anything else you need? I'd like to keep basking.*

She prodded him. *How can you be tired? You haven't done anything all day.*

His ear flicked as if warding off a fly. *I've had to sit in a cloistered and loud chamber all day long, unable to feel the sun. My limbs ache from a cold stone floor and my wings feel like useless appendages. Besides that, I've just done magic for you. What else do you want from me?*

Farren chewed her lip. *Why don't you try flying? There's enough space for you to go a short distance—*

*If I could actually get my wings to work, I would. And if I had somewhere more interesting to fly.*

Frowning, Farren eased closer to the beast, studying his wings. They didn't seem to be malformed, but it would be hard to know without examining them with her hands...and that was assuming gryphon wings were formed the same way as hawk wings. She opened her mouth to suggest he exercise his wings by beating them and then remembered he still had nowhere to fly other than back and forth across the yard.

Sighing, she said, *I'd like to know why you gryphons like bonding with humans. And whether there is a surefire way to break a bond with a gryphon.*

*What peculiar questions.*

*Does that mean you don't know the answers?*

The beast lifted his head once more and assessed her. A breeze carried the scent of his sun-warmed feather and fur. *I know the answers for myself. I like to bond with humans who feed me. I'm also partial to a comfy bed—one that won't tear every time I step on it. As far as breaking a bond, I believe it's much harder to break than your human bonds. Gryphons bond with humans like stone to earth.*

Farren waited for more, but nothing came. Grit rested his head once more, and his mind began to fuzz with sleep. Farren pursed her lips and cast another glance toward the prince. He had started talking to the recruits, and Thella sat calmly listening as if she understood every word.

Over the fortress wall to the west, clouds bulked high, their rolling columns dense and blue-grey with unshed rain. Farren closed her runebond with Grit, letting him sunbathe in peace before the oncoming storm, and sat near him lest the prince looked over and wondered what she was doing.

Tentatively, she reached out with her runeskill and sensed the glowing spheres of the gryphon minds. She could tell roughly where each was without looking. Grit was close, Thella was farther out by the fountain, and—

Farren sucked in a breath. Moving toward Thella was another gryphon mind, but when she looked, only Thella and the recruits were across the yard. She closed her eyes, concentrating, and opened a runebond to the invisible gryphon.

Irritation flushed into her. *What do you want now*, the gryphon snarled.

Farren immediately recognized the tone and held tight to the runebond. Sweat gathered under her arms and on her palms.

*You're invisible*, she told Naronimus.

*Maybe you aren't as stupid as I first thought*, he replied with undeniable sarcasm.

*Why bother if we can sense you with our runeskill?*

A pause. *He asked me to.*

Farren opened her eyes and found Prince Cato watching the recruits with crossed arms. He turned his gaze to where Naronimus paced invisibly along the perimeter. Of course, it made sense; the prince wanted to see whether any of the recruits could locate Naronimus, thereby identifying his magic ability. But as Cato's eyes slid back to Thella, pride flashed over his face.

*It's Thella's magic*, she said. *Not yours.*

*I never said it was mine.*

Farren huffed. *Then what did the prince ask you to do?*

Naronimus was getting closer on his march around the edge of the yard, and Farren's body tightened. Talons scraped the flagstones. Bloodred irises bobbed in a frenzy along the walkway as he passed as if he tried to break them with menacing wing-beats. The connection between them widened, and Naronimus's hostility fell down on her like hard, piercing rain.

*He asked me to tolerate the young gryphon's magic*, he said.

Naronimus's breath bellowed as he eased closer. She didn't like the way their connection expanded and toughened with each passing moment, tugging their minds closer.

*Stop doing that*, she commanded, sending him her anger while tamping down her rising fear. A slight ringing resounded in her ears.

He sent her a small wave of amusement. *Why? I think you should be reminded of your insignificance.*

*And yet, you are the one stuck in a cage.*

Around them, the breeze stiffened, carrying the wet scent of rain. Iris blossoms twirled and bent, nearly breaking in a sudden gust.

Naronimus paused a few paces from her, his invisible talons digging fresh scratches into flagstones already scored by innumerable wounds. *You said you were a prisoner here, too. A puppet to your queen. Weak, just like all the other servants here.*

Glaring at the space where Naronimus stood, Farren rose to her feet. For the first time in years, she wished she was bigger, taller. But she would never be large enough to ward off Naronimus or any other gryphon. She could try waking Grit, get him to help her, but to connect with him, she would have to close her runebond with Naronimus. That would leave her too exposed.

Farren forced her breathing to slow and tried to pull her fraying thoughts together. Naronimus hated people; perhaps she could use his ugly feelings to disrupt the program. But she knew that the only way Naronimus was likely to act was if she challenged him.

Thunder rumbled in the distance.

*If you think humans so distasteful and insignificant, why haven't you killed us all?*

He sent her another wash of amusement. *I don't think that would end well for me. As much as I would enjoy it.*

Farren swallowed. Naronimus was everything she hated about gryphons. Powerful, conceited, and utterly lacking in conscience. She wished the other recruits could hear Naronimus's thoughts, that the queen herself could witness it.

*Have you told Prince Cato that you would enjoy killing people? He doesn't seem to believe you are a monster.*

Naronimus began circling her, his talons and claws carelessly crushing irises in the flowerbeds as he paced around her. *He knows what I am*, Naronimus told her calmly. *And he knows he can't tame me like some gelding.*

Grit appeared to be asleep and completely unaware of Naronimus's proximity. Farren was certain he could sense Naronimus's presence—the animals had telepathy with one another, after all—but would he see Naronimus as a threat or leave the two of them to fight it out on their own?

Overhead, the sun disappeared beneath a tide of grey cloud. Farren shivered in the sudden chill.

*You're trying to scare me*, she said, forcing her feet into a wide fighting stance. Her breath was coming too fast, her legs stiffening. Her body wanted to freeze up; she knew she wouldn't be able to fight this beast if she had to. If he tried to bite her again—

*I think it's working*. Naronimus wrenched the runebond open and peered inside her skull.

Farren screamed—whether aloud or through their runebond, she didn't know—because the way he forced their connection *hurt*. She clutched her head, struggling to take back control. *Let me go! You have no right to be in my head*—

His breath blasted down on her shoulders, and for a vast, frigid moment, his fury melded with hers. *You are a tiny mouse*, he told her, *and I will break you just as I broke your brother.*

Something inside of Farren snapped. Her blood surged like a summer storm. Naronimus was the one. He had attacked her bright-eyed, curious, precious little brother with a hostile nip of his massive beak.

Almost killing him.

Breaking him, forever.

Her throat constricted as too many things washed all at once into the runebond, her feelings mixing with Naronimus's, transmuting them into something savage. Farren broke from her paralysis and vaulted away, charging toward the safety of the other recruits. She longed to rip through the world with the unfairness of it all. Naronimus deserved death, but she couldn't try, not out in the open in front of everyone. Running was her only option.

Naronimus bolted after her, his sudden urge to hurt someone streaking into her. She had to stop him, to stop herself, but his anger fed her anger and looped back to him, building the hatred while each pushed the other to act on it.

They were nearly on the recruits. Farren yelled a warning and flinched when Naronimus's scream resounded next to her. He was still invisible, and Thella lifted her wings and cried out, releasing her magic as she did so.

But it was too late because a moment later, Naronimus appeared, and everyone watched in shock as he grabbed hold of the nearest recruit—Anisha—and swung her into the air.

# EIGHTEEN

ANISHA WHIRLED LIKE A ragdoll. Her hair fell loose from its binding as she spun, and then she hit the ground with a sickening thump.

She didn't move.

The other recruits flushed away from Farren and Naronimus like rabbits from the brush, but Farren caught Camilla and dragged her behind the fountain, out of Naronimus's sight. Naronimus's shriek of rage jolted off the flagstones. Before he could reach for another recruit, Thella splayed her wings, and the recruits disappeared.

White-hot wrath rammed through the runebond, and Farren fell to her knees, clutching her head as she fought to close it. But her skin flushed hot and cold and hot again as the gryphon's feelings rushed into her, catching her insides ablaze. She hated being here. She felt trapped. Afraid. She longed to tear down the walls holding her in, and the only way to do that was to hurt those around her—

"No!" Prince Cato's voice shook into her, scattering her thoughts.

He stood inches before Naronimus, his ink-stained hand held before the beast like a shield. His face was chiseled of stone, his eyes bright swords that met Naronimus's and held them.

She felt Naronimus's hesitation, a sudden restraint that he pulled from somewhere deep inside himself. He had too much respect for the prince to hurt him, too much of a bond that Naronimus had never asked for but had been a part of nonetheless. Besides that, waves of soothing calm washed down their runebond, spilling into Farren and dousing the flames.

She sagged to the ground. The runebond between her and the gryphon softened, and she could finally pull it closed.

A roaring darkness swelled in her mind, but it was just the sudden aloneness of her thoughts and the rapid pulse of blood through her body. White-hot feelings diminished to mere embers.

So much of that fire had been Naronimus's, filling her up until she hadn't known whether it was herself or Naronimus, and... Her head pounded.

"Farren? Are you alright?" Camilla's soft voice wrapped her like a knitted blanket.

"Yes." She rose unsteadily to her feet and lurched to where Anisha lay still on the ground, surrounded by a few recruits.

The woman's arm looked shattered. The sight of her laying there—limbs at unnatural angles and blood seeping over the flagstones—was too similar to the way Desmond looked after his attack. Farren trembled as she knelt over Anisha. She didn't know what to do, so she patted the woman's cheeks, remembering how they had smiled at her just a little while ago, and she held her good hand, wondering whether the other would ever be able to work and if she would end up like Desmond—with a mind that struggled to keep up with the world around it.

"Farren." Prince Cato laid a hand on her shoulder. "Come away now. They'll take her."

Numbly, Farren realized that the other recruits were readying to load Anisha onto a carrier with the help of a white-robed healer. Farren stood and stepped back, lost in a whirlwind while others moved around her. She watched it all distantly with arms clutched around her torso and flinched when Cato's face suddenly floated in front of her. He said something, but her mind couldn't follow his words. She blinked and looked around. The gryphons had been taken away, and the courtyard had emptied of everyone but her and the prince. Wind whipped the garden irises back and forth, scattering leaves and debris around the courtyard. Overhead, the gale shrieked through the iron fingers of the gryphon cage.

"Camilla—?" Her voice was thin as thread.

"She's fine." The prince set his hands on her shoulders. "Now tell me how this happened."

"I don't know." She kept her eyes down and shut them as they burned. Her mind slogged back to the beginning, to what had caused her anger. "He told me something awful that he did. He hurt—" she cut herself off, unable to tell him the truth. He would never understand. Instead, she murmured, "I'm sorry." Even though it wasn't enough. Not nearly enough.

"I just need to know, did you do it on purpose? Was this some sort of ambush—"

Now she had no trouble meeting his eyes. "You think I wanted to hurt Anisha?"

"No, I don't." The prince's hands dropped. Thunder shook the air, but he didn't seem to notice. "Why did you charge us? What did you say to Naronimus to make him angry?"

Farren reeled back. "Charge you? I was trying to escape! And Naronimus—he's angry no matter what I say to him. I told you he's dangerous, and this just proves it—"

"Is that what you were trying to do? Prove how dangerous he could be? Well, congratulations, you've shown all the recruits what happens when you anger a gryphon and can't control him—"

"Why was he here in the first place? He's too much for a recruit to handle. You should've known better. He might've killed Anisha!"

*You fool*, she told herself. *It was* you *who almost killed Anisha. So full of rage about what he did to Desmond.* Just like with her brother's injury, this time, she had let too much of her emotion through, which was why she hadn't been able to control the runebond. But he had nearly killed Desmond, and she would *never* forgive the gryphon for that.

Prince Cato was shaking his head, glowering at her now. "I should've known not to trust you. You don't have enough experience."

"I've been using my runeskill with hawks since I was little," Farren said. "I have more experience than most of the recruits here, and you know it."

The prince crossed his feather-marked arms. "And yet you lost control over Naronimus."

"I never had control over him! I was trying to—" She raised a hand and dropped it, lost for words. "I never meant to hurt anyone. And I wouldn't have if Naronimus hadn't been here. You're the only one who seems to have control over him."

"He's not dangerous," the prince said, dipping his head when she gave him her blackest glare. "I mean, normally. I've known him since he was very young."

"So you have a special bond with him," Farren seethed. "Then why don't you get that he hates people? He completely lacks morals. It's amazing he hasn't killed a recruit by now!"

Heat sparked in the prince's gaze. "Maybe this is your problem, Farren. You have trouble controlling yourself."

"I do not!" Why was she yelling? She didn't have trouble controlling herself; she was a fighter, and fighting was all about control. She had practiced controlling her runeskill with her hawks for years. She had doubled down after her brother's attack, keeping her runebond with Mellion as distant as possible unless absolutely necessary. The prince watched her with tight lips as if she were one of the gryphons he studied. She forced her voice to steady. "I do not have trouble with control."

"Gryphons aren't like hawks," he told her. "You need to listen to my advice. Practice connecting with a different gryphon."

"No. I'm not—" Farren threw up her hands, which, much to her annoyance, still shook. She stepped away from the prince, and the first drops of rain stung her cheeks. "I can't do that again."

"You have to, Farren. It's the only way you'll learn to use your runeskill—" He broke off as she stalked away.

She felt eyes watching her and glanced toward the glass wall separating the courtyard from the fortress. Standing on the other side of it was Isander, dressed in a shade of blue that reminded her of a bottomless lake. He was observing them, his mouth curved in an odd, satisfied smile. As if he had just been proved right.

She wasn't sure what that look meant, and for once, she didn't care. Hot-faced and suddenly nauseous, Farren headed straight for her room.

The rain finally came, soaking Farren just before she stumbled into the gryphon mews. Shivering and wet and aching, she pressed blindly through the hall. All she could see was Anisha flying through the air, her body sprawled unnaturally on the ground. Farren needed to know that Anisha would be okay. But going to see her would also mean risking the knowledge that she *wouldn't* be okay, and Farren knew she wasn't steady enough for that.

Dizziness rocked her, and shadows lurked near the edge of her vision. She gulped air and kept her hand on the white-washed walls.

The sound of light chatter came from down the hall. Farren ducked her head and pressed into her bedchamber before they passed her, then leaned against the closed door, tapping a quick and steady rhythm on the side of her hand.

Breathe in. Breathe out. In. Out. Again. Again.

A soft knock pulled her away from the thundercloud threatening to break loose inside her. When she didn't answer the knock, Camilla's voice threaded through the door jamb.

"Farren, I know you're in there. Please, just let me in."

Farren cursed under her breath, fighting to pull herself together. Her hand refused to cease trembling as she opened the door a crack. "Y-Yes, what is it, Camilla?"

Camilla let out a little breath of air. "I wanted to make sure you're okay."

"I'm fine."

"I don't believe you."

Sighing, Farren swung open the door and motioned the girl in.

"I also wanted to say thank you," Camilla said as she walked in. "For pulling me out of harm's way earlier."

She couldn't meet the girl's eyes. "I'm the one who brought harm your way. You shouldn't be thanking me."

"Well, I'm not thanking you for *that*."

Farren caught a hint of a smile in her tone and risked a glance at her. Camilla's hands clasped loosely in front of her, and she tilted her head at Farren, assessing her with pursed lips. "What happened out there, Farren?"

Farren wandered to the desk, straightening some papers—a long letter she was writing to her father and Desmond. "You saw what happened. Naronimus threatened the other recruits... We both did, and I couldn't stop it."

"I mean," Camilla said carefully, "what *really* happened? Between you and Naronimus?"

Farren hesitated, staring at her handwriting carefully penned over the pages she straightened. The words she had written were about superficial things—the painted walls and plants in the keep, how the hawk mews were run, how big the fortress felt—but contained nothing about gryphons or her struggles with them. She had only told a little of it to Keira in her letters, not wanting to make her friend worry for her safety. Keira already had so much to deal with. Her father and Des would only be upset by how closely she worked with the beasts.

Farren set the stack of pages down. She had spent so much time alone in the mountains, holding everything in. She had been holding things in since Desmond's attack, it seemed.

An eternity.

"Naronimus wanted to..." Farren cleared her throat and turned to Camilla, whose face was a beacon of patience. "*We* wanted to hurt someone. Something. We were angry at each other, and it turned outward somehow."

"But you didn't really *want* to hurt the recruits," Camilla suggested, her tone reasonable.

Farren stalked to the bed and sat on the edge, wishing it would swallow her whole. "I'm not what you think, Camilla. The hate wasn't all Naronimus's, so he can't take all the blame. Part of it was that I didn't know what I was doing, I wasn't prepared, and I panicked."

"And the other part?" she prompted gently, coming to sit beside Farren.

The truth trembled inside her, longing to come out, yet she was afraid to release it. What had happened to Desmond was so close to her heart that speaking of it would hurt, and once spoken, it could never be taken back.

Farren took a breath. "I met Naronimus before my Servitude. He was with a man—Anaxis—visiting my village in the Outskirts. My little brother saw Naronimus and grew too curious. When he reached up to pet it, the beast bit my brother in the head, and it—" The lump in her throat grew thicker, but she pushed past it. "He didn't die, but he hasn't been the same since."

Camilla's hands clenched together in her lap. "You must want Naronimus dead."

Farren stared at her. "What?"

"You must want him dead. Do you?"

"I..." Farren hugged herself. "I don't know."

The girl nodded, her eyes wide and far too dark for their brilliant blue. "I had a sister. Once, I watched my father throw her into a wall." She took a shaky breath, meeting and holding Farren's eyes. "I wanted him dead then."

The thought that someone could be so brutal to a child—their own child—made her sick. "Do you still want him dead?"

"I do." Camilla sniffed and rubbed her chest. "But I mostly want to see my sister again. To make sure..." Camilla's voice dropped to a whisper. "That she's still okay."

"She's alive?"

Camilla gave her a hopeless look. "I don't know. She was only seven when I became Cato's ward. Cato had agreed to take her in as well, but when he went to look for her..." She dipped her head. "I think my father took her and fled. I'm not sure if they're still in Malodai."

"That's awful," Farren said. "If you want, I could help you look for her—"

Camilla stood and shook her head. "I'm sorry. I didn't mean to make this about me. I think you have a lot to deal with. Why not take a day to yourself? After everything that's happened, I'm sure Horat would be understanding."

"I doubt it."

Camilla dropped into a crouch, and her warm hand found Farren's. The touch surprised her, and she found her fingers wrapping involuntarily around Camilla's.

"Farren, you need to do this. You need to figure out what to do about Naronimus."

Farren's heart pounded. "What do you mean?"

The girl gave a tiny smile. "You can't just ignore him while you're here. You can't kill him, either. Cato would never have it."

Despite the dread that had settled over her, Farren laughed. "He would rather have me killed, I'm sure."

Camilla's smile deepened. "Don't suggest it to him, though. He doesn't need more ideas in that cluttered head of his." They chuckled together, then Camilla squeezed her hand, and the mirth faded like the light from a sinking sunset. "But you need to figure out how to live with Naronimus because it's dangerous if you cannot. And Farren? You should tell Cato the truth. Tell him what happened with your brother."

"I don't think I can."

"I know it hurts, but he needs to know. Promise me you'll tell him."

Farren held Camilla's limpid blue eyes, bolstered by the girl's indelible strength. "I will try."

A knock sounded, and Camilla opened the door. For once, Alexon wasn't sucking on a candy, and he almost looked relieved when he saw Camilla there.

"Horat is asking to see Farren," Alexon said.

Rain lashed at the windows as Farren stalked to the Lord Falconer's study. She had forgotten to change into dry clothes, so she hugged herself to keep warm.

Her attempt to learn more about gryphons had failed, miserably. And it was beginning to feel like everything she was trying to do was hopeless. How could she possibly learn about gryphons while being so afraid of them? And how could she bring down a program when doing so might hurt the very people she wished to protect?

Farren reached the study. Voices rose behind the closed doors.

"...have a longer time to train?" Cato was asking.

"We're nearly out of time," Horat said in his gruff voice. "Five weeks won't be enough for her. I had higher hopes for her skill level, but this has been disastrous."

"But she sensed Naronimus despite the invisibility. And he spoke with her, runebonded with her deep enough that they seemed to act as one. That has to mean something—"

"It simply means that she is Naronimus's puppet," Horat said sharply. "She can't stay on, Cato. The queen will never allow it."

A pause, filled by the thunder of Farren's heartbeat.

"Alright then," Cato said softly. "Her father will be sent in her stead?"

"I imagine so. We'll have to send for him—"

Farren threw open the door and lurched inside. A frigid cold took hold of her, and she clasped her hands against it. "Please, you can't—I can't go."

Horat sat at his desk, looking only mildly surprised at her entrance. "I'm sorry, Farren. You're too dangerous to have here, and we haven't the time to train you properly."

"Please," Farren said. "I'll train day and night if you wish. Cato can teach me." She tossed a desperate glance at Cato, but he was staring at her in puzzlement.

"Unfortunately, it's not entirely up to us," Horat said. "Once the queen hears of it—which she likely already has—she'll ask for your dismissal."

"But what about imprisonment? Lashings? I'll take those—as many as you'd like—"

"Cato has convinced me that what happened with Naronimus was an accident. Are you telling me that isn't true? That you deserve punishment? Know that whatever you tell me, your father will still have to take your place to fulfill the Servitude."

Her mouth dried up. She rushed to Horat's chair, knelt and took his rough, scarred hand. "You cannot take my father. He's the only one—"

"Stand up, girl," Horat snapped. "Begging is beneath you."

He was right. When had she ever begged for anything? When had she ever been so painfully desperate? She forced herself to her feet, chest heaving.

"You have the rest of the day to say your farewells and pack. You should be ready to leave by the morning."

She stared at Horat, a thousand words ready at her lips, but he had said not to beg. Cato remained standing by the window with crossed arms. "Prince Cato—"

"I thought you didn't want this, anyways?" Cato asked, gesturing to the mews. "Isn't it better if your father comes?"

"It is the worst if he comes," Farren managed to say. "I wanted to work with hawks, but if it comes to working with gryphons or my father being taken..." A violent shiver racked her, and she clenched her teeth to keep them from chattering. "I will do whatever you think is best to train with the gryphons. But please do not send me home."

Cato's gaze darted to Horat, then he cleared his throat. "Farren, the queen won't want you as part of the guard if you can't control your runeskill. And as Horat stated, we don't have the time to train you properly—"

Farren knew it was futile. Cato already didn't like or trust her. He did whatever his mother told him and didn't even disagree with Horat about her future. Still, she stepped toward him.

"I know I lost it with Naronimus. I can't promise it won't happen again. But I can promise that I'll work with the other gryphons, and that it will go better. Naronimus and I have history, you see." Farren licked her lips. "My father can't come here because he's taking care of my brother, Desmond. Desmond suffered great injury to his skull at Demithya's Festival this past spring. It nearly killed him, and he hasn't been the s-same since."

She needed him to find the truth for himself, to recognize what Naronimus was. Slowly, he seemed to fit the pieces together.

"Demithya's Festival? That was when my uncle was still alive..." His arms fell to his sides. "Your brother was the boy who was injured? Scipio told me that Naronimus had nipped someone." He fell quiet, gathering into his thoughts, forgetting that she was there.

"No, you don't get to do that," Farren said in a ragged voice. "It wasn't just a nip. He nearly cracked Desmond's head open. My brother almost died. He was changed forever by the damage Naronimus caused him. All because he was curious and loved the world and wanted to pet the beast."

"That's enough, Farren," Horat spoke from his desk, his tone quiet but even. "We're sorry that Naronimus hurt your family. Many people were hurt by Anaxis' choices. Unfortunately, your story changes nothing. You need to prepare to return home. You have until sunrise tomorrow."

Cato stared at her open-mouthed.

"It's not just a story," she whispered at him fiercely, damning the hot tears that escaped down her cheeks. "It's everything."

# NINETEEN

LIGHTNING FLASHED IN THE window as Farren spun away from the senseless prince. She needed her room, to be alone so she could sort through the mess in her mind and heart.

Alone. She had been alone in the mountains for months and hadn't worked through any of it. Being alone hadn't helped. It hadn't diminished the memory of Desmond's attack. It hadn't taken away the sharp prick of the moment she had decided to leave him.

Weeks after the attack, Desmond's scar had mostly healed. He had been so sullen, so apathetic that she had decided to take him to the river by their home. They used to love swimming there, and she challenged him to their usual contest: whoever reached the half-submerged wateroak log first was the winner, and the loser had to do the winner's chores that day.

Desmond always won. This time, he didn't.

Farren hadn't noticed anything was wrong until Desmond came up on her in the water, red in the face and huffing as he paddled. Then came the screaming and cursing. Smacking the water with angry fists. And then he pushed her head beneath the water.

The shock of it had nearly overcome her. She heard him yelling above the surface, and he wouldn't let her go. A well-timed assault by a fishing-bird saved her. Desmond had lost some of his coordination with the head injury, and she was able to kick away from him, swimming to shore before he could reach her again. She had run home and sat in her bedroom, shivering and sodden as Desmond howled at her parents and they tried to calm him. That was when she realized he would be better off without her there.

Leaving him had been the hardest thing she had ever done. The worst part was that she had never been completely certain—during all those months alone in the mountains—that she had made the right decision.

Enough of being alone.

Striding down the halls of the mews, Farren's mind flew like the gale, relentless and whirling, and she yearned for something solid and warm. She needed...she just needed...

She slid back the bolt of a door. When she opened it, the wave of musky feline odor made her waver. But she stepped in and closed it. Torch leapt around her legs, ridiculous in his excitement to see her. He had been eating fish and left it to greet her.

For a moment, Farren stood still. Why had she come there? Torch didn't need to feel what she was feeling. Besides that, what if Delphi wouldn't welcome her there? From where the other gryphons were eating at the opposite end of the chamber, Delphi glanced at her from beneath mantled wings before returning to her share of lacy-winged mistfish.

Farren sank against the wall and pulled her knees up. Torch pressed against her and startled as thunder rattled into the chamber. Gray rain rippled like gossamer linen beyond the high slits of glassless windows. The little gryphon's feathers were soft, and his tawny fur warm. Her fingers glided over his back, pausing for a moment to explore the familiar touch of feather, how it blended imperceptibly with fur, yielding so easily to the pressure of her hand.

Torch watched her avidly, eyes bright and fragile as honey moonbeams. He didn't seem to mind her repetitive petting and bobbed his head at her.

No, she wouldn't runebond with him. She couldn't. Instead, she dug her hand deeper into his luscious fur and laid her head against her knees, willing darkness and the hush of rain to roll through her. The storm rumbled, the scent of rain filled the chamber, and Torch didn't leave her side.

Forming a runebond with Naronimus should have helped her learn more about gryphons, or at least about Naronimus, but all she had learned was how little control she really had. How helpless she felt. How terrifying her own anger was. And how desperately she hated being there. And now, it was all for nothing. Her father would be brought there to suffer as she had, and she would have to try to take care of Desmond.

Farren was lost in uncertainty when Torch nudged her. Her knees were warm and wet with tears. She took a shuddering inhale and lifted her head, hardly able to meet Torch's persistent gaze. He nudged her once more with his beak.

"Can't we just do this without runebonding?" Farren asked aloud.

Another push to her arm. She had come here for a reason. Her mind had grown dark up in the Kithyrian Mountains, shadowed by fear and doubt and regret. Inside the tomblike walls of the fortress, it had only seemed to worsen. Perhaps that was why she had come to the nursery. She knew it was one of the only places where the dark might scatter. If she was brave enough to open herself to it.

Torch emitted a mewl with a quavering beak. Farren struggled to organize her jumbled thoughts and pushed the worst of all that had happened to the back of her mind. Then, she opened a runebond with the little gryphon.

He sent her a string of impressions. Tasty, succulent fish flesh. The ripe smell of the storm. A rain-streaked face that he couldn't understand.

*They are tears*, Farren explained.

*Like rain?*

*Rain comes from clouds in the sky.* Farren showed him her memory of the oncoming storm clouds. *Tears are different. They come from within. They are still drops of water.* Sensing he wanted to know more, she widened their runebond. *Droplets form in the air as dew or mist.* She sent him an image of a dew-dotted flower petal and another of breath misting in frigid air.

Unbidden, another image rose of tears clinging to eyelashes. One of so many memories of Desmond, upset or raging because he didn't understand the world anymore, because he couldn't tolerate things that never used to bother him.

*Tears are sad?* Torch sent her hesitant curiosity.

*Tears can be many things. Sad, broken, desperate, tired, or happy.*

*Are your tears happy?*

With aching care, Farren sent him a sliver of her heart, just enough for him to understand. *This is what I feel, but bigger. It feels like everything is wrong, and I can't make it better.*

Torch wedged closer to her as if his strength could help hold her up. He bobbed his head again, seeming to examine the fresh tears that pearled down Farren's cheek.

Another image came to her, bending Farren's perception. A glassy tear clung to her chin, drooping and round, and the dim light from the window reflected off its curved surface. *But your tears are beautiful. They are round, like a ball, but tilted on the inside. Can you see it? Does it make you feel less sad?*

Their connection fuzzed for a moment as if his mind were focusing on something outside of the runebond. As Farren watched him, a speck rose before her.

Farren barely dared breathe lest her breath disturb it. Her perfectly round tear hung in the air, spinning a slow dance between them. Floating, like something otherworldly. Something impossible.

*Torch, is that—?*

Joy burst through their runebond, and Torch leapt away so that he could rise up on his hind paws and cuff the air with his talons. He stretched his wings wide, and beads of raindrops flew in from the window. They joined into silvery threads and wove into the room.

Delphi's stance shifted as she noticed, and she lifted her head high.

*Kee-kee-kee!*

Her cry echoed around the chamber, and Farren clapped her hands over her ears as Torch's siblings emitted a similar sound. Impulsively, she narrowed her runebond. The string of water threaded through the room, and suddenly it danced above her head, forming a circle that expanded around her, encompassing Farren and the little gryphon in a fat silver ribbon of water.

Torch's cry was exultant. The feelings trickling into her were akin to sunshine—white-bright and embracing, and like nothing she had ever felt through her runebond before. She inched their runebond wider, and the sunshine poured in, filling her with beaming rays that banished the cold.

*Do you feel better now?* he asked.

She reached toward the water display around them. *It's wonderful, Torch! How are you doing it?*

*It's my magic! Mother told me it would come soon, that I would know when it happened and that it would feel good and right.*

His thoughts stumbled over one another in his haste to tell her. He danced away, and the water broke apart and coalesced around him like a glittering shield. When he reached his family, the water parted as they touched beaks and bumped shoulders. Wings tangled briefly as the gryphons wove between one another, each calling in excited trills.

Farren laughed. It was as beautiful as a dream. Warmth spiraled down Torch's runebond, and rather than feeling separate from them, Farren felt part of the whole. She spread the runebond wider yet, and Torch looked at her above the milling bodies of his siblings, his perceptions of them flooding into her. They were his family, his kind. And she could be, too.

A wildness rose in Farren that she hadn't felt in months. Without thinking, she lifted her chin and let out a trilling cry that matched that of the gryphons. Delphi and Torch spread their wings and cried out with her, and then Torch galloped back to her. He sent an exquisite wave of something that felt oddly, achingly like love.

*Are you really moving the water?* she asked, standing up as he pushed against her.

In answer, water droplets coalesced above him and formed a miniature river. It poured from the air and dropped over a tiny, invisible cliff in a manner that reminded her very much of the falls.

*Do you like it?* he asked.

*It's wonderful, Torch, I'm so...*

Witnessing the rising of his magic was having a profound effect on the soft spot that had formed in her. She glowed with Torch's joy and excitement.

But his magic also reminded her of why he had been born at all and that he would one day have to take his place with the other gryphons in the guard. Curtailing her sadness before it traveled through the runebond, Farren hugged Torch and received a blissful face-full of feathers.

*I want to try more!* Torch vaulted away from her.

*Of course you do.* She wiped her eyes. While Torch and his siblings leaped among his water circles and fans and swirling drops, Farren's awe never ceased, and neither did her grin.

# TWENTY

ALTHOUGH FARREN LONGED TO carry Torch's joy with her all day long, she eventually had to leave the nursery and close their runebond. The storm-soaked world out the windows turned the mews dim and dreary.

Her elation deflated further when she went to see Anisha. Thankfully, a broken arm had been the only result of Naronimus's attack, and Farren insisted on helping her write a letter to her children. But as she scrawled Anisha's loving words to her family, she couldn't stop thinking, *I almost caused a tragedy, just like the one Desmond suffered.* What if Anisha had suffered worse injuries or died? She would've left behind her children and family business. To make matters worse, Anisha had kept saying thank you to Farren—not just for the letter writing, but for giving her a reason to be sent home. The woman would be leaving in two days, dismissed from the queen's service for her injuries. Her misplaced gratitude had been too much to bear.

Horat had told her to say her goodbyes and pack, but all she wanted was a warm bath and to be alone. By the time she walked over to the servant's bathhouse, the storm had petered to a drizzle, washing the ceiling of the courtyard a dismal gray.

Despite being meant for servants, the bathhouse just north of the main keep was big enough to house two small pools and a sweat room. The scent of lavender petals permeated the humid air inside. Farren undressed near the door and donned a thin bath sheet hanging from the wall. Candles wavered in sconces, barely illuminating the curtained openings of private dressing rooms. Farren padded to the sweat room first, ears perking at the chatter from the pools. Two ladies—one of whom was fellow recruit Callipe and the other whom she didn't recognize—rested their heads on the edge of the cold-pool as they spoke. A sleek otter with fur the shade of chestnuts swam behind them and peeked its head out as Farren walked past them.

The servants' voices grew hushed.

"That's the girl who nearly got Anisha killed!" Callipe whispered.

"Really? She doesn't look very threatening," the other woman replied loudly, her voice melodic and smooth.

"Don't trust what you see."

Farren stepped into the sweat chamber and sank into the shadows of the stone bench there, gratefully giving in to the enveloping humid air. Coals burned on a wide brazier across from her, and she ladled water onto them, drowning her senses in the hiss of water and thick heat of steam.

She had gone over the scenario again and again, trying to pinpoint the moment she had lost control over Naronimus, but it was all too bound up in the anger and the fear and the strangeness of Naronimus melding into her. It was as if the boundaries between them had been pried away by his vicious talons.

Farren shivered and poured another ladle of water over the embers. White steam coiled like a serpent, dissipating until she felt the prickling bite of it over her skin.

She had intended to bond with Naronimus to learn about gryphons, but she had also wanted to cause some sort of disruption, and to use Naronimus to do it. But it had all gone terribly wrong when Naronimus admitted to what he had done. The longing for vengeance twisted through her like a fetid disease, eating away at caution and reason.

Farren pulled the thick air into her lungs, forcing her thoughts to clear. It wouldn't do her any good to mull over what had happened now that she was leaving. She just needed to enjoy one last blissful bath and forget everything so she could focus on what came next. She would have to take over her father's business, raising and training hawks for hunting. But her mother would barely tolerate her, and Desmond would need help.

Farren gripped the warm wooden plank of the bench. No, she couldn't help Desmond. He needed his mother and father. Farren was just...an outlier. An intruder. Hadn't her mother said as much under her breath one time?

Outside the sweat chamber, Callipe's voice rose.

"...saw my skin painting, and then the cobbler raised the price by eight dremmas!"

"Eight?" the smooth-voiced servant echoed. "Those Runeless men are so arrogant. How dare he do that with a queen's servant?"

"He certainly didn't care who I was. All he saw were my skin paintings. When I questioned him about the other customer getting a better deal, he shrugged and said the man was a friend from the Runeless Quarter. So I went to a different cobbler—a Lidellian—who offered a much more reasonable price."

"The Lidellians are so very reasonable," the woman agreed.

"I've heard whispers that there are already a dozen Runeless among the City Watch and that they've been allowing Runeless citizens to hunt animals within the city walls. They say that the Runeless number more than a thousand now."

"Still nothing to match the rest of us—"

"And it's said that the queen has invited one of the Runeless leaders to join her Royal Council, and already he has requested to build a thoroughfare from the Outskirts directly to their Quarter. I'm certain they'll take over the entire eastern portion of the city before long."

The older woman spoke low. "They want Malodai to be empty of life. Fill it with meaningless machines and lofty buildings, refuse runeskills under the guise of bettering themselves."

Callipe *tisked* loudly. "They cannot empty Malodai of everything. The queen would never allow it. Once the gryphon guard is on the streets, we won't have to worry about the Runeless anymore."

The woman hummed in her throat thoughtfully, then said in a barely audible voice, "You think they will be cowed by the gryphons?"

"Wouldn't you be? With their magic?"

"From what you've told me, yes."

Farren stood and eased over to the opening of the sweat chamber, straining to hear their conversation. A soft padding sound drew close from outside the chamber and a little whiskered face peered inside. Water beaded off the otter's oiled fur as they stared at one another. After a moment of silence, Farren scooped more water and tossed it on the coals, and the resounding hiss sent the otter scuttling away.

Callipe hummed in her throat, and there was a splash. "Well, if no one can save us from the Runeless, we'll have to forever listen to their horrid preachers going on about all the ways we'll perish."

"It's they who need to worry about perishing. You've seen how they look."

"Too bad there's no cure for runelack madness," Callipe said cheerily, and the otter chirped as if in agreement. "We should head out. Maybe Livigena has some of that hidden mead. I need a nightcap."

Farren listened to them dress and heard muffled voices speaking at the bathhouse doorway. She breathed in the silence, finally allowing the tension to unspool from her shoulders. The bathhouse fires would be dampened soon, but she would have time to herself while the water began to cool.

She eased out from the sweat chamber, the soaked bath sheet clinging to her thighs. Tugging the knot free, she let the sheet fall to the tiled floor and went to the shelf of oil vessels, pouring a handful of oil into her palm. She worked it over her body with handfuls of sweet-smelling gritroot, then stepped down into the hot-pool.

Torch would've loved the bathhouse. Besides the two pools, there were several fountains placed strategically along the periphery, so that those wanting a quick wash could do so. Along one wall protruded the stone gryphon heads, fed by cisterns hidden in the ceiling. No doubt Torch would've investigated every source of water.

Farren prodded at herself, at the tender spot Torch had created inside her. It made her feel wrong, soft in a way she hadn't been since Desmond's attack. Somehow, in their time together, Farren had begun to feel motherly toward the gryphon. She didn't deserve his love, and she wouldn't—couldn't—be a mother to him.

And yet...he needed her. Not in the way he needed his mother, perhaps, but in this strange, curious way he wanted to be around her, to share his world with her and learn through her eyes. And despite the fact that she wouldn't likely see him again, she couldn't deny the seed of truth that had started to grow inside her.

She needed Torch.

The longing of it struck her suddenly, and she swayed on the pool steps. Spanning her runeskill wide, she sorted through the spheres of nearby gryphon minds. They were all clustered in the mews, but she found Torch's mind easily. His was a bright little bell, and when she touched him, he immediately opened to her.

*Where are you?* he asked. *Are you coming to visit?*

*Bathing*, she answered. She widened her runebond so he could glimpse the water before her, the smell of it, and the sensation of oil on skin. She reveled in his excitement as she waded into the waist-deep pool.

*I want to do bathing! Can you take me there?* He shot her an image of his dim, musty, utterly boring chamber.

*You do probably need a bath. I will ask Horat if I can bathe you tomorrow in the fountain,* she told him, knowing it was a lie. She hadn't yet told him she was leaving. But she couldn't stand to hurt him, couldn't consider what might happen to them with their bond being so new, so tender.

*But Torch, I was wondering... Can you use your magic from afar? Can you use your magic even if you can't see the water?*

He considered her words, then sent her an odd impression, one full of a sense that went beyond vision. He could *sense* the water, almost like Farren could sense gryphon minds; he could feel how much water there was and where it was. The runebond dimmed as Torch's mind focused on something beyond their connection.

A narrow thread of water pulled up from the surface of the hot-pool, growing long as it gathered in the steamed air, and formed into an oval. It thickened and expanded until it rose high above her, and the water spun gently, a living thing flecked with lavender petals. Torch remained silent while he worked, completely focused on his task, but Farren sent him a sliver of her glee.

This was *theirs* to share together, away from the prying, hungry eyes of the queen. Farren didn't have to be with Torch to be close to him, or to share this beautiful ability he had discovered. The preciousness of that gift made her vision blur.

*It is exquisite, Torch,* she said, reaching a hand out to the floating water. It touched her fingers and flowed around them like translucent silk.

A moment later, the oval collapsed, and Torch sent her a wave of exhaustion.

*It's harder than it was before. You are far from me.*

*That's enough for now. You need to rest.* At her words, she sensed him lay down to snuggle with his mother. *Torch? Did you tell Cato about your magic rising yet?*

*Mother wants me to tell the prince tomorrow. But the other gryphons know, so he likely knows already.* He prodded at her, perhaps sensing her hesitation.

*I wish we could keep it a secret, just between us.*

*I don't want it to be a secret!* In a flash, he sent her the memory of his magical rising, when his whole family had gathered and cheered for him, announcing his rising to anyone who could hear it. The rising was about more than the magic, more than the display of power. *I want to tell everyone, to show everyone! And Mother said that Cato could help me learn how to use it.*

Cato, she grudgingly admitted, was the best person to help Torch get a handle on his new ability.

*You can help, too,* Torch suggested. *Mother has been helping me already. She tests my brother, Balyon, by hiding things. He can find lost or hidden things.*

*A very useful magic,* Farren said, leaning back in the water so that she could look up at the great alabaster gryphon heads gaping down from the ceiling.

*All magic is useful,* said Torch. *That's what mother tells us. It's how we use it that is important.*

*You mean using it for good or ill?*

*I mean that if I use it, I must consider if I am helping others or...*

*Hurting them?*

Yes. His mind quieted as he nuzzled down to snuggle with his siblings. *But I don't think I'd like to do that.*

Within moments, his mind faded into sleep, and their runebond disintegrated. As Farren swished her arms in the luscious embrace of warm water, the unmistakable splash of someone entering the pool resounded behind her.

# TWENTY-ONE

THICK, HUMID AIR STUCK in Farren's throat as she spun around.

"Isander!" Her shriek echoed around the bathhouse as she covered her chest and sank beneath the water's surface. "What are you doing here?"

The elder prince wore nothing more than a thin bath-sheet tied loosely at his hips. Delicious hips that dove down from a slender, muscular torso. He held his hands up defensively as he paused on the pool steps. "You won't attack me with water, will you?"

Of course, he had seen Torch's magic. She had been so deep in communication with the gryphon—and awed by his magic—that she hadn't even noticed someone enter the bathhouse. At the edge of the pool were the prince's satchel and plain clothes.

"What are you doing here?" Farren repeated, cheeks heating. Could he see beneath the surface of the water?

"I like to bathe, Farren." He moved down into the pool, causing the water to undulate outward until it teased her shoulders.

"Don't you have a private bath in the keep?"

The prince shrugged. "It's not as quiet or dim as this one after dark. And it's not quite big enough to swim in."

"Swim?"

He propped up a quizzical brow as the water rippled along his torso. Dark hair coiled on his chest and stomach, swirling down to his—

Farren's eyes flashed up, catching the amused quirk of his lips.

"I do other things besides paint, you know," Isander said.

His copper skin gleamed beneath the water, the delineation of his limbs clearly visible. There was her answer to *that* question. She pushed herself away from him, hoping distance would obscure things better.

"Well," she said mildly. "I came here to bathe and think. *Alone.*"

"Of course. It'll be like I'm not even here." With that, he peeled off the bath-sheet and glided into the water, seeming to pay no heed to her as he swept by, the curved arc of his backside sleek and luminous in the candlelight.

Right, as if she could think clearly in the presence of *that*.

Sighing, she pressed along the wall, giving him a wide berth as he swam back and forth. She made herself busy applying clay to her hair, trying rapidly to work it into the strands until she realized how utterly tangled it was. Slowing her hands, she worked out each tangle. No need to rush. Isander's presence didn't bother her, and she wouldn't let him ruin her last bath in the fortress. Ignoring him was the best option. She worked her way more leisurely through her hair.

"I saw you earlier today."

Farren flinched as the prince's voice resonated over the stone tiles. He had pulled himself up out of the water and sat near his satchel as he caught his breath. A dry bath-sheet lay crumpled in his lap.

"You were different," Isander continued when she didn't respond.

He was referring to the Naronimus incident, of course.

"It wasn't what it looked like."

"You were scared," he stated.

Farren held her breath, waiting for more, but nothing else came. "I have trouble working with gryphons."

Isander's brows lifted. "You seem to like Torch, from what I hear."

"Torch isn't as threatening as the others."

Farren dunked her head beneath the water, washing away the clay. When she came back up, he was still there. She smoothed her hair back and wrung it lightly, keeping her body low in the water as she neared him.

"It's normal to be scared," he told her. From his satchel, he tugged out a small book and a piece of charcoal. "It shows that you know what they're capable of."

Farren swallowed. "I thought you saw me as some captain of a guard? That doesn't sound like someone who is afraid."

Isander's hands began moving more rapidly across a blank page, and his brow furrowed in concentration. "Everyone experiences fear, Farren. Especially those with much power to lose."

A familiar look overtook his expression—one Farren had become used to after hours of watching him paint. It was one of fervent need and focus, as if he was captured by something and had to make it real, to replicate it with his beautiful, capable hands.

Oh, she would miss those hands at work.

Farren edged close to the side of the pool, skimming it until she neared his satchel. The corner of a page poked from the bag's opening. She eased the page out. The sketch was of a young woman standing in a pool, hand outstretched to a serpentine form of water in the air before her, not just touching it, but commanding it.

"This is me!" She glared at the exquisite drawing. He had taken something that was hers—hers and Torch's—and twisted it. The image was false. Bereft of the love and awe she had felt, and full of something dark and dangerous. Something she didn't have and didn't want. "And—what—you lurked in the shadows, spying on me? You didn't even ask if you could draw me, much less announce yourself!"

Isander tossed aside his notebook and charcoal and snatched the drawing from her, and was about to return it to the satchel when she plucked it back, holding it out of his reach over the water. "What kind of a prince does that?" she demanded, heat clawing up her neck when he didn't answer. "Why did you draw me like that?"

Isander removed the bath sheet from his lap and lowered himself back into the water, for once looking sheepish. "I promise I see it differently than you. I'm an artist, Farren, nudity doesn't bother me—"

"I'm not concerned about *your* feelings."

He made a dive for the paper, and Farren tried to twist away, but he caught her arm mid-dive and pinned her against the side of the pool. His weight pressed on her, incredibly warm and solid. Breathless, she said, "You have no right to draw me so—"

"Beautifully?" he suggested. "Alluringly?" He tugged on the paper, but she refused to let go. He would have to rip it if he wanted it back.

"Naked." It took effort to ignore the feel of his skin against hers. The way the water trembled between them, licking up her sides with his every movement.

"You had no right to spy on us," she insisted, waiting for an apology. But he was a prince, and apparently above apologizing. Well, that would have to change.

"Us? So it was a gryphon? Torch, I imagine?" His gaze grew brighter, almost feverish as his attention darted between her and the drawing.

Her fingers curled tighter on the page. "You intruded on something that you had no right to."

"Farren, please," Isander said, his cheeks darkening as the page began to crumple.

"You owe me an apology."

"I'm sorry I—"

"A *genuine* apology. I don't like your princely tone overly much."

"But I am—"

"You seem a bit out of practice with it." Farren tilted her head at him.

He sighed and searched her face. "I apologize for drawing you without your knowledge. It wasn't my intention to make you uncomfortable."

"And next time...?"

"Next time... I will ask your permission first, if that's what you wish."

"It is." She retained her hold on the sketch. "And now you must tell me why."

He glanced from her to the page she held captive. His eyes were too perfect. Long-lashed and steady as the stone pressing into her back.

"Because I like to draw you."

The swell of her breasts crushed against his torso as she breathed, yet he didn't move. After all the sparring she had done, she should be used to being this close to a man. The only difference was the lack of a piece of cloth between them. That lack made every nerve in her body buzz.

He gave a half-hearted tug of the page once more, his lips curving ever so slightly as he did so.

"You draw me because you like how I look. Is that all?" Why was she prodding him this way? There was a boundary between them, one that marked him as a prince and her as a servant. Yet every passing moment that their bodies touched, the boundary burned away.

"You know it's not just how you look," he answered. "I can see so much of you—."

"You don't know me."

"I know you better than you think." He released his hold on the paper and ran a thumb down to the runemark on her inner wrist.

"I know you are more than just this mark. More than a falconer. More than a daughter. More than a sister. And certainly more than a servant."

She had told him so much about her life. Too much, perhaps. But he didn't know her secrets, nor her deepest fears.

"You remind me of possibility, of strength and determination," he said. "You think you are a hawker, a fighter, but what I see is regal. A commander, unafraid to protect what is hers."

There he went with his fantasies again, seeing her in some strange, idyllic, impossible light. She didn't want to believe a word of it, but she couldn't stop the way his words made her feel—dark and powerful, unafraid. And utterly, breathlessly alive.

Something burned through her, and she could no longer tell if it was from anger or his touch. "Is this some sort of poetry to woo me?"

"It's just the truth. I can't help it if I sound poetic."

His face inched closer to hers, and her heart thudded in her ears. For a few breathless, angry moments, she wanted to shove him away. Why did he have to show up unannounced? Why did he have to draw her, when he could draw anyone else in the fortress? And why, *why* did it have to feel so good when he caught her face and tilted it up to his?

His thumb ran over her clenched jaw, smoothing the tension there. His gaze swept over her face in the hazy air, and when it rested on hers, it was as if he peered into her rune-made soul.

Resistance crumbled as their lips met. Instead of pushing him away, she leaned in, and the kiss was gentle and heady and delicious. It tugged at the heat glowing low in her belly. She lifted a hand to his face and delighted at the feel of smooth-shaved skin softened by oil and steam. Despite her annoyance—despite everything—she wanted him. Badly.

He pulled away. His face started to close, something in those eyes receding as they traced over her. "Can I tell you a secret, Farren?"

She swallowed, caught off-guard, and forced a smile. "Is it a secret you tell all the women you paint?"

Unsmiling, he held her gaze. "No."

Her heart was hammering so hard she was sure he could feel it. As if sensing her discomfort, he eased back and edged to the side, nabbing the sketch from her hand.

Her body throbbed. It had been months since she had been touched by a man like that. Centuries. She turned to face Isander, folding her arms over her chest as she sank deeper into the water once more. The water's embrace was cooler than it had been. Her skin prickled.

"My runeskill didn't rise until the day Cato was born. I thought the pain was a nightmare, but when I woke up, I felt every bit of what my mother felt as she brought him into the world."

He picked up the slender piece of charcoal he had dropped by his satchel and spun it between his slender fingers, coating them in black dust. "I was only five at the time, and I ran away, terrified of what the pain was and why it wouldn't stop. My nanny found me, hours later, crying in the cellar, and her anger toward me felt as harsh as a whipping." His thumb pressed into the vine of charcoal until it broke. "I was so ashamed that I never ran from another's feelings ever again. From that day, I bore them all rigidly, and when they overwhelmed me, I wished to die."

Farren glanced at his scarred runemark, seeking the pattern that should've been imprinted there from birth. A runemark that shouldn't be possible because it was only spoken about in legends.

"Are you saying... You have a human runemark?" She waited for him to laugh, or for something in his expression to give away his story.

Isander tossed the charcoal aside and expelled a short breath. "My mother had it burned from me soon after. As protection from those who might use me."

Farren pictured Isander as a young boy, frightened of the mark on his wrist—his birthright—confused and hurting as his mother ordered it burned from him. Not only had his mother caused him this pain, but she had sought to erase the symbol that represented his deepest connection to other life. The symbol was meant as a guide, as an encouragement for the bearer to grow and learn from their runeskill. And his mother had taken that from him.

"She had no right to do that," Farren said.

"She had good reason."

"Why not cover it instead? I'm sure there were other methods—"

"No, I'm glad she did it." He pressed his thumb into the scar tissue. "It's a reminder of how dangerous it can be."

Sober acceptance lit his gaze, and she considered his words. "Dangerous for you, or others?"

"Both."

"Your mother was worried you would use it against her?"

"I used to think that, until I realized that I couldn't sense her the way I could sense others. One day she finally told me why. It's a necklace she wears, passed down from her mother."

"Is it...Enchanted?"

"It has to be. I cannot use my runeskill with her, and she cannot use her own runeskill when she wears it. Our relationship has always been...easier...because of it. With others, it's..." His lips tightened, then he gave a slight shrug. "When I was older, I tried using wine and herbs to wash out others' feelings, but that only made things worse. I stay away from those now."

He seemed lost in thought, so she prodded him. "How do you deal with it now?"

His lips quirked. "I paint. Or draw."

She hesitated as questions burgeoned up. This was the closest she had ever been to Isander, and she found that she didn't want to risk ruining it. If she asked him questions, if she pressed him, would he answer her? Would it jeopardize the fragile, uncertain thing that had started to form between them?

*It's not fragile*, a voice said in her mind.

She stared at Isander, who looked back at her like wings bracing against a storm.

*It's not fragile*, he repeated. *It's strong and certain.*

*No, no, no. This can't be real. I can't—* Farren sucked in a choking breath of humid air and pushed away from the edge of the pool. How much of her thoughts had he heard? And how was it that hearing him in her mind made her skin *tingle* while the rest of her body seemed to go into fight mode? His thoughts were intimate, like a touch, but so incredibly—

*Wonderful*? His lips tilted hesitantly as he watched her.

The hot air squeezed the last drops of sweat from her skin. "I was going to say *wrong*," Farren said aloud. "Why can't I feel you with my runeskill?" Her voice started to rise, and she rubbed her throat. "Why can't I feel you in my mind?"

Isander's smile fell. "You can, if you pay attention. At least, that's what others have told me. It should feel similar to what you are used to."

"Others?"

"A few people know. My parents. Cato. And Persepha."

"Persepha?"

"An old love. She's no longer here. Will you focus on the runebond?"

Farren struggled, sensing the barest breath of a presence. The sense of it came through a window of her mind she never knew was there. She tested it, and slid the window closed. And just like that, she felt herself again. Her mind firm and unwavering. She had let it go earlier, perhaps with Isander's kiss, and hadn't even realized she had done so.

Isander smiled. "I knew you would be quick. You have a very strong mind, Farren. The strongest I have known, yet." He waded close to her and pulled her hand. Rivulets of charcoal-tinted water coalesced in her palm as his thumb grazed her runemark. "It makes me wonder. If you can keep me out, what else can you do?"

"I'm not as strong as you think," Farren said. She tugged her hand away and turned toward the steps.

"Because of Naronimus?" His tone was gentle, but pressing.

Farren took the first step up, her skin tingling as it left the water. "Yes."

"I know you think Naronimus is vicious. And he is. My uncle treated him abominably. But I know you could be vicious, too, if you set your mind to it."

She thrust out of the water and grabbed a bath sheet from the nearest wall.

"Farren."

The thin sheet clung tight to her body as she wound it around and around. "You sound just like your brother. But worse."

Isander chuckled. "I'm not like my brother, Farren. He's a lost pup. Let me guess. Did he say that you and Naronimus could be best friends? That you could bond with him and everything would be happy-ever-after?"

"Something like that." Farren found a comb among the pots of oil on a shelf and began tugging it through her coarse hair.

"Well, that's not what I think. I said you both could be vicious. Dangerous. And maybe there's a way for you to use that."

Farren ripped through a particularly stubborn snarl. "And to what purpose? To hurt people? Kill them? I've almost done that, and I say no. Anyways, the Lord Falconer is sending me home, so it doesn't matter."

"What?"

"I'm leaving first thing in the morning."

"The queen ordered it?"

Farren shot him a stern look. "She will. I almost killed another servant."

Isander scoffed. "Naronimus almost killed her. Not you."

Farren knew it didn't matter what she said to Isander, that she still had no control over her Servitude. Before Isander could push her on the topic, she said, "Why did you call Cato a lost pup?"

Isander's expression tightened as he returned to his notebook and charcoal. "His choices—when he has finished thinking enough to make them—are constantly aimed for the approval of our parents. He hasn't learned yet that the queen is impossible to satisfy, and that he should stick to doing what he wants. The problem is, I don't think he knows what he wants. He spends his days bumbling around the mews, pretending to be a gryphon breeder rather than a prince. But you probably think that is cruel to say."

She pulled her hair into thick ropes and began plaiting them together. "Not cruel... Just a bit severe considering you're brothers."

Isander gave a mirthless chuckle. "I swear to you that he has worse feelings for me than I of him. He holds me in high resentment."

"What for?"

"For being the eldest," he said. "And a painter. For my parent's love. For most things, really."

His parent's love. Isander's words reminded her of her mother's love for Desmond, and how such warmth and protectiveness had never been shown to Farren, at least from what she could remember. Had Farren resented Desmond for that love? She frowned as she considered it. No, she would never hold that against Des. It was her mother, not Des, whom she resented, and after the accident—with her mother's constant reminders that Farren was the one responsible, that Farren had failed, that Farren couldn't be trusted to take care of Des—Farren's resentment had sharpened to something akin to hatred. Her mother had made it too easy for Farren to hate her. It hadn't taken much effort for the insidious feeling to creep up, to develop the honed edge of self-defense. Farren was simply protecting herself—no more, no less.

And she would have to go on doing so once she returned to Capai. Her mother would be furious at her arrival.

Farren went to the private sweat chamber to dress in the fresh clothes she had brought.

"I wish you could see yourself," Isander said, breaking her away from her thoughts.

When she peered around the wall of the sweat chamber, Isander's normal intensity lit his gaze as his hand flew over the page of his notebook, making modifications to whatever sketch he had begun earlier.

"I can," Farren said, motioning to the sketch. "Through a rather bright lens."

"That's not what I mean. It's different with the gryphons."

Finished dressing, she emerged from the chamber with hands on her hips. "What do the gryphons have to do with it? With me, I mean?"

His hand froze. "Everything, Farren. Can I show you something?"

With the way he looked at her—earnestly, hesitantly—she knew he wanted to connect with her again. She swallowed and cleared her mind, then pushed the mental window open.

A single impression slid into her. A commander stood, imperial, in the center of a shadowed room. Six gryphons laid at her feet, calm and watchful and obedient. Eerie light rose from the commander's form, ethereal and luminous, and a sword glinted at her side. Just like Farren, the woman was short; the gryphons would've towered over her if they stood. No fear leaked from the commander's expression. Instead, she blazed with confidence and poise. Her mind was expansive, as strong and tensile as iron, holding each gryphon as a warrior grips a sword. The commander lifted a hand, summoning their magic. Water, rock, leaves, and wind whipped and swirled over her head, alive and pulsing, waiting for her to wield them. Through her gryphons, she saw all threats. Using their magic, she defeated them.

*This is how I long to paint you*, Isander's voice said in her mind.

She could almost taste it, could feel the gryphons' magic moving through her. It reached down inside her and touched something there. A shiver rippled over her.

Hadn't Iana warned her of this? That he might try to convince her to be more than she was? More than she ever could be? Farren's hands clenched. She slammed the window shut and turned toward the door of the bathhouse.

"I—I need to get back."

"You can't keep avoiding it, Farren." His tone was resolute, his lips pressed to a thin line as he continued sketching, not even bothering to look at her.

She stalked back to him. "Why do you keep forcing this fantasy on me? Like you're trying to satisfy some strange obsession—" A new thought occurred to her. "Is that why you're trying to get close to me? Because you're obsessed with gryphons?"

Isander finally looked up from his work. "I'm not obsessed with gryphons. I admire them, and I want to paint them beside you—"

Farren waved a dismissive hand at him. "I won't hear anymore. I'm done, so none if it matters now."

"I have a feeling this is far from over, Farren."

She pressed on into the dark cutting air of night.

# TWENTY-TWO

Farren tossed in bed, unable to get comfortable. Isander's impression had caused her stomach to turn, and yet, she couldn't rid herself of it. It was as if Isander had planted a seed deep in the pit of her, and with every passing moment, the seed burrowed a new root into her heart.

What if he was right? What if she *could* control gryphons? What if having more control meant she didn't have to be afraid anymore? That it meant she could no longer be manipulated by Naronimus? The thought was too alluring to let go, circling around and around until she remembered...

She was leaving first thing in the morning and none of it mattered.

Farren rolled over and winced as something dug into her ribs. Earlier in the night, sleep had evaded her, so she had occupied her mind by scouring the remaining books she had borrowed from the Lord Falconer's study. She still hadn't been able to find clues to Mellion's strange disease, which had left her more irritated and restless than when she had started. From her father's letters, she knew the disease hadn't reached her family's mews, thank the Enchanters.

She tugged the tome out from beneath herself and tossed it under the bed, cringing as it thudded onto a pile of books. Now that she was leaving, she should probably return the books. At least she had learned a few useful things from some of them. Like how a respiratory illness could lead to a gryphon's beak changing color. Or that gryphons could suffer madness or prolonged despondence if one of their family—or a human they bonded with—died.

Farren tossed on a short chiton, gathered up the books, and peered out the door of her chamber. The hall, dimly lit by a few scattered sconces, stood empty and quiet. She clutched the stack of books and eased out, bare feet silent on the cold flagstones.

The Lord Falconer's study door was closed, and she braced the stack of books beneath her chin as she moved the handle. It was unlocked as usual and dark as night inside, except for thin silvery moonlight needling between the window curtains near the bookshelves. She cursed brusquely as she stubbed a toe on a stool. Where in the Enchanter's poorly-lit realm had the stool come from?

Something rustled behind the desk, and Farren grabbed a book from her stack, wedging the binding against her palm. The book might make a good weapon if someone decided to grab her.

A blackness moved in the shadows, and Farren caught a soft glint off a damask cloak. She relaxed, but only a fraction.

"Prince Cato. Why are you sitting in the dark?"

A sigh emitted from his shadowy form, as if he had been hoping to remain undiscovered. "I think better in the dark. Why are you sneaking like a thief into Horat's study?"

"The door was unlocked." He didn't reply, so she added, "I'm not sneaking. I'm just returning his books."

"Books that you stole."

"*Borrowed*, actually, with Horat's permission," she replied tartly. "You're just like your brother, sitting there without announcing yourself." She could practically feel him prickling at her words.

Light flared as the prince struck flint to light a candle. His eyes lit yellow in the glow, rimmed below by deep shadow. "You've been spending more time with him."

Farren went to the bookshelf, hiding her face in shadow as she began sliding the books back to their proper places. "You disapprove of a servant speaking with a prince?"

The irony wasn't lost on him. "Of course not. But Isander isn't..."

"A normal prince?" Farren asked. "It seems that you aren't, either."

Prince Cato shuffled the papers on his desk, which did little to tame the clutter there. "No, neither of us is well-suited to the role," he said. He set the papers aside suddenly. "I wanted to say that I'm sorry about what happened with Naronimus. With your brother's injury, I mean. If I had known about it before, I would've never had you two in the yard together."

Farren peered at him over her shoulder, catching his imploring look. He seemed genuinely apologetic, at least—better than his brother's attempt at apology earlier in the evening.

"I didn't know it was him until too late," she said.

"Why didn't you tell me about your brother when we first met?"

"Would it have made a difference?" Farren shoved another book into the row on the shelf. "The queen wanted fighters, yes? Horat still would've denied my request. And if not, then someone else might've been unlucky enough to form a runebond with Naronimus, so all of it might've happened anyways—"

"I know," Cato said quietly. "I made a mistake. It was foolish, and presumptuous, and I wish I could change what happened."

Hardly believing his words, Farren turned to face him. He looked down at his papers and fidgeted with their alignment. She could leave him there in silence and let him brood in the sour-sticky feel of his regret. If he sank deeply enough into that mind of his, into the darkest corners of things-he-couldn't-change, would he ever come out?

She pressed her lips together. She wouldn't leave him hanging, but she wouldn't forgive him easily, either.

"So, you admit that Naronimus shouldn't have been training with us?"

The prince sagged over the desk and ran his hands through the dark crop of his hair. "I was hoping that he would find someone to bond with. Someone that would convince him that not all humans are worth hating."

"I'm certain that as long as he breathes, he'll hate humans. Alth ough...he doesn't seem to hate *you*. You said you were bonded to him, and even that hasn't been enough to improve his opinion of people."

The prince sighed. "I thought maybe he needed someone smarter. Or someone who felt the same anger as him. But any recruit who tried speaking with him grew too afraid to attempt a true bonding." The prince's solemn gaze held nothing back as he stared bleakly into the candlelight. "My Uncle Anaxis didn't have a runeskill with gryphons. But when I was a young boy, he traveled frequently to the Blades to trap gryphons and brought them back to raise them in the fortress. He got some sort of sick satisfaction from owning them, from trying to get them to submit under the rule of his fists. One day, he brought home Naronimus, who was only a few months old at the time."

"Torch's age," Farren said. She slid the last book into place and sat on the stool, close enough to see the ink blots staining Cato's fingers.

"Yes," Cato said with soft surprise. Farren tried not to fidget under his measuring gaze. "I was the first to connect with Naronimus, and what he showed me was...unspeakable. My uncle had slaughtered his parents, then captured Naronimus. His magic had only recently risen, and he didn't yet know how to control it. Unfortunately, it made things worse."

"What is his magic?" Farren asked.

"He can manipulate emotions. Anger, especially."

"Anger? But he didn't make me angry. I was already there." Some of the anger had been rightfully hers. Naronimus had caused far too much pain for her to ever deny it.

"He might've made it more pronounced, focused it." He leaned forward. "He blames himself for what happened to his family because he believes he didn't have a good handle of his emerging ability when my Uncle Anaxis trapped him. He thinks that his magic influenced my uncle, convincing the man to slaughter his parents."

"Is it true? Did Naronimus cause their deaths?"

"I'm not sure. Anaxis certainly killed some gryphons when he was out in the Blades. But what matters more is what Naronimus believes. When I runebonded with him, he showed me everything—his guilt, his fear and anger, his hatred of humans. My uncle was the first human he ever saw." The prince's tone curdled with disgust. "He was far from being a decent man. He abused all the gryphons in his care. He kept Naronimus in this little metal box, only letting him out for short periods of time. So I fed Naronimus when he was starving, and I treated his many, many wounds. I tried to help him, but my uncle made it difficult, abusing my mother and everyone else who angered him."

Cato rubbed his arm, where tawny gryphon feathers fanned over rounded muscle. "I helped Naronimus understand his magic, allowed him to practice on me. We both benefited from the exercises."

"And you bonded with him," Farren prompted, fighting against the sickening sensation rising in her at Cato's words.

The prince gave a weak smile. "Yes. We bonded over pain, and fear, and discomfort. And I was hoping he could bond with someone else in a more positive way." His lips twisted. "Too much to hope for, I suppose."

Farren frowned, turning over Cato's words. "I think Naronimus is finished bonding with humans. But what about other gryphons?"

"He's not interested. Elya has already been injured by him—she was lucky it was only a torn ear she walked away with."

"What about Thella? He tolerated her using invisibility on him."

"After what happened with Anisha, I'm not sure he'll get along with her again, either."

Farren forced herself to stand. "Well, when my father comes to take my place, be sure that he isn't put with Naronimus, either. My father's anger is quieter than mine, but no less dangerous."

The prince looked surprised for a moment, then frowned. "I suppose Horat wanted to wait until morning to tell you."

Farren's heart nearly leapt from her chest. "Is it worse news than you've already given me?"

The prince's frown deepened. "I learned of Torch's magic rising."

Farren lowered her gaze. How much had Torch told him? Had he shared an impression of the moment with the prince? Had he shown the prince how it had felt, or how his joy had poured from him like rays from a midday sun?

*It isn't just mine*, Farren reminded herself. *The memory isn't just mine. It is Torch's, and Delphi's, and his siblings'.* Torch could share it however he wished. He loved Cato, so why would the young gryphon keep it from him?

Cato's chair creaked as he leaned forward. "You were there."

"I was."

"And you were runebonded to him, which means you are truly bonded now."

"Truly bonded?"

"Yes." He tapped the desk lightly with a finger as he said, "Gifts, adventures, births and deaths—none of those are so potent for bonding as the mutual experience of a magical rising."

Farren's heart beat faster. Torch was a part of her now; she had felt that when he welcomed her into his family. But hearing it from Cato's lips, recognizing the shape of it in her life, made it all the more real. It was a solid, tangible thing. What had Grit told her once? Bonds between gryphons and humans were like stone to earth. A shiver stroked through her.

"You should tread carefully, Farren." The prince's distant gaze had sharpened to a talon's point.

She licked her lips. "I always try to."

"This is different. Bonding with a gryphon isn't like anything else you've experienced before. It goes deep, much like when a chick imprints on a human. Torch will trust you, perhaps naïvely. He will want to be with you much of the time. He will need you, and love you, if he doesn't already. If you shut him out, it will hurt him. If you betray him, it may break him. If you—"

"I would never—"

"Are you certain?"

Farren held his frank gaze. "I've never been more certain of anything."

The prince reclined in his chair and rubbed the scruff on his face. "Good."

Why was he talking to her like this—like she wasn't leaving forever? With a huff, Farren slapped her hands down on his untidy papers. "What does this mean? That I'm not going anywhere?"

"Right," he said, a note of apology in his tone. "A gryphon needs to feel secure and trusting in order to bond, and even more so for the magic rising to take place. Once we knew that you bonded with Torch, Horat decided that perhaps you weren't hopeless after all. That you might be able to bond with another gryphon. Safely."

"But I thought it was up to the queen?"

"It is. That's another thing. She called Horat to a late-night meeting. It seems she hardly needed convincing to keep you on. She said the entire incident proved you had mettle, and that bringing your father here would only set us back."

Farren's ears rang. She stared blindly at the desk. "I'm staying."

"So Horat and I discussed further. You'll be training with me one-on-one with an adult gryphon. Preferably Elya or Thella."

Her throat worked. "Thank you."

"Don't thank me. I had little to do with it. And now that I know your history with Naronimus, I think it's best if you keep distant from him. No more yard time together."

It was like a fresh gust of cool air during a heat wave. "For once, we are in agreement," Farren said.

There was no killing Naronimus, as Camilla had already pointed out. The thought of doing so made her stomach turn. It would be far too great a risk, even if she could bear ending a gryphon's life. But there was no living with him, either. She would just have to try to avoid him, physically and mentally. Instead, she could focus on getting to know the other gryphons. Perhaps she could get close to Thella or Elya—without endangering anyone's life. Only four weeks remained before the Festival of the Forging, when the queen would allow the new gryphon guard to walk the streets of the city.

"About what happened," Cato said, scrubbing a hand over his mouth. "With your brother, I mean. I want you to know that you can come to me, if you need anything. If you aren't sure about how to proceed with a gryphon, or if something is upsetting you... I can try to help. I promise you that I will listen next time."

He leaned forward, his expression warm and soft in the candlelight, open to her in a way that caused a slow heat to rise in her. She swallowed against the tightness in her throat. "I appreciate that. Very much."

"We'll start training first thing in the morning, as soon as sparring practice has wrapped up."

Feeling light as a wind-blown feather, she asked, "Why don't you ever practice combat training with us?"

"I don't care much for fighting." His eyes narrowed when Farren snorted. "I train alone, with Scipio."

"You probably aren't learning much more than snobbery from him."

"I'm a prince." He scooped dark curls away from his face. "No one knows snobbery better than me."

Farren couldn't help smiling at his sudden sense of humor. It made him a bit less annoying. "How will the rest of us learn how to fight important people if we can't practice sparring with them? And, I know he thinks so, but Scipio is not an important person. Besides, I could use another fighting partner."

"Your bum getting too sore finally?"

"Oh, there's that snobbery. Maybe you should stick with Scipio, after all."

He gave a lopsided grin. "No, my bum's getting sore, too."

Farren laughed, and the prince stood to snuff out the candle. As she removed her hands from the papers on his desk, a familiar name scrawled on one of the pages caught her eye.

"Wait," Farren said, voice unsteady.

The page was a list of names, written in even handwriting. The very last name had caught her eye.

Persepha.

The name was burned into her mind, a mysterious shape she wasn't sure how to fill, and wasn't sure she wanted to.

"Why is Persepha's name on this list? What is this?"

In the candlelight, his face was a mask of copper and shadow. "The missing."

"The missing from Malodai?" Farren scanned the page again; there were dozens of names. "I don't understand. Is this Isander's Persepha?"

"It is. The others I gathered from some of the folk across Malodai. It's bad, Farren."

"There are more than I thought," Farren said. "But I don't understand why Persepha's name is on the list."

The prince sank back into the chair and pinched the bridge of his nose. "It's my suspicion. There were many rumors. Some said that she wandered too deeply into the keep, or that she was swept away by the Kithyria. Others speculated that she was kidnapped for a ransom." As Cato slanted toward the candle-flame, the shadows on his face sharpened. "But there was no ransom request, nor even a body. Nobody found her."

"So you think she's one of the missing. That whatever happened to them may have happened to her?"

"It seems too coincidental to think anything else."

"Do you have any ideas about where they are?"

"I have some of our best *Canids* searching, when they can be spared."

Farren expelled a breath. It was all too easy to remember the look on that grieving woman's face in the inn. The way the innkeep had laughed when Farren asked about whether the queen was searching for them.

"I want to help."

The prince shook his head and tugged the list from her hand. "You have enough to focus on with the gryphon training. And you did tell me that you would do whatever training I asked, remember?"

She couldn't argue with that.

"But," the prince went on, "you should be careful around Isander. You don't really know him."

The hair on Farren's arms rose. "You think I can't handle myself?"

His eyes flashed to hers. "He's capable of more than you can imagine."

"I already know about his runeskill. And I'm..." She dropped her gaze. "I'm fine with it."

"He told you?"

"Is it really that hard to believe he trusts me?"

The prince's lips formed a hard line. "Yes. Especially with his runeskill. Not many know of it. Persepha was bold, direct, and witty, but those things... They didn't save her."

"Save her from what? You think Isander hurt her?"

Cato studied her, as if wondering how much he should say. "Persepha was smitten with him. I think they had been intimate with one another, and the last time I saw her, he was taking her to his room."

"So they were a couple. That doesn't mean he had a hand in her disappearance. And he couldn't possibly have known all these people," Farren said, motioning to the list. "Unless you found proof?"

The prince flushed and remained silent. Perhaps what Isander had said was true, and Prince Cato was jealous, looking for fault where there was none. Isander was always polite with the servants that visited them during painting sessions, and she had never even seen him squish a mosquito. His runeskill meant that he could feel others' pain—and that would make him more understanding.

Farren glanced at the list again, crumpled beneath Prince Cato's balled fist. "I think this is bigger than any one person. Don't you?"

Prince Cato's words were clipped. "Just be careful."

# TWENTY-THREE

THE NEXT MORNING AT sparring practice, the tension of what had happened to Anisha pressed against her. Alexon didn't approach her as he usually did, even though he had taken to offering her a honeyed sweet before every practice session, and when she approached him, he quickly partnered up with someone and scuttled to the farthest area of the courtyard. The other recruits avoided looking at her. She hadn't been close to any of them before, but their side-glances and silence made her feel more alone than ever since arriving at the fortress.

She practiced sparring with Scipio, this time with wooden knives, and had no trouble giving it little effort. Letting him win should've made him tire of her quickly and move on to another sparring partner, but unfortunately, it only seemed to irritate him.

"Feeling more Outskirts drift than fighter today, eh?" he jeered. He wore a liver-colored sash around his neck that reminded her of a rooster's wattle, and she longed to tear it off and stomp it into the dirt.

"I'm not in the mood for your condescending remarks, I suppose." Farren ducked as his wood knife whipped out toward her cheek. She sent a fist into his torso, not feeling her usual satisfaction when he grunted.

Prince Cato lingered by the fountain, watching the recruits with a very distant expression. How he could stand there motionless with all the activity perplexed her. She had never *not* been able to say no to a fight right in front of her. Not even when she was supposed to be watching Desmond.

A movement out of the corner of her eye caught her attention, and she missed Scipio's shift. Just as she saw the queen's distant figure enter the gryphon yard, Scipio's shoulder barreled into her, flinging her to the ground. He dug the tip of his wood knife into her sternum.

"Worse than usual today, wastrel." Scipio lifted the knife and stood, brushing off his shoulder as if touching her had dirtied it. "I just hope that the next time you really injure someone, you don't take this long to get over it. There's no time for that when you're a royal guard."

Farren lurched up, wincing at the pain that grated along her back. Her skull felt wobbly, and she rubbed her neck. "Thanks for the tip. Maybe you should see what your queen is doing here."

Scipio turned to look where Farren nodded, too startled by the sudden nearness of the queen to take offense at Farren's words. Prince Cato woke from his trance-like state and walked stiffly to the queen's side, towering several inches over her. Yet, his shoulders were hunched like a hawk stooping over prey.

The queen barely glanced at him as she spoke, too quiet for Farren to hear. Prince Cato drew back, replying in a hushed tone.

"Why is she here?" Farren asked Scipio.

The guard had taken on an erect stance, hands locked behind a stonewall back. "It's not my business unless she tells me so."

Cato's voice rose, and the queen retorted with something low and sharp. By now, the other recruits had taken notice and stopped practicing. Farren pretended to stretch, but she watched the prince and queen from beneath her lashes, unable to stop herself from wondering—and worrying—about why they were fighting. And then the queen turned from the prince, lifting a dismissive hand as she headed deeper into the gryphon yard. Prince Cato's face had a pale sheen, and he stared after her only a moment before storming her heels.

The queen moved like water over the flagstone path, utterly graceful and without thought to the recruits around her. Her high brow was plucked to a thin line, her chin jutting like a sword as she pressed through them.

Farren lowered her eyes and curtsied—giving it the special dip from the waist Camilla had taught her. The queen's shoes came into view: flat sandals threaded with golden beads, nothing to add height to her short stature.

"Farren Blackburn," Queen Aurelia said.

Unsure if she should look up, Farren glanced at Scipio, who nodded once. She managed to lift herself out of her curtsy without wobbling. Their eyes leveled, and Farren repressed a quiver as she met Queen Aurelia's expansive green gaze, wide and observant as a cat's.

"Yes, Your Majesty." The words felt prickly on her tongue, but she kept her face still.

Prince Cato halted beside them, his cheeks tinging the shade of a rusthawk's feathers. "Mother, I must insist—"

The queen cut him off with a lift of her finger and spoke to Farren. "I heard about your accident with the servant." Her tone was curious, with no hint of anger or suspicion.

Farren licked her lips. "Yes, Your Majesty. It was an awful accident. I never meant to hurt Anisha, and I'm very sorry—"

"None of that," Queen Aurelia said shortly. The icy glint of the gem on her necklace waxed and waned from where it nestled over the scarlet iris imprinted on her chest. "It seems that you have remarkable potential. It's not easy to push a gryphon to action."

"Your Majesty, I didn't purposefully—"

"And I know what a beast Naronimus can be," she continued, as if Farren hadn't spoken. "I would like you to train with Naronimus from now on. You both have potential and he needs reigning in."

Prince Cato shook his head. "Farren and Naronimus can't—"

"Quiet, Cat. I am done with your whining," the queen snapped without sparing him a look. "You see, Farren, Naronimus could be very useful to my realm. But his temper is...undesirable. He needs someone like you to control him."

"Control him?" Farren's voice sounded much too high, although she was having trouble hearing since her ears had begun to ring. "I can't control him. No one can." Never mind that she and Naronimus hated one another. And that she had zero intention of ever being around him again.

Queen Aurelia lifted a hand, startling Farren as she reached for a lock of Farren's hair and tucked it behind her ear. "My dear," she said sweetly, and her hand drifted down Farren's arm and squeezed lightly just above the bronze bangle on her wrist, shackling it. "I don't think you understand. I'm giving you an order. Your first of many if you succeed with this."

Farren, disbelieving, looked at the prince, but he stared hopelessly back at her and shook his head.

"Cat cannot help you," the queen stated without emotion. "And I find I have a hard time trusting his...competence." She gave a delicate sniff, oblivious to the way the prince's jaw bulged as if cracking nuts. "But that poor woman has been injured, and now I'm short a recruit. Therefore, you will train with Naronimus, and little Cat will help you. I want to see progress with your control of him. Prove to me that he is useful. Disobedience will result in thirty lashings and a year without pay. And I will be forced to execute the gryphon due to his aggressive nature."

The heat drained from Farren. *Executed?*

Prince Cato reeled back as if slapped. "You can't do that, Mother. The gryphons will never cooperate if you threaten them—"

"I have every right." The queen's eyes pinned on him. "Perhaps I should remind you of someone else Naronimus hurt. Killed, rather."

Cato glowered. "Uncle Anaxis treated him horribly, and you were glad Naronimus finally gave him what he deserved—"

"Watch your tongue, you fool." The queen's tone was scathing, and the prince's mouth snapped shut, his cheeks darkening to crimson.

She returned her gaze to Farren, who was feeling anything but steady. The whole world seemed to be shifting beneath her feet, a crater opening before her, and it took every ounce of focus to keep from falling in.

"I must emphasize how important the gryphon guard is to me and to all of Malodai. Only yesterday, two guards from the City Watch were caught trapping and killing innocent animals within the city walls. When questioned, they were found to be members of the Runeless Sect. They admitted to killing almost a hundred animals, ridding the city of *vermin*, as they called our beloved creatures. Now, knowing what you know about gryphon magic, do you think they would've killed so many animals before the gryphon guard found them?"

"No, Your Majesty. But I think someone more comfortable with gryphons would have better success—"

A slight wave of the queen's hand cut her off. "Do I have your obedience, Farren Blackburn?"

"Yes, Your Majesty," Farren said, her voice sounding leagues away.

"Good. You have until Prince Isander's birthday feast to get it done. I will make my decision then."

The queen left them, and Farren bit the inside of her mouth hard enough to draw blood. The prince glared at the back of his mother as she quit the gryphon yard. A muscle worked in his jaw.

Farren took a breath. "When is the prince's birthday feast?"

"Four weeks," Cato said shortly. "On the eve of the Festival of the Forging."

Farren tasted the metallic tang of blood. "Did you tell her about what Naronimus did to Anisha?"

Cato turned bright eyes on her. "No, I did not. I didn't have to. She has many eyes and ears."

*Like Scipio.* Of course.

A part of her wanted to argue with Cato, to find out what exactly he had said to the queen to convince her that working with Naronimus was a horrible idea. Another part of her grappled with the idea of Naronimus's execution. The more she learned about Naronimus's past, the less certain she felt about what he deserved for hurting Desmond. Execution would mean that Naronimus was hopeless. That he could never change. Could he? Would he? And who would help him? Her anger toward him had already proved that they wouldn't work well together. Someone was bound to get injured or killed—unless she could learn to control her feelings.

Farren's stomach churned. She wasn't sure what Naronimus deserved, and now it didn't seem as if it mattered. What choice did she have in any of it? She was a puppet, and the queen was her master.

# TWENTY-FOUR

FARREN SAGGED IN RELIEF as she entered the stone gryphon mews, alone. She had grown accustomed to the acrid, feline smell of gryphons, and had even begun associating it with Torch. She rubbed her wrist. The queen's touch lingered from earlier that morning.

Prince Cato had left shortly after the queen unleashed her orders, and Farren finished up sparring practice with all the brutal force the queen's words had given rise to. After she nearly dislocated Virilus' shoulder, Scipio dismissed her. With the keen edge of her rage spent, she went looking for Cato, but the Lord Falconer informed her that he needed the rest of the day to prepare. Horat didn't offer her any advice on how to proceed with Naronimus beyond telling her to get it done without getting anyone killed.

Very helpful of him.

Cato would likely have told Naronimus by now. Would the gryphon be furious or amused by the queen's threat? Not that knowing his feelings would help her prepare. Only one thing could give her strength before she had to attempt the impossible. As she entered the gryphon nursery, warmth lit into the runebond she opened with Torch.

*I told her! I told Mother!* Torch said, bouncing around Farren as she came in.

*About what?* She crouched down, longing to touch Torch's feathers, to embrace him.

*The bathhouse!*

*And what did she say?*

*That my magic is strong, and that I need to keep practicing. Can you take me to the fountains?*

When Farren widened their runebond and reached out to him, he dove into her arms in a whirl of feather, fur, and claw, and she breathed in his warm gryphon scent. For a moment, the whole shining world fit in her embrace.

*I will try to*, she told Torch. *I need Prince Cato's permission first. And the Lord Falconer's.*

*I can't wait! I can feel the water from the fountains, but it's much easier to do things with it when someone shows me.*

*Yes, and you might frighten the other gryphons or recruits if they see water moving differently than it usually does.*

*Or they might like it. Especially if I made puddles for them to jump in, or...*

Farren listened as he went on, soaking in the effervescent glow of his chatter. She found comfort in the patter of his heart, in the way he wriggled next to her, barely containing his excitement. She found clarity, too, in the steadfast love he held for her, a blazing candle that warmed her rune-made soul.

*Mother wishes to speak with you*, Torch said suddenly. *Can I play?*

*Of course you can. Gently*, she added. When she closed the runebond, the quiet cold of her own thoughts returned.

Delphi stood from where she had sprawled near the fireplace and roused, sending clouds of dust and feathers swirling up to the large tapestry depicting the Blades. Farren sneezed, then scrabbled to her feet when Delphi began walking toward her. At her full height, it was apparent that Delphi was the largest gryphon in all the mews. Long, thick limbs curved with muscle, and her back paws were four times the size of Farren's head. Her crest nearly touched the high rafters.

Farren squeezed against the wall and inched closer to the door. Damp palms found the handle and gripped it, just in case she needed a quick escape. The great beast paused a few arm-lengths away and sat. Bright phosphorous eyes watched her, waiting. Reluctantly, Farren touched the radiant sphere of Delphi's mind.

*You do not need to fear me.* Delphi's voice was a deep-toned bell, so different from Torch's brightness.

*I'm not afraid*, Farren said. *Just cautious.*

*I'm sorry Naronimus did that to you.*

Farren swallowed, unable to respond.

*I was just speaking with Cato from afar*, Delphi continued, her thick tail moving to rest on her hind paws. *He believes the gryphon is doomed to execution. The prince's thoughts sometimes fly in downward spirals. Do yours fly higher?*

It seemed a strange question from a gryphon. Then again, she hadn't spent much time speaking with gryphons.

*I will keep going until I can't anymore*, Farren said.

*Camilla told me you are a fighter.* Delphi bobbed her head, appraising Farren with bright eyes as if in approval. *You are small, but maybe smart. Naronimus, too, is smart.*

*And stubborn*, Farren said. *And hateful. Fighting with him almost got someone killed.*

*So do not fight.*

Farren crossed her arms. *I don't want to fight with him. But what he says and does—he makes me furious!*

A wave of something washed through the connection, pulling her thoughts away from her own words.

*He cannot make you feel. Only you can do that.*

*But his magic—*

*Is perception*, Delphi said. *He dangles thoughts, memories, whatever he can to get a rise. Don't give in to it.*

Farren bit her lip. *I'm not sure I can runebond with him without being angry. I can't put it away.*

*I didn't say not to feel*, Delphi said. She stood and went to the short log resting by the fire and began feaking, rubbing her beak back and forth on the rough bark to clean it. *Only to not give in to what he tries to get you to give into.*

*And how do I do that?*

*It's not something I can teach you. You must learn to do it on your own.* Delphi placed a talon on the log, crushing the bark beneath it as she stretched her wings, opening them to the heat of the fireplace. The spread of her wings nearly filled the chamber. *You cannot do it through fighting. You must step back from the fight, recognize your feelings but don't fall into them. Since you cannot fight him, you have to work with him. That means finding out what you both want and working towards it together.*

What they both wanted? Farren repressed a snort. They had nothing in common except for not wanting to be at the fortress in the first place.

Farren's stomach tightened. Freedom. If not for herself, then for Naronimus. If he was freed, would he leave humans alone? If she made a bargain with him—his freedom for leaving and never returning—would he honor it? Farren ground her teeth, knowing she was once again at a disadvantage for having little knowledge of the beasts. Hawks, she knew. With gryphons, she felt all the trepidation of dealing with an entirely new type of animal—one that was far more wise, capable, and dangerous than raptors.

*How do you know so much about working with* Naronimus? Farren asked.

Delphi's wings lowered slightly. *When Anaxis was still alive, he forced Naronimus and me into a chamber and wouldn't feed us until we mated. Naronimus didn't care about starving, but I did. So, I had to convince Naronimus to work with me.*

*Naronimus is Torch's father? Does Torch know him?*

*Torch knows of him, but they do not speak.*

*How did you convince him to mate with you?*

*I promised him that if the opportunity ever arose, I would help him kill Anaxis.*

Farren stared at her. *Did you do it?*

*I did.* Delphi moved away from the hearth and folded her fire-gilded wings. *In a moment when Naronimus was freed of his box and fear froze him, I pushed him through it.*

Thankfully, the gryphon chose not to show her what had happened. Farren sent her a wave of gratitude and turned her attention back to Torch. The little gryphon had become entranced by the water tub in the back corner and was using his magic to pull out fist-sized balls of water, teasing his siblings with it. When his sister pounced on the ball, it splashed all over her chest. Torch made a high chittering noise that could only be laughter.

Farren couldn't help smiling. Once he had more practice...

Her mirth faded. *Practice.* Torch wasn't just a young gryphon that she was beginning to love. Torch was owned by the queen and destined to be one of her guard. Queen Aurelia would learn of his magic ability and want to use it for her own gain. She wouldn't care about who Torch was. And if Torch ever hurt someone—or if the queen suddenly decided he was unfit for his designation—she would have him killed.

If she was going to try to free Naronimus, all the rest of it would still remain. Freeing Naronimus wouldn't stop the gryphon guard, or the queen's misuse, or the captivity. Torch would still be in danger. All the gryphons would be.

Unless she freed them all.

Farren's skin tingled, and she rubbed her throat. Without Anaxis trapping more gryphons, it could work. But it would take time, and that was in ruefully short supply. She needed to connect with more gryphons, gain their trust, and learn more about each of their magical abilities. To do so might take months, but she only had a handful of weeks. And then, she would have to convince them of her plan. Above all, she needed to be very careful because if her plan was revealed to Camilla or the prince, everything would fall apart before it even began.

With a start, Farren turned to Delphi. The gryphon had gone quiet as she worked at preening her shoulder. Their runebond had narrowed, but Farren couldn't be certain that her thoughts had stayed private. Who knew what an adult gryphon was capable of sensing or understanding? Probably only Prince Cato.

*Why are you helping me?* Farren asked suddenly.

Delphi ceased her preening. *Hold out your hand.*

*What?*

*Hold your hand out to me.*

Despite a tremor of unease, Farren did as Delphi asked. The gryphon approached, and Farren's neck craned as she kept her gaze on the gryphon's massive curved beak. With surprising grace, Delphi bent down and curled her head toward her chest until the smooth part of her beak touched Farren's palm. Farren's heart thundered as Delphi's breath poured through her fingers. The lingering heat from the fire emanated from the beak's solid, smooth surface.

*This is how my kind have always shared their trust with humans,* Delphi said.

Speechless, Farren sent a rivulet of curiosity.

*I remember the time before Anaxis,* Delphi explained. *I was the oldest gryphon captured, with one molt already completed. My family used to live among people in the Blades. They worked together to build, hunt, and flourish as one.*

*I thought the Blades were uninhabitable by humans?*

Delphi finally lifted her head and gave Farren a long and thoughtful look.

*There were humans and many other things that I remember. I dream of it sometimes. That I'm flying there to return.*

Farren's eyes tore away to rest on Torch once more. *With Torch?*

*With them all.* Delphi's ears pricked toward her, eyes molten.

Something brittle fluttered in Farren's chest. *Thank you for sharing that with me.*

*We are family now,* Delphi replied. *We are of the same feather. I can feel your love for him grow each day, and it strengthens our bonds. You have a choice, and it is a choice that others have seen before. No one has ever been strong enough to make it. If you think you are strong enough, I promise to help you in whatever way I can.*

Farren's hands tightened to fists. *I am strong enough.*

When she headed back to her room, she found a folded missive outside her door. The seal was broken. Taking it to the light of her window, she read her father's steady, blocky writing and took solace in his familiar words. He had caught a few more hawks to train as he tried to re-grow his business, and Desmond was doing as well as could be expected. They had received her last letter, which—despite being five pages long—had been too brief for Desmond, who longed to know more about life at the fortress. Mostly, he wanted to know how exactly the falls looked and if they were as huge as he had heard.

Farren smiled. As dark and prison-like as the fortress felt to her, she knew Des would love to explore it. He would probably even try to swim in the river and—

No, he couldn't swim like that anymore. Although she wouldn't put it past him to try.

Farren sat at her little writing desk to pen her response. She wished fervently that Desmond could visit, but she didn't want him anywhere near the gryphons. Farren wouldn't be able to handle his outbursts well, anyways; that was, after all, one of the reasons why she had left home in the first place.

So she wrote of the falls and of the little she knew about the Enchanted quill Prince Cato wrote with and the broom from the kitchens. She wrote, too, of Camilla and Prince Cato, but only briefly and nothing of the gryphons. They had all been deeply affected by Desmond's attack, and she didn't think her father would understand her relationship with Torch. That was something too intimate to share, even with her father.

A knock sounded on the door, startling her. She set the quill into the inkwell, then on second thought, grabbed it and held it firmly in her fist, her mind flashing through at least three different ways in which she could use it as a weapon. She eased open the door.

Isander leaned against the door frame, one hand behind his back. She let out a breath.

Dark hair lapped the sides of his lean face, framing eyes that roved over the room behind her. His gaze landed on the quill clutched in her hand, and he lifted a quizzical brow. "Did you think someone would knock if they intended to hurt you?"

"You can never be too careful. There are many dangers in Alidonia." Farren's hand tightened on the door. She made sure her mind was closed to him.

She didn't think it was possible, but his brow quirked higher.

"I think we all know that you are one of the most dangerous people here," he said in an even voice, his gaze pinioning her.

"What do you want?"

"First, I'm glad to see that you're still here."

Farren fiddled with the quill. "Did you have something to do with it?"

"I may have mentioned a word to the queen."

"That was generous of you," Farren said. Had he done it for his own sake or for hers?

Isander gave her a strained smile. "I wanted to apologize for my behavior the last time I saw you. It was thoughtless. And..." He hesitated, then pulled his hand out from his back. He cradled a flat, square-shaped parcel. "I made this for you, in hopes of your forgiveness."

The light parcel was wrapped in a cream-colored fabric as soft as the silk chiton he had gotten her. The ribbon wending around it reminded her of the stream of water Torch had awed her with in the bathhouse. Where the prince had seen her naked. No, where he had *studied* her, naked.

"Thank you, Your Highness," she said as she untied the ribbon, "but I'm not sure I'm in the mood for gifts..."

Her words faltered as she found the small painting inside. A replica of Farren stood on a hillside, dressed in comfortable leggings and short woolen chiton, with a hawk on her gloved fist. Farren envied the confidence and ease in the woman's eyes. It was how she always felt while flying hawks—something she missed sorely. And Isander had depicted each strand of her dark hair, each ruddy hawk feather, with exquisite detail. The hawk herself carried that quintessential look that was at once intimidating and beautiful.

"It's lovely," she said, unable to lift her gaze from it. She could just make out the strokes of paint he had used to form her face, angled perfectly to her features and blending seamlessly with one another. He had painted it scrupulously, and she wondered if he had had that fevered look about him while he did so.

"We never had a chance to finish our discussion," Isander said, holding his hands behind his back as if he was a servant waiting on her.

She wasn't very interested in finishing that particular conversation with him, but she also didn't want the prince lingering outside her door. She glanced into the hallway, hoping no one had heard their exchange.

"Come in, then," she told him and took the painting to her writing desk. She dropped the quill back in the inkwell and faced him, crossing her arms as she remembered Prince Cato's words that she shouldn't be alone with him. But Prince Isander was all cordiality as he quietly closed the door and hovered there, keeping his eyes averted from the bed. Strangely, she wished he *would* look there. Did he remember their kiss the way she did? Did his lips still tingle when he thought of it, and did his mind wander to the other parts of their bodies that had touched—no, *pressed* together?

A dirty pair of underclothes had been left on the floor by her bed. She nudged it with her foot until it disappeared under the bed.

"I wanted to ask you to reconsider my request that you pose with gryphons," he said, his spring-mountain eyes hopeful in the fading light of her window.

"Why don't you explain why you're so obsessed with them first?"

He clasped his hands in front of him. "Obsession is an extreme term, Farren. I would call it more of an interest."

"Why?"

"The better question is, why not? They are beautiful, unique creatures with high intelligence, and many of them have powerful magic."

"Sometimes no amount of magic can make up for their less savory qualities," she pointed out.

Isander abandoned the door and meandered toward the desk. "I know you don't like them, that they make you uncomfortable. But it's important to me."

His eyes trailed over the letter she had been writing, and she fought the urge to cover it. Let him see it. He needed to know that he wasn't as important to her as other people, that she had pieces of her life that he knew nothing about.

"I wish you would tell me what happened," he said.

Farren went rigid, double-checking that her mind was sealed like a tomb. "About what?"

His fingers skimmed the back of the desk chair as if studying the robust curve of the wood. "About why you are so frightened of gryphons. It must've been something that happened before you came here because you were afraid long before the incident with Naronimus."

"I thought you said it was normal to be afraid?"

"It is. But I hope you know that you can trust me, Farren. Maybe telling your story will ease your fears."

"Maybe it will make my fears worse."

He nodded once, and Farren was too aware of how his wide hands splayed along the back of the chair, squeezing lightly. The folds of his chiton stretched between his shoulder blades, hinting at the strength and resilience there.

Her past lurked like a shadow between them, and she had to admit that she wanted to tell him. The more she thought about doing so, the more she ached for it. She had already told Camilla, and even Prince Cato. But telling them wouldn't be the same as telling Isander. Would Isander understand? Something in her chest lurched. Perhaps she could *make* him understand, without even using words. But would he see her differently—not strong and skilled, but weak and broken?

As if sensing her hesitation, Isander turned to her and smoothed his hands down her shoulders. Her skin tingled beneath his touch.

"If you don't want to tell me, that's okay. I just want you to feel comfortable. I want you to know that I care about how you feel."

"Then you can paint me without gryphons?"

Isander gave a half-smile. "I can."

He was disappointed. He expected more. He wanted her to work through her fear, and the restless edge of his impatience burned beneath the forced calm of his gaze.

She hated that she wanted to meet his expectations. That she craved his closeness because the past months of living alone in the mountains, bearing the burden of her brother's attack, had left her feeling like a hawk with a shattered wing.

Her breath hitched as she grabbed Isander's wrist. "I want to show you something."

She could feel his pulse quicken, and the set of his mouth tightened as if he were afraid to speak. Carefully, Farren selected the memory of Desmond's attack, slid open the window of her mind, and released it.

It was as if she lived through it again, but this time, Isander was beside her, holding her hand in the shadows.

They shared the sweaty-slick pressure of Thestor's arms and torso as she grappled with him. The way the flies buzzed and nipped at her skin. The golden-winged sparrow fluttering, fluttering madly to tell her where Des had gone. They both looked out over the street, heard the shouts as a parade of affluent silk-and-brocade-dressed revelers flanked by the royal guard marched by, showing off their prized possession: a gryphon with painted feathers—one so massive and mean-looking that Farren looked twice.

And there was Desmond, willow-limbed and bright-eyed, reaching a hand from the edge of the crowd of onlookers. Then the confusion, the anger and fear permeating everything as she runebonded clumsily with the gryphon and he...

A shudder rocked her as the beak dove down. It was a little nip for the gryphon, but Desmond's head twisted as the beak nearly crushed his skull, and he started falling, but Farren was too far from him, her body moving as if through water.

She had wanted to catch him. Her heart rode high in her throat as she raced there, watching him spill to the ground as rivulets of blood ran down his face and neck. She didn't remember hearing sounds. All she remembered was the weight of Desmond's body in her arms, the way her throat burned as she screamed for help, the inevitable seep of warm blood from his wound as she pressed on it. The silent, still, maddening crowd that did nothing. Until the healer. Then rushing to the infirmary. She had been out of herself by then, shaking and muddled and terrified of losing the only brother she had ever had.

She pried herself from the memory. It faded between them.

Isander's eyes were closed, and his hand a fist. When he opened his eyes, they were lit like fiery mirrors, reflecting the turmoil she held deep in the core of herself. A wound that had not yet scabbed over.

He took her hand in both of his and held it to his smooth cheek. "I'm sorry," he rasped. "Did he make it?"

"He's alive. But not the same."

Silence spread, then Isander said, "You know it's not your fault."

Farren's eyes burned. "Yes, it was." She fought not to tug her hand back. Isander's grip was firm and sure. Nothing like her quaking heart. It shocked her how easily she could share something so deep, that she didn't even have to use words to do it. And now he held that memory of hers, and she was terrified of what would come of it.

"You didn't know what the gryphon would do," Isander said, trying to reason with her.

"I knew they could be dangerous. I was distracted by the boy I was fighting with."

"You tried to stop it."

"But I didn't. I think I made it worse. I caused the gryphon to lash out at him—"

Isander sucked in a breath and his hands tightened on hers. "Farren, it makes no sense to blame yourself. You can't go back and change it. All you can do is learn to use your runeskill better." He swayed and closed his eyes. "Farren, you need to close it now."

In a panic, she realized she hadn't shut her mind. She did so, cursing her recklessness. What if he had seen her plans for the gryphons? The hate for them that still lingered?

When he opened his eyes again, they seemed clearer. "Thank you. I know that was hard to share."

"It wasn't."

Instead of letting go of her hand, he stepped closer. "I was worried that my runeskill was the real reason why you left so angrily."

Her cold fingers, still cupped by his hands, curled against his skin. "You didn't need to worry about that."

His eyes roved over her face, intense and restless as always. "Then it was my request to paint you with the gryphons?"

Unlike before, there was understanding now, the soft lilt of grief in his tone that echoed the ache inside of her. And beneath the glassy sorrow in his gaze, a red haze of anger burned where it hadn't been, a slow fire that she had ignited.

"Yes, it was the gryphons," she answered. "And...the fact that I believed I was leaving. It felt like we had too much unfinished business, and I had no control over anything."

Isander sighed, and she could taste the *birali* on his breath. "You have more control than you realize."

"I'm a servant, Isander." She waved her shackled wrist to remind him.

"And you're a fighter. You know that sometimes when you have the least control...there's a breath of a moment that opens up for you. A chance to take back the balance, to bend it in your favor. All you have to do is take it."

She couldn't argue with him. And she wasn't sure if they spoke of gryphons, of her Servitude, or of something else entirely...

The pressure of his hands on hers grew more noticeable. Nothing lay between them now. Every moment he didn't move away from her, her body pulsed with the need to be closer to him. Their minds had connected, and he had felt something she had experienced.

It left her aching for more.

The way his eyes drifted to her mouth and lingered there told her it was what he wanted, too.

His voice was husky as he said, "Do you mind if I—"

Farren wrapped her hands around the gilded folds of his chiton and tugged him down, warmth blossoming through her as their lips connected. He pulled her close, his hand finding her head and cradling it as delicately as he had her portrait. Embers burned low in her belly. What she wanted from him—what she wanted to feel, to see, to touch—caused her face to flame. She pressed her hands against his chest until he reluctantly pulled back with a smoldering, impatient look.

"Isander, we shouldn't be doing this. The queen wouldn't—"

"We are just kissing. And we are in your room, so no one will know."

"Unless they see you leaving." She bit her lip. The risk of discovery was almost as tantalizing as the kiss itself, and it surprised her. Not because she had never had secret trysts before, but because that part of her life—that part of who she was—had disappeared long ago with Desmond's attack. Or so she had thought. Perhaps it was that she was already angry at being trapped in the fortress, and this was a way of breaking out from her entrapment. But she liked Isander—prince or no—and liked what he could do with his hands.

Her heart ran wild as a hare pursued by a hawk. Once they had each other's bodies, would anything else remain burning?

He kissed her again, and her thoughts scattered. He was a lure for her, one that made her forget where she was, and all she wanted was to chase him. Especially if chasing him felt as good as the kisses he started planting down neck. Her mind buzzed with the scent of him, dark and clean and utterly forbidden.

"Isander?"

"Hm."

"Do you sleep with all the women you paint?"

She could feel him smile against her neck.

"Never."

Before she let her mind slip into the abyss of pleasure, she wondered if it was true.

# TWENTY-FIVE

ISANDER LEFT SOMETIME WHILE she slept, and when she woke the next morning, her bed felt cold as a winter's morning. She sniffed the sheets, seeking out the prince's clean smell—a scent that reminded her of a warm breeze twining down a mint-filled mountainside. The memories of the past night grew closer as she sank her nose into the pillow.

He had been surprisingly tender. Fastidiously attuned to every detail of her body. The way her hair slithered just so between his fingers, the sleek muscles sculpting her back, how his hand fit perfectly around the mound of her breast. He had blessed her with kisses and words, and she had lost herself in it as a honeybird in a pipeflower—drinking deep of the warm sweet insistence of Isander's hands and mouth and...

*It was real*, she told herself. *Every blissful, heated moment of it was real.*

And temporary. She had let herself go for a time, wrapped in his arms and the hard press of their bodies together. And it wouldn't happen again. She was certain Isander felt the same way; his leaving in the middle of the night only proved that it would be something they would probably pretend never happened.

But as she dressed, a knock sounded on her door. A servant left a tray outside, and the scent of *birali* welcomed her as she lifted it into her room. Spread next to the steaming cup of tea, Isander had sent a round of flatbread, a little dish of olives, and a quick sketch of her profile, sleeping. She set it on her desk and stared at the drawing.

Maybe this was Isander's way of saying thank you. After all, he had sent her breakfast before. It didn't mean that something significant had happened between them.

Regardless, she sat and enjoyed the small meal, grateful for the way the *birali* woke her mind and bolstered her for the task ahead. Today was the day her training with Naronimus would begin.

When the sun peeked through her window, she left for the mating chamber where training would take place, lingering outside the kitchen for a moment to listen to gossip. No one mentioned Isander coming or going from her room, thank the Enchanters.

The mating chamber, an expansive room set partly into the ground, was similar to the other gryphon chambers. There was only one door, and the windows—located high above—were barred. Camilla had told her that the chamber used to be a granary before the queen had it converted, removing the window panes and barring it in—much like a dungeon. Slanted grids of flaxen morning light fell over the walls and dirt floor. Beneath a massive wooden beam stretching clear across the chamber, fat silver-blue fish circled inside a dingy pool lined with stones. The chamber was otherwise bare and desolate, not at all the kind of place that Farren imagined gryphons would enjoy finding a suitable mate—unlike the mountainous wilderness of the Blades where wild gryphons lived.

Prince Cato led her inside the chilled stone walls, and shock swept through her at the sight of Naronimus, standing like a huge, grizzled statue next to Camilla.

"Camilla!" Farren fought the urge to grab the girl. "Come away from him."

"No, it's alright, you don't need to worry."

"I really don't think—"

"I'm fine." Camilla let out a breath. "Naronimus didn't hurt me. We have an understanding."

"That's all well, but he isn't exactly trustworthy—"

"Farren." Cato stepped forward, his tone soft.

She glared at him but bit her tongue.

Camilla smiled tentatively and turned to Cato. "He came without complaint."

"That's good," Cato said. "He's had enough time to process the news from the queen about his behavior. Maybe he'll be easier to work with today."

"Doubtful," Farren commented, crossing her arms as she gave Naronimus an assessing look. He did the same to her, of course. Could he already feel her rising anger?

Cato scrubbed a hand over his mouth. "Listen, I know that Naronimus hurt your family, and that this is hard for you. But we've been given an order. You need to put away whatever feelings you have toward him, and try to make this work."

"I think I should speak with the queen, tell her what happened to my family. Maybe she'd understand."

"She won't care, Farren. Naronimus hurt my family, too, and did that make her care? It only gives her more reason to have him killed. No, talking to the queen won't make a difference in this. She's already made up her mind."

"Farren," Camilla said, taking her hand. "We're here to help you. We'll work at it together, okay? You don't have to do this alone."

Farren squeezed the girl's hand. "You shouldn't be here, Camilla. You should be doing fun things, like sneaking sweets from the kitchen and playing snake bones with the other servants' children."

"Or hiding away in the dovecot?" Camilla suggested with a wistful smile. She shook her head. "I would rather be here. Just in case you and Cato try to kill each other."

They all laughed at that, and a bit of the tension eased from her shoulders. Naronimus had begun pacing the outer edge of the chamber. Despite her hatred, her fear of him still needled her. What would he do to her? To Camilla? Would she be able to see it coming next time? Delphi had told her not to give in to what he wanted. To see her feelings, but not fall into them. She wasn't sure she could.

From the darkness swirling in her mind, she sought out an image—the only one, perhaps, that gave her a mote of hope: Isander's bright, strong commander. The woman he thought she could be. *That* woman controlled her fear, because she controlled the gryphons. Farren took a deep breath, sensing the tenderness of her emotions: they were malleable, ever-shifting beneath her attention. Like water, they seeped into places they didn't belong. She needed to contain them. Store them in a vessel that couldn't be shattered.

She formed a vessel in her mind and poured it all inside. Searching the corners, she found more of it, and poured that in too. Only then did she touch the sphere of Naronimus's mind.

*Finally.* The acrid brimstone of Naronimus's impression burned into her, igniting little fires that she forcibly stamped out.

*The queen wants us to work together*, Farren said.

*I've heard. Although I'm not sure why she chose you.* He sent a wave of doubt and pity, and came to stand beside Cato, tail dipping left and right like a swallow snatching gnats from the air.

*She threatened to kill you*, Farren told him, sending his pity back at him.

*So why not let her?*

The question startled her. *You don't care if you die?*

*Better dead than shackled here. I'm old, and tired.*

Farren snorted. *You don't look it.*

Naronimus flicked an ear. *Neither threats nor flattery will convince me to work with you.*

*Is that what you were in a hurry to tell me?*

*I'd like to get back to my midday meal in my chamber.* He sent a vibrant image of a half-gutted, decapitated mistfish and accompanied it with the feeling he had while shredding its translucent wings and viscera.

The sensation was meant to disgust her, no doubt. Luckily, Farren was used to the sensation of birds decimating their prey and had had much practice watching gryphons doing the same since starting her Servitude.

*Cato wants you to work with me*, she said.

Naronimus, apparently bored, stood and walked to the pool across the chamber, where fat, silver-blue fish swam in the depths.

*He told me about your magic*, Farren prodded.

The gryphon closed their runebond and cast a long look at Cato, apparently conversing with him privately. The prince's face grew tight with worry and then quickly changed to irritation before he turned away, shaking his head.

Naronimus leapt up to the long beam spanning above the pool, his talons and claws grasping at the deeply scarred wood. The crisscross of shadows and light from the window fell on the beast's back and hind quarters, and Farren glimpsed the wiry patchwork of scars along his legs and neck.

She bit her cheek and glanced sidelong at the prince. Holding her breath, she touched Naronimus's mind once more, and he opened to her. *What if I could convince you to work with me?*

Naronimus watched the fish swim in slow, hesitant circles below him. *I'm not interested.*

Farren let out a huff. *You would rather die than try?*

*I'm not afraid of your queen.*

*You don't think she would go through with it?* she asked.

Naronimus sent her something akin to amusement. *I know she would.* A vibrant impression shot into her: the queen laughing as she stood over the bloody remnants of a body. *I killed her brother, and that's how she reacted.*

Farren remembered the story Cato had told, that Naronimus had lashed out at his uncle, Anaxis, after suffering abuse. Farren clenched her hands, struggling to understand. *Then why aren't you afraid? You don't fear death?*

*I don't fear something that won't happen*, he answered.

*You seem to think you're in control here*, Farren said, her annoyance threatening to rise with their circular talk. *That you can stop the queen from killing you.*

He looked at her pointedly, his ears twitching in slender blades of golden light as he sent her a wave of contempt. *I am in control.*

*Yet, you're still here. Shackled, as you said.*

Naronimus's tail whipped back and forth over the beam, and as he stretched out his wings—an intentional display of his might—Farren saw the way he looked toward Cato, and it reminded Farren of how two nestling hawks regarded each other just before taking flight from the nest. A bit resentfully, but also something edging toward attachment.

A thought struck her. *You stay for him.*

One of Naronimus's talons slipped, and his claws dug deeper. Wood flaked into the pool.

No, he said. *The prince doesn't need me.*

*Not even to save him from his mother?*

His ears pressed back as hot embers of rage blew into her. *You know nothing, human.*

Farren beat back the embers, cooling herself with a steady pattern of breath in and breath out—a technique her father had taught her when dealing with an irritable hawk. Enchanters, but she wished he was there with her. He more than anyone could help her deal with this awful creature. Her father had always remained calm, no matter how maleficent the hawk.

What was it, then? Was Naronimus's magic faulty? Was it something more than saving Cato from his mother? Why else would he stay? If his manipulative magic was everything Cato said it was, he could use it to convince the servants to free him. To convince Cato to...

Knowing buzzed through her as she grasped the truth. *You don't want to use your magic on him.*

Naronimus bristled, and in one giant leap he cleared the pool and landed ten feet from her. *Just like every other useless human. Too much prying. Too much poking.*

As he came closer, Farren forced down her hatred of him. She avoided thinking of Desmond or the attack, avoided considering all the ways she could hurt the beast, the ways he could hurt her. Those things she had sealed in the vessel. They wouldn't serve her now.

Farren clenched her hands against the cold fear trying to claw into her. She called up the image of the commander that Isander had seen in her. Shoulders back, head up, and legs braced for impact. Mind sharp as a talon.

*What if I could set you free without Cato?* Farren asked him.

Naronimus didn't stop his approach until he was a few arm-spans away. Farren could feel herself freezing up, just like last time, and inhaled deeply, allowing her breath to pool into the tense parts of her, to form the calm stillness she wanted to feel.

*Why would you help me?* Naronimus asked.

*I don't have much of a choice. The queen threatened me, too.*

*With execution?*

*Lashings*, Farren said. *And no pay.*

Naronimus snorted, blowing air through his beak. *That doesn't sound like much of a threat.*

Farren grit her teeth. *It is, and so is your execution. It would change things for all of the gryphons.*

His golden eyes bored into hers, and she allowed her feelings of protection toward Torch to simmer through their runebond. She saw the moment he understood as his ears twitched back—a slight, brief flicker. There was something else in the movement, a fragile thread in the runebond she couldn't quite grasp before it ebbed away.

*You will be caught if you try*, Naronimus said.

*I'm making a plan.* She didn't elaborate but sent him the wide impression of the wheat fields on the north side of Alidonia, outside the fortress walls where there was open sky and the feel of the wind on her arms. The city, of course, surrounded the river on either side, but if he escaped to that part of the island at night...no one would know. He could fly off, unseen, to wherever he wished beyond the city.

*Where is that field?* he asked.

*Not far from here. Just north of the fortress.*

His tail slithered on the stone floor.

*You won't have to use your magic on Cato*, Farren said.

His breath streamed out like bellows on a fire. *When?*

A *few weeks*, she replied, *before the prince's birthday feast. We'd have to work together until then, so the queen doesn't suspect anything. And we cannot tell anyone our plan. Especially Cato.*

She met Naronimus's trenchant gaze. He tried to wedge their runebond wider, but Farren kept a hold of it, every ounce of her unwilling to reveal the secrets that must remain hidden. For Torch, for her brother, and for all the gryphons. Her body quivered with the effort, but unlike last time, she felt steady enough to hold onto what little control she had.

*Then let's begin*, he stated.

*One more thing. When you are free, you must promise to leave humans alone. Forever.*

*You don't have to worry about that. I want nothing to do with your kind.*

The words snapped hot and restless at her mind, and Farren quickly narrowed their runebond.

*It seems to me you want to kill them very much*, she said. Would the City Watch be enough to keep him away? Was he malicious enough to try evading them?

Naronimus blew air from his beak and shook his head, causing dust and a few stray feathers to whirl from his great head. *I'm not fool enough to waste any more time on humans, should I have freedom.*

Farren pursed her lips, seeking in his words some sort of deception, but she found none. As if sensing her doubt, Naronimus moved closer to her, forcing her to crane her head. Her heart beat so hard it shook her body, but she refused to flinch or step away. The stench of fish nearly made her gag as his hot breath flooded over her. Silvery fish scales flecked his beak, which arched down to a spear-like point a few hand-spans above her head. Was this what Des had seen just before Naronimus had attacked him? Farren narrowed their runebond to a needle's width, forcing thoughts of her brother back into the vessel.

*You must promise me*, Farren said. *Otherwise, no deal.*

Feathers rustled as he gently lifted his wings to expose the creamy feathers beneath. *I promise that if I have turned into such a miserable wretch as to waste my freedom by coming back here, you can kill me yourself.*

Farren inhaled sharply, but before she could respond, Naronimus went on.

*It's best done with an arrow or blade to the heart, with no hesitation.* With a bob of his head, he swiveled his beak down to touch the side of his chest. The spot was close to the bony protrusion of his keel, but not protected by it. He lifted his head once more to peer at her, as if he waited for her to acknowledge understanding.

He was serious.

Well, so was she. I *will not hesitate.*

# TWENTY-SIX

"HE'S AGREED TO TRAIN," Farren informed Cato. Naronimus had returned to the beam over the pond, his eyes glittering as he studied the fish, but one ear swiveled in their direction.

"Really," Cato said, crossing his arms.

Camilla sighed in relief. "It's a good thing, Cato."

The prince fell silent, and the feathers inked on his forearms bulged as he stared intently at Naronimus, apparently communing with him privately. An aggravated huff a moment later showed that he hadn't gotten anywhere with that, either. "Why did he agree to it?"

"He doesn't want to die." Farren forced conviction into her tone.

Cato's prickly silence was too tenuous to trust. She needed to be sure he didn't pry in case Naronimus decided to reveal their secret.

"Are you jealous that I was able to convince him, when you were not?"

Cato scowled. "Of course not. I just don't understand how you, of all people—"

Camilla put a hand on his arm, and he bit his tongue.

How much should she tell Cato? If she stayed closer to the truth now, would the final truth be easier to digest, once he learned it? Farren's stomach tightened. His feelings about it didn't matter, because he would never understand what she was planning to do.

"I think I convinced Naronimus it was in his best interest," she said. "Perhaps I can convince the queen to use him only for good. After all, she doesn't have the ability to use him the way I do."

She was well aware of how she suggested Naronimus was a power to wield and control. It might upset Cato—his eyes flashed at her words—but it was the truth, because that was exactly how the queen saw the gryphons, and Cato needed to hear it.

"The queen always finds a way to get what she wants," Cato seethed. He fell silent once more, but Farren could tell by his rigid stance that he argued with Naronimus.

Her heart raced at the risk she had taken, giving a part of her plan to Naronimus. She would never trust Naronimus completely, but she hoped to the Enchanters that she could rely on his avid interest in freedom—and his love of Cato—to keep their plan a secret.

"We need to begin," Farren said. "You can go brood about your insecurities up there." She indicated the open, barred windows cut into the wall high above them, accessed by a separate stairwell in the mews: the observation area for mating pairs.

"I'm not insecure—" Cato began, but Camilla cut him off again with a muttered word, and then they left.

At least he listened to Camilla's reason. Alone with Naronimus, she sucked in a fortifying breath and opened a runebond to the beast once more.

*You sent the girl away*, Naronimus snapped, giving a short burst of his wings as he leapt onto the floor, talons and claws sinking into the dirt. Dust billowed as he folded his wings into his sides.

*She's not safe here with you*, Farren said.

*Who else will we practice on?*

Farren stared at him. For some reason, she hadn't realized they would need to practice on *someone*. She thought through what they needed to accomplish: somehow demonstrate to the queen that Farren could use Naronimus to influence other people. More than that, as she had to show she could *control* the beast.

Of course they would have to practice on other people. Or...

*Why not try another animal*, she suggested.

Naronimus flicked his ears back. *Do you always dip your talons in first?*

*I like to learn things without hurting others.*

He gave a skeptical twitch of his tail. *Is that true when you fight with other humans, too?*

*How do you*— she cut herself off. When Anisha had gotten injured and their minds had melded together, he must've seen some of the times she fought. *Fighting is different*, she said. *You only learn by throwing yourself into the fray.*

*That is how magic works*, too, he countered.

*It didn't work very well last time you did it. My goal is to not hurt anyone.* She held Naronimus's glare. *Your magic is more nuanced than that, anyways. You can't just be rage all the time.*

*Why not? Rage is more potent than the others, and has far more interesting results.* He preened some errant feathers that had rumpled from his wings.

*Devastating consequences, you mean.* She could hardly believe how twisted his perception was. Most people had a moral lens through which they viewed the world. Naronimus, it seemed, had none. Perhaps no gryphons did. *Rage isn't what will free you.*

Naronimus, apparently bored with where their conversation was going, finished preening and stretched, the muscles in his hindquarters bulging. *If not rage, then what? Submission?*

Farren scrambled to think of what the queen would want. They needed to learn quickly, to practice whatever it was the queen would find most useful. *Devotion. Trust. Would that be too difficult for you?*

In answer, Naronimus snapped their runebond closed. Great, now he was obstinately refusing to—

A fuzzy feeling blossomed in her chest. It started as she looked at Naronimus, then expanded, warming her from head to toe. She liked Naronimus. Loved him, in fact. He was strong and intelligent and would protect her no matter what. He was like a father figure, or a king, someone who could lead her to her highest dreams, if only she followed him.

He wanted her to bend the knee, to show her devotion to him. Her loyalty. With barely a waver, she felt one leg bend, and she looked up at him, high and mighty above her. She had never seen a beast so beautiful, wings radiant in the light slanting through the windows above. It was enough to convince her that no one should threaten him. If they did, they would see the edge of her sword.

A moment later, the feeling fled. Farren gasped. Her own feelings—dark rage, shock, and fear—spiraled up with such speed that her stomach flipped. She rose from her sickening pose, swallowing back bile as her normal awareness returned. Who she was, what she wanted...everything that he had so easily made her forget.

Like Desmond's attack. Her fear and hatred of gryphons.

Her head swam. She heard a rustle beside her, and realized that Naronimus had neared. He sat calmly while she regained her composure.

When she opened her runebond—wide enough for the smallest of thoughts to pass through—he asked if she was satisfied.

*I think I'm going to be sick.*

*That is what you wanted. Would you rather I practice on the girl?* He twitched an ear up to the windows.

Despite herself, Farren glanced up at Camilla through the barred window, wondering if the girl would be able to handle the onslaught of Naronimus's magic better than she could. No wonder the queen wanted to use Naronimus. If she knew even a fraction of what Naronimus could do, if she could use it as a weapon, she would be the most powerful person in all the Enchanted realms. The thought sent a shiver down her spine.

*We'll find someone else*, Farren said, knowing she probably wouldn't handle another round without bringing up her breakfast.

*Very well.* He sounded pleased.

*But no harm is to come to anyone*, Farren stated, trying to sound stern even though she was shaken.

Silence answered her, doing nothing to dispel the leaden weight in her chest.

"Absolutely not." Cato's sharp voice cut down the hall, probably alerting everyone in the mews that they were fighting. Again.

"Practicing on other people is the only way to use his magic," Farren explained, clasping her hands together in front of her. Cato sat behind Horat's desk, looking far too comfortable in a chair that wasn't rightfully his. The conversation would've gone smoother with Horat, but the Lord Falconer had taken the afternoon to attend the city market.

"Why not have him practice on you?"

Farren's belly squirmed at the idea of Naronimus using his magic on her again. "That wouldn't work. The queen wants to see that I can use Naronimus, not that Naronimus can use *me*. She has to see me act as wielder of Naronimus's magic, otherwise she will never believe that he can be controlled."

Cato dragged a hand through his hair and sighed. "What about an animal? We can pull some mutts from the kennel—"

"Your mother doesn't want to control mutts," Farren snapped. "She wants to control people. And that is what we will show her."

"Since when are you so in league with what she wants?"

"Since she threatened to kill a gryphon."

He cocked his head, inspecting her as he would a treacherous insect. "I thought you disliked gryphons?"

"I do. Or, I did." Farren unclasped her hands to cross her arms. "If she kills Naronimus, how easy will it be for her to kill another, and another?"

Cato shook his head, his lips pressed into a thin line. "Why would she want to kill more gryphons? She wants them in her guard, remember?"

"She owns them, Cato. That means she can do what she wants with them when they displease her." Farren tugged the stool out and sat on it, burying her head in her hands.

Cato rustled. "She doesn't own them."

Slowly, Farren lifted her head and gazed at him, wondering how in the Enchanter's realm he could be so blind. He fussed under her stare, crossing arms over his broad chest and tucking his hands into his armpits. "She doesn't," he reiterated, as if that elucidated his extremely flawed reasoning.

"She owns them," Farren said quietly. "Just like she owns me, and even you." When something flared in his gaze, she almost smiled. There was a trail she could take easily, but it wasn't why she was here. Before he could offer a rebuttal, she continued. "When one of them doesn't perform to her expectations, it will be the end for that gryphon."

"She can't kill whichever gryphons she wants. They are far too valuable. And she cannot replace them, not with the only wild gryphons left being out in the Blades. She knows I would never help capture more."

A hysterical laugh caught in Farren's throat. "Cato, she wouldn't need to capture more! You're breeding them for her, so she'll never run out."

Cato swallowed, his gaze dropping down to the desk, and he started fiddling with his papers, rearranging them into neater stacks. "It still doesn't explain why you're helping her," he said in a low voice. He dropped a stack of pages casually to the side of the desk, causing them to shift into disarray once more.

"I'm not helping her," Farren bit out. "I'm following her orders. Maybe I don't want lashings and a year without pay. Besides those obvious reasons, I don't trust what will happen if she follows through with her threat to Naronimus."

No one had the power to protect the gryphons from Queen Aurelia, and it meant that Torch would never be safe. Anaxis had been the mallet that had warped Naronimus's mind and rune-made soul. Would the queen grow to be like that? And if so, would it change Torch, altering his bright, curious mind into one that was twisted and bitter like Naronimus's?

"I don't trust that..." She swallowed past a sudden tightness in her throat. "I am concerned that if another gryphon slips up and makes a mistake, the queen might decide he or she is unfit for the guard. Do you really want a culture of execution here? Is that any different than how Anaxis would have ruled, had Naronimus not killed him?"

Cato went very still at her words, and his jaw worked as he stared hard at her. "My mother is nothing like my uncle."

"Yet both would put gryphons in danger," Farren said, her voice rising a notch. "Both have threatened them."

He glared at her, unmoved. She had been too careless with the prince, too callous by far about the gryphons. Her bullheadedness had eliminated any ease that might've existed between them, and he would never believe that she could change her views on gryphons. She needed him to understand, so she said the words that burned brightest in her heart, even though he wouldn't accept them. "I can't let anything happen to Torch."

His expression softened and his shoulders sank down from his neck. "It's about Torch, then?" His words cradled a sliver of hope that shivered through her.

She nodded, not trusting herself to speak.

He blew out a breath and closed his eyes. "Fine. Use one or two of the recruits." He looked at her once more, and when he spoke, his voice had the strength of a worn leather leash that refused to yield to the tug and lash of a bating hawk. "But they are to wear armor at all times."

Cato reluctantly helped her gather the recruits, making sure they voluntarily participated in the exercise and overseeing the selection of armor. The other recruits trusted Prince Cato, and he had little trouble finding volunteers—Alexon, and the newer recruit, Virilus. Farren knew she wouldn't have had such luck.

By the time they arrived at the gryphon yard, it was late afternoon and Naronimus was pacing a track around the iron grate dome as he always did.

Farren took a moment to breathe and gather memories and feelings into her vessel, then touched the sphere of his mind.

*You'll get out of here soon enough*, she told him. She despised how much her body tensed when she saw him. Things would perhaps be more civil between them now, but would her fear ever subside?

*Is it wise to be practicing here? To be showing them how to use me?*

*That is the whole point*, Farren said. *We'll show her enough so that she decides not to kill you. Then, we'll set you free.*

*She will send people to hunt me.*

*You think she could find you? Go somewhere far. Like the Blades.*

Naronimus continued his restless saunter. *Aren't there humans in the Blades? An entire city?*

*The Blades are impenetrable stones, there's no city hidden inside of them. Delphi said there are people around the Blades, but the Blades are enormous. You can find somewhere quiet.*

He had nothing to say to that. It was almost reassuring that Naronimus felt uneasy about the queen witnessing his magic. Maybe he did have a conscience, after all. Too bad he hadn't used it with Desmond. Farren stuffed the thought back into the vessel.

Naronimus finally ceased his pacing as they began training. Alexon—sucking hard on his honeyed candy—and Virilus listened as Farren spoke, shifting uneasily in their heavily padded leather armor. Cato had overseen their armor, but Farren had demanded they wear metal helmets. The men sweat beneath their weight.

As they worked, her skin prickled under the sensation of being watched—a feeling she forcefully banished from her mind.

First, Farren asked Naronimus to have the recruits pledge loyalty to her.

Alexon and Virilus bowed, and Alexon spoke first.

"My Majesty is the most beloved creature, shining as a star in a soup pot. My sword as your hair is the most silken tower in all the realms..."

*Naronimus, why is he speaking in riddles?*

A mental grunt and their runebond twinged and sharpened.

"By your good graces," Virilus interrupted Alexon. "Please accept my sword so that I may fight in your honor."

*Better*, Farren said.

Next, she had Naronimus march them in formation along the stone paths of the gryphon yard. At one point, Alexon stumbled and looked around, confusion filling his features.

*Naronimus—*

*One moment.*

A pause, and their runebond rippled as he did something with his magic. Alexon began marching again, this time moving his legs stiff as a puppet.

*It is difficult to keep both their feelings and beliefs synchronized,* Naronimus explained.

*Do you need to rest?*

*Of course not.*

*Let's try something different, then,* Farren said. *Can they demonstrate subservience to me?*

Alexon and Virilus raced to her side, their eyes warm and fuzzy. Virilus pawed at her hair and Alexon bent so close she could smell the honeyed candy on his breath.

"Such beautiful skin. Radiant," Alexon murmured.

"Your hair is too fine to be bound back," Virilus said, tugging her binding out so forcefully that her scalp shrieked. More tenderly, he worked her dark hair out of its braid. Alexon gasped as it fell loose.

*Naronimus, what is—*

"Like a night sky," Alexon breathed.

"A wondrous black ocean," Virilus said.

"Spectacular dark waves," Alexon agreed, studying her hair as if it were the vista of the Kithyrian Mountains.

*Why all the focus on my hair?* Farren asked, resisting the urge to pull her hair out of their fingers.

*Would you rather I have them compliment your human baldness?*

*That wouldn't be much of a compliment. I said* subservience *to me*, she told Naronimus. Not...*adoration.*

Naronimus scoffed. *What is the difference?*

*Subservience shows respect and reverence. They would never dream of touching my hair.*

*Submissiveness, you mean,* Naronimus corrected.

*In simpler terms, yes. But it's important that they believe me superior to them.*

Through their runebond, his magic shivered. The recruits stepped back, and as they looked at her, their expressions unfolded into something—

Breathtaking. Their eyes grew wide and bright, their faces loosening as self-awareness receded beneath glimmering awe. As if they saw the world in her. She was Queen. No, Enchantress.

"Take the knee," she ordered. They did as she asked.

If it weren't for the queen's Enchanted necklace, Naronimus could have the very same effect on Queen Aurelia. The queen would bend a knee and look at her with this awe, forgetting herself and her title and everything else. How far could Naronimus go before the queen realized it was all a lie?

*That's enough*, she told Naronimus, wishing for one of Alexon's honeyed candies to wash the sourness from her mouth.

Alexon and Virilus blinked, and as the wonder dropped from their features, a cold dread took its place. Virilus' blond curls trembled as he shoved to his feet, and Alexon sputtered as if choking on his candy. The looks they gave Naronimus and herself were full of fear.

"I know that was awful," Farren said hurriedly. "But thank you. We will need to practice again tomorrow if you're up for it—"

"But y—you were different," Alexon said, pale as a dove. "I wasn't—"

"Me," Virilus finished for him. The two looked at one another, then back at her. "It's not right. What kind of magic does that?"

"Naronimus's magic," Farren said grimly. "You don't have to do it again, if it made you that uncomfortable. I'm sure Prince Cato could find other recruits ready to take on the risk of working with the beast."

Virilus considered her words, then puffed his chest. "Prince Cato can count on my help."

"Yes, of course," Alexon added a bit faintly, "anything the prince needs."

As they left to remove their armor, Farren prodded Naronimus. *What would the queen do if she used us and then her people hated her? Could you hold sway over them for longer?*

Naronimus dipped his head into a fountain, gulping water. *Perhaps an hour or two, but no more. Magic takes a toll, you know.*

*Really? You seem no worse for the wear...other than being thirsty.*

*The longer I use my magic, the more my head aches. The more my head aches, the less I can focus my magic.* Naronimus lifted his head, beak and feathers dripping. *But you said I would be gone before she could actually use me.*

*That's the plan.* The plan. She would have to work on that. And on how she would explain things to Cato if he kept pressing for answers.

After the prince took Naronimus away, Farren bound her hair once more and sat next to one of the fountains, considering how exactly she could release Naronimus without him using magic on Cato. The easiest thing, perhaps, would be to remove Cato from the situation. Give him a reason to head out of the fortress for a time, long enough for Naronimus to get far away—

Something sharp prodded her shoulder, and she jerked, wincing as it dug in deeper.

"Careful now." Scipio's words slithered over her, a low warning. He held a wooden knife, its blunt point bruising her shoulder as he forced her to remain seated.

Farren tried to compose her features. "I'm surprised I didn't hear you approach. Usually, your arrogance is louder."

Scipio pretended not to hear. "We're about to begin practice with weapons." He sneered, glancing at the mews. "But I see you've already started with yours."

Farren's arm throbbed, and she fought the urge to bat the knife away. "Oh? Should I call him back to join us?"

Something flashed in his slate-gray eyes, and the tip of the wood knife twisted. "I think that wouldn't be very fair for your fellow recruits. They've all seen the damage you and Naronimus can do. In fact, it looked like you two were getting along splendidly just now," he remarked. "Tell me, did it feel pleasurable to have people kneeling before you?"

"I'm following the queen's orders."

Scipio nodded, his smile not reaching his eyes. "And I applaud you for doing what you should be. As long as you continue to do so. I wouldn't want you getting confused, wastrel, about your role here. Naronimus's power isn't for you, but for the queen."

"I assure you, I do not want Naronimus's power."

He gave her a considering look. "Well, I'm glad we cleared that up. But I'll be keeping a close eye on you in case you change your mind."

Heat flushed through her as the pain at her shoulder spread. "And here I thought you had more important things to do, being the queen's personal favorite."

His lip curled, and he pulled the knife away. "My job is to protect the crown, no matter how insignificant the threat."

"Strange, then, that the last two royals died so suddenly," she ventured. "Were you distracted by insignificant threats then?"

The *Canid* growled and flashed his teeth. "Just watch your step."

"Like a dancer," Farren replied, rising to her fullest height—nearly a foot below Scipio's.

She forced ease into her gait as she headed toward the other recruits entering the yard, breathing through the pain in her shoulder. Well, if she had thought Naronimus's release difficult before, it would be even more challenging with Scipio lurking around. Especially if she failed to hear the steady tread of his swagger.

She would have to be more vigilant than ever, and focus on her promise to Naronimus—and make a plan when she was safely alone in her room. One thing was certain: her plan could not fail, because at the very least, it would mean imprisonment for her, and at its very worst, a queen with power far beyond what one person should ever hold.

# TWENTY-SEVEN

Days of training passed and blurred into weeks. The air began to turn cool with the coming of autumn, but the gardens in the gryphon yard remained full of vibrant blossoms, kept that way by the queen's relentless bouquet of *Planteri*.

Farren had missed Calipion's Sun Festival in midsummer due to being in the Kithyrian Mountains, and now missed Tyrili's Festival—which Horat did not give her permission to attend in the city. At home, the village would be adorned with garlands of nuts and berries, and all the forested hills around them would be flushed gold and amber as pika trees prepared for dormancy. The festival itself, Farren missed sorely. The sweetly spiced potatoes, warming cider and birch beer, not to mention the silly apple-bobbing she and Des always did together. There would be a great hunt with the hawks in the mountains, and the entire village would share the quarry over bonfires and stories. Then, of course, there were the fighting matches, a tradition that Farren treasured with the turning of each season.

Instead of the beautiful mountainsides, all she could see were the immense black walls of the fortress and the never-fading gardens. Even the air remained humid and cool, the crisp scent of autumn lost beneath the tang of the river. It was no wonder the days had started to run together. First, she endured rough sparring with Scipio, then suffered training with Naronimus, and by the end of the day she would drop into bed, exhausted. It wasn't just the physical challenges that took it out of her.

Hating Naronimus—or rather, hating him and holding it back—wore her thin. When she wanted to argue, she didn't. When she longed to push him out of her head, she kept her runebond open. Whenever she wanted to remind him of what he did to Desmond, she chose not to. Not because he didn't deserve to see it, but because she knew that she might lose the little control she had.

Her plan to free the gryphons had to come first, not her feelings. Her father would've told her the same thing if he were there. Personal feelings had no place in the training of a difficult hawk, even when the hawk inflicted wounds.

Farren managed to learn about some of the gryphons by listening to the other recruits and visiting with them herself. Blessed Camilla came with her the first few times, but after that, Farren was comfortable enough to go alone, and even brought them gifts she had purchased from a visiting peddler. She learned that gryphons enjoyed collecting items that were related to their magic. Grit, with his ability to manipulate stone, had a wonderful collection of colorful rocks lining the shelves along his walls. Elya could move air, and her chamber was filled with wind baubles: wind-tubes and pipes, pinwheels made of thin slips of wood, and rafters filled with different colors and sizes of chimes. Farren gifted her a set of silk streamers that danced whenever Elya tossed a breeze up to the rafters. A pregnant female, Phynx, could start a fire, but her vanity made a mirror the perfect gift. The gryphon liked looking at herself so much that she admitted to Farren she dreamed about flying over a lake just so that she could watch her reflection move along its surface.

They were nothing at all like Naronimus.

And the more she spoke with them, the more they confided in her about other things. The noise of the mews bothered Hylas to the point of plucking out his own feathers. Bald spots marred his feathered chest, and Cato had to apply a healing salve to the open sores every day. When Farren runebonded with Calipsa, who shrieked incessantly, the gryphon shared with her the pain of her joints. Only a recruit she bonded with was kind enough to come to her chamber to rub soothing ointment on her talons and wings.

Eralius, a young male gryphon, had such deep dreams about hunting that his body would waken while his mind slept, resulting in frequent injury to himself as he tried to fly in his chamber. He would often wake to find himself clawing the wood door as if he were attacking a bear.

More gryphons complained of aching wings and stiff legs. Like Hylas, others couldn't stand the noise, making them irritable or loud, which only added to the chaos. Several of them admitted to destroying the items in their chambers—baubles and gifts from recruits, or bedding, or anything they could get their beaks and claws on.

Farren knew they were all symptoms of one thing: captivity. She had seen it in captive hawks, and exercise was the best way to combat it. Well, exercise and hunting. But the latter would be impossible, at least for now. Still, she encouraged them to stretch their wings and asked where they would go if they could get away. The river, some said. Others wanted the deep forests to the east, where they could fly into the sunset or perch high on the steep mountains of the Blades.

She wasn't yet ready to propose her plan to them, but each time they spoke to her about their dreams, the words and impressions they shared caused a small spark of hope to rise in them.

At night, Farren couldn't escape the scent of Isander that lingered on her bedsheets. Day after day stretched by with no word from him, and then one night, she returned to her room after cleaning the gryphon nursery and found a neat letter folded on her pillow. She knew before she read it that it must be from Isander.

*I wish to see you again. Tonight. I know it is hard, but if there's any chance you could bring me one of the beasts you're most comfortable with, I would be eternally grateful.*

*Yours,*

*Isander*

She read it twice more, then tossed the note on her writing desk, biting her lip as she considered his request.

The painting he had given her was propped in the corner of her desk. Rather than the woman in the painting, she felt like the hawk on the woman's glove, leashed and owned by a situation she didn't want to be in. They had slept together, but of course, he still wanted to finish his painting. He probably would pretend as if none of it had happened, just a princely mistake or some foolish excuse.

Still, she brushed her hair and braided it tight to stay out of her face, then fetched Torch. Over the past few weeks, Horat had begun to trust her more and more as she followed orders and put in effort with Naronimus. She spent a significant amount of time with Torch when she wasn't training—taking him for walks around the yard and fountains, even falling asleep curled against him in the nursery after a particularly exhausting day—but hadn't taken him beyond the mews and gryphon yard yet. It would be good for him to get out and see new things, and she trusted him unequivocally not to hurt anyone. She had the letter from Isander, anyways, if anyone stopped her.

When Farren walked into Torch's chamber, he had just finished a meal with his siblings, who lounged around the chamber, full and sleepy by the warm hearth. Torch wasn't so sleepy, and her arrival made him jump around her feet, talons scratching tiny grooves in the stone.

*You are getting bigger*, she said, grinning as he cried out and dove between her legs, nearly pushing her over as he did so.

*Mama says I'm an expert at flying now. Watch what I can do!* He gallivanted away, spreading his wings and beating them fiercely while he ran. He lifted off the floor and had enough time to scramble to a stop before running into the wall on the other side of the chamber.

*We must get you out to the gryphon yard again*, Farren said. Prince Cato had begun allowing Delphi and her little ones a daily hour in the yard after guard training was over. Torch spent his brief time there switching between flying and using his magic. *I can try to convince the prince to give you an extra hour there if you come with me tonight. And if you behave yourself.*

*Where are we going?* he asked as she put the gryphon band on his leg and hooked it to a long, thick chain.

She sent him an impression of the prince's art chamber. *Just for a short while*, she reassured him.

His tail drooped. *No water?*

*Just paint*, she told him and realized with alarm that paint might be something he could control since it had water in it. *Which you must not use your magic on.*

*Paint?* His ears pricked toward her and he cocked his head.

Farren sighed and led him out of the chamber with a reassurance to Delphi that he would be back soon. Torch's stream of questions still hadn't let up by the time she reached the keep doors. Thankfully, Iana wasn't there this time. The guard read the letter she handed him and gave a brisk nod before leading them inside, past the expansive, evening-lit atrium. As they rounded a corner to a corridor, the guard bowed suddenly, and Farren looked past his shoulder to see Prince Cato.

Farren clutched the leash as the guard stepped aside to let the prince pass. Torch darted forward.

*Slow down!* She stumbled and cursed as Torch dragged her in front of the prince, who didn't notice them until Torch was nearly at his feet.

Although his face remained as stubbled as usual, he had begun to look a bit more rested these past weeks. Farren expected a reprimand for bringing a gryphon out of the mews, but Cato just blinked at her as if his mind struggled to emerge from whatever thoughtful depths they had been swimming in.

"Farren. What are you doing here?"

She pulled the leash tighter, urging Torch to return to her side. He did so, though very reluctantly. "I have a meeting," she told the prince. She hesitated, wondering how much she should tell him. "Your brother would like to paint him."

Thoughtfulness fled Cato's expression as something darker took its place. "Paint him? Where exactly?"

Heat crept into her cheeks. "In his art chamber."

He cursed and dashed a hand through his hair. "Did you ask Horat first?"

"No, I—"

"You can't just take gryphons wherever you please."

"But I've taken Torch out around the mews before, plus the yard, and didn't think it would—"

"It doesn't matter if Horat approved it before. This is different." He held out a hand for the leash.

Farren pursed her lips. He should be happy that she was making an effort to spend more time with a gryphon, even if it was one whom she already liked.

"The prince requested us. I don't wish to disappoint him."

"You think Torch is going to willingly sit still for a painting? How long will he have to sit for?"

Farren shrugged. "We will manage. He's curious about it."

The prince's face tinged a dusky red as his scowl dug deeper. "I keep telling him no for a reason," Cato said. "When forced to sit in a room, they get more aggressive, less predictable."

Farren absorbed this new information. "I can take him to the yard afterward and make sure he gets some exercise."

"I'm coming with you."

Farren stiffened. "To Isander's room?"

His eyes narrowed, and she realized she had used his brother's first name, again. Too informal.

Now her cheeks burned. "Come along if you wish. But you'll probably be more bored than Torch."

Cato dismissed the guard and led them up the stairs to Isander's chamber. Farren wished desperately that he would change his mind and turn around. She enjoyed being alone with Isander and wanted to see whether or not he would pretend nothing had happened between them. Now, with Cato tagging along, he most definitely would.

Cato rapped on Isander's door, looking like a bristling wildcat that had just discovered an intruder in its territory. Torch was picking up on Cato's anger—or whatever it was that made the prince's nostrils flare and the feathers marked on his arms ripple as he clenched his fists.

The door swung open. "Brother," Isander stated, carefully unemotional. He looked down the stairwell and met Farren's gaze with a smile—one that widened at the sight of the gryphon.

"We need to talk," Cato said, practically shoving his brother aside as he barged in.

"Of course," Isander said easily, but his mouth tightened. His beautiful, seductive mouth that she just wanted to kiss. Again.

Isander gave her a sly grin as he ushered her into his chamber, and Farren rushed to double-check that the window between them remained closed.

"Thank you for coming," he said into her ear, making her nape prickle. "But why did you bring *him*?"

"I didn't," she started to say, but Torch strained toward the window, so she shrugged helplessly at Isander and followed the gryphon's lead.

Torch barraged her with questions about the view of the River Kithyria and Malodai. Farren drank in the sight of giant dewfall trees, their green drooping branches brightening to butter-yellow with the touch of autumn, and focused on answering his questions while keeping an ear on the princes' discussion behind her.

"I told you I don't want the gryphons sitting in rooms," Cato said.

Farren glanced back and saw Isander bent over his table of art tools, briskly mixing brown paint in a wooden bowl. "It won't be for too long, brother. I will, of course, stop if the little gryphon becomes agitated."

"If he's agitated, he'll be harder to handle. That's exactly why I don't want gryphons cooped up in rooms. They're not meant to be inside the keep."

"What do you think will happen when the queen uses them for her guard?" Isander asked, his tone reasonable.

Cato only bristled more. "That's different. Torch isn't even trained yet. He's still half-wild."

"It's the only one Farren is comfortable with, I believe."

Farren swallowed as they both glanced at her. "I will stay runebonded to him the entire time," she told Cato. "And take him to the yard after."

"See?" Isander said. "You don't give her enough credit."

"You always do this." Cato's words cut toward his brother. "Twist things around until they are exactly how you want them. You never listen to me. You just do whatever you want."

"What I wanted was to paint them in the yard. But you didn't like that either."

"Because we use the yard for training, not posing for pretty pictures. And it's the same issue—I can't force my gryphons to sit still like that. It's unnatural."

"More unnatural than keeping them in a cage?"

Farren's brows lifted at Isander's rather fine point. She glanced sidelong. The *Felid* had his teeth bared, and his hands curled into claws at his sides, ready to scratch out his brother's eyes.

She narrowed her runebond with Torch. "Let's get on with the painting." She stood exactly where she had when Isander had painted her last and told Torch to lay next to her. She hoped Isander wouldn't try to get her to wear the fancy dress with Prince Cato there.

Isander gave her a warm smile. "Excellent, Farren, thank you. Cato, we can continue our discussion later if you'd like." He motioned to the door.

"I'm staying," Cato said as he crossed his arms.

Isander paused on his way to the easel, his jaw flexing. "I will be able to focus better without you here, brother. Your anger is rather...distracting."

"I find it hard to focus when one of my gryphons is out of the mews," Cato returned, pulling a chair out and seating himself stiffly.

Isander sighed and set his paints by the easel. He took in the sight of Farren and Torch, then adjusted the position of her arms and head. His fingers were light but insistent under her chin and lingered for a moment longer than necessary.

"Perfect," he murmured.

She looked for a hint of something more—some warmth that lingered from their night together weeks ago, and she found it in the way his eyes roved over her mouth. Then his gaze leapt up to hers, and his lips quirked.

"I haven't forgotten," he stated aloud, making Farren flinch.

She fought the urge to glance at Cato. Instead, she closed her runebond with Torch and took a moment to press her worries over Naronimus to the deep recesses of her mind. Then she opened the window that connected her to Isander.

*That's not what I'm wondering*, she said privately, fingers pressing into the cold, hard chain.

His smile deepened, and so too did the heat in his gaze. "After I paint, we can talk," he suggested aloud, and the way he said *talk* made her think of much different things than talking.

Face hot, she spent the next half hour immobile, holding the pose until Torch rose with a rush of curiosity toward the window panes as a flock of pigeons burst into the fiery glow of the setting sun.

Cato leapt up. "That's enough, Isander. He's had enough, clearly."

"He just wants a view of the sunset," Farren said before Isander could reply. She eased the tension from the chain, but Torch wandered from the window toward Isander's desk. She sent him a wave of calm, feeling his curiosity brim as he moved to an unexplored part of the room.

"It's time for him to get some exercise," Cato insisted, holding his hand out to Farren for the chain.

Isander waved a paintbrush at them, eyes still on his canvas. "I'm nearly done for now, Cato. Take him if you wish."

Relieved, Farren went to pass the chain to Cato, but just then, Torch darted forward, sending her a flare of mischievousness. The chain flew from her hand as he scuttled toward the art table, half-opening his wings as he stood on hind legs to peer into the wooden bowls of color.

*Torch, don't even—*

Streams of paint rose in glossy rivulets, winding higher and higher.

*Can I paint, too?* Torch asked. *Do I need paper? Mother told me all about paper and words and—*

"My paint," Isander said, staring open-mouthed at the spectacle quickly growing toward the ceiling.

Cato lurched toward the gryphon. "This is exactly what I was talking about!"

*Torch, put the paint back*, Farren demanded, but Torch's attention was already somewhere else. He darted underneath Cato's outstretched arms, chain rattling along the floor as he scampered to Isander's desk, apparently looking for paper.

*Torch, put the paint—*

Rivulets of paint collapsed and plummeted toward the bowls. As they landed, paint splashed the table and Cato with purple, blue, and brown. Farren scrambled after Torch's chain, watching with dismay as Torch used his beak to grab a book from Isander's desk.

"Torch!" Farren admonished as Cato swore aloud.

Torch spread his wings half-open and ran into the curtained changing area. Cato went after him, but not before a ripping noise resounded through the room.

"No!" Isander shouted, dropping his brush and sprinting to where Torch had hidden.

Farren cast Torch a spark of her anger and urged him to release the book. She sent him the impression that the book was absolutely forbidden, that he must not touch it. Despite Torch's burning shame, his insistent curiosity lit through her, and she tugged the curtain aside. Cato and Isander grunted and swore as they grappled the book from the gryphon.

*Drop it. Now*, Farren said. *Or we will not play in the fountains.*

Torch gave it up, ears slinking back as he emerged from behind the curtain. Farren fell to her knees, opening her arms as a wave of sadness hit her.

*I'm not angry at you*, she told him, warmth blossoming in her chest as he trotted straight into her arms. *And I'm so glad you listened to me.*

*I really want to visit the fountains*, he said tremulously.

*Yes, we can visit them tomorrow. But you must never steal another person's things.*

His tail tucked between his legs. She ran her hand between his ears, smoothing the feathers all the way to his back. Cato stood over them, his expression wary. She pushed to her feet.

"I'm sorry I dropped the leash. It won't happen again."

Cato shook his head and held his hand out for the chain. "This is exactly why—"

"Cut it, Cato," Isander barked. Scowling and tight-lipped, he examined the torn page of the book, which appeared to be blank. The unfamiliar look he wore made her skin prickle.

Cato took the leash and looked at the book over his brother's shoulder. "It's empty? Why—"

"None of your damn business." Isander snapped the book closed, and Farren glimpsed the cover, which held an odd rune she remembered seeing on the binding of one of his books before. It must've been the same book. He strode stiffly to his desk and returned the book to its neat row.

Farren continued speaking to Torch and found that he had been looking for paper, but once he had the book, he had simply been curious about what was inside. He had tried turning the pages with his beak but ripped them by accident. He quivered next to Cato, his wings half-open and beak gaping as he breathed heavily.

*He's not angry at you*, she reassured the gryphon, *just at his brother.*

*I don't like him much*, Torch said.

*Cato?*

*No, the other one.*

*Because he shouted at you?*

Torch didn't answer but sent her a wave of unease. *He has a book without words.*

*We use empty books sometimes, to write in.*

Torch shook his head as if to clear it and folded his wings down. *Can I go to the fountains now?*

*I will ask Cato.*

Cato's crumpled silk chiton dripped paint. Despite his appearance, he had grown very still while Isander returned the book to the desk, staying there even while Isander began cleaning the mess of paint from the table. The *chink* of bowls made him flinch, and he blurted, "Will you listen to me now and not force a gryphon to sit for you?"

"I will paint the gryphon until the piece is complete," Isander replied, his back turned to them.

Farren stood. "He wants to go to the fountains," she told Cato. "I'd like to take him myself."

Cato turned wild eyes on her. "After this?" he shook his head. "I will take him to the yard myself. And I don't want you bringing him here—"

"You will not hold this over Farren," Isander cut in, turning to face his brother. "She's following my requests and will continue to do so as long as she wishes."

"She's not *your* servant, but the qu—"

"Perhaps I'll have a word with Mother and you can take my place at the next three Council meetings. The one today only took three-quarters of the day," he said with irony.

Cato's knuckles whitened as they gripped the chain leash. "She would never agree to that."

"Really? The Council has been riddling her with questions about the gryphon program—when it will be ready, how safe it will be for the people, what exactly the gryphons will do—and who better to answer them aptly than yourself? Or, if you'd rather, I can simply remind her that if something ever happens to me, she'll only have you to inherit the throne."

Cato scowled and opened his mouth in retort.

"I'll be going now," Farren said. "As much as I adore watching you two squabble like roosters. Torch needs to get settled with his family."

Farren reached for the chain leash, but Cato pulled it away. "No. I will take him. You may return to the mews."

"I would like to stay with Torch. He's still frightened—"

"I will see to him." Cato's stony expression remained as he strode to the door. Farren runebonded with Torch and felt the faint shadow of Cato's prickly mind as the prince runebonded with the gryphon at the same time.

"I got it, Farren," Cato said shortly, apparently feeling her presence as well.

*Goodnight, Torch*, she said to the little gryphon, who sent her a wave of alarm at Cato's temper. *Maybe use your magic to cheer him.*

*Will I see you tomorrow?*

*Of course, silly.*

The door slammed shut behind them, and she stayed with Torch for a bit longer until the gryphon's mind eased as he headed for the yard.

Silence had grown in Isander's chamber, and she turned from the door. The elder prince had cleaned up the table, washed his hands, and stood near the darkened window, looking at her with cautious warmth. A faint pressure on the left side of her head, and she knew he wanted to connect.

"We can just talk," Farren suggested as she clasped her hands together.

"I know," he said, walking toward her. "But there's something more intimate about using my runeskill, and... I never get to use it this way."

Isander took her hand, wrapping her in his heat. *About earlier*, he said through the runebond, *when I told you I didn't forget about what we did. What were you wondering about?*

*Not whether or not you remembered*, she told him, repressing a chuckle. Speaking with him this way was more complicated than speaking to a gryphon. His feelings, warm and wary and excited, were as nuanced as hers.

*Then what were you wondering*? he asked.

*Whether or not it meant anything.*

*I hope it did*, he said, and then he kissed her hand.

How could a prince care for a mere servant? For someone who had come to the fortress by force?

*I'm not right for you*, she told him, her hope slipping.

*This feels right to me. Nothing else matters.*

And he pulled her so close that their bodies pressed like a glove to skin, and he bent his head to kiss her. When their lips met, she knew he was right. Every space between them was a pocket of cold. If she stopped touching him, her hands were empty and aching. She wanted the scent of him—the mingling of *birali* and musk—on her tongue, to breathe him into her lungs. Each stroke of his skin on hers sizzled along her nerves, and she ate it up.

Isander saw her the way she was and the way she could be: someone strong, commanding, and confident. She wanted to drink deep of that potion, to let it fill her. Even if it was forbidden, she would take it. She would take whatever he offered and give what she could in return. He knew her better than anyone living in the damnable fortress, and he still accepted her. He deserved her love. And she, Farren Blackburn, thought she might deserve his.

# TWENTY-EIGHT

OVER THE NEXT WEEK, Farren split her time between Naronimus and Scipio, holding in all her ugly feelings while throwing punches. At night, she spoke with the gryphons from the privacy of her bedchamber, continuing to learn more about them.

Delphi spoke to them as well, protecting Farren's identity while suggesting to them that there may be a point in the future where they could finally leave this place. Each time Delphi runebonded with her, Farren paced and sweat, waiting for word that a gryphon agreed to leave if given the opportunity to do so. Relief strung through her every time there was an affirmation. Hylas agreed first. Then Elya and Grit. Phynx, Eralius, and Calipsa had enthusiastically agreed and inquired more about the plan. To keep their plan a secret, Delphi wouldn't give them more details but worked with Farren to secure them a way out.

Farren would open each gryphon chamber door, and Hylas, who could manipulate sound, would dampen the noise of talons and claws. Delphi would help her lead the gryphons out of the mews. Naronimus—the only gryphon to whom Farren gave details besides Delphi—had agreed to manipulate any recruit or guard on duty in the mews when the time came to leave. The birthday feast would draw Cato far from the gryphon's magic. Carrying out her plan during the feast would also mean that Naronimus would be freed before the queen made her final decision about what to do with him.

Farren would lay in her bed in the dark, ruminating over all the ways it could go wrong. Eventually, she would fall asleep and wake bleary-eyed to start it all over again.

During one of her ruminating sessions, she had realized there still remained an issue: anyone from the fortress might be able to spot the gryphons leaving, especially if their rune animals were with them. The only gryphon who could help with that was Thella, and Farren hadn't yet spent time with that young gryphon. Her invisibility display during the Naronimus incident weeks ago had spurred a wave of interest from the recruits, which meant that she always had visitors and gifts.

But without Thella's invisibility magic, Farren's plan had a thread-thin chance of success. And Prince Isander's birthday feast—only two days away, on the eve of the Festival of the Forging—was fast approaching and left her little time to convince Thella to help with the plan. Part of her wanted to ask Delphi to speak with Thella, but that would do nothing to build trust between herself and the young gryphon, and they would certainly need trust if the plan was to succeed.

She finally found Thella alone one evening when the recruits were in the kitchens excitedly preparing for the feast. Thella was curled tight in a corner of her stone chamber. The faded glow of sunset washed through one high, pane-less window, lighting up row upon row of glass figurines, mirrors, and polished crystals lining shelves along the opposite wall. More crystals dangled like raindrops from the bare rafters above, sparkling and tinkling as they swung in a gentle breeze. Farren gazed at the splendor as she eased into the room.

Despite the beauty, a chill emanated from the walls. Thella lifted her head when Farren closed the door and opened a runebond. A shiver ran through her as the gryphon's fear trickled in.

*I will not hurt you*, Farren said.

Thella flashed her a memory: Farren and Naronimus lunging toward the recruits, rage filling their faces as they plunged ahead. Thella had known they meant harm and hadn't thought twice about leaping to protect the recruits, throwing out her magic to cloak them all with invisibility.

*I'm sorry for what happened*, Farren said, trying to steady her drumming heart as the impression cleared from her mind. *I never intended to cause the recruits harm. I was lucky you were there to protect them.*

*It was the right thing to do*, Thella replied, the impression of her words steady and assured.

The gryphon unfurled from the corner, wings fanning as she stood and shook the dust from herself. Gold-limned feathers rimmed a face as delicate and sharp as a dagger, and at her back, the feathers gave way to fur the shade of sun-lit wheat. She was smaller than the other gryphons, but elegant and poised. Glints of crystal-reflected light danced on her slender form.

*I didn't bring you a gift*, Farren said. She'd have to remember to get something the next time a peddler came by.

As daintily as a dancer, Thella stretched out the leading edge of a wing and brushed a string of crystals hanging from the ceiling. They twirled and tinked and scattered light all around the room.

*They are just trinkets. Mostly from the queen, gifted when my magic was born.* Thella tucked her wing back against her body. *I care far more for company.*

*What sort of company do you like?* Farren asked. *Glum like Cato, stern like Horat, or sweet like Camilla?*

*I'm not particular to that.* Thella came and sat in front of Farren, as calm as if they were sitting down to tea. *Why are you here?*

Farren hesitated, unsure where to begin with her request. *When you helped the recruits with your magic, you showed your devotion to humans. Unfortunately, not all gryphons feel this devotion.*

*You mean Naronimus. He is not like the rest of us. Just as you are not like the other recruits. But I heard that you are getting along with him better now. Is it true?*

Farren felt herself stiffen. *We are tolerating one another. But he hurt me deeply, and I cannot forget that.*

*He is ill-suited to human life*, Thella said. *He doesn't get along with all the gryphons, either. He scares many of them.*

*Like Elya?* Farren asked.

Thella sent her a wave of regret. *Elya is very close to her humans, and she is far too meek for the likes of Naronimus. That is why she's been injured by him. If it hadn't been for Delphi*, she added, *I'm not sure Elya would've survived the attack.*

*Delphi defended her?* Something about that steadied Farren.

*Yes, though she was pregnant at the time. I've never seen her as fierce as she had been then. She charged Naronimus and pinned him with beak and talon before Naronimus could do more than bite Elya's ear.*

Farren could picture Delphi this way with startling clarity—huge with her kits, her angry and powerful limbs unstoppable as she knocked Naronimus down. It was something she instantly admired.

*Then you agree that Naronimus shouldn't be a part of the queen's guard?*

*I think that would be a wise decision. And I have told the prince my thoughts. So why are you here?*

Farren pursed her lips. The fact that Cato didn't listen to Farren or even Thella—

*Is it my magic?* Thella's tail swished softly along the ground. *Many have asked me about my magic.*

*Recruits?* Farren asked.

*Many would like to use it for their benefit.*

*Have you done what they wanted?*

Thella bobbed her head. *Some. One wished to leave Alidonia without being noticed, to visit a dying family member. Another wished for me to make the iron cage of the yard invisible, just for a few moments, so that she could see the sky better. One wished to be invisible so that he could sneak into the kitchens for a morsel of spiced tart, and I didn't see the harm in it. I rather enjoy using it for their benefit, if it is morally sound. That is why we are here, isn't it?*

Farren wrapped her cold arms around her torso. *Not to help anyone who asks—*

*I am bonded to them. I know them. I wouldn't have done it otherwise.*

Farren still doubted the young gryphon's judgment, but tried not to let that seep through their runebond. Instead, she decided to use it. *Perhaps since we are not bonded, I shouldn't ask anything of you, then.*

Thella was silent a moment, assessing her. *What would you ask me to do?*

Every nerve in her body shivered as she considered what to say to Thella. And yet, as she stared into the beast's eyes, she began to feel a strange sort of calm that folded into her.

*I would like your help releasing Naronimus,* Farren said, and she held her breath.

Thella's head inched back, her tawny ears flattening slightly. *How?*

*You can use your magic to make him invisible while I take him outside the fortress.*

Thella stood, and the runebond narrowed to the point where Farren could only receive a trickle of the gryphon's tranquil demeanor. Thella walked to the slender window and peered out into the evening sky.

*What if he hurts humans out there?* Thella asked.

*He has promised to leave humankind alone.*

Thella snorted—an odd, breathy sound through the nostrils of her beak. *His promises are meaningless.*

*I threatened to hunt him down myself if he returned.* Farren would never fully trust the beast, but the more time she had spent training with him, the more she believed he would keep his word.

Thella swiveled her head to peer at Farren, but said nothing. Farren clasped her hands, wishing she had her father's way with words as she broached the next pressing issue. Instead, she built an impression for Thella: the queen's gryphons casting off into the sky, finally free to be and go where they wished.

*I want to release you all*, she said as she sent the impression.

Thella tensed and her ears whipped back. *All of us?* No. The answer was firm. Final.

Farren swallowed. *Think about it. The queen threatened to execute Naronimus. What would it take for her to decide the same fate for another gryphon?*

Thella glared at her in a way that only a gryphon could do, with feathers bristled above her beak, deepening the furrow of her golden brow. Her head hunched down threateningly.

*If we do what we are told*, Thella reasoned, *then we wouldn't be threatened in such a way. Naronimus nearly killed a recruit. Does Prince Cato agree with this plan?*

Farren's mouth went dry, and she licked her lips. *He doesn't know, and he can't know. He doesn't see all the things wrong with this place, with the way you're all treated. Captivity is only hurting your kind. Please just think about it—*

*I will not help you release all the gryphons*, Thella said. *We were raised to be among humans, and this is our home. We have been here since we were babes, and even though the queen's brother treated us horribly, the queen has given us so much. A comfortable place to sleep, food, fresh air, when all we had before were chains and meager scraps of fish.*

Farren wedged their runebond wider, showing the gryphon more of her anger, her fear, and her growing sense of protection—not only toward humans, but toward gryphons, too. She switched tactics.

*Delphi and I have already spoken with the other gryphons. They all wish to leave.*

Her tail flicked up. *Even Elya?*

*Yes. They know that freedom is better than this.*

*How can they? They've never had it, or were too young when Anaxis took them to recall it.*

*Delphi remembers. She has shown them, and she can show you. Once you have seen it, you might understand. You might wish for freedom, too—*

*I won't.*

Farren crossed her arms. *But it's not just up to you. Shouldn't every gryphon be able to decide whether to stay?*

Thella looked out the window once more, her posture stiff. *I need time to think on this.*

*There is no time,* Farren said, fixing her gaze on the unmoving gryphon. *The feast is in two days. The mews will be empty and no one will be watching.*

*This cannot be rushed.*

*I'm not rushing,* Farren said. *I've been planning for weeks. But none of it will work without you.*

Thella's tail lashed side-to-side. Finally, she turned to Farren, the feathers over her sharp eyes still bristling. *I will speak with the others. I need to hear their reasons. I had thought most of us happy here, or at the very least content. We need to be among humans. They teach us how to use our magic, and they provide for us. And to be among them feels...right.*

*It feels right to be locked in a room all day?*

*We go to the yard daily,* Thella pointed out.

*In a cage.*

The gryphon emitted a soft keen of frustration. *I cannot leave Cato. Nor Camilla, nor Virilus. There are too many that I love.*

*And I don't want to leave Torch. But I know he will be better off away from here.*

*How will he learn his magic?* Thella pressed. *He will suffer tremendously to be torn from those whom he's bonded with.*

Farren's eyes had inexplicably begun to burn. *It is still better than staying here, where the queen could have him executed on a whim.*

Doubt seeped through the runebond, and Thella roused herself. *I will think on this, and discuss with the others. You said you have a plan. I need to hear it.*

Farren tried her best to show Thella her plan using impressions and words. When she finished, Thella walked to the door and sat expectantly.

*That is enough for now. Thank you for your honesty.*

Shakily, Farren opened the door. *You're the only one who can help us. It's the right thing to do.*

Thella flicked an ear and closed their runebond.

# TWENTY-NINE

THE CONVERSATION WITH THELLA left Farren feeling on edge, but she found release in Isander's arms. Over the past week of training and getting to know the gryphons, he had found her at odd times—at late hours in the bathhouse, at dawn in her bedchamber, or even as she trudged to the kitchen for a midday meal. No matter how busy she was, he would find her alone, and they would kiss in secret—and sometimes, blissfully, more—until Farren had forgotten whatever had been occupying her mind. Always, he would reach out to her with his runeskill, and Farren began to learn how to feel him there, hovering just beyond the window of her thoughts.

It was rather distracting. *Very* distracting, in fact.

Farren cursed as Scipio's fist nearly connected with her nose. Apparently, the cup of *birali* from the breakfast tray Isander had sent that morning wasn't enough to keep her from the distraction. She stopped trying to guess if Isander watched her from the royal atrium and refocused on the way Scipio moved.

The guard seemed to be growing bolder, but his anger was getting the best of him. Probably because he couldn't stand to see the progress she made with Naronimus. Her sparring had improved as well. After six weeks of eating three meals a day and sparring day after day, she had grown stronger. Besides that, she was learning Scipio's weaknesses—the most obvious of which was his smugness. But she still held back from him, waiting until he grew bored with her. It worked, most of the time, and he let her practice with another recruit. Then she could lose herself completely in the fight—and finally win.

Scipio pulled out one of the wood knives they practiced with, twirling it between his fingers with a sneer before striking. His fancy moves gave her ample time to prepare her parry as she pulled out her blunt knife. With a lazy motion, she grabbed his knife hand as he jabbed, twisted it away, and lifted her weapon toward his armpit—just slow enough that he could send his fist into her side. She braced herself and grimaced with the impact.

Scipio broke away from her with a huff, then called out to the recruits. "Let's switch!"

"My pleasure," Farren murmured, rubbing the new bruise on her torso.

"Care to dance?"

Farren whirled to face Cato, who gave her a strained sort of smile. "Did you finally get sick of watching us?"

"Actually, Scipio thought the practice would be good for me."

"Hm. Knives?"

"Of course."

Despite the cold day, his sparring shirt was already dark with sweat—just like hers—and his hair looked especially disheveled. Still, he eased into a fighting stance like any well-rested *Felid*, his body tensed and head lowered, eyes latching onto her every move.

"You look like you got more sleep last night," Farren said, trying to distract him as she assessed the best route for her first attack.

"I can't say the same for you."

Farren's cheeks warmed, and she attacked. Cato knocked her hand away. Across the yard, the recruits grunted in the chill autumn breeze as they sparred, and every so often, a shout punctuated the air as one went down on one of the hard stone paths.

"I've been trying to find out where the missing went," Cato said, easing back with knife poised in front of his chest. "No one seems to know anything. There are no patterns, no hints, no trails. It's as if they disappeared into thin air."

"Impossible." Farren swiped up toward his side, and their knives clacked together as he blocked her. She recalled something Torch had told her. "Have you tried asking Balyon? I heard he can find lost things."

That did the trick. Cato's eyes grew wide, and his knife dipped a couple of inches as he considered her words. "I hadn't thought of that—"

Farren grabbed his knife hand and thrust hers. She paused, holding the wooden blade against the stubbled side of his throat, and the scent of his sweat reached her. The knife moved as he swallowed.

"That wasn't fair," he said.

"I honestly thought you'd be faster." She gave him a moment to regain his fighting stance and repressed a smile at the way his jaw clenched. "You must be excited for the feast," she said, attacking once more. A fraction of a second too late, he tried to block her and failed.

Cato winced and shook out his knife hand. "Not exactly. I'm not overly fond of feasts. And this one will be worse than usual. She wants a couple gryphons there."

They both knew who *she* was. Farren gripped her knife. "I thought she wouldn't put them in public until the Festival of the Forging?"

"She only wants two. I think she sees it as a test."

Farren jabbed the knife toward Cato's belly, but he quickly slashed her arm. She attacked again and again, anger biting into her. The plan wouldn't work. She wouldn't be able to release all the gryphons.

"Which ones?" she asked, letting up on Cato.

"She wants Elya."

Farren's heart fell. Docile, wind-loving Elya, whose chamber was full of wind-chimes, bells, tubes, and the silk ribbons Farren had given her. Elya had dreamed of the way the wind would flow free beneath her wings when she soared.

Cato's weight rocked side-to-side as he waited for Farren's next move. "And Thella."

"Thella?" Farren tried to control her voice and cringed when she heard a slight tremor. "Thella only recently discovered her magic. Wouldn't she be a hazard?"

"She has excellent control over her magic. She's been practicing with half a dozen recruits. I will be with her the whole time," Cato said. "The queen has requested that all the recruits attend as well. In uniform."

"But we aren't ready. Nothing is ready. We need more time—"

"Farren, we've had weeks of practice. I agree that you and some others could use more time bonding with the gryphons, but we knew the queen wanted us ready by the Festival of the Forging. It's only a day early, anyways."

"I know, but Thella can't be at—" Farren bit her tongue. "I was hoping to runebond with Thella more during the feast. I've had a hard time pinning her down."

"She is popular," Cato said, gripping his knife. "I'll be with Thella during the feast, and Horat will be runebonded to Elya. But you can spend time runebonding with her afterward. Why can't you be excited like all the other recruits about going to such an *important* feast?"

"You know why," she said tartly. Although she did get a little excited that Isander would be there. What would it be like to be near him again, unable to touch, surrounded by all the nobility who would be mortified if they knew what lay between her and the prince?

Cato lunged, and they went back and forth for a few moments while Farren's mind raced. Thella wouldn't be able to help her during the feast unless she could use her magic from afar. And neither Thella nor Elya could escape with the other gryphons unless Farren's plan happened after the feast—or whenever the gryphons were allowed to return to their chambers. That meant Cato would return to the mews with the gryphons, and likely wouldn't go back to the party afterward. She had hoped for Cato to be far away from the mews when she implemented her plan. The only way around these new issues was to postpone the release until after the birthday feast and somehow find a way to get rid of Cato. He had an annoying tendency to linger in Horat's study until late in the night.

Farren feinted an attack. He moved to parry her blow, but she turned and dug her knife toward his ribs. He spun out of the way, grinning.

"Why don't you let me work with Thella during the feast instead?" Farren asked, panting as they circled each other once more. If she was runebonded to Thella, she could at least try to convince the gryphon to help her. "I can be runebonded to her the entire time if need be."

His brow popped up. "Now why would I do that?"

She cleared her throat. "I know you don't trust me, but I've been practicing with Naronimus. I've really improved my ability to—"

Scipio's shout rang over the yard. "Knives down! Hand-to-hand!"

Cato tossed his knife away and crouched into a fighting position. "I see the work you've been doing with Naronimus, but your ability isn't why I don't trust you."

Farren grit her teeth and pounced. She knocked him down, and they tumbled. He was surprisingly strong, considering how much time he spent wandering aimlessly around the halls. She managed to grapple him into a position beneath her, but he kicked his leg up and around her, twisting her off him. Before she could get up, his weight fell on her back, and he blocked her elbow as it went toward his face. The *Felid* was damnably fast.

"I've done everything you and the queen have asked," Farren said breathlessly, wriggling beneath him. His cursed thighs locked her in hard as stone. To make matters worse, they had landed in a garden bed, and velvety iris petals threatened to suffocate her with their perfume.

Cato grunted in acknowledgment. "It's strange, isn't it? You used to be so against everything. It made sense when you told me about what Naronimus did to your brother. But now you want to do things I only let the best recruits do. I would've expected submission, but you're pushing back in a way that has me questioning your motives."

"Scipio has been filling your head with lies," Farren said. She took gulping breaths of cold autumn air. She needed to clear her head, think of how to renegotiate, how to get out from his infuriating weight.

"Scipio? He hasn't mentioned anything to me. Should I have a talk with him?"

"Talk all you want." Then she threw her head back, using the momentum to twist and aim an elbow toward his head. His weight shifted as he recoiled, and she bucked. Triumph sailed through her as he tumbled off, crushing more iris blossoms. Farren rolled away and pounced to her feet.

He looked dazed as he stood and went to the closest stone fountain to sluice a handful of water over his face. "That was...i nteresting."

Farren brushed the remnants of mashed petals from her leggings. The queen's flock of *Planteri* would no doubt bring the flowers back to life, just as they had continuously done after each hard frost. She swore softly as her fingers caught on a fresh rip in her chiton. The worn fabric had torn and left a gaping hole along the side of her stomach. She shot a glance at Cato, meaning to berate him for sitting on her, but her tongue stuck to the roof of her mouth.

His gaze lingered where the bare skin of her torso showed. Something akin to hunger flickered there—and the sight of it caused her to flush with heat. He dragged his eyes away.

She pinched the fabric closed, struggling to control the quickened pulsing of her heart. Absurd. This wasn't an unusual way for a man to react after sparring—especially for a younger man who was fresh at it, who hadn't touched a woman's body in a way that didn't involve bedding her.

But her body's reaction...

She shook her head and crooked a brow at him. "You're too much in your head when you fight."

"I could say the same to you. Although I have noticed some improvement since you've been practicing with Scipio."

Farren smirked. "He's taught me a lot about what *not* to do. And you're right that I've been pushing back. I've gotten to know many of the gryphons, and I've worked hard to show you and the Lord Falconer that I've changed. That I feel differently about gryphons than I used to."

Cato gave her a look of disbelief. "Does this mean you've forgiven Naronimus?"

"Oh, I still despise him," she said. "But I don't despise all gryphons." Like dear, exuberant little Torch. "Maybe I'll discuss the feast with Horat instead."

Cato picked up his knife and sheathed it at his hip, his brows sinking into their usual dark glower. "You can try. But I've no doubt he'll agree with me."

"Right, because he would never disagree with a prince."

Cato's prickliness at her words was more than a little satisfying. She would just have to speak with Horat herself; she would convince him of her progress and show him how far she had come in working with Naronimus. Her plan hinged on it.

"You're not ready." Horat's voice was gruff as he continued his hobbling pace down the mew hall.

Mid-afternoon sun streaked through the windows, barely warming the chill air of the mews. Autumn wind gusted in from that cursed Enchanted window that opened itself at whim, and as they passed it, Farren tugged it closed, wincing at the ache in her arm as she did so. The tenderness echoed through her body, all the way down to her toes. It was a feeling she normally relished after sparring practice, but with exhaustion weighing heavily on her—from early mornings sparring, afternoons working with Naronimus, and late evenings spending time with Torch or other gryphons—she could hardly muster appreciation for it. Even her mind felt wrung from the frequent and strenuous mental exercises with Naronimus.

Farren rubbed stiff hands over her arms and caught up with Horat. "I've been practicing for weeks now, and you know how difficult Naronimus can be—"

"But you haven't been practicing with Thella or Elya."

"I *want* to. I just haven't had the time. But I have spoken with Elya on several occasions and even brought her a gift."

Horat shook his grizzled head. "You should continue focusing on Naronimus. That is your priority."

Farren fought to keep the impatience out of her tone. "It has been my priority, but how do I know when the queen has made up her mind?"

Horat grunted. "She's giving you until the prince's birthday feast. You have two days left, and you'll know her mind then."

Farren strangled back a wail of frustration and halted in a thick band of sunshine, folding her arms over her torso as she willed the sun's warmth to spread through her body. It never came.

Horat's gait slowed, and he paused beyond the reach of sunlight. "I will tell you that she isn't quite satisfied yet. She hasn't seen anything that has really proven Naronimus's worth."

Farren's mouth fell open, then snapped closed. "Nothing? But we've made recruits bend the knee! We've had them carry me on a litter, feed Naronimus out of the palms of their hands, and all the while, they believed we were king and queen..."

Horat hobbled to her, and the bright light revealed every crinkle and scar born on his face. He seemed impossibly old in the harsh light, and beneath the years he wore, Farren sensed an unwavering strength and wisdom that reminded her keenly of her father.

"She needs to see more. Do whatever you can. Whatever you're willing to do."

Her skin prickled.

She didn't follow Horat as he headed back to his study. What was she willing to do? Not hurt another innocent person. Besides, why would the queen want to see another of her recruits disabled? Farren turned on her heel and dove through the halls to the gryphon yard. She was apparently late, as Naronimus and Cato waited for her with two heavily-padded recruits—Alexon and Virilus, who had persisted with the trainings despite being manipulated and drenched in a sweat she knew had nothing to do with heat after each session. Alexon had foregone his candies and instead clenched his jaw and waited stiff-faced beneath his brass helmet.

She had tried to convince Cato that he didn't need to come to every training session, but he had insisted it was for the safety of the recruits. He shifted his stance when he saw her approaching, an undeniable tension pulling him taut as a bowstring.

When she had asked him why he didn't train with Naronimus himself, he had given her a bristling stare, and claimed that it didn't matter because the queen had never asked him to.

But she knew that he would say yes to the queen if she had asked because he wasn't capable of saying no to her. A rankling thought, but one Farren quickly reigned in as she approached Cato. At least he had been smart enough to leave Camilla elsewhere this time. It made it easier to focus and clear her mind—an effort that was becoming reflexive at the sight of Naronimus. Carefully, she opened a runebond with the beast as he trotted on the opposite side of the yard. His head snapped toward her, and great golden eyes hammered into hers.

She dug nails into her palms. *Are you ready to begin? Or would you like more time to take in the view beyond your bars?*

*I'm always ready.* His tawny ears twitched back. His impressions always came with a dose of irritation and each time, it sparked anger in herself as if her body were a mirror to his. She didn't want to be connected to him this way. She didn't want any of it, really. But she had to deal with it.

She gave a cursory nod to Alexon and Virilus and ignored Cato altogether, knowing it was best for both of them if they didn't speak. Doing so would likely incite yet another argument when all she wanted was to finish practice.

*We need to do something different*, she explained to Naronimus, who had approached at an easy canter.

He paused a few feet from her, well away from the recruits. Farren felt a little better at the distance between them, even though she knew Naronimus could clear it in a moment with his speed.

*Like what?* he asked.

So far, they had manipulated the recruits to bend the knee, to repeat things Farren had said, and to feel unwavering devotion to Farren's cause, whatever that might be. They had influenced the recruits to do simple, repetitive tasks, pushing them—pushing Naronimus—to carry out the tasks for longer periods of time. Shorter sessions under Naronimus's magic meant that the effects faded quickly once his magic stopped. Pushing for longer sessions strained them all to the point of exhaustion. Naronimus's magic would eventually fail as the pain in his head grew unbearable, and the recruits took longer to shake back to reality. The lies Naronimus imbued them with would cling sometimes for an hour or more after his magic faded.

Perhaps it was more useful to focus on the feelings of devotion than on following mindless tasks. Farren knew they could *feel* devotion, but how could she get them to prove it?

*Can you make them feel something different?*

*Of course*, he replied. With ease, Naronimus laid down—a position she had never seen him in before—with all the relaxation of a cat watching two mice.

*The one on the left. Virilus*, she said, stating his name as a reminder to both of them. He was a human, a recruit, just like her. He trembled slightly in his shiny brass helmet, and sweat glittered on his beak-like nose. She wasn't sure Naronimus noticed or cared. *Can you make him feel devotion to the Runeless Sect? To hate runeskills and all that might entail. Animal bonding. Possibly animals. He needs to believe that animals are beneath humans.*

Naronimus flicked his tail. A *preposterous belief. And the second recruit?*

*Alexon should have complete devotion to me. He will do anything I command of him.* It shouldn't have, but the words sent a rivulet of excitement through her. She squashed it.

Naronimus waited while she walked to the recruits, her back facing Cato as she pulled out the blunt wooden knife she used for sparring practice. She held it out to Alexon, who hesitated.

"Take it," she ordered, knowing that Naronimus would make it happen.

The confusion cleared from Alexon's face, and Farren swallowed down queasiness as he took the knife and held it tight in one fist. She moved some distance behind him and saw with dismay that Cato had seen the knife. The prince's face flushed red with fury, and she swore.

*Don't let Virilus get hurt*, she ordered Naronimus. *Do you understand? It must look like an attack, but that knife is not to hurt him. Alexon must believe that Virilus is a threat, and only Virilus. Can you do that?* Farren shot a wave of insistence, filling her words with skepticism.

*Yes, I can do that.*

She could tell by his brief message that he was trying to focus on her request, but she caught the hint of condescension. Which made her feel oddly calm. Oddly, almost sickeningly, trusting.

But she had no time to focus on that feeling because Cato was lunging for Alexon's knife. Farren whipped a leg out, sending Cato sprawling, and at the same time, shouted, "Protect me from the Sect!"

She had taken the prince by surprise, and when he fell, she leapt onto his back, pinning his shoulders to the ground with her knees.

"Enchanter's curse, Farren," he yelled, "get off me! Why did you give him a knife?"

Farren couldn't answer because her eyes were locked on the recruits, her heart pounding in her ears. Cato tried to jostle her off but then saw with horror that the recruits were fighting each other.

As if their lives depended on it.

Virilus roared in fury and charged into Alexon, unheeding of the knife. A few moments later, the knife jabbed forward, meeting padding, and slid through, somewhere on the other side of Virilus' torso.

Farren's heart was in her throat as Virilus screamed and fell to the ground. No, her instincts had told her to trust Naronimus—

*He's not really hurt*, Naronimus informed her, a little peeved. *You needn't have worried.*

Her eyes bulged at him. *I always worry with you.*

When she looked back at the recruits, Virilus clutched his side, his face lined with agony. Alexon scowled over him with the clean-bladed knife.

She leapt off Cato and raced to crouch over Virilus. Almost as soon as she got there, his face cleared, then clouded once more.

He rubbed his side, looking as if he might cry. "He didn't really stab me? I didn't get—?"

Alexon gasped and dropped the knife. "Virilus, are you alright? I don't know what happened—"

"It was just an illusion of sorts," Farren cut in, wanting to clear the air as fast as possible. "An emotional and physical illusion. He made you feel the pain and fear you would from being stabbed. My apologies. We had to make it look real for the queen."

She was barely aware of Cato standing up until he spoke, his mouth tight with rage. "How could you do this?"

"It had to be done." She flushed hot, loathing the impending argument. "Otherwise, the queen will never believe the progress we've—"

"Do you realize how you sound?"

Farren ignored him as she stood and offered a hand to Virilus, who stared and shook with shock. He didn't take her hand or even meet her eyes. Alexon seemed not to see her either, wiping his knife hand on his armor as if it was covered in poison.

"Stop by the kitchen," she said, willing them to look at her. "Have a bit of their strongest wine. We're done for the day."

Alexon helped Virilus up, and they exchanged glances before rushing from the yard.

"I'm not letting this go," Cato spat. "You can't just walk in here with a *knife* and expect not to be reprimanded."

"It was only a wooden knife." Farren held it up between them by the hilt. "The same one you and I practice with during sparring."

"And next time, you'll bring a real one." His eyes, the same green as Isander's, were like chiseled gemstones.

"Go on then, reprimand me," Farren challenged. "I won't be listening because I have more important things to think of. Like what we'll do if the queen is still not convinced of our progress."

Cato waved his hands around. "The queen isn't even here!"

Farren's gaze snapped to the glass wall of the royal atrium and found what she was looking for. The slight, astute frame of the queen stood between the thrones, and her eyes mortared to Farren's. She was close enough for Farren to make out the flash of a necklace gem among scarlet iris petals. Close enough to see the queen's slight nod.

Approval.

Warmth blossomed in her and was quickly followed by a cold wash of dread. "Let's hope we're done for good," Farren said, and she wasn't sure if she said it to Cato or herself. If the queen decided not to execute Naronimus, then she would decide to use him, and Farren couldn't let that happen. She knew how enticing that power was, how it could be wielded to devastating effect. No one should have that power, not even if they were fighting the Runeless Sect.

# THIRTY

TORCHES LINED THE WINDING path through the queen's gardens and cast twitching shadows among the shrubbery. Her breath puffed white in the damp, chill air. Distant voices threaded through the night as servants finished the last of their work and headed to their rooms, no doubt to warmth and firelight and company. Farren shivered and pulled her linen cloak tighter around her body as she strode from the servant's bathhouse back to the gryphon mews.

The bath had helped clear her mind and refresh her purpose, but as soon as she left, uncertainty leached the warmth from her skin. She couldn't stop seeing the queen's nod, her slight smile of approval—a small movement that had caused her stomach to drop.

Nor could she stop hearing Cato's words, tight with accusation. She knew how their exercise with the two recruits must've looked to him, probably little different than when she had first connected with Naronimus and everything fell apart. It was wrong...but thrilling too, to taste the kind of power that came from being Naronimus's savage and ruthless partner. It twisted inside her, begging to come alive again, to be given another chance. *We can get better*, it said. *We can do more. We can become stronger.*

Torchlight flickered wildly as she rounded a corner where another path joined hers, and her spinning thoughts halted when she ran headlong into Camilla.

"Oh, sorry!" Camilla exclaimed, jumping away from her. An armload of fabrics—dainty lace, blue satin, and a viridian brocade ornate with silvery fish—nearly spilled from her arms.

Farren reached out to steady the girl. "I wasn't paying attention," she muttered, her face feeling stiff as she forced a smile.

Camilla peered at her. "Are you alright? You look like you might be sick."

"No, I'm fine. Just heading to bed." Farren continued walking toward the mews, and Camilla fell in step beside her. Farren had grown close to the girl over the past weeks, but because she was the prince's ward—and more than that, a close friend of his—Farren couldn't trust her with everything. Certainly not with her plans.

High overhead, Farren thought she could hear the low talk from the royal guard pacing the top of the fortress wall. When she looked toward the sound—high up on the western wall—two cold eyes and dusky fur glinted from the shadows. Was it Scipio with one of his lurking coyotes or just another of the *Canid* royal guards? Farren shivered again, certain that the animal was watching her.

"I'm heading to bed too," Camilla said, pulling Farren's attention back.

"With those fancy fabrics?"

"Oh, these? They aren't for me." A grin suddenly split her face. "And I may have stolen them from the royal seamstress' lair."

"Won't she notice?"

"I don't think the queen will ever stoop low enough to wear fishy brocade. She wants to represent a gryphon, not a gryphon's food. The seamstress won't miss it because it was in one of her rubbish heaps."

Farren eyed the pristine fabrics. "Right. And are you going to be the one wearing a fishy brocade dress?"

Camilla's laughter resounded in the quiet night, startling a pair of sunsparrows from the thick shrubbery. "It's actually for Livigena. She's desperate for a well-made dress to impress Aktin for the prince's birthday celebration—"

"She's going to the feast?"

"Oh, no. The servants have their own gathering in the kitchens after the feast is over. She'll have the nicest dress, so of course Aktin has to pay attention to her..."

After the feast? Farren fought back a sigh. Another potential knot in her plan. The kitchens were connected to the mews, so she would have to find a way to be sure none of the revelers ended up in the mews while the gryphons were freed from their chambers. Although...she could try to use the party to entice Prince Cato out of the mews for the night.

"...and Livi is hoping he'll ask for her hand soon," Camilla was saying.

"So she'll sew herself a beautiful dress," Farren prompted, smiling at the girl.

Camilla glanced at her in alarm. "Of course not! I offered to do it for her."

Farren frowned. Camilla was already looking sleepless and had a bucketload of other chores to be done. "You only have two days before the feast. Surely, Livi can do it on her own—"

Camilla shook her head adamantly. "She's had a headache for nearly three days now. Besides," Camilla added conspiratorially, "we both know that she would melt into a puddle if no one helped her."

"But it doesn't have to be you," Farren said, rounding the last bend in the path that led to the mews.

Camilla shrugged. "I don't mind. Livigena has been kind since the prince brought me here. I can always come to her when my dreams trouble me."

And just like that, Farren's argument died. "Are they bad? Do you get enough sleep?"

"Oh, plenty," Camilla said, suddenly studying the fabrics with intensity. "I haven't told anyone this before, but... Sometimes, when the dreams are very hard, a voice speaks to me. He calms me, and I feel wrapped in cloud. Do you think it's possible for the Enchanters to speak through dreams?"

The girl was looking at her with wide, glittering eyes.

"I don't know," Farren said, and gently touched Camilla's arm. "I'm just glad that something makes things better for you."

The girl let out a breath. "Well, it's probably my own mind. I've been meaning to ask... Have you noticed a change in the mews? Things feel...different."

With Farren's encouragement, the gryphons had spent more and more time out in the yard. They begged Cato for extra time, and even Delphi had arranged to be in the yard with the others, expressing concern about her kits' wings developing properly. The gryphons spent hours running and flying to gain strength. After days of this practice, the mews had begun to change.

The noise had subsided. The gryphons complained less of aches and pains. They ate voraciously. And a peculiar restlessness touched her every time she runebonded with a gryphon. It took her a couple days to realize that their tiny sparks of hope had flared into robust, crackling flames.

"What do you mean?" Farren asked.

"The gryphons seem like they feel...happier. Or, excited? I'm not sure."

"Maybe they are excited to be out of the fortress once they begin their work as the gryphon guard on the streets."

Camilla considered this as they reached the doorway to the mews. "Well, whatever it is, I like it. Although sometimes it does feel like there's something they're not telling me..."

Farren bit her lip. She hated lying to the girl, but she couldn't know whether Camilla would agree with her plan or not, and certainly didn't trust the girl to keep it from Prince Cato.

A familiar pressure prodded the left side of Farren's head. Farren paused on the threshold as heat rolled into her.

"Are you coming?" Camilla asked over her shoulder. From somewhere inside the mews, laughter and chatter erupted; everyone, including the servants, had been growing excited over the upcoming twin celebrations—the prince's birthday feast and the Festival of the Forging.

"Actually, I think I'll stay out a few moments more, just to enjoy the starlight."

Camilla shrugged and left her behind. As Farren watched her go, she considered letting Isander in. He couldn't know about her plans, or feel her worry over Thella and Naronimus and the feast. Probably best to keep him out.

She sank into the shadows pooling along the side of the mews building, where the gardens gave way to purple sedges and untended snake vines.

"Isander?"

A warm hand caught her wrist and pulled her into a nook formed by a clump of vines. Farren could hardly make out the smooth edges of Isander's face, but the soft satin of his green chiton gleamed in the faint moonlight. He wrapped his arms around her hips and pulled her to him, and she breathed in the scent of soap, musk, and the minty snap of Lidellian *birali*.

"What are you doing here?" Farren asked.

"I've missed you."

"You saw me two days ago." The cloak she wore suddenly felt too heavy and thick, and the long chiton beneath it unwieldy. "Why didn't you come out just now? I was only walking with Camilla. She knows you like to hang about."

Isander's body tensed, and his misty breath rolled between them, catching the cold blue light of the moon. "I prefer to keep my distance from her."

"From Camilla?"

"I call her my Night Muse."

Farren sought his eyes in the shadows. "Is it because of her night terrors? Are you the one who speaks to her?"

"I do."

Jealousy jolted through her. But when had she started thinking of her connection with Isander as being special, as herself as being the only one? No, she was glad that Isander could help Camilla.

"Farren, it's not something I want to do. It's something I *have* to do. When she has her bad dreams, her mind opens like a chasm and screams for help. The chasm pulls me in and I..." His breath in the silence stirred the snake vine leaves, rousing them to whisper and twirl. "If I don't calm her, I get lost in her dreams. I see and feel it all, and it's"—he shook his head—"too much."

"I thought you painted to help?"

"Paint, or draw, that's why I call her a muse."

"I see. I didn't realize that you couldn't close your mind to her."

"My runeskill is different from most. Because it's with other humans, I can't seem to avoid heightened emotional experiences. I try my best to stay away from her."

Farren let her hands run up the front of his chiton, which was stitched with row upon row of thumb-sized irises. "Did your mother give you this?"

He recoiled slightly, then huffed a laugh. "I was afraid you would notice that. Yes, she did. I wore it to mollify her earlier. She was going on about how one of her healers might be a member of the Runeless Sect, and is obsessing over whether or not the healer will kill her with one of her herbal elixirs. It's just a rumor, or course. The healers are nothing other than petrified of the crown. They can hardly meet her eyes when they speak with her."

Farren's fingers froze over the irises.

Isander's hand covered hers. "What is it?"

"Nothing. It's just... I'm not sure if I'd like being feared that way."

"It's wise for people to fear power," Isander said, rubbing his thumb in little circles over her wrist. "If they don't, they're more likely to get hurt."

"I don't want to hurt people."

"But you're a fighter, Farren."

"This wasn't fighting. It was manipulative and treacherous."

"Did something happen this morning?"

"No. Well, yes. Naronimus and I..." Enchanters, why did her voice just quaver? She cleared her throat and lifted her chin. "We did an exercise that I'm hoping will convince the queen not to execute Naronimus. Your brother was furious with me, and now the recruits look at me differently. But we didn't hurt them...at least not physically."

"But you wouldn't have done it unless you had to."

"Wouldn't I have?"

"You said you don't want to hurt people. I believe you. Most people don't *want* to hurt others, they are compelled to. If someone was threatening your father..."

"I would do whatever it took."

"See? I knew she was in there."

"Who?"

"The Commander."

Farren sighed and began to move away, but he pulled her closer and bent his head down to hers until their foreheads touched.

"We both know she's in there." Isander's voice was like a breeze sighing through a pine tree. "I know you can feel her there, because I've glimpsed her. She's trying to waken, Farren."

"You sound like one of the Runeless going on about the Enchanters."

"I'm not suffering runelack madness," he stated, unoffended. "I only want you to acknowledge her. You have to trust yourself. Your instincts and strength are already there. You and Naronimus have something together. Why not embrace it?"

"Because I am a servant. Because I don't want to hurt anyone. Because I can't be anything more than I already am. Because..." She wouldn't mention that she was already busy trying to free the gryphons and take down the queen's program. That if she was to suffer consequences for her behavior, those would be more than enough, if she was found out. "I don't want to work with Naronimus any more than I already have. It's difficult enough as it is. And now the other recruits fear me and it's all so strange and wrong and... I wish I knew when it would end."

Isander was silent for a moment. "You don't need to worry about Naronimus being executed, if that's what you mean."

"What?"

"I spoke with my mother this afternoon. She mentioned something about you and Naronimus, and seemed impressed. There's no chance she would rid herself of something so valuable."

"Really? Were you able to...connect with her?"

A low laugh rumbled in his throat. "I can't connect with her, even if I wanted to. That Enchanted necklace she wears blocks me out.

I've never seen her take it off. But I do know her well enough to say you should have no worry in this."

Heat burned Farren's eyes, and she leaned into Isander's embrace. For a moment, she didn't speak, but savored the lightness sweeping through her. A burden, gone. Now, she could focus on her escape plan. Farren breathed in the crisp air, willing it to clear the clutter from her mind.

It didn't work.

But Isander's hand had begun to move down her backside, and that caused something completely different to spark low in her belly.

Farren traced one of the ivory pins fastening the chiton at his shoulder, her pulse thrumming. "The way you can feel Camilla's night terrors... Does that happen when you and I are intimate?"

His grip around her tightened. "Your mind is usually sealed like a tomb. Your ability to close your mind...it's one of the reasons why I enjoy your company so much. I've never met someone with a mind that strong."

Farren studied the ivory pin, recalling all the times Mellion had been upset with her for not runebonding, or for having too narrow a runebond. And she could never forget that her father had tried to send her messages about the letter from Alidonia, asking her to come home. Only she hadn't opened herself to them.

"After Desmond's attack, I kept my runeskill closed more," Farren said. "I thought that doing so would help me with control. But it-it didn't. It just shut me out from the birds. From my family."

"Farren, mental exercise like that *would* give you more control. You mind is like any other muscle. Don't let your issues with Naronimus make you think you are weak. Not only do you two have history, but he has *magic*."

She savored his words, wishing with all of her heart it was true. If all the practice with her runeskill had indeed helped her mind strengthen, if it would help prevent another attack like Desmon d's...then it was all worth it.

"So you cannot feel anything from me when we are intimate?"

"I can only catch echoes of your feelings, not unlike the lingering pink in the sky after the sun has settled."

"Do you like feeling the echoes?" she asked. Knowing that he could feel something of her beyond the physical sent a shiver coursing down her spine.

He tilted his head down to hers. "It is as gentle and beautiful as anything I could hope for."

"Maybe you should paint it."

"I should."

She felt the curve of his smile as their lips met, and tasted the zing of spiced mint from the lingering *birali*. He turned so that her back pressed against the cool stone of the wall. While his lips traced a pattern down her neck, she sighed into their green-spun nook, glad to be hidden from view of the fortress wall and the pathway to the mews. Here, in the privacy of shadow, they could have each other freely, if only for a short while. She could forget about Naronimus, Cato, and the queen. Her mind could wander blissfully in the night-washed forest of Isander's skin, in the way he pulled up her chiton, in how her leggings slid so easily down and off.

The air was crisp and biting. He whispered to her little details about her body, kissing each in turn. Her tumbling hair, dark as shadow. An achingly soft bosom that smelled of ralai flower. The graceful arc of her hips, which framed her with perfect symmetry. He worshiped her body as only a painter could, with beautiful words and hands that worked until they both blazed. The cold stone wall pressed against her backside as he lifted her. Then her senses were consumed by fire and driving force and ripples of pleasure that carried her high, high into the starlight.

# THIRTY-ONE

ISANDER HAD BEEN RIGHT. The following morning, Horat informed her of the queen's decision not to have Naronimus executed. Somehow, Cato had kept silent, pretending to be buried in books when she could see him perched on the edge of the stool as if it were covered in barbs.

Horat also mentioned two other important details. First, that the queen had requested to speak with her during the feast. Second, that what had happened with Naronimus and the recruits hadn't convinced either him or Cato that she was capable of being in charge of Thella during the feast. The prince had broken his silence then, and went on a five-minute speech about how she could no longer be trusted after her trick with the knife.

As if he had ever trusted her to begin with.

After sparring practice, she spent the rest of the day finalizing plans with the gryphons and checking in with Thella. Farren had managed to find an odd ornament from a peddler who had loitered near the East Tow, just outside the fortress gates. The ornament—a column of translucent material made by a simple Lidellian artform—was crafted of glassweed, which had been smashed, dried, and rolled into a fat tube. When held up to the sun, it shimmered. The peddler had instructed her to look into it, and when she did, there were all manner of shapes and colors that glinted and flashed in the afternoon light.

Now, she watched Thella peer through the tube, which Farren had carefully anchored to a rafter so that it hung at Thella's height. Through their runebond, Thella sent her a wave of curiosity and wonder.

*Have you made your decision yet*? she asked the gryphon.

Reluctantly, the gryphon pulled away from the tube and sat in front of Farren as primly as a housecat.

*I have. I will help you. But I will not go myself.*

Farren closed her eyes as something cool soared into her.

*You understand that the queen will use you,* Farren said. *To do whatever she asks.*

*I do. But I am not staying for the queen.*

So, Farren wouldn't be able to completely rid the crown of gryphons. But she knew that the other gryphons all wished to be freed. That had to mean something, if she could free all the others. And if the only gryphon remaining was Thella...

Farren recalled how quickly Thella had jumped to protect the recruits from herself and Naronimus. If any gryphon could be trusted not to hurt people, it was Thella. The queen would have a very difficult time forcing her to do something her morals disagreed with.

*Tell me the plan once more*, Thella said.

*Can use your ability from afar?*

*For all the gryphons?* Thella's tail twitched on the ground. *My magic is strong, but I cannot use it from a great distance. It works best when I am close and can see the light with my own eyes. And with so many gryphons at once... It would be harder the farther they went. I'm unsure if I could use it past the River Kithyria, unless I was out in the open.*

*I see*, Farren said, glad she hadn't depended on that strategy. *And Elya wishes to go, as well. So we have to wait until you both return to the mews. Once everyone is good and drunk, and the night deep, we can begin.*

*And Cato? You said he cannot be in the mews.*

*No one should be in the mews. I will see to that. There will be a party in the kitchens after the feast. I can encourage Camilla to take the prince there.*

Farren took her time picking through the plans with Thella, making sure everything would go smoothly. She left Thella's chamber feeling lighter than ever, and headed to the gryphon nursery. In the few remaining hours of the day, she played with Torch, sang him songs, and snuggled with him next to the hearth.

She didn't have the heart to tell him what would happen the following night, but she knew that he would do what she and Delphi asked when the time came. As he slept on her chest—his delicate feathers ruffling in her shallow breaths—she savored the comfort she gleaned from him. Tomorrow, she would tell him. Tomorrow, she would say goodbye. For tonight, she just needed to pet his silky fur and feel his breath move in a steady rhythm in and out and in and out until her eyelids fluttered and sealed off the world of tomorrow.

The following evening, Farren fought not to slouch as she stepped into the royal atrium. Dressed in the leather vest and bracers of the royal guard and reeking of the bitterseed wax used to harden it, she felt entirely out of place among the brocade chitons and finely embroidered cloaks of the queen's guests. Beneath the leather armor, she wore a new tawny chiton and leggings, which may have allowed her to pass unnoticed in the crowd but for the dazzling orange cloak of the royal guard that hung on her back.

She might as well have been wearing the sun.

Flicking the cloak back from her shoulders, Farren lifted her chin and pressed through the crowd gathered in the royal atrium, searching for Thella. Candlelight twinkled around the atrium, shone off the polished stone floor, and turned the water in the rain-pool a gleaming yellow. Hanging potted plants thrust into the warm air, and vines spilled down in profusions of emerald strands studded with purple and red blossoms. Above the rectangular rain-pool, the ceiling opened to the velvet sky. Autumn night drifted in, fluttering the candles and stirring the musky air.

Farren followed the edge of the atrium, sidestepping a guest whose swarm of bees buzzed around her flower-laden headdress, and nearly slipped in a wet trail left by a small family of otters. Camilla had informed her that the queen had invited two hundred guests, and apparently, each one decided to bring their rune animal.

Farren bit back a curse as vines from one of the potted plants tangled around her head. The fine tendrils seemed to move with a life of their own, searching for purchase in her hair. Luckily, she had it pulled into a tight plait, and the vines broke free on her third abrupt tug. She pushed deeper into the crowd, aiming for the sprawling dais to the right side of the atrium, where the queen and king sat on their thrones.

All that day, the excitement about the feast had grown nearly palpable in the gryphon mews. The recruits moved with more alacrity while cleaning the mews, and even Scipio seemed lax during sparring practice, letting her spar with others so that she was able to beat three separate opponents.

That had helped her relax, a little.

Now, her leather armor felt like a vice around her torso. She tugged it down and sucked in the warm, cloistered air.

She had never seen so many people in one place, nor so many animals. A red-gold fox brushed past her, trailing a young woman with a cloak fashioned of white rabbit fur. Farren stared after her, marveling at the display of predatory power. Even in her small village in the Outskirts, wearing a rune animal's prey was considered a bold and ostentatious move, especially if it was flaunted in front of someone whose runeskill was with the prey animal.

The wealthiest among the crowd wore the most revealing silken chitons, to better show off their elaborate skin paintings. One man's neck and arms were covered in writhing snakes of all kinds—red vipers and blue moccasins and vine-like green snakes. They even threaded beneath his sandals and wrapped his toes. An elegant woman's chiton draped to the very bottom of her back, revealing a snarling and ferocious wolf. The hem of her chiton was studded with pieces of deer antler that clacked as she walked.

Farren stepped carefully through the crowd, nearly treading on a scattering of round excrements, and halted when a strange barking rang out from the group of men next to her. A venomous swamp salamander with a silvery-blue tail twined around a man's neck. The creature stared at her as she gave it a wide berth.

Luckily, there didn't appear to be many more dangerous animals.

She spotted Thella and Elya above the crowd, their feathered faces colored bright with a yellow powder, and continued pressing along the wall. Sweat broke out under her arms at the press of bodies and the noise of voices, laughter, and the buzzing, cheery music of the queen's royal chorus—a collection of a hundred finches perched high above the crowd.

Ahead of her, a man spoke lowly with two others near the wall. He had a jutting chin and a wide brow, and his broad shoulders were draped in a dusky grey chiton. No hint of a rune animal was painted or sewn anywhere on him. The starkness of him among the crowd drew her eye.

"...and is it true that the Runeless Sect is experimenting with runes?" The stout man standing next to him had spoken, a circular eye-glass clutched beneath a scowling brow. "Trying to find a way to rid us of our runeskills?"

The starkly-dressed man stiffened. "Changing our runes?" he scoffed. "What a nonsensical accusation. Unless you know about an Enchanter that has miraculously returned? Then, by all means, do let us know."

The stout man reddened and muttered something under his breath. As Farren moved around them, the starkly-dressed man noticed her stare, and gave a cursory nod. She dropped her gaze, but not before looking at his wrist.

No runemark. Nothing.

Her stomach knotted at the emptiness there, and her eyes darted back up to his. His lips twisted into a smile that didn't reach his eyes.

Farren's thoughts scattered as she ran into a thicket.

She pressed branches away from her face, glancing around wildly as a few songbirds shrieked and batted her with their wings. She reached out to calm one of them with her runeskill. A woman's loud voice penetrated Farren's confusion.

"Oh my goodness, I *am* so sorry!" The thicket moved out of Farren's face, and she saw that it was an enormous headdress made of woven sticks that protruded in all directions.

"Are you hurt? They are nesting now, so they're a bit peevish. Oh, I know it is a little risky, but I just love them so!" The woman motioned to her headdress, jowls waggling as she gave Farren a sheepish grin.

"No, I'm not hurt," Farren said, trying not to sound too curt. She dodged another branch as the woman's head swiveled toward the dais. When she looked back at Farren, her plump cheeks turned crimson.

"But aren't you the same woman...?" She pointed vaguely toward the dais, then squinted at Farren with a knowing glint. "Aye, you certainly are. It's those eyes. Although the prince made them look a bit more...commanding." The woman shuddered, but her puce-painted lips puckered in glee. "Is it true you two are...?"

Farren swallowed. "I'm not sure what you're speaking about."

"You...and the prince." The woman spoke as if Farren were slow-witted.

Farren shook her head, blood suddenly thundering in her ears. How had the woman guessed about her and Isander? "The prince and I are simply acquaintances," Farren told her.

"Oh, I see. But are you sure he feels the same way? The way you look up there is stunning, my dear." The woman giggled, and her songbirds tittered from the high branches of her headdress.

"Excuse me," Farren said shortly, muttering apologies as she shoved through the remainder of the crowd to get to the dais.

When the crowd finally thinned, Farren nearly barreled straight into it. The painting was propped on a golden easel, otherwise unadorned. Farren stopped breathing as she took it in. Dark colors poured from the painting, and in the middle stood a woman, one that Farren had seen before, one that Isander had sent her from his mind.

The commander stood bright, strong, and assured, her leather armor glistening in light that seemed to rise from within her, not only pressing back the shadows, but controlling them. At her sandaled feet lay three attentive gryphons, and the commander had her hand on one of their heads, the only hint that the woman was more than a commander. A mother, of sorts.

The detail was perfect. Isander had again captured every angle of her, and she even thought she could recognize the gryphons. Naronimus, Thella, and the third—

Torch. His unmistakable tuft of curling head feathers protruded beside his perked ear. But in the painting, he was older.

"I wonder who it is," someone behind her asked.

"I've heard the prince will paint anyone," another said, "even beggars on the street, if they pique his interest."

"So she's wearing a costume?"

"Do you think he's *involved* with her?"

"The prince! Of course not. He wouldn't be cavorting about with beggars—"

"Or servants—" someone added.

"The queen would never allow it!" a third person admonished, shushing their speculation.

So much for trying to avoid more of the queen's attention. It was as if Isander tried to deliberately anger his mother by putting the painting on such display. It was cruel and thoughtless of him. Now there would be even more whispers about her, new speculations about who she was and what she wanted from the prince.

For an instant, she regretted ever having kissed Prince Isander.

Farren turned away without looking at any of them, her face hot as ember, her chin jutting in spite of it. She tugged her leather vest down, and scanned the dais. Isander was nowhere in sight, and a little wave of relief swept through her. It made it easier to sweep her feelings about the painting—about him—out of the way so that she could focus on her duty.

"Where in the Enchanter's realm have you been?" Cato seethed, an ink-stained hand racing through his unruly hair.

Farren glanced through the mass of moving bodies cluttering the atrium. "Trying to get through the crowd. I've never seen so many—"

"The queen's been asking for you," Cato said. "You were supposed to come with us before the guests arrived."

Farren had been stalking around the gryphon mews and yard, trying to route her way out with the gryphons when the time came, but of course she wasn't going to tell Cato that. "I had some business to see to," was all she said.

His eyes narrowed. "I want you here, where I can see you."

"Do you want me to stand with Thella while you mingle?" she asked innocently.

He grimaced. "No. You should speak to my mother."

"What does she want?"

"When you're done, come right back here. No wandering."

Farren bit back a snide reply, knowing it wouldn't help his opinion of her. Not that she cared what his opinion of her was... Besides, whatever he thought of her was probably right. Considering her plans tonight.

She looked up at the dais, and was taken aback by the sight of the queen and king on their thrones. Their elaborate masks depicted gryphon faces—the queen's narrow and sharp, much like her actual features, and the king's wide and sleepy-eyed.

"Don't look too surprised," Camilla's soft voice said over her shoulder.

The girl was dressed in a ruffled chiton dyed the shade of sun-lit moss. Despite the beautiful dress, Camilla looked ghostly, with deep shadows lingering beneath faded-sky eyes.

Farren's smile faltered. "Are you alright?"

"Just tired. I wasn't able to get much sleep last night."

"Your dreams again?"

Camilla gave her a lopsided smile. "No, actually. I was finishing the dress for Livigena."

"Oh." Farren fought the urge to chastise the girl for wasting her sleep. "Was she at least happy with it?"

The girl's smile widened. "She was as pleased as I've ever seen her. But it wasn't without cost." She held her hands up and wiggled several bandaged fingers.

"Camilla! You've got to be more careful."

Camilla shrugged. "It's not the worst pain these hands have suffered."

Farren's throat tightened. "You are too generous."

"No such thing."

Farren shook her head and decided not to spoil Camilla's evening with an argument. She tilted her head toward the queen and king. "Do they usually wear the masks at feasts?"

"They do," Camilla said. "I'm unsure if the queen does it to make herself look fiercer or to make the king look less so. I think it's her not-so-subtle reminder that she is the one who matters. That it's her bloodline that traces back to the Enchanters."

"But the king's bloodline isn't important?" Farren asked, suddenly wondering why she had never heard much about the king. She didn't imagine he had much control over the gryphon program, so had never considered trying to speak to him.

"Not unless you think falling asleep suddenly is a special ability. They call it a sickness, but really, most people find humor in it. He falls asleep at odd times, without warning."

"That does sound like a sickness. Listen, the queen has asked to speak with me. But can we talk after?"

Camilla dipped her head. "Good luck with that." She gave Farren a teasing grin before her slender frame slipped away into the crowd. Farren balked for a moment, fighting the urge to follow Camilla. To protect her from whatever darkness crawled in the crowd. Like thickets and venomous lizards.

She forced out a sigh, then took herself up to the dais. The glass wall at the back of the dais threw up her shadowy reflection, and she barely recognized herself. Who was this short, armored woman who approached the queen with a steady gait? No one important, Farren told herself. Just a servant. Just a guard. She caught the flash of her own eyes, the set of her jaw, and the glinting hilt of her dagger and knew what she told herself was a lie.

As she neared the queen, she grew keenly aware that every single person in the room had a good view of her as she approached the throne. Farren forced herself to focus on the queen's elaborate dress, which matched the bronze of her mask. Cut at the shoulders, the dress revealed the queen's skin-painted shoulders and arms: an elegant dance of irises winding over her like a cloak and trailing all the way to her fingers. In the heart of the iris imprinted on her chest, the clear gem of her necklace sparkled faintly in the candlelight.

"Farren Blackburn." Queen Aurelia's tone was clipped.

"I am here, Your Majesty."

"Good." The queen deigned to turn her head slightly, assessing Farren through the slits in the bronze mask. Narrower slits showed in front of her mouth, allowing her voice to carry through the metal. "I saw your work with Naronimus. I am quite happy with his display of magic. You two make quite the pair."

For a wild, panic-stricken moment, Farren wondered if Scipio had told her his suspicions. Where was Scipio, anyways? She hadn't seen him since arriving in the atrium.

The queen added, "I only hope that Naronimus will work as willingly for me."

"Of course, Your Majesty. He is well-tamed," she lied.

Her mind leapt to what would happen when Naronimus was gone and the queen found out she helped him escape. But she quickly pressed the thought away, unable to consider the future when so much hung over her head.

"Excellent. You are an adept fighter, Farren. I would hate for you to lose your place in my guard. And you show exceptional talent with those gryphons. Even my son was impressed."

Cato? Farren glanced to where he stood and flinched when she met his stare. She doubted he would've gushed about her to the queen. Isander, on the other hand...

"What about Elya?" the queen asked suddenly, her tone thoughtful.

"Your Majesty?" Farren looked toward the gryphon, swallowing involuntarily.

Elya looked demure as always, larger than Thella but her frame gentle and delicate. Elya was always the quietest gryphon, and she had bonded with the timidest of the recruits. Besides that, she was young, only a few years into maturity.

"I've heard she can manipulate the air?"

"Yes, Your Majesty," Farren replied, afraid to say more.

"Is she fecund? Would she conceive if mated?"

Farren's heart thumped unsteadily. "I'm...unsure. Prince Cato would know more about—"

"Cat will do whatever I ask of him," the queen said in an acid tone.

Farren bit her tongue, knowing that the queen was probably right.

"No matter. I've made my decision." Before Farren could wonder about what, the queen glanced toward the painting. "I thought I warned you about getting involved with my son?"

Farren's face flamed. Her eyes darted around the crowd, seeking out Isander. She couldn't find him, and a moment later, she pulled her attention back to the queen. *I don't need Isander*, she told herself. *I can protect myself. It's just a painting.*

She cleared her throat. "My apologies, Your Majesty, but your son was very insistent about painting me." She tried to make her tone emotionless, but an edge formed on each word.

The queen gripped the arms of her throne. "Don't get confused, girl. You are nothing to him. A toy to tinker with. Something to distract him."

Farren tried not to scowl, wishing the queen's words didn't prick her like needles. "It seems that the *distraction* has been fruitful," Farren risked saying, motioning to the painting.

The queen barked out a laugh, startling her husband, who must've been dozing. "What did you say, dearest?" he asked, his voice thick with sleep.

"Nothing, you." Then her bronze mask tilted toward Farren, feral and furious. "Next time you write to your father, do invite him for a visit. Perhaps he can bring along your mother and brother as well. They would love to see what you've been up to behind these walls." The queen lifted two fingers off the armrest. "You're dismissed."

Farren grimaced. She had known her letters to her family weren't private, as they never arrived sealed. But knowing that the queen's eyes had read her father's words—and likely her own—made her skin crawl.

She forced her mind to clear as she returned to Cato. Unlike her royal guard ensemble, he wore an embroidered cloak embellished with gold-threaded feathers and a billowy cream chiton with ruffled hem. It looked far more comfortable.

"Well?" he asked, crossing his arms.

"She asked about Naronimus. If he was ready."

"And what did you say?"

"That he was."

Cato cursed and shook his head.

"Was Balyon able to help find the missing people?" Farren asked.

"I tried," Cato said. "But he's still so young in his magic. And he's a bit slower than his siblings. I couldn't get any information from him."

"Hm."

"It's hard to ask for his help when I don't know any of the missing. Well, except for—"

"Persepha."

"Right." Cato tossed her an inquisitive look. "I tried sending my memories of her to Balyon but..." He blew air through his lips. "I couldn't get anything out of him."

An errant breeze moved down from the opening over the cistern pool and rushed to the dais, turning Farren's skin to gooseflesh.

"Do you think Balyon's magic might be limited to...living things?"

Cato's brows drew down. "He can find objects, so I don't think so."

"But a human isn't an object...alive or dead."

"He can find lost things. These people are lost."

"But they could be dead."

"I don't know."

Cato's grim look made her grow quiet. Through the windows, the evening light was fading to dusk. The Runeless man—a grey smudge among the bright, festive colors—was having his chalice of wine refilled from a servant's curved vessel.

"Why is there someone here from the Runeless Sect?" Farren asked Cato, and he looked at her sharply.

"Where?"

"Over there by the wall."

Cato was silent for a moment, his dark eyes steady on the half-hidden figure. "Diocleto. He's one of the Runeless leaders and a newer member of the Viridian Council," Cato said quietly. "He comes to many of the queen's functions."

"The queen doesn't mind?"

"The queen is the one who invites him. The late king put him on the Council, much to her annoyance. Diocleto has already influenced the other councilors to clear out some of the wilder places within Malodai."

Cato didn't seem reassured by that information, so Farren wasn't, either. "Why would she invite him?"

"She likes her enemies close to keep an eye on them. Try to keep things civil."

"She doesn't seem like the civil type," Farren said quietly, motioning to the people around the atrium. "It doesn't seem civil to have dangerous animals at a gathering, and there's certainly no civility in allowing half-trained beasts in the same room as—"

"Don't get started on that again, Farren. Now is not the time." Cato's short, tired tone made her hesitate. Whatever was bothering him must be the same reason why he looked like a week-old corpse.

The moment Isander entered the atrium, the air shifted. Murmurs erupted as the gold slash of Isander's slender form moved like a flame through the chaos of the crowd. He spoke with everyone he passed, nodding and shaking hands. Did he runebond with each of them as he walked, stalking their minds like a lion in the grass? Farren shivered, and his eyes shot toward her suddenly. She had let the window of her mind open, and she snapped it closed, but not before a small wave of longing hit her.

Longing and lust.

Isander's gaze drove into her, and a flash of heat struck deep in her belly.

A moment later, he was back to speaking with his guests, and Farren glanced surreptitiously at Cato. The prince was glowering as usual at his brother, but there was open suspicion on his face.

Much the same way Cato looked at her.

Before she could ask Cato what he was thinking, the queen clapped her hands and made a grand speech about the prince. Then, the people began bringing forward gifts. Isander stood just below the dais to accept them, thanking each person and remarking on each gift, no matter how dull.

No wonder people liked him.

He received plenty of gifts she knew would likely bore him—candles, soaps, furs, statues, and sparkling jewelry. But she noticed a subtle shift in him when a different gift was brought forward by the Runeless man.

Diocleto carried a small glass bowl in his hand, and he spoke loudly enough that his voice echoed off the atrium walls.

"Prince Isander, it is with pleasure that I present a gift from the Runeless Sect. It is a special mineral brought from our mines in the northeast. We thought you would enjoy it for your majestic paintings."

The prince stepped forward avidly, and dipped a finger into the bowl. As he brushed the powder from his fingers, he gave the man a puzzled look. "I thank you for your generous gift. It is an...interesting shade of brown." Isander's brief pause was a mere flicker, a hint that he had expected more from the man.

Diocleto smiled with a sharp, cunning mouth. "If you take a step back, I will show you something magnificent."

Farren felt the crowd tense, and she connected with Thella.

*Something seems off*— she started to say, but before she could finish the sentence, Diocleto threw something into the bowl. Fire exploded in front of the crowd.

# THIRTY-TWO

GASPS AND SCREAMS ERUPTED as flames burst from Diocleto's bowl. The fire sounded like a thousand rain drops hitting a tin roof, and it burned from white to molten red.

*Is it magic?* Thella asked, curious and not at all alarmed.

Farren stared at it, unsure. *It is something*, she said.

She held her breath until the flame died, and Diocleto held the bowl out once more, triumphant.

When Isander dipped a hesitant hand into the bowl, a glittering powder coated his finger. The shade was one Farren had never seen before, like a kiss between a pink rose and a burning sunset.

"Magnificent, indeed," Isander muttered, and he clapped the Runeless man on the back.

"What an excellent and thoughtful gift, Diocleto," the queen spoke up, a slight edge to her tone as the acrid stench of burnt minerals reached the dais. "We can always rely on your...group...for the most interesting inventions."

"It is a pleasure to bring it to your attention, as always," Diocleto said, giving a slight bow.

"Now that we have the gifts out of the way," the queen continued, "I would like to make a special announcement."

The crowd hushed.

"I have made some improvements with my guard, as you can see." Queen Aurelia swirled her hands gracefully toward Thella and Elya. "And it is only growing stronger. My aim is to keep you all safe and to ensure a secure throne for my sons so that they may continue to do the same. As we've done for generations.

"And now I would like to invite all of you to a very special display, which will happen tomorrow evening. You all are welcome back to Alidonia after the Festival of the Forging parade to celebrate the mating display of two of my most talented gryphons, Naronimus and Elya."

A frigid wave washed over Farren as the crowd erupted into applause.

Cato swore viciously. "Naronimus already injured Elya. What is she thinking?"

"I-I don't know. She asked if Elya was fecund—"

"Bloody enchantments, Farren. If you told her—"

"I didn't. I told her that only you would know if Elya could mate. I had no idea what she had in mind."

"What do you think he'll do to her if Delphi isn't there to protect her?"

"I don't know! How can the queen decide who gets mated? I thought that was your task?"

Cato inhaled sharply and looked toward Elya, apparently speaking with her. His jaw clenched.

"She's scared. She doesn't think she would—" He shook his head. "I'll speak to my mother." His tone hardened with resolve as he turned to climb the dais steps.

"I'm coming with you," Farren said.

"You've said enough to her already," Cato shot over his shoulder.

Grinding her teeth, Farren opened a runebond with Thella and immediately felt the gryphon's panic.

*Elya is very upset*, Thella told her hurriedly. *She thinks she will die, and I don't disagree.*

*We won't let it happen, not if we are releasing the gryphons tonight.* Farren was unable to stop herself from what she said to the gryphon next. *Do you see why Naronimus must go, why all the gryphons must go? The queen doesn't care who gets hurt. She doesn't see you the way I do, or the way Cato does. You are just tools, weapons.*

*Weapons? But she knows we protect people. Why would she want to hurt them? Or us? Doesn't she realize—* Thella's ears flattened suddenly and her head lowered as fear speared down the runebond, shaking the poise that had always carried Thella's thoughts.

*What?* Farren prompted.

*Doesn't she realize that we're stronger than her?*

The thought was said so quietly, so tumultuously, as if Thella had realized as she said it how treasonous it was.

No, Farren answered her, just as quietly. *She believes she is the strongest of us all. That everyone bends to her will.*

Thella had begun to quiver, her feelings spilling into Farren like hot water from a kettle. *I can't let Naronimus injure Elya.*

*Then we must release him tonight. Before the mating is to take place. Do not tell Cato*, Farren demanded, glancing in Prince Cato's direction to see if he made any progress with the queen. His mother wasn't even looking at him, but she could tell by the hunched way he stood that the queen spoke to him.

*But won't Cato try to stop the mating?* Thella asked.

*He is trying.* She chewed her lip, wondering if Cato felt dread the way she did whenever she was with her own mother. *You comfort Elya*, Farren told Thella, *and I will try to help Cato convince the queen.*

As Farren neared the throne, the royal guards watched her. They didn't stop her from approaching—likely because of her royal orange cloak. Still, it felt wrong to be treading so close to the thrones, but as she neared, Cato's tension became palpable. The queen's voice cut low beneath the lively chatter of the crowd, too quiet for anyone else to hear.

"Why can't you be more like Isander? You've always been such a disappointment."

"Maybe your expectations have been too high, Mother," Cato replied, and Farren blinked at him.

The queen made a noise of disgust. "If my expectations are too high, then you shouldn't be working in the mews at all. Would you like that, Cat? What would you do with yourself then?"

"You can't take that away from me." Cato's hands were balled, and he hadn't yet noticed Farren standing behind him.

"I can take away anything I damn well please, and I shouldn't have to remind you of that. One word with Horat and he will do as I say. You will be barred from the mews, forbidden to have anything to do with gryphons. You'll be stuck inside the keep, expected to attend the bare minimum of events as befits your title. Are those expectations low enough for you?"

The queen's words were acid, and Farren could sense Cato crumbling beneath them.

"Your Highness," Farren said, and the queen seemed so startled to hear someone else that she turned her bronze head.

As she glared through the slits, she hissed, "Remove yourself from the dais this instant."

"Please, Cato knows the gryphons better than anyone else. If you do this, Elya will be injured, if not killed—"

"I've had enough of your impropriety," the queen said tightly. "I suppose Cat's leniency has something to do with that."

Farren ignored Cato's cold look. "They aren't compatible. Naronimus and Elya. He has almost killed her before."

The queen tilted her head up. "The strongest always try to kill one another. That is how animals behave."

"Elya's magic may be strong, but she is timid. She will not use her magic on Naronimus out of fear for his retaliation."

"That is precisely my reasoning for this mating pair—not that I need to explain anything to you. Naronimus's magic is invaluable, and Elya's magic is strong. His personality leaves much to be desired, but Elya's personality," the queen tilted her head in the gryphon's direction. Elya sat hunched, her beak open as she panted, her gaze riveted to the dais. "She has the perfect temperament. Calm and submissive. When paired with Naronimus's abilities, her offspring will make perfect gryphons for the guard."

Farren stole a glance at Cato, waiting for him to speak up. He stood unmoving, his expression one of disbelief and a cold, dawning understanding. Something hardened in Farren's belly.

"He will still hurt her," she said to the queen, but her words were like raindrops on hot stone, hissing away to nothing.

"I will put Naronimus on a leash." The queen's bronze face turned away. "Now leave me alone before I have you removed. I will not change my mind about this. Cat, bring Thella here. She has the perfect demeanor to stand beside me. It is a shame she is too young yet to breed." The queen motioned for another guard to come. "Remember, Farren, how easy it would be for me to call your father back here. I hope you haven't forgotten your contract."

Farren stalked off the dais before the guard could reach her. She watched as Cato led Thella to the queen's side. The gryphon loomed high over the queen's head, her beak pointed and her paired talons splaying wider than the throne. At least she didn't have to worry about Thella hurting the queen; that would complicate matters. She had to calm Elya, to reassure Cato that they would make things work out. The last thing she needed was Cato lurking around the mews late because he was worried about the gryphons.

Elya shook with terror but tried not to show it. *I won't let this happen to you*, Farren said. *Thella has agreed to release Naronimus tonight. He won't touch you.*

The gryphon didn't respond, so Farren sent the beast a wave of calm, like the steady drafts of wind high up in the sky. She lingered just beneath the dais as she closed their runebond and reached out again with her runeskill.

Around the mews, thirteen gryphon minds stood out like silvery spheres. She was getting better at discerning them, and she was immediately pulled to Torch's bright bell of a mind, surrounded by his little siblings. Instead of touching him, she focused on the hot-sharp feel of Naronimus's sphere, relieved to find him in his normal chamber. She had bargained with Naronimus—he had worked with her as the queen ordered, and now Farren must free him—and Farren would not go back on her promise, especially now that Elya's life was at stake. Naronimus must be freed with the others as soon as Thella had returned to the mews.

There was no time to waste.

*Naronimus, our plan will be happening tonight. Thella has agreed to help release you.*

Muddled and dizzying, Naronimus's words spun down the runebond.

A *plan...tonight? I can't...*

*Naronimus? What's wrong with you?*

He tried to send her an impression, but all she received were shadows and a low muffled voice. It was as if Naronimus reached toward her from bottom of a murky lake.

Her palms sweat as she moved slowly away from the dais and along the edge of the crowd. When she ducked behind a group of tall *Rodentids* wearing ridiculous bowl-shaped hats full of tree squirrels chittering over oaknuts, Farren whipped the royal orange cloak from her shoulders and tossed it behind a pillar. Then she slunk from one clump of revelers to another until she reached the atrium doors. Hoping against the worst, she ran to the mews.

# THIRTY-THREE

FARREN SPED DOWN THE gryphon mews and stepped into Naronimus's chamber. Moonlight poured through the barred window high above and swayed on the bare floor. Naronimus had no baubles hanging from the ceiling nor comfortable furniture. The hearth was cold—she couldn't remember it ever being lit. When she opened a runebond with him, his mind sloshed and tilted.

Movement to her left caused her to leap back and brace into a fighting stance.

A figure peeled himself from the shadowy wall. "Ah, the country bumpkin. Or should I say something else, now that you've been *elevated* by the prince's painting?" He tisked. "That is bold of you to flaunt around with him so openly. Tell me, did your mother teach you to bed richer men, or is that something that all desperate country lasses do?"

Farren longed to sink her fist into Scipio's teeth. Instead, she straightened, and tried to make herself look calmer than she felt. Her runebond with Naronimus was still open, and he sent her a wave of bitterness.

*Not freeing me*, Naronimus said, his words wobbling through the runebond.

*I am. It will happen later tonight. What is he doing here?*

Scipio continued, "I am surprised to see you entering a gryphon chamber at such a late hour."

"You shouldn't be surprised to see me in the place where I work and live."

*Can you use your magic to get him to leave?* Farren asked Naronimus fervently.

*I can't...use magic. He can't feel forever...what I want.*

*Enchanters, Naronimus, I cannot understand you!*

Scipio tilted his head. "Does your coming here have anything to do with the queen's order?"

Farren sniffed, trying to pretend innocence. "You mean the mating display? Of course. I've come to tell Naronimus of it. To make sure he doesn't hurt Elya."

She started to look toward Naronimus, but Scipio said, "Don't worry about it. I've already informed him. And took precautions to make sure nothing happens before the display."

Confused, Farren looked at Naronimus, and saw the massive chains bound above each talon, the shackles overlapping the scarred and bare skin that had formed on Naronimus's legs from years of Anaxis' abuse. Grim desolation swelled in the runebond, grey and so unlike Naronimus's normal white-hot anger.

"I'm surprised he didn't bite you," Farren said, her voice sounding too high as it echoed around the chamber. She could see it now: Naronimus swayed as he stood. His eyes were dim and all of him seemed to droop toward the floor.

*He used magic on me*, Naronimus told her, fear biting at his words.

"What's he telling you?" Scipio asked, stepping closer to the gryphon and leering up at his beaked face.

"What did you do to him?"

"It's very effective, isn't it?" Scipio pulled a vial from his leather vest. "A special potion from the Runeless Sect. They really have some excellent inventions. Despite being mad and depraved."

"What does it do?" Farren demanded, the hair on her neck prickling.

*It's over*, Naronimus was telling her, looking at her as if he were already dead.

Farren clenched her hands. *No it's not; we just have to wait for Thella—*

"It causes sleepiness. Docility. Submission." He sneered at her. "All things you would benefit from."

"Right. Because the queen wants her guard to be docile toward threats." Farren wished fervently that she could fight him, right there and then. She was certain she might actually kill him.

Scipio frowned and tucked the vile away. "Anyways, I have this covered and don't need you here."

"How long will he be in chains?"

Scipio looked at her slyly. "Why does it matter?"

"Because it's cruel. Isn't the chamber enough of a prison for him?" Farren waved around at the talon-gouged walls.

"Queen's orders." Scipio shrugged. "He'll be this way until the mating. She wanted to be sure he didn't try escaping...and that no one tried to take him."

Farren glared at him, her chest tightening, and decided to ignore his insinuation. "How is he supposed to mate while under the influence of your poison?"

Scipio shook his head, his finger ticking side to side. "Potion, not poison. He'll be fine, like a man who drank a bit of wine before putting a wench on her back."

Oh, but if only she could knock the smirk right off his face.

*Where did he put the keys to your chains?* Farren asked Naronimus, but the beast only dipped his head as his eyes started to slide closed.

*Naronimus!*

The gryphon flicked an ear. *Horat.*

Farren spun wordlessly from the chamber, a shiver slithering up her spine as Scipio's chuckle followed her down the hall. Horat was nowhere to be found—likely he had retired to his room—and she slid into the study, closing the door quietly behind her.

She lit the candle on the desk and searched the drawers, beneath stacks of paper, and in every crevice and cranny of the shelves. No key.

Breathless, she stepped back and looked around the disheveled room. Was the key in Horat's bedchamber? She couldn't risk going there when he was in the room; he would reprimand her and probably tell the queen what she was up to. What if Naronimus had seen wrong, and Scipio *did* have the key? How would she get it without fighting him? Without alerting him more than she already had?

Farren sagged onto the stool.

*The poison.* What if she could take the vial from Scipio? If Farren could steal it, she could use it in Scipio's food, or Horat's, if he had the key. Or both of them.

The only problem was that she didn't know how much she would need to use without killing them. And that she was certain she couldn't steal it from Scipio without fighting him, and she had already decided that was too risky.

But he had said it was an invention from the Runeless Sect. So it was possible she could find more. Newly determined, Farren set about straightening the mess she had created in the study and snuffed out the candle.

The feast had petered to a thin crowd by the time Farren returned to the atrium. She stuck to the shadowed servant corridor and peered out at the guests. The queen was likely retired, and the king stood beneath the dais, guffawing at some joke one of his friends told.

Thank the Enchanters that she hadn't seen either Cato or Isander. Farren was just starting to think that the Runeless man, Diocleto, had left when she heard his voice coming from the open doorway of the back atrium. The expansive room was dimly lit by candles, but Farren couldn't get her eyes on him without being seen. She hung back in the front atrium, pretending to look at a large tapestry while straining to make out his low words.

"—over her son's death. I could send...in the next two days."

Farren shuffled closer, and winced as another voice spoke clearly.

"I trust your judgment," Isander said. "I will let you know if..."

His voice faded, and then their feet shuffled away. Farren pretended to be utterly engrossed by the tapestry, but toward the distant front doors, Isander emerged from another doorway into the front atrium. He clapped a hand on Diocleto's shoulder and said farewell, then left through a servant hall.

A moment later, Farren dodged through the front atrium doors, startling the guards on either side.

"Wait," she called softly to the Runeless man.

He turned, an easy smile on his face. A false smile, if Farren had ever seen one.

"Yes?"

"Are you friends with the prince?" She didn't know why she had asked; perhaps it was curiosity, perhaps it was the insanity of what she was about to do. Who she was about to get involved with.

Diocleto's lips tightened. "We are acquaintances," he said in a curt voice, glancing at the guards behind her. He turned away from her and strode down the torch-lit path toward a covered litter flanked by four servants.

Farren dodged in front of him before he entered the litter. "I need something that I think you have. I'm willing to pay."

Diocleto's expression shifted to pleasure—a transformation that was so deftly done, she wondered if it was genuine. "The Sect has many things to offer, for the right price. What are you looking for?"

"There's a potion," Farren said in a surreptitious voice. "One that a guard uses to make the gryphons sleep. I would like to buy some."

"For gryphons?" The man's voice matched hers.

"No." She didn't dare say more.

He studied her quietly for a minute, his face like a mask. Only one corner of his mouth lifted slightly, and she couldn't tell if it was a tick, or some sort of glee he tried to suppress.

"And I want to be sure," Farren added quickly, "that the potion doesn't cause harm, only sleep for a while."

The man nodded once, then glanced at his litter. She moved back, and a servant parted the curtain for him.

"Tomorrow," he said quietly, "one hour after dawn, meet me by the statue."

Disappointment gnawed at her. "You don't have any potion now?"

He frowned at her. "It would be very foolish to bring such a thing to the queen's home, don't you think?"

"Of course." She should be more careful of what she said. "How much does it cost?"

His smile curled up. "No charge for first-time customers."

That left her speechless as the servants carried him away.

Farren spent nearly the entire night pacing her chamber as she discussed new plans with Thella. They had confirmed that Elya had also been chained up once she returned to her chamber and that a guard was posted outside her door. Every so often, she would close her runebond with Thella to connect with Delphi, frustrated that the gryphons could speak to one another simultaneously, but that her runeskill would only let her runebond with one gryphon at a time.

They all agreed that it was best to wait for Farren to free Naronimus to enact the plan. Farren's idea of using the poison on Scipio and Horat was risky, but Thella had agreed to make her invisible so that she could creep into the kitchens where their breakfast would be prepared. Once she found the key and released Naronimus, he would use his magic to compel any lingering servants to leave and attend the festivities in the city for the day. If everything went according to plan, the gryphons would all be gone long before sunset, when the mating display was scheduled to occur.

At dawn, Farren roused herself and dressed in her short chiton, leggings, and leather armor by the flickering light of a lumpy candle. She would go first into the city, before Horat and the others awoke.

Once she dosed Scipio and Horat's meals, she would have to find the key to Naronimus's chains, free him, and, once he was able to fly, gather the gryphons. Then they would head north of the fortress where the gryphons would have plenty of room to take flight over the river, all under the cover of Thella's invisibility magic.

Her plan had to work, because it was the only one she had left.

A rapid knock on the door made her flinch. She finished tightening her belt and cracked the door open. "What is it?"

Livigena offered a small tray with a steaming cup of *birali* and a stack of buttered flatbreads.

"Another breakfast from your special admirer," Livigena said, her charcoal-lined eyes crinkling slyly. "He said he wants you to start the day off strong. I was not happy to be in the kitchens so early this morning, but he came around and cheered me right up."

In the chaos, Farren had completely forgotten about Isander. Had he expected to see her after his birthday feast? Farren took the tray, noting with dismay that he hadn't left a sketch for her this time.

"Thanks."

"You're welcome! Oh, you missed the gathering in the kitchens last night! Camilla sewed me the most wonderful dress of brocade, and of course Aktis was fawning all over me because of it. She's such a wonderful girl. I've given her every ounce of my love since she's arrived, and just look at how she's blossomed!"

Farren pulled her lips into a smile. "I'm glad it all went well, especially since Camilla spent so many hours sewing the dress for you."

Farren waited for the woman to acknowledge the suffering Camilla had endured, but Livigena suddenly became preoccupied with a stray curl of hair and excused herself. Farren shut the door and set the tray on her desk. As she sipped the *birali*, she studied the pink-tinged sky through her little window, her skin turning to gooseflesh at the autumn draft that slid in between the panes.

Farren found she could only drink a few sips of the *birali* and nibble at the bread, her stomach turning in tandem with her worry over the plan. Farren tied up her sandal thongs, grappled her hair into a braid and headed for the door.

A few steps from it, she stumbled.

Dizziness rocked into her, rolling waves that caused her to tilt. Something warm fuzzed up her legs, and she grabbed the bedpost, a whimper escaping as weakness flooded her knees. The warmth crept into her back and arms, and when it reached the base of her neck, tiredness folded over and over her thoughts. Smothering them.

Farren gripped the bedpost and forced herself to stand. The floor wobbled, threatening to come up to meet her. Mind sluggish, she looked around the room. The blurry bed. The swaying chair and desk. Her eyes snagged on the cup of *birali*.

"Enchanter's curse," she tried to say, but her tongue fumbled the words.

She pulled herself up to sit on her bed, but her legs shuddered as she did so, and she rolled onto the bed instead, turning until she lay on her back with feet flopped over the edge of it. Her limbs prickled hot and cold. Her eyelids dragged down.

Vaguely, she heard the door open and close. Sandals thumped across the floor, and then a face loomed above her.

"It's time for the country bumpkin to sleep," Scipio said, his sneer a bone-white slice over his face. "It's important that you don't cause trouble today."

Farren couldn't speak. She had never hated anyone as much as she hated him in that moment—even his father, Anaxis.

Her fingers twitched. She longed to reach for her knife and plunge it into Scipio's chest. She had never killed anyone before. Not that she hadn't wanted to. Just once, after Desmond's attack. And now.

Tears pricked at her eyes. Fires sparked and sputtered in her, smothered by the potion cooling her veins. Her heartbeat slowed. Shadows started to move in, pooling at the edge of her vision as she forced herself to stare at the man above her.

"Oh, and I'll let Horat and the prince know you aren't feeling well today. That they shouldn't disturb you. Sleep, little bumpkin. Have sweet, trouble-free dreams."

And she did.

# THIRTY-FOUR

WHEN SHE NEXT OPENED her eyes, she was alone. She blinked around the room, trying to remember where she was.

Distant voices shouted down the halls. A draft swept in from the window, and Farren shivered violently, coming fully awake as her body shook.

She was in the mews. In her bed. And Scipio had poisoned her.

The poison was still in her blood; it slogged in her limbs and wended between her thoughts like carded wool. Something lit in her, and the shivering intensified, making it difficult for her to stand. But she did, clenching her fists and sucking in air, willing it to clear her mind.

Out the window, the sun hovered over the horizon. It was nearly time for the mating display to begin. Farren stumbled across the room, dizziness rocking her, then cracked open her door. The hall was empty. She headed for Naronimus's chamber. Too much time had passed; she had lost her chance to get the poison from Diocleto. But that didn't mean she couldn't try to free Naronimus some other way. Besides that, she still had to free the others.

The only problem was that her limbs couldn't quite keep up with her. Nor her mind.

When she reached the hall with Naronimus's chamber, she nearly ran into a cluster of recruits. She fell back and peered around the corner. Chains rattled as the recruits tugged Naronimus down the corridor, where a large metal box stood open, its gaping mouth a black hole. Huge wooden wheels held the box aloft.

"Come on you stubborn bastard!" Scipio's voice rang down the hall, and Farren grit her teeth.

"Stop!" a voice shouted.

Farren teetered as Prince Cato appeared next to Scipio.

The prince gestured wildly at the metal cage. "The box will make everything worse—"

"It's the only way we'll get him there!" Scipio spat. "He nearly trampled a recruit coming out of the chamber."

"You should've waited for me like I told you. There's no rush—"

"Are you going to help, or not?"

Clenched fists and a face of stone. "I will not put him in there, cousin."

"So you won't help us. Do you really want to be a traitor to your mother?"

Prince Cato glowered at him, but said nothing, and then Scipio shouted at the recruits to push Naronimus forward.

When Farren touched the heat of Naronimus's mind, fury lanced through her, but a rill of cold ran just beneath it.

*I can't go*, Naronimus told her in a short burst. He was in pain from the chains, his head ached from the potion Scipio had been dosing him with since last night. But none of those things bothered him the way the box did.

*Your magic, Naronimus!*

His thoughts were too scattered and slow, and his body not much better. *I can't. Or maybe, just one, but it won't be enough—*

*You must try!*

She felt the nudge of his magic, and Scipio suddenly quieted, swaying for a moment before shaking his head. Then he yanked the chain taut once more, bellowing in fury at Naronimus. He sounded just like Anaxis, his voice dripping with venom and spite, his knuckles turning white as he gripped the chain leash—

Farren bit her lip and clumsily narrowed the runebond, clearing it of Naronimus's memories. If Naronimus couldn't use his magic, there was no way for him to get out of this. Even Horat was there, overseeing the process with a grim expression. Cato had backed away, but Farren could feel his shadow in Naronimus's mind, speaking to the gryphon just as she was.

*Just do what they want*, Farren begged.

Naronimus's talons slipped on the stone floor, and he took one hesitant step forward, then another. His hind legs froze up, and he pressed back.

*I can't. Don't let them do this—* He was pleading with her, but Naronimus never did that. He was never frightened. *Please don't let them put me in a box again!*

Naronimus widened their runebond, and an impression collided with her thoughts. A dank box of metal enveloped him in darkness.

It was so small that he couldn't open his wings or turn around. His whole body ached. The worst part was that he knew that when the box opened, he would see something worse: Anaxis. And an entirely different level of pain would come after.

Farren reeled as the image left her. Her nails scraped the wall as she fought to hold herself still. It was just as Cato had told her—Naronimus had been kept in a box for far too long, and now he was being forced into a box again. Strangest of all was that the donkeys pulling the box were facing the wrong way—toward the entrance of the mews rather than the door to the mating chamber.

*Why aren't they taking you to the mating chamber?* Farren asked.

*The falls*, he said.

Farren's stomach churned as she imagined Naronimus flying over the falls, chained. *Isn't that too dangerous? Can you even fly with the poison in you?*

*Please!* The blackness inside the box nearly swallowed Naronimus's head.

Farren lurched forward, half-stumbling, half-running to Naronimus. She would drag Scipio down if she had to, if he wouldn't listen to the prince—

"Farren," Prince Cato appeared in front of her and grabbed her by the arms. "What are you doing here? I thought you were sick?"

His face was far too close to hers, nearly spinning. "Cato, we have to stop this. We can't let Scipio—"

"I've already tried, Farren. It's the queen's orders. I'll make sure Naronimus doesn't hurt Elya. The recruits and I will try to calm them as much as we can."

"No, you d-don't understand. I made a promise to him—" Her voice had begun to slur, and nausea somersaulted her belly.

"Are you drunk?"

She turned away from him and heaved. Nothing came up. Enchanters, she needed to rid this poison from her body. Biting back a frustrated cry, she grabbed at Cato, using him to steady herself. The neck of his chiton crumpled in her fists. Behind them, Naronimus screamed, and talons scraped metal as he entered the tomb-like box. A small part of her still melded with the gryphon's mind, and she felt a piece of Cato there, too, shivering in the waves of desperation and fear.

"Naronimus doesn't deserve this," she said, putting effort into how her tongue formed the words. "We must let him go."

Cato searched her face, and she willed him to see, to *feel* through the runebond what Naronimus truly needed. For a breath of a moment, his brows lifted and a strange light entered his gaze.

"Are you saying that..." His gaze narrowed. "I can't, Farren. Even if I wanted to."

"You need to. He is suffering. Let him go, Cato."

He expelled a breath. "I have no control over this."

Hadn't Isander said something about control to her once? Farren's mind reeled to the memory.

"Sometimes when you have no control," she said, trying to echo Isander's words, "there's a chance to...bend things to your will...a nd you just have to take it."

He stiffened beneath her hands and pried her fingers from his embroidered chiton.

"You're drunk, Farren. Go back to bed. That's an order."

He tore away from her and stalked back to the recruits. Farren braced herself on the wall, wincing as the door to the metal box screeched on its hinges and closed with a bang.

Inside it, Naronimus shook with memories. She widened her connection with him.

*I'm so sorry*, Farren said, wishing poison didn't weigh her down, wishing Scipio wasn't in the hall, wishing Cato could do more. But wishing didn't help her or Naronimus.

The gryphon didn't respond, but Cato was there with him, muttering things that sent calm fluttering into him. If anyone could help Narominos to be unafraid, it was Cato. She trusted him with that, and trusted that he would help Elya, too.

As the others disappeared down the corridor, sounds faded from the halls, and then, the mews fell silent. This was her only chance. Farren might not be able to stop the entire gryphon program, but she would sure put a massive dent in it.

Still runebonded with Naronimus, Farren sent out one last impression. *I will be back as soon as I can*, she said. *Do not hurt Elya. If you have a chance at freedom, take it*. She let loose an image: Naronimus breaking free from his chain to sail across the falls. A tiny flame of hope that pushed at the darkness in his box. She left him then, reassured in his growing calm, with her promise to return spurring her into movement.

The spinning had receded somewhat, and she lurched back to her room, her mouth parched. She guzzled water from her leather flagon and strapped it into her belt. With any luck, it would help leach the poison from her body.

Naronimus's reluctance to leave had likely delayed the mating display, which would give her more time. When Farren reached Thella's chamber, the gryphon confronted her with bristling feathers.

*Where have you been?!*

Farren grimaced and leaned against the chamber wall. *Scipio poisoned me. And the plans have changed. They are taking Naronimus to the falls as we speak. And Elya—*

*They've already taken her*, Thella said, affirming Farren's fear that two gryphons would be left behind. *She's in chains, too.* Thella paced her room once more, her ears brushing the glittering baubles hanging from the rafters. Fiery specks swiveled over the walls. *She won't be left behind*, Thella said finally. *I still plan on remaining.*

*You haven't changed your mind about staying?*

*I stay for Cato and Elya. Who knows what damage Naronimus will do to her?*

*I will return and try to free Elya and Naronimus as soon as I can.* Dizziness rocked her, and she swallowed tightly against a sudden bout of nausea. *Right now, all eyes are on them. I would be imprisoned if I tried anything. Cato said he would do what he could to keep her safe.*

It was too late to convince Thella to change her mind about leaving. And she had nothing left to say to Thella that the gryphon didn't already know. She had seen for herself how demanding and selfish the queen could be.

Farren guzzled more water, took a breath to steady herself, then swung open the door. The servants had gone, and silence engulfed the entire mews.

It was time.

Thella eased out behind Farren, and moments later, gryphons filed out of their chambers. The air thickened as Hylas' magic doused the air—dampening the sound of scraping talons and rustling feathers.

By the time Farren reached Torch's chamber, the shaking caused by Scipio's poison had left her body, but when she saw Torch, sleeping peacefully in the last strip of sunshine coming through the window, she wanted to weep.

How could she possibly say goodbye to him? How could she ever face another day without seeing him, without feeling his joy and curiosity and energy? The thought of him not being in his chamber, not being within easy reach of her every moment, left her feeling unbearably cold. The life she could return to after her Servitude, with the hawks and her family and familiar village life, suddenly seemed empty. Farren knew, in the deepest part of her, that it wouldn't be enough.

But it would have to be. She would have to let him go.

He woke as she stepped into the chamber, and he nearly tripped over his talons as he scrambled to greet her. Under the ministrations of his piercing cries and bracing wing beats, Farren dried her eyes and made sure he knew what was happening.

*Mother told me everything*, he said excitedly. *I wouldn't go, at first, but she promised I would be able to see you again.*

Farren's chest hurt as she looked over to Delphi, who stood waiting in the doorway. The gryphon met her gaze, steady and knowing and fierce.

*That's right*, she told Torch, hating that she had to lie to him. As long as the City Watch disallowed gryphons, as long as Queen Aurelia reigned, it would never be safe for him to return to the city. *Now we must walk quickly and quietly until we are out of the fortress walls.*

He stuck by her side as they went down the halls. Farren opened the outer door of the mews and checked the pathway to be sure no one was around before telling the gryphons to follow. Invisible, she led the eleven gryphons through the gardens. The path led them past the stables, where the horses nickered and stomped in their stalls. Farren pressed on, knowing that if someone looked too closely, they might see the hedges bend or the irises crush underfoot.

Fog rolled in from the river, clinging to her skin and clothes. She tucked her cloak more firmly around herself. A few spare guards walked along the outer wall of the fortress. Because of the late hour and likely because most were at the mating display, the gate to the West Tow was nearly empty. A lone guard stood facing the opposite direction. Beyond the gate, the expanse of river was framed by the western portion of Malodai, where mossy gables emerged from patches of autumnal forests and half-tamed scrub.

All they had to do was walk past the guard without being noticed—

A low growl rumbled through the thick air, and an enormous coyote emerged beneath the arched gateway, ears flattened and head low to the ground. It looked directly at them.

*Don't panic*, Farren said to Thella, even though her own heart beat as fast as a honeybird's wings.

*It can't see us, but I cannot hide our smell! And the sound—*

*Hylas is trying to cover our noise, but the coyote may still hear.*

The guard turned, squinting in the direction the coyote moved—for it was creeping low, hackles raised.

*Whatever you do, don't drop your magic,* Farren urged. *The guards on the wall have bows and arrows, and you could be a target. And I cannot be spotted—*

The coyote's growl intensified, and Farren halted as it grew closer. The guard followed, and Farren saw that it was Iana.

*You must lead the others away,* Farren said to Thella. *Now! Otherwise, they won't make it—*

A wisp of a cry erupted—the noise feathering above Hylas' dampening magic. It was one of Torch's young siblings—and the faint noise spurned the coyote to a run.

Farren broke off the path and connected with Torch. *Fly now, fly!*

She couldn't see him, but sensed with her runeskill that he obeyed, running back along the path until he gained the speed to rise in the air.

"Who is there?" Iana shouted, tugging her sword from its leather sheath.

Shrubs crashed and soil churned as the gryphons leapt and ran from the dodging coyote. The beast was quick, its maw snapping as it tried to find the thing it could not see.

Through her runeskill, Farren sensed Torch and Delphi lift away, followed by Eralius, Grit, and—

Phynx, heavy with kits, was too slow. The coyote headed straight for her, around a little dewfall tree, where a rusthawk watched the coyote with avid eyes.

Farren snapped a runebond open with the hawk. *The coyote is hunting beneath you. It will scare away all your food.*

The rusthawk sent her a flash of annoyance and burst from the tree. It dove and scratched at the coyote's head, then swooped away to gain height before diving again. From Iana's outcry, it drew blood. The coyote fell back, giving Phynx just enough time to get into the air.

By now, the guards on the wall had their arrows nocked, but Thella's magic still cloaked the gryphons, who winged high above. They were all in the air, except for Torch's three siblings. Farren reached with her mind, and found them in the distance, in the direction of the mews. They must've turned back, too frightened to take flight.

Delphi's panicked cry trumpeted briefly—still softened by Hylas' magic, but it was just enough for the guards on the wall to point up. Three arrows flew toward them, and Farren stifled a scream.

The arrows arced and then fell, missing the gryphons. The gryphons rose higher, beating fast and hard at the air. Iana's large frame filled the gateway, and her sword pointed out, ready to strike down whatever invisible enemy came her way. Farren darted back to the mews. She had to find Delphi's other young and get them out.

She runebonded with Thella, her head spinning. *You can drop your magic from me. Lead the others beyond the wall until they are out of reach of the City Watch—*

*Farren!* Thella's impression was urgent, causing Farren to stop in her tracks. *Something is happening back at the fortress. Elya is hurt, and...I think Naronimus may be drowning.*

*Drowning!* Farren's heart hammered in her ears. *Why is Elya hurt? Did Naronimus hurt her?*

*I'm not sure. We can feel her pain, can't you?*

Panic seized her. Closing her runebond with Thella, she stretched her mind toward the falls—no, past it—and opened to Elya. Thella was right; pain lanced through Elya's hind leg, and she couldn't move from where she lay downstream from the falls. Naronimus was closer, and when Farren closed her runebond with Elya and connected to him instead, she nearly lost herself in the sensation of water pulling and pulling down. Naronimus could barely move beneath the massive pounding of the waterfall. The chains held him pinned beneath its weight.

*Naronimus!* She sent a burst of fear toward him, and followed it quickly with anger. He couldn't be in trouble. He was stronger than that. And he had probably hurt Elya, so she shouldn't even care about what happened to him. *Move, Naronimus! Move your wings.*

Naronimus couldn't respond. Farren clutched at a tree so hard that the bark flaked beneath her palm. He knew he was dying. He was too weak to resist.

A sob lodged in Farren's throat. It was the poison Scipio had fed him, making him weak and sluggish, and he couldn't resist the pull of it, especially not after having suffered that box. Once inside the box, memories assaulted him, and would've broken him again, but the poison had been a refuge, and now all he wanted was to sink into it forever. Even Cato hadn't been enough to pull him out of it completely.

Farren swore. She closed her runebond with Naronimus, sensing all the gryphon minds swirling above her, waiting. Reluctantly, Farren runebonded with Thella.

*Farren*, the gryphon said quickly. *We can't—*

*I know. I must go back. But the others should go on, get away while they can—*

*I told them such, but they cannot abandon an injured gryphon any more than you can. And Delphi will not leave her children. I will go to Elya. The others wish to come with me.* Thella wasn't asking, and Farren couldn't argue with her. If they felt even a fraction of what Farren was feeling—what Farren was trying *not* to feel through the runebonds—then nothing would stop them from trying to save one of their kind.

As the gryphons wheeled toward the falls, Farren swept down the path toward the keep like a falcon stooping toward prey. Her breath formed a bellows within her, her mind a talon of intent as she gathered every morsel of anger she had, pulled from her most painful memories. Desmond's attack. Her mother's rejection. Every fight. Scipio's wretched face. Even Naronimus himself, selfish and hateful and brutal. She reached until she met the very depths of her rune-made soul, then sent it spiraling down her runebond to Naronimus, breathing life into his torpid body.

*Use me, you fool. Use my anger and live!*

# THIRTY-FIVE

NARONIMUS'S PARALYSIS BROKE AS he shrieked to life. He swung against his chains and grappled along them until he gained purchase on the rocks.

Farren gasped as he breathed, dispelling fear as he shook water from himself. Along the balcony's edge above him, little men with pale, taut faces held Naronimus's rattling chains. Behind them, the crowd moved out into the open and pointed at the sky where gryphons swarmed overhead, forgetting about him entirely after he had plummeted down and not returned. They had assumed him dead, perhaps.

*You can fly away*, Farren urged him, forgetting that she ran to the keep, forgetting where she was as she sank deeper into their runebond. *Shake them free of your chains.*

*And then what? Drag chains around until the day I die? I will not wear chains in freedom.*

*But now is your only chance—*

Naronimus bunched his wet body and leaped up to the balcony, pivoting toward one of the men who held his chains. His beak sank easily into flesh, breaking bones and tearing ligaments. The sound of the freed chain hitting stone shivered into him. One binding, reduced to a heap of nothing. It was the least the human had deserved, after pulling at him like a human doll and forcing him into a metal box.

Farren's fingers dug into her palms, and she tried to distance her mind from Naronimus. But their runebond widened, pulled by the fire surging between them as Naronimus inflicted his destruction.

Bile burned the back of her throat as she ran toward the keep—her legs heavy with the residue of poison, her mind there but not there as her mind moved with Naronimus. He took satisfaction in each twitch of his beak, in the crush and snap of bones beneath the weight of his talons. He took down one guard, then another.

Camilla held her hands up, long braids flashing in the dying sun as she ran in front of him, and Naronimus hesitated. But the heat in him was too hot, and the girl was only getting in the way. He spread his wings, cried out his fury at being chained, at being poisoned, being held hostage in the damnable fortress. All he wanted was to rip through things, to destroy all he hated.

Ice speared into Farren: the same terror she had while watching him attack Desmond while she lay too far away, entangled in a game of sparring, and she could do nothing to stop what she knew was about to happen.

Except that wasn't true, now.

She wanted to scream at Naronimus through their runebond, but that would only make things worse. Instead, she filled her lungs with a calm that reminded her of the black starry skies of night. She imbued a command with it, and shot it down their runebond with all the authority she could muster.

*Naronimus, do not touch her.*

Her impression hit Naronimus as he lunged at Camilla, and it dragged him down beneath the wild tide of his recklessness. Instead of cutting through Camilla, he swiveled past her, his intention to harm her gone. But the side of his wing knocked into her, and Farren's heart dropped as Camilla tumbled over the edge of the balcony and disappeared into the roar of mist.

Something pricked Naronimus's neck. A moment later, Farren lurched forward, spasming as their deep runebond shattered.

She had fallen on the stone path leading to the keep where the balcony was. Farren scrambled back up, scraping her hands on the rough-cut stone. Her breath came short and fast, and a ringing resounded in her ears, the pitch of it rising high above the crash of the nearby falls.

"She... She just..." Farren tried to swallow past a massive lump in her throat.

Her hands tingled. She looked hard toward the falls, seeking sign of Naronimus flying, reaching out to him with her runebond, needing to know if he could see Camilla. But she felt only other gryphons, not Naronimus. There was no gryphon cry she could hear, and no screams.

The mist to the south was too thick to see through, and the crash of water would mask any sound, no matter how desperate. The falls were long, the water going down with a speed and heaviness that Farren could hardly imagine.

There was no way Camilla would have survived it.

A scream rose up inside her, and she longed to release it into the void of the mist. But she was no longer invisible, and couldn't risk drawing attention to herself. Guards walked along the outer fortress wall. Farren crossed her arms against her shaking body and reached out to Torch. She faltered as she felt his fear.

*Where are you*, she asked.

*Mother is looking for Elya. She can't find her!*

*You need to stay close to her. I'm on my way.*

Farren burst through the unguarded doors of the keep. Screams echoed around the front atrium, and the thrones stood empty. Farren veered toward the opposite side of the keep where the back atrium opened to the long stone balconies jutting over the falls.

Hundreds of people pressed back from the balconies, where gryphon wings flashed between spears and arrows. Farren bit back a screech as one nearly hit its target. Apparently Naronimus had frightened them into losing all logic. Where was he now?

She reached out to a gryphon flying close to the balcony—Eralius—and tried to squash the gryphon's fear. Her own limbs still shook with shock, and her mind spun like a hawk lure, round and round and round, every time flashing with Camilla's pale, pinched face.

*You will be killed!* she screamed at Eralius. Hylas and Calipsa flew just beyond him. *I know you want to help Elya and Naronimus, but the queen's guards do not care, and this is your only chance! Fly away while you can.* She urged him to take the others toward the mountainous Blades where the queen would be unable to touch them.

Near the balcony doors, guards pulled people inside the keep while they wielded weapons outward.

"Stop!" Farren's voice didn't rise above the noise, so she thrust against the press of bodies to get to the guards. "STOP!"

One of the guards just outside the doors turned toward her, frowning.

Scipio. His face went slack.

"Don't hurt them!" Farren screamed, her outcry finally cutting through the noise.

The guard frowned at her, and he aimed the long shaft of his weapon at Eralius, who had stubbornly ignored her and now reared on the balcony. One of the guards who threatened him with a spear swore aloud as the wooden handle splintered—Eralius' magic at work.

Without hesitation, Farren leapt through the doorway and yanked Scipio's arms down. He turned on her with a snarl and twisted away. Farren tripped and fell onto a mound of sodden feathers and fur. Naronimus lay prone on his side, pink water coalescing on the stone floor as the lingering blood-red powder applied to his feathers dripped away. She put a hand to his chest, warmth flooding back into her when she felt his heart beating.

He had been sedated for his ruthlessness. If she had just let him die, then Camilla wouldn't have fallen. She would still be—

Unable to finish the thought, Farren turned back to Scipio, jumping up when she saw his weapon once again pointed at Eralius. A moment later, Scipio put the weapon to his lips and blew a burst of air. Something burst from the shaft and flew straight for Eralius' heart.

She reached to yank the weapon from Scipio before he could hurt another, but a hand tugged on her arm.

"Farren! Leave him!" Cato shouted in her ear.

Farren looked at him, feeling crazed. "He's hurting them!"

"No, he's putting them to sleep!" He jabbed a finger toward Eralius, who slumped to the ground and closed his eyes. Scipio must've gotten more poison. Had the strange shaft weapon been an invention from the Runeless Sect, too?

Just beyond the balcony, Hylas and Calipsa paced in wide arcs. Their focus was on the falls below, not on the chaos of the balcony. The others—Grit, Phynx, and Thella—were not in sight, and Farren couldn't rest a moment to sense them with her runeskill.

"Why are all the gryphons free?" Cato spoke quickly in her ear, his voice edged in panic. His face was stricken and sickly white. But he was concerned about the wrong thing. He didn't know that—

"Camilla," Farren started, but found she couldn't form the words to tell him what happened.

Cato shook his head, wide eyes turning toward the falls. "She—she went over," his mouth wobbled, but he gripped her arm. "I couldn't stop it."

Farren swallowed the truth down, knowing it would doom her. "I just... I need to..."

She dragged away from him, something propelling her across the balcony. She slid as she reached the banister and gripped the cold, wet stone with trembling hands. Mist shrouded the bottom of the falls, but a wind whipped up and stung her face, powerful enough that Farren had a sense of how far down the falls were.

It felt like leagues.

Her eyes burned. What had she expected to find? Camilla still there, hanging in the air, waiting to be rescued? There was no second chance for Farren to save Camilla, just as there hadn't been a second chance to save Desmond.

A shudder racked her body, and she gripped the banister so hard that the rough stone cut into her fingers. The sharp pain brought her back from the precipice just enough that she could think about what to do next. She reached out beyond the damnable mist and found Delphi.

*Have you seen Camilla?* she asked the gryphon, not bothering to hide her panic.

No, the gryphon answered. *I have found Elya. She's badly wounded. I cannot reach her mind.*

Heart in her throat, Farren tore away from the banister and turned to find Scipio and Cato staring at her questioningly.

*Enchanter's curse.* She had to be very careful now. Her breath was coming far too quickly, and she fought to slow it. She needed to think clearly, but all she could think about was how Camilla had been flung into the falls.

She forced herself to check Eralius first, confirming the gryphon's slow, steady pulse, then made herself speak. "We have to go get Elya," she called out to Cato, trying to hide the way her hands shook. "She's hurt."

Cato's brow furrowed and his eyes closed as he apparently opened his runebond to Delphi. "This way." He grabbed her hand, and Farren allowed him to pull her away, trusting his runeskill to find the gryphon. She avoided Scipio's sharp gaze as they passed.

"The queen got to safety," Cato shouted above the din.

As if she had asked. As if she cared.

She glanced at a man who sat shivering against the wall, his arm bloodied. Across the room, a woman exclaimed in a shrill voice how gryphons were monstrous beasts, and the queen must be mad. Cato pulled her around a tussle where a man tried to steal a guard's sword to kill the gryphons himself.

Farren watched it all, an unbearable cold creeping into her. Her leather armor was slick from the mist, and the only thing tethering her to the ground was Cato's firm grip.

"We need to get the other recruits, and Muta," he said, referring to the stale-breathed animedic whom Farren had asked, unsuccessfully, about Mellion's death. "We'll need a few supplies."

Farren clamped her mouth shut and focused on communing with Torch, keeping their runebond narrow so that he wouldn't feel her panic about Camilla. She tracked him using her runeskill, and sensed that he was somewhere below the falls.

*We are coming*, she tried to reassure Torch, but it was far, and it would be difficult to reach the pool at the base of the falls.

"What if we don't reach Elya in time?" she heard herself ask Cato. The prince had gathered Alexon, Virilus, and Callipe. Muta ambled up to their group in the atrium with surprising alacrity for his large size, carrying a large sack.

"We'll get there quickly," Cato said to her in a hushed voice. "This way," he motioned with his head at the group, and they all followed at a brisk pace.

"How?" Farren struggled to keep up with them as her legs wobbled like jelly.

Alexon, who worked nervously at one of the honeyed candies in his mouth, glanced back at her warily. He hadn't looked at her the same way since she and Naronimus had begun practicing with the gryphon's magic on the recruits. "We'll have to take the East Tow and find horses to get us through Malodai to the border wall. Then somehow find a way down the steep, stony hills to the base of the falls—"

"None of that," Cato said, his tone clipped. "There's a different way. Much more direct."

Farren followed them out of the front atrium, where guests still clustered beneath the dais as if waiting for the king and queen to arrive. Many spoke in small groups, with hushed voices as they passed. A few of the injured waited on lounges for the royal healer to attend them, while others pressed toward the keep doors, eager to be out of harm's way. Cato had left several recruits with the guards on the balconies to help commune with any gryphons who might decide to land there.

Cato veered down a wide hall, and Farren's gaze roved past each door, seeing but not really noticing the riches beyond them. They passed what appeared to be a ballroom, a private library, then a sitting room. A small group of men argued by the door. One of them looked familiar, and Farren reflexively swallowed. It was Diocleto. He noticed her stare, and his scowl shifted minutely. Had he just winked at her?

Cato's grip on her arm was a vice. "We have to stick together. It's late, and there are people who are very angry about what happened with the gryphons."

Farren gave him a frank look, her mind clearing for a moment. "Like you?"

"I don't have time to think about my feelings right now. We need to get to Elya."

"And look for Camilla," Farren added, knowing that Elya needed help, but unable to stop her words.

Cato grit his teeth, then pulled her into a chamber where the rest of the group already waited. He closed the door to the study. "We'll take the stairs down."

"What stairs?" Farren peered around the room, which seemed to be a sort of study.

A large fireplace framed by two stone gryphons cradled a tiny fire, and a man wearing a servant's plain chiton stirred the embers with a poker. Books lined the wall on either side of the mantle, but the other walls were filled with portraits. One showed the queen and king, another the two princes together, both paintings dull and lifeless. But the others held a characteristic Farren immediately recognized. Isander's perfect details shone out from his portraits—one of a brown-haired young woman with a pointed chin and a gardener's apron, another of an old wine merchant with a knobby cane, and a third that Farren was drawn to like a jay to a chattering mob of sunsparrows.

The woman stared back at her with warm, feeling eyes, high rosebud cheeks, and a delicate mouth. Etched in the brass plaque beneath the portrait was a name that sent a shiver down Farren's spine.

Persepha.

"Before we go," Cato was saying, "I need your promises that you will not tell a soul of this passageway. This room is little used, except as the entranceway to the Healing Caves. Only a few know of its existence, and I'd like to keep it that way."

"What about him?" Virilus asked, nodding his head at the man by the fireplace.

"He's one of the few," Cato said. "A guard of sorts."

The man stood up and gave Cato a curt nod before backing away, and Farren caught sight of the leather sheath hanging from his belt. Before anyone could ask more questions, Cato bent over one of the stone gryphons and tugged on a talon. Stone ground as the fireplace and mantle broke apart from the wall and began to rotate. A chill gust of air swept into the room.

It smelled as dark and ancient as a tomb.

# THIRTY-SIX

AS THE FIREPLACE DISAPPEARED, the stone wall behind it rotated toward them and came to a stop. A semi-circular stone platform lay at its base.

"We'll have to go two at a time," the prince stated.

The group had fallen quiet, but Muta stepped forward.

"I'll be damned if I miss an opportunity to be first," the animedic muttered, sidling right up onto the platform as if he had done so many times. "Don't think there's room for a second though, unless the little lass wants to join...?"

All five of them looked at Farren questioningly. Her cheeks warmed, and she straightened her back, eying the slight space between Muta's roundness and the edge of the platform. She couldn't forget the stench of his breath, either. "I think I'll just wait."

The looping lines of the animedic's symbol on his forehead wrinkled as he glowered. "Death won't wait for Elya, girl."

"It's alright, Muta," Prince Cato said, saving her from having to answer. "You go down first, and we'll hurry after."

With Muta's nod, the prince plunged the gryphon's talon down, and the stone groaned in answer. Virilus and Callipe went next, and then it was Farren's turn. She huddled next to Alexon, groping for something to hold onto. Then Cato stepped up to the platform, wedging himself between her and the other recruit.

"We need to make haste," he said, and reached up to grab the wall above him. There seemed to be a sort of ledge there for grasping, but it was too high for Farren to reach comfortably.

The man with the poker pushed the stone talon down, and the platform began to move. Farren pulled closer to the steady, warm body next to her. As the bright study turned away, a dank, cold air enveloped them. Dim light unfurled as the platform completed its circuit. A few paces away, a graceful iron archway lined with tiny candles framed the start of a stairway. The winding, deep-cut steps disappeared into shadow as chilled and dense as the stone itself.

The thick scent of ancient stone stuck to the inside of her throat. An echoing whisper cascaded around them, a shushing susurration that must have been the sound of the falls.

Farren followed Alexon off the platform, steadying herself with a hand to the rocky wall. It buzzed beneath her skin—wet, cold, but strangely alive. She pulled her hand away.

"It's Enchanted," Cato said, his voice bouncing off the walls. "The Enchanters built this long ago."

Farren hugged herself and began the descent, hating how the damp air seeped into her clothes. It took all of her focus to keep her leaden legs stable on the steps, which was why she didn't notice the way the stone glowed until the recruits' exclamations echoed up to her.

The glow silhouetted her sandals. Such a strange glow, like moonlight, and they seemed to emit a gentle heat that reached beyond the soles of her sandals. The farther she went, the less her legs ached, and they began to feel lighter—so light that she was able to go faster, touching her foot for only a moment to each stone until it felt like she was floating down and down and down—

She landed at the bottom and fell forward, crashing into someone in front of her.

Virilus turned and glared at her over his beak-like nose as if he had been rudely woken from a dream.

"Sorry," Farren muttered, and a moment later, they both smiled at one another. Her mind felt like springy, soft wool. Worries fell away, and something in her chest spread its wings, itching to fly.

Muta and the rest of the recruits gathered close as Cato eased up beside Farren, looking unruffled from his descent. At their questioning, awed looks, he cleared his throat.

"It's the Moon Fall Stair," he explained. "A shortcut to the Healing Caves. The mouth of one of the caves isn't far, just this way." He pointed in front of them, where the narrow path was lit by candles perched in miniature alcoves along the walls. "Elya is close now."

Indeed, so was Torch. His anxiety trickled into her, disrupting the peace that had begun to wrap her body and mind. Farren surged forward along the path, frowning when the cave began to veer in the opposite direction of Torch. She followed it a few moments longer, Muta and the others tailing her, until the pathway split, one going left, the other continuing right.

Above her, the cave reared up, disappearing into a hush of darkness...or what would be, except for the bright green dots glowing all around it. The dots moved along the stone, although not in any certain pattern. The susurration she had heard before grew clearer now, and the endless cadence rose and fell like a great beast breathing. She paused, staring at the green dots, ears perking at the peculiar noise.

"They're beetles," Cato murmured, his shoulder brushing hers as he came up beside her. "They eat the moss in the caves, so they are harmless to you and me."

Farren realized her mouth had dropped open, and she closed it. "I wasn't afraid of them."

"Good. It's this way." The prince nodded at the path to the right.

"It's going farther from the gryphons," Farren said as Muta and the three recruits moved ahead of them.

"It curves back around. I know where I'm going. My father comes down here regularly, and I with him. You've heard he has an illness?"

"Camilla told me."

"He falls asleep in fits and bursts, but being in the Healing Caves seems to help him. It helps everyone."

Almost everyone, Farren thought. Isander had said he tried the Healing Caves and that it hadn't worked. Had it been his runeskill he had been trying to heal rather than a wound?

Farren looked once more down the path that veered left. No candlelight lit the passage, so she assumed it was never used. Deep in the shadows, the verdant glow of beetles skittered over the walls. Within the shrouded layers of darkness and rock, she could almost sense the tangle of paths—as curving and unpredictable as the movement of serpents—beneath tons of earth and the rush of the Kithyria. Vast caves were hidden all around.

Something stirred in Farren's belly—a mere twitch of certainty that this place held something that she must heed to, something that she could almost reach if not for the—

The fleeting certainty died almost as soon as it was born. It left an echo aching inside her. Farren took a shuddering breath and wrapped her arms tight around herself, and by the time she exhaled, the feeling was gone entirely. In its place, tranquility pooled in her, warm and nourishing as a heated bath.

"Farren, you'd best keep close," Cato called from where he had started to follow the others down the right-hand pathway. "The walls are Enchanted, and it is far too easy to get lost."

Right. Enchanted. No wonder she was having trouble focusing.

Farren hurried after Cato as they went down a twisting walkway and came out into a cave. The space was wide and deep, the top sloping down as they pressed toward the mouth of it. Fresh air swept in, bringing the damp scent of ash from the fire-pit in the center.

Cato led them out, and as soon as Farren's feet left the cave, worry crashed back into her. The roar of the falls swallowed all sounds, and mist billowed thick as rain around them, soaking her instantly. A hand gripped her arm and she clung to it as they walked a narrow dirt path cut along the side of the pool, barely visible in the thin moonlight.

As the path widened and they moved out from behind the hammering water, Farren could make out gryphons in the distance. Farren stumbled toward them with Cato and the recruits, steps urgent over the slick path. The pool of the falls was deep but small in diameter, and it took them a short while to reach the point where the pool emptied into a thick river as it churned down the land.

There on the river's edge, Elya lay on her side, feathers and fur sodden as her wounded leg seeped blood into the water. Delphi and Torch surrounded her.

*Thank the Enchanters you are alright*, Farren told Torch as she gripped him in a hug.

*I stayed close to Mother like you said*, Torch told her, pulling away before Farren could ruffle his feathers too much. *My siblings are in the mews.*

Farren glanced at Delphi, who stood as staunch as ever over Elya.

*They tried to follow with me*, Torch said, *but grew too afraid. They returned to the mews to wait for us.*

A quick check with her runeskill reassured her that his three siblings were safe in the nursery—for now. *I am glad you stayed with your mother*, Farren told Torch.

She bent over the wounded gryphon. Deep grooves in the dirt showed how much Elya had struggled to get up and move out of the water. Her chest rose up and down, and when Farren tried to sense the sphere of the beast's mind, she could find nothing. Elya remained unconscious.

Cato snapped out orders to the recruits, telling them how to make a frame of saplings on which to carry the gryphon. When Farren moved to join them, Cato shook his head.

"I need you with Elya as soon as she gains consciousness," he said, tearing off a long strip of his chiton. "I will be focusing on her injury."

Delphi nudged Farren's arm. Farren broke away from Torch for a moment and runebonded with her, sending only a questioning impression.

*Did you find Camilla?* Delphi asked.

Farren sent her an image of the falls, buried in mist. *I couldn't see anything.*

Delphi sent her a wave of reassurance. *We will find her.*

The impression had a grimness that made a knot form in Farren's throat again. She scanned the river. Her eyes snagged on something in the moonlight, but it was just a fallen tree bobbing in the waves.

*Cato can't know that I saw her fall*, Farren told her. It was for the better that he didn't know about her runebond with Naronimus when Camilla went down.

*But he saw her fall, too*, Delphi answered, and the feeling she sent with it was complex and strange, like stern sympathy, with an expectation of understanding between Farren and Cato.

*That's not how it would be if he knew I saw it through Naronimus's eyes.*

The gryphon remained silent.

*How many escaped?* Farren asked, glancing up at the now-empty night sky.

*I am unsure.* Delphi twitched an ear as if listening to a far-off sound. *Some, at least. I cannot feel all of the gryphons, but I fear a few are not conscious.*

Some? Farren's eyes burned suddenly. She must have convinced them to flee, but the others...? Put asleep by Scipio, perhaps, or Cato had convinced them to return.

Farren broke off her runebond with Delphi. She had risked everything to try and free the gryphons, and now they would all be locked under chain and key. The queen might even punish them, just as she would surely punish Farren if she found out the truth. If Farren hadn't revived Naronimus, everything might've turned out differently. But because she couldn't leave Naronimus to die, the queen would use him and the others however she liked.

She ripped her thoughts away from it and reached out for Torch. When they connected, his love smoothed over her roiling mind like a salve. The little gryphon was torn between fear for Elya and excitement at getting to see the falls for the very first time.

*You can be excited later*, Farren told him, chiding gently that he should remain calm and stay close to them. They didn't need any more gryphon injuries or deaths, and Farren couldn't bear the thought of anything happening to him.

"Where is Muta?" Cato asked, tightening the knot of his makeshift bandage on Elya's leg.

Alexon scurried back down the path, shouting toward the cave.

"I'm coming, you bloody young'un." Muta's deep voice boomed over the crash of the falls.

"Hurry up, you old fool," Cato muttered, scowling as he scooped water over Elya's leg, washing away the blood. "How is the frame coming?" he called out to Virilus, voice sharp as a whip.

"Halfway there, Your Highness."

"Muta has the rope for the joint bindings. Use strips from your chitons to fortify the saplings along the bottom. She'll be heavy, and we don't want the litter falling apart next to the falls."

Farren stared at Cato as her fingers smoothed Elya's feathers. She had never seen him this way before. Efficient. Clear-headed. A lion steering through the chaotic waters of a river, eyes fixed on the opposite shore. It steadied her, and she clung to that feeling like a drowning woman.

He glanced at her. "She'll be alright."

"Who?"

"Elya."

Farren swallowed hard.

Over the reverberation of water, Muta huffed and crashed down the path in a mockery of running.

"Move aside," Muta ordered as he neared the gryphon and set down his heavy bag.

Farren shifted, testing her stiff, cold muscles. She scooted far enough that she didn't have to smell the man but close enough to continue reassuring Elya. The gryphon stirred, and Farren closed her runebond with Torch in order to speak with her.

*Farren?*

*I am here with Cato*, Farren said. *Muta will heal you.*

*I need to tell you...* Elya struggled for a moment, her impressions thin and gauzy. *I saw her when she fell.*

Farren stared down at Elya's glossy golden eye, her heart hammering in her chest.

*Camilla?* she asked, sending an image of sweet Camilla laughing in a shaft of light coming through a pigeon hole of the dovecot.

Elya lifted her head, wincing at the pain, but twining rays of love and grief shone down the runebond. The gryphon had bonded with the girl, and sensing Camilla plunging down the falls had felt akin to falling herself.

*I tried to help her*, Elya said, her impression so weak that Farren widened their runebond.

*What do you mean?*

*I tried to stop her fall, but I'm afraid my magic wasn't enough, not while wounded and trying to get to shore. I couldn't save her...*

A last whisper of sorrow slipped through the connection, and Elya sank once more into unconsciousness. Farren bent over the gryphon's great head, her jaw clenched so hard that her teeth should have cracked.

But she wouldn't crack. She couldn't.

"Will all of us be able to lift her up the Moon Fall Stairs?" Farren asked Cato, forcing steadiness into her voice.

He dipped his hands in the water, scrubbing the blood off. "We're not taking her back to the fortress."

Farren stared at him. "So you'll just tend to her out in the open? We need blankets, clean water—"

"We have all that and more. In the Healing Caves."

Muta hummed agreement as he riffled through his bag.

"You believe the caves will heal her?"

"I believe that Muta can heal her. But she needs time and stability. She's been under far too much stress."

"That much hasn't changed," Muta said, giving them both a pointed look. "I prefer quiet while I work."

Farren obliged to silence while Muta sewed Elya's wound and dressed it with some sort of green compress. He applied a fresh bandage, then cleared away his things so they could transfer Elya to the frame.

Moving her onto the frame proved to be the hardest part, what with her heavy head, wounded leg, and sharp talons. Three of them lifted on each side. Farren's limbs shook under the weight of the litter, but when Delphi shoved her beak beneath the frame and helped lift it, the load lessened. Torch followed, hugging the sloping bank to stay far from the water's edge.

They made their way down the shore, growing so close to the water that the pound of the falls reverberated up Farren's sandals. The path narrowed as it rounded a rocky outcrop and snaked behind a curtain of water until the black maw of the cave appeared. The litter creaked and groaned from the weight as they ushered

Elya inside. The moment Farren stepped over the stone floor, she felt a little less cold, and her worry over Elya and the other gryphons began to dissolve.

She hadn't taken time to look about the cave before, but now saw that it appeared recently used. Crates with blankets were propped up on stone slabs, and a giant stack of wood and kindling piled close by it. A stone ledge held several jars, each looking clean and new. In the center of the cave, a small ring of stones marked where previous fires had been lit, although the charred stone seemed to have been scrubbed nearly clean.

"Place her here." Cato indicated a place by the firepit. "Farren, can you grab a few blankets? I'll get the fire started."

Within moments, a small fire crackled to life, and Farren tucked thick wool blankets around Elya's chilled, wet body.

"Won't it get too cold tonight?" Farren asked.

"I'll have to tend the fire all night, keep it warm in the cave," Cato said. He added a final piece of wood to the flames and then turned to the animedic. "Muta, thank you."

Muta nodded gravely and pulled a clay jar from his bag. "Use this three times daily. Be sure to clean the wound well. Boiled water only. I'll return in the morning to check on her."

"You're not staying?" Farren asked. What if Elya suddenly took a turn for the worse?

"I have others to attend to," Muta said shortly.

"Yes, please see to Naronimus first," Cato said, practically shooing the man away. "Then check that none of the others have been injured." Cato lowered his voice. "And keep your ears sharp. If you hear anything about how the gryphons got out, I need to know."

Farren swallowed as Muta walked toward the cave entrance. "What if we need him?"

"You won't need me," Muta said over his shoulder. He waved at Elya. "She's stronger than she looks."

Cato blew on the fire, causing the embers to flare. "I trust Muta's opinion."

"Well, then I guess I trust him completely, too," Farren said, lacing her voice with sarcasm. She wouldn't forget how Muta had dismissed her concerns about Mellion's death as fragmented memories from an injured mind. Cato ignored her, but his face reddened.

"Everyone else, you can return to the fortress," the prince snapped. "See to it that all the gryphons have been safely returned to their chambers. Be sure they are all accounted for."

Farren cringed, but she didn't have time to ponder how furious the prince—and the queen—would be when they found out that some of the gryphons hadn't returned. Far too many other things occupied her mind. Like the body that might be floating somewhere in the pool or down the river that led away from the falls. An urgency propelled Farren to find it—to find *her*—and she wouldn't rest until she did.

"I'm not leaving Elya," Farren heard herself say. Torch's beak touched her hand, and she dug fingers into his neck feathers.

Cato sighed. "I don't need you here, Farren. You should go back, help the recruits."

"I told you, I'm not leaving Elya. You can't tend to her all by yourself—"

"I can, and I will."

"I will help. We can take turns. One of us tends Elya, while the other looks for Camilla."

Color leached from the prince's face, and unshed tears rimmed his eyes. "She's not there, Farren."

"You don't know that." Her voice snagged, but she pushed on, uncaring that the recruits shifted awkwardly near the cave's entrance. "She could've...gotten stuck, o-or—"

"It doesn't matter," Cato said, his words turning ragged, "because *she's not there.*"

Understanding hit her. Camilla wasn't alive anymore, so finding her body would mean nothing to him. Farren narrowed her eyes as heat flashed through her.

"I need to find her. So I'm staying." She sat on the cold stone floor to prove her point.

The prince barely glanced at her. "Fine."

"Fine." Farren stared numbly at Elya until Muta and the recruits left.

# THIRTY-SEVEN

TORCH NUZZLED BETWEEN FARREN and the fire while Delphi lay beside Elya to help keep her warm. Delphi's eyelids drooped, and Farren sent her a wave of reassurance that she would watch Torch. Beyond the heat of the fire and the endless shushing of the falls, the caves emanated their own blanket of calm, which Farren pushed against. She had too much yet to do, and far too much she needed to think about.

Cato hadn't stopped moving since they had entered the cave. Perhaps he resisted the tranquility pouring from the cave walls as much as she did. His pacing ceased for a moment when he put a hand beneath Elya's blankets.

"She's still too cold," he said.

"I'll grab more blankets." Farren grabbed one for herself, too, hoping to quell the trembling that still had hold of her body.

"Her heart is beating fast," Cato said, speaking almost too quietly for Farren to hear.

She added more wood to the fire, watching Cato hover over Elya, his eyes closed and one hand covering her chest. After a few moments, his shoulders relaxed.

"Better," he said, smoothing the feathers down her neck. "She's thinking too much of what happened with Naronimus."

*She's not the only one*, Farren thought to herself. She returned to the fire and pulled her blanket tight over her shoulders as the heat sank into her. Torch lay against her once more, the curve of his beak hugging her knee.

"What did you see, Cato?"

Cato stood, his mouth pressed tight as he shook his head. "It was...difficult to watch."

Farren smoothed her hands along the point of Torch's back where glossy feathers met thick, tawny fur. "Why did she choose the falls instead of the mating chamber?"

"Why do you think?" Cato looked sick. "She was giving a show."

"They could've drowned."

"I know that," Cato snapped. "There was nothing either of us could've done."

Farren gripped the rough wool of her blanket. "Just tell me what happened."

Cato grabbed a stick and prodded the fire, causing sparks to fly at her. She didn't flinch as one landed on her wool blanket, but eyed it until the ember faded to black. The prince sank into a crouch, his gaze turning pensive. He twirled the stick between his fingers, reminding her instantly of Isander twirling his paint brushes. Even his hair fell in a similar way, dark waves of it tucked behind his ears and curling around his neck. She banished the thought.

"Naronimus didn't like the chains, of course," Cato began quietly. Farren leaned forward, straining to hear him over the muffled roar of the falls. "And he was still woozy from Scipio's potion, or from being in the box." He frowned, tapping the stick against the stone floor. "He tried mating with Elya, but she kept dodging him. I tried to calm her, over and over again, until finally she was just about to give in to him. But he lost his grip on the rock, and he tried to hold on—injuring Elya by accident in the process. He fell into the falls, and only the chains kept him from falling to his death."

He went on, telling her things she already knew: Elya had been unchained and fell into the pool after her injury, narrowly avoiding the falls herself. Her escape had roused the crowd, then chaos came with a swarm of gryphons. He hadn't been able to get an answer out of the gryphons as to how they escaped.

Farren carefully changed the topic away from the freed gryphons. "Do you think she will have him killed?"

His gaze met her squarely. "I don't know. Honestly."

"Did Scipio poison him again? Is that why he was lying on the balcony like that?" That would explain why her runebond with him had failed suddenly after Camilla was pushed off the balcony. Her sense of his mind had disappeared completely.

Cato nodded. "After he lashed out at the guards, Scipio put him down. I just hope that means my mother will keep him alive."

"That might not be for the better," Farren said without thinking. She bit her tongue, but too late.

"Really, Farren?" His brows sank into a scowl. "I can't tell if you love gryphons, or truly hate them."

"I hate a queen who would use gryphons to her advantage."

Cato tossed his stick into the fire, and the flames devoured it. "We all use the gryphons, Farren. Don't you see that?"

Farren's lips twisted. "Not to rule a kingdom. Not to sway people."

"You used Naronimus to sway people. Remember?"

"That was different."

Cato shook his head emphatically. "You're just like her. Justifying your own actions, accusing everyone else."

"I am nothing like her." The heat of the fire started to make her sweat, and she tossed off the blanket. "I don't want to use the gryphons." She lurched to her feet, unable to sit still. "They are suffering, Cato. They cannot be kept in captivity like dogs."

Cato stood, his mouth as serious and firm as ever. "They are treated far better than my uncle treated them—"

"That's not good enough, Cato! They are surviving, but miserable. They have aches and pains, their wings aren't as strong as they should be. They need to hunt and fly."

Torch had gotten up when she did, and tried to follow her as she began pacing. Delphi, no longer looking sleepy, watched them with perked ears. Tossing more wood onto the fire caused sparks to flare wildly between them.

"It was you," Cato said quietly, his tone filled with surprise and betrayal.

Farren paused, not looking at him. Her heart beat sluggishly.

He forced out a guffaw and shot her a savage look. "I should've known. After what you said about Naronimus."

She dragged in a breath and met his hard eyes. "What I said before is true. They need you to let them go. You're holding on so tightly—"

"It's called a bond," Cato spat, "and it's unbreakable. You know, I actually had them here for a reason."

"What reason is good enough to imprison creatures who need to be free?"

"They *don't* need freedom, Farren. How can you not see that? They need people. That is how they thrive. It's in all the lore, in all the books I have read—"

"Stories are not the truth, Cato."

"They aren't just stories. They are all the writings of those like me, who have spent their lives studying gryphons. Stories are based on the truth. I've found old ones—written hundreds of years ago—that talk of Enchanters working with gryphons."

"We are not Enchanters," Farren pointed out.

Cato's face closed, and he turned away from her. The dark ink of feathers along his arms shone in the firelight, gilding the intricate patterns needled into his skin. "What if Torch had left? How would you have felt?"

"I would still have him freed."

"Then who would look after him?"

"His mother, who would also be freed."

He turned back to her, his mouth tight. "So you would just abandon your bond with him? As if you never needed it."

She opened her mouth to deny it. To deny ever needing it, or him, or any of this. But she couldn't, because that would be a lie. "Of course I need it," Farren said softly. "I love Torch. He is my family."

"And you would abandon those you love? Your family? Desmond?"

A hard lump formed in her throat. Her eyes burned, and she blinked them fiercely. "You know that keeping them here against their will isn't right."

Cato threw a hand up. "It's for a good cause! We can all bond with one another, and their magic can be used to protect Malodai from the Sect—"

"And who would stop the queen from using it to enslave her people?"

Her words stunned Cato to silence. He shook his head. "She wouldn't do that—"

"Why do you think she wants me to use Naronimus?"

"To protect Malodai from—"

"It can't just be to protect Malodai from the Sect. She doesn't care about her people, Cato, not like she should." Farren drew a breath, and said, more softly, "Not like you do."

Cato's eyes turned wild. "I don't care about the people!" His voice reverberated into the vaulted ceiling of the cave. "Enchanter's curse, Farren, I only care about the gryphons! This is where they belong, and I swear I could throttle you for what you've done—"

"You care about Camilla, and all the people who are missing," she reminded him, knowing that his words were a lie, an excuse to avoid the truth. "Just say it, Cato."

He clenched his jaw as he stared at her, withdrawing inside himself as his expression washed from doubt to anger, then finally, resentment. His shoulders hitched high as he approached her, his breath fast and tight, his cheeks a dusky red-gold as he held her gaze.

"There's only one thing I'm good at, Farren. And that is working with gryphons. If they were all released, I'd have nothing. Nothing." His hands cut a line in the air between them, emphasizing his point.

"That simply isn't true," Farren said. Perhaps it was the blanketing pressure from the Healing Caves, or it was that she was beginning to understand this man before her. Whatever the cause, her anger fizzled, and something warm and malleable began to take its place. "You have your people. You have the recruits."

He snorted and started to turn away, but she caught his arm. "I need you, Cato. The gryphons still need you. We can't... I can't do this alone."

Cato regarded her in the flickering firelight. His skin radiated heat and tension, and she had the urge to press her fingers in, to coax the hardness of him to soften.

"What you're asking," he said slowly, "is impossible."

"If you won't listen to me, at least listen to Delphi."

He glanced at the gryphon, who astutely observed them from where she lay beside Elya. Her golden eyes met Cato's steadily, waiting.

"I need to sleep," Cato muttered. He pulled out of her grasp and marched to the crates along the side of the cave, tugged out a blanket and returned to cast it out on the opposite side of the fire. Then he laid on his side, facing away from her. As if there was nothing to do now but sleep. As if he *could* sleep. How very *Felid* of him.

She stood abruptly. "I'm going to look for Camilla."

He didn't reply.

Farren shuddered in the cold, damp air that lingered along the river. Her body was soddened, hands like lumps of ice and mind ragged with weariness.

She had been searching for what felt like hours, with no sign of a body anywhere. The weak light of the moon had helped her see a little, but every suspicious movement and shape in the water had turned out to be a log, or an otter, or a tattered clump of leaves and sticks.

Tucking her hands into her armpits, she glanced back at the long, winding way she had come, and flinched as a tall shape moved in the brush. She caught the glint of a curved beak, and was comforted at once by the feel of Delphi's stone-steady patience through her runebond.

*I can't find her*, Farren said, sure that the coldness from the water had seeped into her very bones.

*I have searched, too. Are you sure she fell into the falls?*

*I saw it through Naronimus's eyes.*

Delphi remained quiet for a moment. *Might her body have sunken like a stone?*

Farren shuddered. *I don't know.* If that was the case, they would never find her.

*You should go back to the cave*, Delphi chided gently. *You are shivering.*

Farren curled her toes in her sandals, willing warmth to move into them. *I'm fine. I need to keep looking.*

Delphi turned her great head toward the sky. *The sun will be rising soon. We can look again.*

Delphi was right, of course. She had searched as much as she could in the dark, but she'd be more likely to see something in the light of day. Besides, the cold was beginning to distract her from everything else. A hawk would never keep hunting for prey if it was cold and wet. Far better to rest and dry off, then return to it when the senses were sharp once more.

Farren ground her teeth, trying to stop them from chattering. *Maybe just a few minutes by the fire.*

With a satisfied flick of her tail, Delphi turned on the path—hopelessly crushing some of the brush—and led the way back. Farren had expected Cato to be sleeping when they entered the cave, but instead he bent over Elya with closed eyes.

The cold and stiffness in her body receded the moment her sandals hit the cave floor. Her tiredness, on the other hand, seemed to amplify with the waterfall hush emanating from the cave walls. Farren dropped down next to the fire and pulled the wool blanket up to her neck, too tired to pay any attention to Cato as he moved about the cave. Torch rose and lay snuggly against her, his body nearly as long as hers. She folded her arm over his belly, comforted by the musty smell of him and the soft brush of his feathers against her cheek.

Torch's breath grew long and even, and his connection to her fuzzed and faded in a way that she knew meant he dreamed once more, his mind and feelings unreachable. Enchantress' blessing, it felt so comforting to be close to Torch, to know he was safe and sound. The fact that she had almost left him behind—that she had been ready to abandon him—

No, she hadn't been ready.

Tears pricked her eyes. She hadn't been ready, and she hadn't been willing to leave him. But she had been determined to do it for the sake of all the gryphons. For the sake of the people who might get injured by them, or by the queen's ruinous program.

Relief spun through her that he was still there with her. But what did it mean for the gryphons? Her fingers clutched Torch's burnt-gold fur. She couldn't bear the thought of Torch going back to the fortress, to the prison of the queen's gryphon mews. Farren dragged her eyes to Delphi, reluctance pulling at her as she opened a runebond to Torch's mother. The gryphon had returned to Elya's side, and the clinging mist on her feathers steamed in the fire's heat.

*You must flee while you can*, Farren said.

Delphi met Farren's gaze with all the force of a winter gale. *I will not abandon Elya or my other children. And I promised to help you find Camilla.*

*What about Torch? Now is your only chance to leave the fortress, to escape whatever the queen might do—*

Delphi regarded her kit, her tail twitching on the stone floor. *I will not break my promise to you. Torch must learn from this, too.*

Farren's arms tightened around Torch's warm body. *Will you take him back to the mews?*

*We will stay in the Healing Caves*, Delphi stated. *Until Camilla is found and my other children are free.*

*Have you told Cato yet?*

*I have*, Delphi said, flicking her tail. *He doesn't agree, of course. He's very stubborn, but he doesn't have a choice in this.*

Farren chewed her lip. *I'm not sure we can free your children—and any others recaptured—without his help. Can you convince him to help us? He won't listen to me.*

*I will try. But you may have more influence on him than I.*

*He certainly prefers gryphons to me*, Farren said.

*If that is so*, Delphi said, bobbing her head, *it is only because he hasn't seen where his own kind can take him. Keep trying to speak to him. Already he doubts the way things have been, and where they will be going.*

Farren dug her fingers into Torch's feathers. She wasn't sure whether Cato would ever listen to her, but she wasn't ready to give up yet.

# THIRTY-EIGHT

EVENTUALLY, FARREN'S EXHAUSTION AND the unending press of serenity from the caves undid her resistance. Her imperfect mind tumbled and sank into the abyss of sleep. It seemed she had just gotten there, in that tranquil, dark space, when light tugged her toward the surface.

There was something she needed to do, now that light had arrived. Little by little, awareness returned to her, and with it, memories. Perhaps it was the cave's doing that she sat up slowly, not with the urgency she knew she needed.

Torch flicked a sleepy ear at her movement from where he lay next to her. The prince was crouched in front of Elya, pulling off the old dressing on her wounded leg. He hadn't noticed her stirring, and she was grateful for that as she collected her thoughts.

She pulled herself to the mouth of the cave, her tired eyes peering through the curtain of water. It was useless, however; the falls were a wall between her and the majority of the pool. A small, feathered head pressed beneath her hand, and she impulsively smoothed Torch's feathers, noticing the uneasy way his ears twitched between her and Cato.

*You stay here with Cato*, she told him.

His head bobbed in denial. *But I want to go with you—*

*No*, she answered firmly. *You cannot swim. Stay with Cato. I can't keep you safe while looking for Camilla.*

He didn't argue with her, but slunk back to where Cato finished redressing Elya's wound. Farren stepped out of the cave's entrance, and the oppressive serenity fled. Her body ached from searching for Camilla during the night, and her head throbbed with weariness. Her stomach was hollow, but the thought of food was unappealing. She hadn't fully realized how the Healing Caves had lessened her physical pain...and her emotional duress. She sucked in a breath, struggling to keep it all from surging up at once.

She took another step from the cave. Mist hung over the pool as ever, an unrelenting veil that clung to her skin and clothes. The rushing water vibrated the stone beneath her feet and set her bones on edge.

"Farren, wait." Cato's voice was rough as a toothed blade.

She paused, unable to break her eyes from the moving water as it churned into the pool. He stepped up behind her, and she wavered, inexplicably drawn to the solid warmth emanating from him. She shivered and folded her arms over her stomach.

"I'm sorry for what I said before..." Out of the corner of her eye, she saw Cato's hand dart through his hair. "I want to help you look. It'll be more efficient with two sets of eyes."

"What of Elya?" Farren asked, her voice scratchy from lack of speaking.

"Delphi and Torch will remain with her for now."

Silence folded over them once more as they left the cave. They followed the narrow path out past the pool to where they had found Elya. Farren inspected the markings in the muddy trail, but could make out nothing beyond claw marks and the deep tread of their own sandals. Ahead, the path moved farther from the water's seething edge, and cut through the brushy, cumbersome bank as the land rose sharply to meet the rockface of cliffs above it.

Farren pressed off the path, taking a different route than she had during the night, now that she could see the distinct edge of the frothing water. Cato kept behind her, occasionally going up the bank to better see across the river. The expanse of rapids was wide—several times wider than the height of the tallest tree there—and there was no way to cross it.

"What if she's over there?" Farren asked Cato in a distant voice. The longer they searched, the more hopeless she became that they would ever find Camilla. The sense that she was out there somewhere, her body alone and frigid in the water, was maddening.

"I haven't been able to see anything. She was—" Cato's voice snagged briefly, and he cleared his throat. "She was wearing a blue dress. It would stand out."

Blue. Camilla's favorite color. Like the sky. Like her clear midsummer eyes.

They would never be bright again.

Farren clamped her lips together. They continued searching, weaving around shrubs and through dense stands of rushes. The pathway had petered out as the bank grew too steep to walk on, and they were pushed into the edge of the river, which tumbled and spat until it met the resistance of a log or a riffle of rocks. Still, they clung to the saplings and growth along the banks, knowing that a misstep could send them sliding too far into the river, just enough where the current would sweep them away. Their sandals grew sodden as they waded into shallow pools and patches of flooded banks, and Farren's body began to grow stiff with exhaustion.

"Farren..." Cato's voice was too distant behind her. She turned, her mind slow to process what she was seeing.

Cato had stopped in the relative calm of a bubbling riffle. His hand pointed to the bank, where a small piece of fabric snagged on a sapling branch and twitched in the breeze.

It was blue.

Farren's heart pounded as she stumbled to get to it. She grabbed for the fabric the moment it was within reach.

"Is it—?" She stared at the soft fragment of linen, knowing the answer.

"It's hers," Cato said, his voice not as cold as it had been. "And look." His finger pointed to the sloping ground at the edge of the river. Farren stared hard at the mud, barely making out the shape of a sandal-print.

A slight, slim impression in the soil. Farren peered closer, barely breathing as she made out another print, and another, all traveling in the same direction—uphill.

"Enchanter's curse," Farren breathed. "Did she—? Is she—?" Without waiting for an answer, Farren started to scramble after the tracks, but Cato's hand stayed her.

"Wait." His cheeks were flushed, his eyes wide and glistening with the same warmth spreading through her chest. "I think there's more. We can't trample them if we want to understand them."

Again, he pointed to the bare ground at the edge of the riffle. Where Farren had almost stepped, another set of tracks dug deep in the mud. Big enough to be a man's. Farren crept carefully, following the marks out of the riffle. The man had come from the direction of the Healing Caves, and then the prints disappeared in the brush.

"Did someone help her?" Farren asked.

Cato was inspecting the tracks closely where they met—where Camilla and this mysterious person had come together.

"There's no sign of struggle that I can see." He frowned, lost in thought.

"This isn't the time to get thoughtful," she said, hastening to follow the set of tracks. But these, too, grew lost in the brush. She made a frustrated noise.

"It just doesn't make sense," Cato said. "Why would someone be out here at all? This edge of the river is dangerous, and the land itself belongs to the queen. No boats come up this way..." As if uncertain of his words, he stood and craned his neck, searching the water.

"The trail ends here," Farren stated, waving her hand at the thick brush.

Refocused, Cato followed the tracks up to where she stood. He squinted, his breath hitching. "Look there, the broken branch. You can see where they went by the crush of plants. They had to go on hands and feet because of the steepness." Now Cato was leading the way, grabbing onto saplings and thick roots to haul himself up.

"She's alive. She has to be," Farren said as she scrambled after him, certainty growing inside her. There were footprints, a piece of her dress. Who else's could they be?

After a few moments of following the trail of tracks, Farren realized where they were headed.

"This is going back the way we came," she said.

He paused, clasping an errant boulder as he looked down the steep bank. Down by the river, the ground started to smooth out and form the bare dirt trail once more. "There's the path. But these tracks keep going to..."

He had turned back to the trail of disturbed mud they followed, and his whole body tensed. Then he bolted forward, diving through the brush like a mountain lion after prey. Who had known he could move so fast, so lithely? For a brief moment, she had a twinge of admiration for the *Felid*.

Too bad she couldn't sprout wings and fly like her rune animals. She swore and struggled after him, her sodden sandals slipping on plants and mud and catching on rocks. She reached Cato and clung to a sapling that bent with her weight. In front of her, Cato stared at something.

"Please tell me you found something."

Cato flinched. "It's a stairway."

Farren craned around his shoulder. An inconspicuous series of split-log steps climbed up the steep rise of the bank. The stairway was narrow, wide enough for a single person to climb, and the wood was covered in moss. It wouldn't have been visible from the pathway unless one was looking for it. If Camilla and the man had come this way, they must've gone up the steps, not back to the trail. Otherwise, they might've found her while out searching for Elya.

Farren peered up through the brush, but lost sight of the steps. "Where does it lead to?"

"I think I know, but..."

Cato began walking up the steps, and Farren followed, hoping the stairway was shorter than the Moon Fall Stairway beneath the fortress. After a few moments, the log steps ended where a stone step began. Like the log steps, this stone stairway was narrow, chiseled into the face of the cliff as it went up and up. The stairway wouldn't be very visible from afar, and the ascent would be treacherous. This far from the falls, the mist was thin high above them. The cliff stretched overhead, ending only where a great wall began.

Farren gasped. "Is that...?"

Cato's grim gaze pinned to the high wall. "Malodai."

Relief spun through her. "So she returned to Malodai? To the fortress?"

"I don't know. If she went up the steps..." He shook his head, brow creased. "There's no gate on this side of the city. But they must've made an opening, otherwise why the staircases?"

"They?" Farren frowned at him, amazed he could still get side-tracked from finding his ward. But as she watched him, something dark unfolded in his expression, and the hair on her neck prickled.

"The Runeless Sect." His words were oddly thin, his mouth tight around them. "This portion of the boundary wall is in their Quarter."

There was something else he wasn't saying, and Farren repressed the urge to shake his shoulders. "We have to get back to the fortress. She is probably there, waiting in her room, wondering where we are." Farren stepped down the log path, her limbs re-awakening as hope blossomed. "I will go when Muta returns. He should be here soon. When I get to the fortress, I'll send a bird with a message to let you know of her safe return."

For the first time since Camilla fell, weight lifted from Farren's shoulders. Elya's magic must've saved her in the fall—cushioning her blow with the water—and Camilla had somehow pulled herself out. Farren didn't know what sort of luck had brought the man to the water's edge, but he had led Camilla back to the city so that she could return to the fortress. Farren began to feel light, although Cato didn't speak as they made their way back to the Healing Cave.

By the time they returned, late morning sun whitened the falls in their plummet to the pool. Mistfish jumped and flew in and out of the water, silvery wings flashing in the light before they snapped closed as the fish dove back down.

It wasn't long that they had to wait for Muta's return. Alexon came with him, and when the young man emerged from the back entrance of the cave, sweaty and sleepless beneath his mop of black curls, Farren's heart skipped a beat.

"Cato," the recruit said breathlessly. "Five of the gryphons are accounted for—Delphi's young, plus Naronimus and Eralius. You have three here, and four more of the gryphons are missing."

Farren closed her eyes. That meant that Phynx, Grit, and Calipsa had gotten away. And Thella—had she escaped, too, even though she had wanted to remain?

Cato stood, his face grim as Muta pushed into the cave and checked on Elya. "That's only twelve gryphons. There should be thirteen."

Alexon bowed his head. "Hylas was found on the eastern city wall. He was shot dead."

Cato rubbed a hand over his haggard face. "It must've been the City Watch."

"They're killing the gryphons?" Farren asked, heart plunging at the news. "But I-I thought the queen had made it a high crime to kill one—"

"She did. It's a high crime, but gryphons have never flown to the city before. They've never been a danger. Until now."

Farren swallowed. "Is it because of what happened at the keep?"

"I'm not sure. We know that the Runeless Sect has begun to infiltrate the City Watch. The queen thought she caught them all, but there could've been more. They certainly have no interest in gryphons prowling the city, much less any other rune animal."

"About that," Alexon said, scratching at his cheek. "The queen has postponed the gryphon guard entering the streets. There's too much unrest and uh...distrust of gryphons after what happened."

Cato swore. The recruit shuffled his feet, and Farren had the distinct sense that this wasn't the only news he brought with him.

"What else?" she pressed him, already feeling her belly grow cold.

Alexon's eyes flicked to hers, then back to Cato. "It's Camilla, sir. She's been missing since yesterday. We couldn't find her in the mews or the keep."

# THIRTY-NINE

THE WEIGHT THAT HAD left Farren moments ago came crashing back, roaring as loud as the falls.

"But w-we found sign of her... She's alive. We know she's alive," Farren babbled, wondering why Alexon looked at her as if she were crazed.

"We've looked all over the fortress," Alexon said.

Farren looked wildly at Cato, who stood frozen in the moving light of the fire.

"Cato," she snapped.

He blinked, and his gaze flashed to her. "I'll send guards to search the city," he said, then turned to the recruit. "I want them prepared by the time I return to the fortress. Every *Canid* ready with their animals."

Alexon stiffened. "But what if the queen—"

"This is about Camilla," Cato said, face reddening. "Not the queen. Do whatever you have to. I'll lead the search in the Quarter myself."

"The Runeless Quarter?" Farren asked. "You think she's still there?"

"Do you have a better idea of where to look?"

"I don't know!" Farren kicked the nearest rock, wincing as it caused pain to lance through her toe. "I'm not capable of sensing other people."

A thought struck her at the same time it did Cato, and it turned his face to stone.

"No," he said.

"He's the only one who can. He can come with us into the Quarter."

"I don't want his help."

Farren scowled. "Well then, he will help *me*, not you. Besides, it's Camilla he's really helping. I'll even go ask him, so you don't have to bother."

Cato's lips twisted. "Of course you will."

"What is *that* supposed to mean?" Deciding she didn't care, she shook her head. "Never mind. You can keep your opinions to yourself."

Not that he was good at that, being a prince and all.

Farren tapped her foot as the black-bearded guard squinted down at the note she had given him—one of the old ones she had received from Isander—and cursed Cato for leaving her to find Isander alone. Granted, she was glad he had gone straight to the barracks to take the guard into the city. With any luck, he would find Camilla swiftly, but if the girl had indeed disappeared like one of the other missing, Isander was their best bet for finding her.

They had left Muta with Delphi, Torch, and Elya and taken the Moon Fall Stair back into the keep, but she had been stopped by two guards in the atrium as she made her way to Isander's art chamber.

"Is there an issue?" she asked, exhaustion wearing her patience thinner than a feather. She was wearing her guard's uniform after all, but the men didn't seem to pay it any mind.

"Just have to be careful, is all." The guard sniffed. "What's your business with the prince?"

"As it states in the letter," Farren said, "the prince has requested my presence. I know only as much as you about why."

The other guard stuck his thick hairless chin at her. "Isn't she the one in the painting?"

Farren ignored him. "I don't think the prince will like being kept waiting."

The bearded guard folded the note back and offered it to her. As Farren reached to take it back, his hand whipped out and he grabbed her arm, exposing the runemark imprinted on the tender flesh of her inner wrist.

Farren yanked her arm back, but not before the guard saw the bold markings, and smirked. "You're an *Avid*, then. Your kind aren't supposed to be in here."

Neck prickling, Farren did her best to look furious. "I don't think the prince will take that very well." She glanced between them, noticing how they bent closer to her, as if they could sniff out something she had done. "I don't think Scipio would approve, either."

The bearded guard's smirk widened. "Scipio is the one who told us not to let any of you in. You'd best be behavin', little birdie. There's an investigation going on, and they'll like be looking for you."

"An investigation?"

"You didn't hear?" The second guard's fleshy jowl wobbled. "The gryphons attacked the keep yesterday."

"Oh, I think she heard about it. She might've even been there." The bearded guard stepped closer.

She glanced down at his wrist, which was carefully covered by an artful band of leather. He was a *Diptid* most likely—annoying, selfish, and petty. The worst he could do was set a swarm of mosquitoes or biting flies on her. Farren straightened her back. He wouldn't scare her into running off. She swallowed down words she knew would only provoke him into a fight, and tried to disarm him by lacing her voice with praise.

"You must be a *Canid* with your keen sense, sir. I was with Queen Aurelia, as a matter of fact. I am in her gryphon guard."

The guard's frown slackened, and Farren rushed on.

"I helped Prince Cato when we discovered that the gryphons had escaped. They appear to be much wiser than we previously thought. I am actually helping Prince Cato with tending to one of the injured. He is on his way here now to gather the guard, and he will be *very* upset when I tell him I was not admitted to the keep. It is absolutely vital that I speak with Prince Isander. It's regarding Camilla, Prince Cato's ward, who has gone missing. Being royal guards, you must know how deeply the prince cares about Camilla, and to what lengths he will go to in order to find her."

Farren reveled in the way their faces changed from smug skepticism to trepidation. The second guard glanced at the bearded one, who still hesitated. She tucked the note back in her pocket and stepped back. "As you wish. I will report to Prince Cato immediately what has happened. I will let him know that two guards, by the name of..." She squinted at their leather baldrics, where their names were stamped into the leather. "Tyron and Esmond, were not willing to comply with the Crown Prince's wishes."

The guards glanced at one another, and Esmond's fleshy chin waggled when he spoke again. "I will take her."

"Be quick about it," the bearded guard said, eyes narrowed as he watched them head down the corridor.

They went to one of the stairwells that led up to Prince Isander's art chamber, but found it empty.

Esmond's breath was heavy from his climb. "I'm sorry, miss, but I'll have to escort you back out."

"Doesn't the prince have a chamber he sleeps in?"

Esmond's lips pursed. "He does, but we don't have access to it. It's deeper in the keep, where we're forbidden to go."

Farren stared at him. Why would a prince want to sleep somewhere that no one was allowed to go? Her tired mind tumbled around the thought. She supposed it made sense, with his rune-skill being what it was.

"Fine." She motioned for Esmond to escort her back, and as they passed a corridor at the end of the stair, she glimpsed a silk chiton fluttering around a corner. The crisp scent of *birali* tickled her nose.

She opened the window of her mind, but nothing was there.

Farren's eyes darted around the corridors as she followed the guard. If she slipped away now, would the guard follow her to the forbidden part of the keep? Isander couldn't have gotten far, so she might not have to delve too deeply into the keep anyways.

It wasn't difficult for Farren to slip away, first down one corridor, then across another. She drove deeper into the shadows. Her breath echoed against the cold stone walls.

She navigated the corridors, some lit with mellow candlelight and others in pools of shadows. Windowless, like most of the areas deeper in the keep. The air grew dank, and old doors with rusted hinges and peeling paint appeared. Another hall had fresh, white doors, lit by the lapping light of a few candles.

A tall, dark-haired figure—undeniably Isander—walked to the end of the corridor and turned into another hallway.

"Isander?" Her voice was swallowed by the air as if the hall were lined in rugs rather than wood and stone.

She ran after him. Another hall doused with black, and at the end of it stood a closed door. Her slick palms slipped as she turned the round handle. It opened to a small room with a simple bed and chair. A door stood closed on the other side of the room, which must've been where Isander had disappeared to. She crept across the chamber, cursing as her knee met the corner of the shadowy bed, and through the door, which opened up to a different corridor limned by weak candlelight.

The still, close air felt too thick to breathe. Farren closed the door behind her and headed down the hall, going only a few steps before she realized there were no other doorways.

"Cursed Enchanted walls," she muttered.

Wood creaked overhead, and she froze, staring up at the blank white ceiling. Had it moved just then? She forced herself to look away and turned back to the door that led to the bedroom, fighting the sudden certainty that the hall was narrower than before. All she had to do was stay calm and go back the way she had come—

Instead of the bedroom, a new space spilled open before her. It appeared to be a dance hall—wide flagstones checkered blue and white beneath a curtain of tiered candles, flickering like stars as they hung from the ceiling. Farren gripped the door handle. She wouldn't go back to the doorless hallway. The hair on her nape prickled with the sensation that the hall behind her was shrinking.

Even though that was ridiculous and impossible.

Wasn't it?

A wild glance over her shoulder didn't ease her. The hall looked no wider than the length of her arm.

The dance hall, then.

No windows marked the walls, but a set of double doors stood at one end. The patter of her sandals echoed on the flagstones as she raced to the doors and flung them open. Shelves full of linens stared back at her. She whirled away and searched the walls for another door. There wasn't one. When she went to find the entrance she had come through, she found only a wall.

The doorway had disappeared.

# FORTY

FARREN STRODE BACK TO the double doors of the linen closet. Spots appeared in her vision, and she closed her eyes, forcing the stale air of the dancing room in and out of her lungs. It smelled of mildew and dust mites and why in the Enchanted realms was there a linen closet in a dance hall?

No, better not to ask those kinds of questions.

She tore out the bedsheets and blankets and pillows. They might be wonderful to sleep on should she simply give up. When she reached the top shelf, her feet balancing precariously along the bottom one, she saw a blackness where there should've been wall. She pushed her hand into it, and nothing pushed back.

She shouldn't do it. But she couldn't stay in the dance hall forever, even if the silken sheets and fluffy blankets were calling to her.

Pulling herself up to the top shelf, she squeezed into the blackness. It was just wide enough for her to crawl through, and in a few moments, soft fabric gave way to her. She stuck her hand through it until she felt an opening. Something firm formed beneath her hands, and she pulled herself out of the fabric.

Pillows tumbled away from her as she emerged from a cushioned couch. She had somehow wormed her way out through the cushions, but when she stuck her hand back between them, searching for the hole, she felt only the hard wood of the furniture frame.

Her throat constricted as she looked around. If this place had no doors, she would be trapped there forever, and wither away in the dark stuffiness of the keep's bowels until only her bones were left. Perhaps that was how Persepha—Isander's former love—had truly gone missing. If Farren wandered around for long enough, she might even find Persepha's body, shriveled and curled up in the musty corner of some long-forgotten room.

She spied the doorway and struggled to her feet.

One lone candle burned away at the shadows of the windowless room. It appeared to be a parlor of sorts—two couches, a long table, and a glass case. Knives gleamed inside the case, and on a velvet-covered tray, a beautiful necklace glittered green with gems. She had no intention of finding out if that was the same necklace that had nearly killed the queen's mother, despite it feeling like the cursed Enchanted walls had *wanted* her to see it, open the case, and put it on.

She scrambled out the doorway and emerged into a wide hall. Her hand shook as she rubbed at her throat.

The hall rolled on forever, and candles stood at each unpainted door, which glistened as if freshly oiled. As if lived-in.

She moved down the hall, and the air shifted. A fresh, cool breath swept over her. It smelled of the rich River Kithyria, so unusual in the cloistered keep that she paused. The candles flickered: proof that one of the doors had been opened just a moment before.

Between each door hung a painting, and a scarlet one drew her eye. The moment she saw it, her heart hammered. Moving closer brought the painting—a blood-red flower—into sharp focus. She *knew* that flower. The exact color of it, the way the bee lay frozen in the middle. Her breath hitched in her chest.

She bent closer, examining the painting. Each brush stroke was evidence that it was Isander's work. Smooth strokes. Effortless perfection. Nothing was out of place, and the colors, shadows, and curves were as real as when she had bent there over Mellion, terrified at what her hawk had experienced as she died.

She reached out a finger, fighting her body's tremor. She winced when her finger touched the flower, but this time there was no pull, only the ridges of paint like a miniature landscape beneath her fingertip.

"Do you like it?"

Farren whipped around to face Isander, who stood just down the hall looking calm and unruffled. She hadn't heard anything, and the doors remained closed as they had before.

"Where were you? I've been looking all over!"

Isander approached, eyes narrowing. "Are you alright? You look—"

"I don't care how I look, Isander!" Farren didn't know why her voice was rising, just that she had to have answers, and have them now. "What is this painting of? I've seen this flower before."

"It's called a blood-flower. It grows in spots around the hills."

"Why is it here? In this hall? Is this where you sleep?"

Isander smiled. "No. These halls aren't used for anything. I like to keep some of my paintings here, where no one can see them. They are my private collection."

The way he said it didn't make her feel any better about the painting. "I don't understand. What are you doing here?"

He quirked a brow. "Shouldn't I be the one asking that of you? How did you get into this part of the keep? It's far too dangerous to wander around by yourself."

"Camilla has gone missing. Can you help me look for her? In the city?"

"Missing?" Isander took a step back. "You mean she's alive? I thought that she—I mean I heard that she fell from the balcony?"

Farren had never seen him look so perplexed. She reached for his arm, relieved when he didn't pull away. After nearly being lost forever in the keep, the solid feel of him did more than steady her.

"She did fall"—the image flashed in her mind, and her voice wavered—"and I thought she was dead, but she's actually missing, and we think she must be somewhere in the city. You're the only one who can find her. You're the only one I trust to help—"

"Shhh, alright. Come here." His face relaxed as he pulled her into his arms. "I can see—and feel—how much she means to you."

Farren pulled back sharply. She had stupidly left her mind open. Vulnerable. "Oh, I'm sorry, I didn't realize—"

"It's alright."

Isander gave her a smile that didn't reach his eyes. Triple checking that her mind was closed to him now, she leaned into him, and noticed the same scent she had smelled before: the unmistakable whiff of chill autumn air, weighted by the wet smell of the river.

Farren glanced back down the hall. "Have you been outside?"

Isander went very still for a moment, then cleared his throat. "If you mean to ask whether I've been outside today, then yes." He gave her a peculiar look. "When was the last time you slept, Farren?"

"I don't know. I don't have time to—"

"You need to sleep. You look like you haven't in days, and the mind doesn't do good things when it doesn't get sleep."

"I don't care about my mind right now. I just care about finding Camilla—"

"How will you find her if you aren't well-rested, Farren? If you go too long without sleep, you start to see things. Hear things. In fact, are you sure she, ah...fell from the balcony? You said she's alive?"

"We are fairly certain," Farren said, face heating.

"We?"

"Cato and I."

"Ah. But...what makes you think she's alive?"

"We found tracks leading up to the Runeless Quarter. She was with someone else. I know she hasn't been missing that long, but you called her your Night Muse, and I was wondering... Have you felt her at all in the past day?"

He dipped his head. "You know how difficult it can be for me to handle high emotion. The Night Muse is...not someone I normally reach out to."

"Can you try? Please?"

Isander swallowed, then cleared his throat. "I won't help until you've had some rest. And a bit to eat."

"This is important, Isander."

"So are you. Besides, I cannot reach minds that are very far away, and you said she is likely in the Runeless Quarter."

Farren crossed her arms, and her breath made the candlelight flicker and twist. "I will try to eat, but I'm not sleeping."

"We'll see."

Her irritation dwindled when he held his arm out to her. She took it, trying not to cling to him as they walked toward the end of the hall. Getting there had been a complete mystery, and she knew that if she ever tried to get out again by herself that the keep might well swallow her whole.

"You can relax now." Isander placed his warm hand over hers. His fingers were clean, scrubbed of paint, and she caught the faint whiff of soap from his skin.

She tried to pay attention to where Isander led her, but after the first few turns, her mind didn't seem able to hold anything more. This time, at least, doors weren't disappearing, and he didn't bring them into any odd rooms.

"I had trouble finding you," Farren said.

"Very old Enchantments are in these walls and doors and stairs. They are meant to protect the royal family in case anything happens."

"So the keep sees me as an intruder?" Farren's skin prickled.

"Not really," Isander said. "Just that you are not part of the royal family. It does take a bit of practice, anyways. You have to walk with intention, and once the walls determine you're not a threat, they will bring you quickly where you need to go. At least, that's how it works for me."

"Oh." Farren felt too tired to contemplate the intricacies of the keep walls. She was just relieved to have someone guiding her out. "The guards were awfully hesitant to let me into the keep."

"After the gryphon incident, the queen was quite angry. She doesn't know what happened, or who to blame."

"What do you think happened?"

Isander glanced at her, his eyes guarded. "I think that if the gryphons escaped, they are far more dangerous than we realized. If they were released, it was a bold move, if a bit reckless. And it apparently didn't go according to plan, unless whoever released them wished to cause havoc. In which case, it was a complete success." He stared at her sideways as if waiting for an explanation.

*Enchanter's curse.* Perhaps he had seen something earlier while her mind had been open. Foolish of her. Maybe she did need sleep, after all.

After a little while, the halls grew less stuffy, and finally they emerged into the servant corridors by the front atrium, which brimmed with midday light. Farren peered out the glass wall behind the empty thrones, her heart skipping a beat. Hours must have passed since she had gone into the keep. Cato would be wondering where she was. And Camilla... She couldn't waste a moment longer.

She wove her fingers through Isander's and pulled him into the shadow of a pillar. He glanced around, and gave her his full attention when he seemed satisfied that they were alone.

"Isander, we don't have time to eat. The day is growing late and I desperately need your help. We won't find Camilla without you."

He considered her for a moment in perplexing silence. "I believe you can find her. On your own."

"It might take days," Farren whispered, fighting to keep her voice low. "And I'm worried that she's in danger."

Isander stroked her cheek, sending an infuriating flash of heat down her body. "And you can save her."

"What are you saying? You won't help me, then?"

"You need to trust yourself, Farren."

"I know what I'm capable of, and this isn't it. I can't sense other people like you."

"You don't need to be able to do that. Just use what you *do* have. Like perception. Fast reflexes. The gryphons."

She scowled and tugged away from him. "I thought I had *you*."

"You have me, Farren. Just not for this. There's something I need to do."

"Right now? Can't it wait—"

"I'm afraid not."

He already seemed to be thinking of other things. His gaze swept around the atrium once more, and his body tensed with his familiar restlessness. Now that he had painted her, was he done with her? Had she been a momentary obsession of his, just like the gryphons? Suddenly, she missed those painting sessions. She missed the close attention he had given her, the way his words had dug into her, finding the deepest, strongest things in there that she hadn't seen.

That she hadn't been willing to see.

He had always made her feel strong. Like she could be stronger, like she could have control over things. Over everything.

"Isander." Her voice nearly cracked. "Why did we never runebond when we were intimate?"

His brows lifted. "I didn't think you wanted it. And I... I have trouble keeping myself afloat in such intimacy."

"So you never wanted to runebond with me?"

"I didn't say that. I said it was hard." He frowned, then smoothed hands down her shoulders and sides. "I would always rather connect, if you want to. Just not while we're intimate...yet."

"Yet?" Her stomach fluttered.

He planted his hands on her hips and pulled her against him. "I want there to be more. Don't you?"

He looked at her with those spring-in-the-mountains eyes, warm and earnest and full of things that had yet to take flight.

"I do," she said. "But I'm not sure I'll be able to forgive you for not helping me find my friend."

"I will make it up to you. I promise."

Farren chewed her lip. Hopefully, Cato was able to find Camilla in the Runeless Quarter. But if he hadn't...she would need all the strength she could muster. "At least could you... Can you show me the Commander?"

"Of course." He took her hands, gave her a knowing smile, and pulled her close once more. "Open yourself to me, Farren Blackburn."

Repressing a shiver, she cleared her mind of everything except for the feel of his hands, strong and nimble in hers. His minty breath punctuated the air, and she could almost taste the *birali* he had sipped after his last meal. When she was certain secret thoughts were locked away deep, she opened her mind to him. His voice was honey and fire and stone.

*This is how I know you.*

The Commander flared to life between them. Proud and strong, she lit the dark with her essence. She wore her armor inside and out, and melded her mind to the gryphons' like a hilt to a blade. The Commander was small like Farren, poised and ready, awareness penetrating the shadows around her. When the Commander spoke, Farren was uncertain if it was Isander speaking or her own imagination.

*I am here,* The Commander whispered. *See me. Feel me. Become me. We are one.*

A tremor shook Farren. It didn't feel like Isander. The voice—the feeling of certainty, of reaching—emerged from somewhere inside herself, but it was distant and only touched Farren briefly before it faded.

When the voice receded, Farren steadied. The Commander's light shone on and on, and Farren savored it, taking the burning image into herself like the sun.

# FORTY-ONE

After Isander left her, a restless energy warmed Farren from head to toe. She was about to step out from the shadow of the pillar when commotion resounded at the front doors of the atrium. A group of well-dressed people surged inside, demanding to speak to the queen. They gathered beneath the dais expectantly, arguing amongst themselves about something that was *beyond reparation* and *despicable* and *utterly outrageous.*

In the same moment, Farren became aware of hushed voices from the corridor just beyond the pillar, where the library, ballroom, and several small rooms were held. She left the shadow of the pillar and wedged herself next to a tapestry just outside the corridor, ears pricked at what was unmistakably the queen's voice.

"How could you be such a fool?" Queen Aurelia seethed, her voice a barely-restrained whisper. "First you stole my guards—like some traitorous thief—and then you searched the city without my approval or knowledge. It makes me sick to think what damage you have caused to my position!"

Farren had never heard the queen so furious. She swallowed, cringing internally as Cato spoke up.

"I had no time, Mother. Camilla could be out there, hurt or taken—"

"To make matters worse, you caused a skirmish inside the city! You know as much as I do how much the Runeless Sect hates us, how they disapprove of our runeskills. And that on top of the gryphons escaping—the gossip is rampant about the ineptitude of the royal family. Now I have to contend with their leaders because you so mindlessly tried to breach their walls. You'll be lucky if they don't retaliate, and with whatever strange new things they've developed—like that Enchanted curse of an explosion they demonstrated at your brother's party—we are not bloody ready for a rebellion, Cat, not even close. And this," the queen exhaled, in a way that Farren thought she was trying very hard not to strangle her son, "all this for that silly girl you adopted like a pet."

"She's not silly, and she's certainly not a pet, Mother," Cato retorted. "Th—This is exactly why I didn't ask your permission. You've never cared about her and I knew you would never allow me to take guards—"

Farren flinched as a sharp slap rang in the air.

"Control yourself, Cat. The girl is not worth the risk of war. If you had even a quarter of the sense of your brother, you would understand that. Go back to the mews. Do what I told you and help Horat question the servants. We need to find whoever is responsible for what happened with the gryphons." The queen sniffed, apparently mollified by her own words. "I will deal with the Sect leaders, and when I'm finished, I expect to hear something from you about your progress. I'll have no more talk about the girl. Do you understand me?"

A pause and then a begrudging murmur.

Farren pressed herself against the wall as the queen stalked past—an erect column draped in a green and black brocade cloak, with a simple silver circlet adorning her head. Something about the queen's rigid posture and raised chin reminded Farren of a serpent readying to strike.

Luckily for her, the handful of visitors demanding to speak with the queen preoccupied the guards in the atrium. If Farren went by the visitors' plain appearances, unadorned by skin paintings, runemarks, or any other sign of rune animal, they must've been the leaders of the Sect. She walked quickly past them, her head bent like a servant on an errand, and loosed a breath when she left the keep behind.

She trod down the path toward the East Tow, hoping she would be able to cross the Kithyria without issue into the city. Since Cato hadn't been able to get into the Runeless Quarter, Farren would have to try. From what she had heard, they didn't usually admit those from outside their Quarter, but she figured she could try using Diocleto's name to get inside, and hunt for Camilla once there.

As she headed for the East Tow, her mind probed the mews for Naronimus. She found him in his chamber, shivering with wet and cold. His mind was fuzzy and addled, spinning with more of Scipio's poison.

*Are you alone*, she asked him.

*Alone...with chains, with pain,* he said, sending her a bleary impression of the shackles on his legs, the pain slogging into his shoulder and limbs from bruises and cuts. He wanted all of it to end.

*I'm looking for Camilla now,* Farren explained. *And after, I will find a way to free you—*

*Don't,* he said. *No more lies. Should've never trusted you... Empty promises.*

Her breath hitched. *It wasn't an empty promise.*

*Useless.*

The cruel word tumbled into her, and she cringed. *As soon as I can, I will find a way to help—*

"There you are!" Scipio darted from beneath the shadow of the eastern gate and clamped onto her arm. "I've been looking for you," he said, holding tight so she couldn't run. "Did you have a nice visit in the keep? With the prince, I assume?" He sneered, glancing back the way Farren had come. "Where are you off to, now?"

"None of your business." Farren fought the urge to tug her arm away. Naronimus's feelings still trickled into her, so she closed the runebond.

"Actually, it is. The queen charged me with making sure all the servants are accounted for. I'll be bringing you to Horat's study, unless you want me to tell the queen that you've run away...?"

Gritting her teeth, Farren looked longingly back at the shore of the East Tow. It bustled with servants and the wealthier visitors of Alidonia, many of whom were already loading onto the raft before its next trip off the fortress island.

"Are you going to tell me how you did it?" Scipio said in a cloying tone as he dragged her back to the mews.

"What are you talking about?"

"The gryphons, foolish Outskirts girl." His hand tightened, making her wince. "It was my mistake for not dosing you with enough potion—"

"Poison."

"—and I know you must've woken up right around the time of the gryphons storming the keep. I didn't think you would ever do something as stupid as try to lead an attack on the fortress."

Farren's heart thumped, and she fought to bolster her voice. "So why aren't you taking me to the queen?"

"I will, once you have spoken with Horat. First, he'll make you admit to your folly."

"What, that's not *your* task?" Farren asked, sharpening her tone to a point. "Is it because the queen didn't trust you with it or because that sort of thing makes you squeamish?"

His fingers dug into her arm, bruising it as he wrenched her faster down the walkway.

Inside, the mews were strangely subdued. She sensed Eralius, Naronimus, and Delphi's three other young. Still no sign of Thella, Phynx, Grit, or Calipsa. Delphi and Torch remained with Elya in the Healing Caves. She would have time to speak to them later, once she had dealt with Horat. Then she could work with them to come up with a new plan—one that would release the remaining gryphons from the queen's control.

Virilus passed them, eyes diverted as he carried a bucket of meat that she presumed was for the gryphons. The five remaining gryphons had extra sentries posted outside their chambers.

Farren dragged her eyes away from the closed doors. She needed more time to formulate her lie about the gryphon release because if Horat found out the truth about what she had tried to do, he would certainly take it to the queen. She could say she had been asleep the whole time until she had arrived at the atrium. Had any of the gryphons given away her role in their escape? If so, she was doomed.

By the time they reached the Lord Falconer's study, Farren was sweating from the pain in her arm and had failed to come up with a good lie. Scipio swung the door open and practically threw her inside. Horat sat at his desk, a scowl etched beneath the scar on his forehead. Beside him, Cato straightened from where he had bent over a smaller gryphon—one Farren recognized as Balyon, Torch's brother.

"Found her trying to escape," Scipio said to Horat.

Farren rubbed her arm. "I wasn't trying to escape. I was going to the city—"

"That's enough," Horat cut her off, then turned to Scipio. "Thank you for bringing her. You can close the door on your way out."

Scipio's eyes flashed, but Horat stared at him menacingly, and he did as the Lord Falconer said.

"Did you find Isander?" Cato asked in a hushed voice after the door had closed.

Farren glanced back at the door, perplexed. "I thought I was here to be questioned about—"

"We don't have time for that right now," Cato said.

Relief unfurled in her. So, he was still looking for Camilla despite the blow the queen had dealt him.

Cato leaned forward. "Isander?"

"He didn't agree to it."

Cato let out a huff and dug a hand into his hair.

Horat looked at the prince, his mouth tight. "Can she help with Balyon?"

Cato shook his head, looking skeptical. "If I can't make it out, how can she?"

Farren crossed her arms. "Excuse me. I'm right here."

Cato tossed her an apologetic glance. "Fine. I did try using Balyon to find the missing children. I never got anything from Balyon, as I told you, but this time..."

"Does Balyon know where she is?"

"Balyon's magic is different from the others'," Horat told her. "It's muddled."

"We can't understand what he's telling us," Cato added. "It's like a riddle, and I've been trying to figure it out since I returned to the fortress. Horat worked with him while I searched the city and..." Cato scrubbed at his face. He probably hadn't slept since... Well, two nights ago.

Horat lifted a hand and dropped it. "I'm just as uncertain about the meaning. He only gives us one clue, nothing else to go on. It's a single piece of a story."

She eased toward Balyon. "Let me try, Cato. You should sit, maybe have some of that tea." She indicated the steaming cup on Horat's desk.

"I'm fine. I just need an answer."

Gently, Farren opened a runebond with the gryphon and bent so that their faces were level. Balyon's coloring was darker than Torch, his feathers shining with the luster of polished cherrywood. Wide, muddy eyes peered at her as curiosity trickled down the connection.

*My name is Farren*, she said. She opened their runebond wider and felt an undercurrent of fear.

*You don't need to fear me*, she reassured him. *I am bonded to Torch*. Surely, he remembered her from all the times she visited?

Still, no response. Farren turned to Cato. "Can he not communicate well?"

Cato's face tightened. "Scipio used his potion on them all. The queen is afraid they will get loose again."

A flame lit along the simmering embers inside her. The queen, who always wanted to be seen as fierce and wild and untamed, was afraid. Afraid of the gryphons, which had been deliberately taken from the wild and which she had tried to tame to use as weapons.

Balyon's fear grew, and Farren responded with soothing ripples of calm. No doubt Cato had already done so, but she figured it wouldn't hurt. His attempted escape and re-entry to the fortress had likely been traumatic for him.

*Balyon, we are searching for Camilla.* She sent him an impression of Camilla's simple, sweet face—her glistening blue eyes, laughter like finger-bells, her small hands as they petted a dove in her lap. *We cannot find her*, she urged Balyon. *Please help us find her. She is lost.*

Lost? The word echoed distantly down the runebond, and Farren sent him a surge of encouragement.

*Yes, she is lost. No one can find her. She is in danger.* She didn't hold back her fear for the girl, and let her puzzlement wash over him, prodding him to use his magic. *Please help us. Help her.*

Something stirred in Balyon. It was pale and cool like moonlight, illuminating the darkness of the unknown. It stretched down the runebond, tendrils reaching into Farren until she felt certain in whatever it had to tell her. Because it did have something to tell her.

Balyon pushed the light at her, urging her to look into it as it filled their connection and spilled into her mind.

*Here*, it said. *Here is what you seek.*

Red petals unfolded around a butter-yellow center, a bee perched among powdered stamens and sticky pistils. A flower and bee she had seen before. On a hill. In the Kithyrian Mountains.

Her mind tilted. It couldn't be right. Camilla wasn't in those mountains. Farren started to pull away from the image, but Balyon dragged her closer, insistent.

*Here*, he said again. *She is here. This is the truth. Don't look away. You know it. You know this path. You know where to find her.*

Hardly breathing, Farren peered closer. Yes, there was the flower she knew. And the bee, like ice, unmoving. Like a painting.

A painting, yes. It was the painting she had seen before. She caught the raised lines of paint where the brush had traveled along the canvas, replicating reality as if by magic. With exquisite skill and immeasurable patience.

*Yes*, Balyon said, allowing his magic to fade between them. *You know. You know where to find her.* He sent her a tremor of approval, his feelings dampened by whatever poison slugged through his blood.

Farren sank back onto her heels. Her ears rang, and she closed her runebond with the gryphon, not wanting him to feel the sickening sensation rising in her belly.

She breathed in. Out. Stared at Balyon's glossy dark eyes, knowing what they knew. Not believing it.

She would go and see and prove to herself that everything was fine. That Camilla wasn't with Isander because what would he want with her? To paint her? But then why would he have lied about wanting to look for her? Why keep it a secret?

Someone was shaking her shoulder. "Farren!"

Farren stared up into Cato's exasperated face, and his voice cut through her spiraling thoughts. "Did you see it? The image of the flower? I can tell you recognize it," he hurried on. "Farren, we need to find her. Just tell me what you know and—"

The door burst open, and Farren winced as Scipio strode into the room. "That's enough. The queen has given you ample time to question all the servants on their—"

"We're not finished here," Horat said, grimacing as he forced himself to stand. "As you can see, we are making progress."

Scipio hesitated, looking down at Farren. What did he see? Farren felt unsteady and weak. She hated feeling that way, hated the way Scipio sneered down at her.

"Then I'll stay," Scipio said. "I'll be a witness to whatever she admits to—"

"You'll do no such thing." Cato's voice rose to a sharp pitch. He sounded remarkably like the queen when he spoke that way.

Scipio scowled at him. "I'll do whatever the queen asks. She wants to find answers."

"We've had answers," Cato said. He put his hands beneath Farren's arms, helping her stand.

Why did her legs feel so wobbly? She needed to find Camilla. And to do that, she would have to go back to the painting.

She bit her lip until it smarted.

"And Farren can help us," Cato was saying, some of the edge leaving his voice. He was starting to become less certain, and Scipio would notice. "We just need to let her go, and she'll be able to give us proof of what happened."

Scipio's frown turned to a slow, sickly smile. "Let her go?" He held out his hands as if confused. "So she can run again? What game are you playing, cousin? I thought you hated her."

"You know how I feel," Cato said. "And right now, Farren has something that will show us what happened. She can go get it and—"

Scipio wasn't believing any of it. He strode forward, reaching for Farren once more. On instinct, Farren grabbed Scipio's hand, pulling it and twisting her body at the same time, and used his momentum to send him sprawling behind her. He rolled and popped back up, glancing between her, Horat, and the prince.

"Is this how it is, then? You three are working against the queen now? She'll be outraged to hear about your treason."

"I'm not working against her," Cato said, stepping toward him, his hand out in a show of peace. "This is what's best right now, and my mother will see that once we find out who took Camilla—"

Scipio laughed, and Cato's hands curled into fists. "You think that bloody girl is important to the queen? When you almost caused an uprising among the Runeless? Enchanter's curse, you probably *have* caused an uprising, you stupid fool."

Horat slammed a hand down on the desk. "Have a care of your words," he said, his face dark as thunderclouds.

Scipio's grin widened. "What, would you like to fight me, too, old man? Let's see what you have to offer."

Farren stepped backward toward the door, the breath of tantalizing freedom on her back. Scipio caught her movement and lunged.

Two steps back and her foot snagged on the stool. She cursed and lifted her hands to ward off Scipio, but as he passed Cato, the prince's leg kicked out.

Scipio went sprawling, and suddenly Balyon pounced, his taloned claws landing inches from the guard's stunned face. Scipio tried to scramble to his feet, but the prince jumped and pinned him to the floor.

"Go!" Cato yelled at Farren. "Find her!"

Without a word, Farren spun away. She drove through the halls, barreled past surprised servants, and flew out the door like a kestrel bursting beneath the reaching talons of a hawk.

# FORTY-TWO

AIR RUSHED INTO FARREN'S lungs as her feet stomped on the stone path. Running had never felt so good. It fed the urgency inside her as she made her way toward the keep.

People started to turn their heads, so she slowed to a brisk walk and tucked her head, looking like no more than a guard running late for duty.

The painting was inside the keep of the fortress, but she couldn't go back inside those doors, not without drawing the notice of the guards. Besides that, the keep was likely to swallow her alive.

While inside the corridor where Isander had found her, she had smelled fresh air—both in the corridor and on Isander himself. Yet, when she had asked him about it, he had been oddly vague. Perhaps one of the doors *did* lead outside, and if so, that could be her way in. Other than the fortress wall itself, there was no outer wall surrounding the keep, so there must be another door somewhere.

As Farren rounded the side of the keep, gardens of well-trimmed shrubbery and evenly-spaced irises gave way to tall brush that filled the space between the keep and the outer wall of the fortress.

Shrubs clawed at her hair and chiton and snapped as she pushed through them. Why would Camilla be with Isander? Was Isander helping her with her nightmares? If so, why had he kept it a secret from Farren? None of it made sense.

It wasn't just Camilla's disappearance that bothered her. It was that damned painting. The thought of it made the world tilt beneath her. But she couldn't think too closely about it because if she did that, if she did...

Her breath rattled as she met a sudden curve in the otherwise straight wall of the keep. She put her hands against the curve, her head dropping back to follow it up and up and up.

It stopped short and was open at the top. Beyond the shushing of the falls, no sounds stirred beyond it. She climbed a tall, spindly tree and scooched along one of the limbs until she was above the wall and then dropped to land on the ledge.

A large, untended garden sprawled beneath her. It must've been a private garden at one point, full of herbs and flowers and butterflies. Now, untamed weeds and shrubs ruled, obscuring the order that must have cut it into manageable sections, meandering pathways that one of the royal family had undoubtedly walked. The tang of greenery and rot hung heavy in the air.

As she stared at it, her skin prickled. Perhaps it was the disorder of the space that bothered her, but something about it felt off.

Farren swung down to the garden floor and landed in a crouch. The weeds stood tall, but there was a spot where they appeared cut down to make room for a little statue.

A rabbit, she saw. Gray and glassy-eyed and incredibly detailed.

She edged closer, holding her breath. No moss grew on its surface. Rain hadn't pocked the stone like it had the fountains in the courtyard.

Farren bent close and saw the fine strands of the rabbit's whiskers.

*No, no, no.* It couldn't be. Not here, not now, so far from the mountains of the north. Unable to stop herself, she reached out a hand and touched a whisker. Fire lit up her finger and seared down her palm, hungry and searching and reaching down, down, down—

She yanked her hand away, gripping it as she ground her teeth. Her finger ached, but it appeared unharmed. Unlike the rabbit, which was dead.

Just like Mellion.

She forced herself to stand and look around the rest of the garden. Blood thundered in her ears. Camilla was here. She must've been. That was what Balyon's magic had shown her. There must've been other—

Her eyes snagged on a second statue. A not-statue. She stumbled there, to a blue-bell shrub that grew beside it, almost touching. A glassy-eyed fox snarled at her. Each strand of fur burned orange like the setting sun. She pressed through the weeds away from it, only to find a frog and a butterfly, frozen on a yellow lily, and a little patch of roses that no longer moved in the breeze, a line of ants marching along their crimson petals with legs still as ice. Farren found one statue after another. The whole garden was filled with them.

Still life. Stolen life.

Beautiful things, captured forever.

The plants that touched them were frozen, too, as if whatever disease had killed the statue creatures had eaten its fill and moved on to the next living thing. A breeze stirred the living things, and Farren avoided stepping close to anything that didn't move. Her foot caught on something, and she fell forward, yanking away from it. Her sandal had caught on a limb.

A bare limb, on a woman whose simple chiton was pocked with holes. She held a bundle in her arms, and a tiny face showed in the opening, eyes closed and mouth sealed like a flower-bud that would never open. The woman's face lifted to the sky, a cry of anguish frozen on her face.

Farren scrambled upright, something lodged in her throat. A few more steps and she saw a hand. She followed the hand up to an arm that reminded her of a smooth and slender dewfall sapling, and from there to a face she knew, but didn't know. The painted eyes that had been so full of warmth on the canvas now shone with terror and pain, high cheeks and delicate mouth stretched in mortal fear of an invisible force.

Whatever the woman had seen, Farren could tell by the tilt of Persepha's head that it had been above her, and very close. Intimately close. Curtains of dark hair tumbled around her shoulders, and the brocade dress crumpled around her thighs, marked only by summer's rose petals that had fallen and frozen there among its gilded folds.

"Persepha," Farren said, as if the woman could hear her and be broken from paralysis.

Shaking, Farren pulled away from Persepha's half-hidden form. More petrified figures sat or lay in the garden, unmistakable beneath the weeds. A child holding a limp dog, a man with a peg for a leg, an elderly woman covered in oozing blisters. All stamped with the same expressions of terror, loss, and pain. All buried forever in this horrible secret garden.

Perhaps it was all the fortress keep, fooling her mind just as it had inside its walls. The statues weren't real; none of it was real—

A scream pierced the silence. It rose from behind a single door set in the inner keep wall.

Farren pushed herself up, stomach churning. She could see more of them as she stumbled to the door. She wouldn't look anymore, couldn't bear to witness—

What? What was it? She didn't even understand what she saw, felt—

She grabbed the door latch and yanked it open.

Camilla sat on a chair, and Isander clutched her hand. A whispered slurry of words surged from his mouth as he read from a book, and they were unfamiliar, unbalanced words that ran together like water over a crooked brook. For a moment, the world began to bend, and the normal downward pull of the earth tilted toward him. Farren's skin tingled at the change in pressure. The girl's hand shimmered.

Her face contorted with pain as she screamed again, and the sound stabbed into Farren. She threw herself at Isander and thrust him out of the way. His book went flying as he spilled over the floor, but Camilla's scream went on, filling the void left by Isander's strange words. Camilla clutched her arm, holding up the hand Isander had touched.

"Camilla!" Farren shook the girl gently. "What's happening?"

"My hand!" the girl shrieked, her face white as a dove-wing. "It's burning!"

Her hand wasn't on fire. But it was becoming oddly, completely still. Her fingers didn't move.

"It's too late, Farren." Isander's voice was ragged as he picked himself up from the floor. "She told me she wanted this. It'll be over in just a few minutes if you let it be—"

"Help me, Farren!" Camilla sobbed. "I can't feel it; I can't feel my hand except for the burning, and it's coming up my arm, Farren! Please do something—"

She cried out in agony again, and Farren searched desperately for something—*anything*—that would save the girl from whatever monster crept up her arm.

There was a lit fireplace. Shelves of books. Stacks of paintings. A table with a washbasin. On the wall were more paintings, a sconce, a mantle with figurines. Her eye snagged on a long, slender knife braced on the wall above the mantle. She raced to it, grabbed it and rushed Isander, an easy task while he stared dazedly at Camilla. Farren anchored his shoulder with a hand while she tucked the blade's honed edge against his throat.

"Woah, Farren." His eyes glistened as he held up his hands. "Let's talk about this, please—"

"Make it stop!"

"I can't, Farren. Once it starts, it—"

Farren tilted the knife up, intending to prick him with the point, but the blade jerked away from his skin. Confused, she brought the tip close to him, but again it swung to the side.

The prince's lips twitched. "It's Enchanted, Farren. The blade won't cut royal skin."

Of course. Farren threw it aside, ignoring Isander as he dashed after it and picked it up off the floor. She searched the walls again, grinding her teeth at every cry Camilla emitted as the fire worked its way up the girl's arm.

An axe rested on the far wall. Farren gripped its handle as she yanked it off its golden mount. "Is this one Enchanted, too?" she asked Isander, wishing her gaze could hurt him, that it could make everything stop.

Isander swallowed and held up the knife defensively. "It cuts clean, but I promise you that hurting me won't stop the Emptiness from..."

Farren stopped listening and stalked to Camilla. She pulled the girl to the floor, ignoring her wailing. "Hold out your arm!" she shouted, and used her sandal to pin the girl's damaged hand to the floor.

Camilla shrieked as the axe swung down.

The wedged blade bit through bone and sliced the lower arm free. Farren stared at the cut. No blood seeped from the muscle and bone that were now exposed, and she worried for a moment that the monster had worked its way higher than she had realized.

Camilla stared at her, glassy-eyed. "It doesn't burn anymore." Then the girl looked at her arm, saw that it was no longer attached, and swiftly fell unconscious.

"You can try to fix the Night Muse all you want, Farren," Isander was saying, "but she's still broken."

Farren checked Camilla's nonbleeding wound, and touched just above the cut, making sure the skin still felt alive, unfrozen. Relief flooded into her—though it wasn't fair that Camilla had to lose her arm, after she had already suffered so much. Farren knew that if she hadn't done it, the girl would've ended up like Mellion.

She pulled Camilla's unconscious body away from the arm, not wanting her to touch it and risk the same thing happening to her other hand.

"Why don't you explain this to me, Isander?" Farren's voice trembled beneath the force of the storm inside her.

"Explain what, Farren?" He stalked to the chair and sank into it, looking at her hopelessly.

"Why do you have Camilla?"

"She was brought to me, and I could finally help her. I heard about her falling off the balcony, and everyone assumed she was dead. You know I suffered from the Night Muse's pain. Every time she had night terrors, I was pulled there with her. She carries the past like a festering wound, and she wanted it to stop hurting. So I offered to help."

"You mean you offered to freeze her, just like those statues—those *people* out there?" She stabbed a finger toward the motionless garden. What he could do didn't make sense. Runeskills couldn't freeze people—at least not that she knew of. "What did you do to them, Isander?"

"They were hurting, too," Isander's voice rose. "You have no idea what it's like to live with this runeskill. How hard it is to be around other people. I've done everything I could think of to make it better, to dull the way I can feel others, but nothing has worked. Not like this. Please, Farren, try to understand."

He reached out to her, but she backed away. A small painting of Camilla stood on an easel in the corner. She posed quietly in the chair, looking forlorn and hopeful and full of wistful adoration. The paint was still wet.

Bile crept up her throat. Sweet, innocent Camilla had wanted him to paint her, and he had obliged.

"Is that why you freeze them?" she asked. "So that you can paint them?"

She had thought he was just a prince—a talented prince whose impatient passion bordered on obsession. But he was so much worse. How could she have been such a blind fool, after seeing the painting of the red flower and the bee—the very thing that had killed Mellion in the mountains?

"Farren, please. I—I do it to help them, but they want me to paint them, too. I can take away their suffering and preserve their beauty. And it helps when I can see their pain—the raw feelings they have—and not feel them myself. It helps me deal with them better."

Isander was looking at her, his spring-mountain eyes too full beneath furrowed brows. He had uttered sounds she had never heard before—ones that altered the fabric of air between them. What sort of power did he have, that he could do such a thing? How could he unravel the very thing that made a living thing living?

"You're a monster," she heard herself say.

He shook his head. "No, Farren, just listen. I was having a hard time, drinking and taking things to dull my runeskill, but then I found out I could feel runes. I didn't know I could take them away—destroy them—until it was too late."

"You're an Enchanter?"

"No, I'm a human, just like you. But my mother always told me we have Enchanter blood, that dark things were in our past. That was why the book was hidden away, deep in the keep with old, dangerous Enchanted objects. I couldn't read it at first, but once I started to sense runes—so many of them, everywhere—the words on the pages began making sense. It's written in the Tongue of Runes, Farren. The same language used by the Enchanters to create and destroy runes."

The fire in the hearth popped and crackled.

"You sound crazy, Isander."

"I'm not, Farren. You have to understand. I just want to change the runes, is that so awful? I don't want the runeskill I was given—this connection to other people. I just want to be normal—to have a runeskill with a cat or a bird or even a fish. Maybe if I practice this magic enough—whatever it is I inherited from my ancestors—then I can finally alter my runes...or even others who might want them changed."

Her fingers dug into the wooden handle of the axe. She tasted bitterness as she wondered if she had ever truly known any part of him.

"How? How can you kill people?"

"I didn't kill them!" Isander threw up his hands. "I just...emptied them."

"You killed them. You killed Persepha."

"I never meant to hurt her!"

"She's out there." Farren jabbed a finger toward the garden. "A statue. What did you do to her, Isander?"

"It was an accident! I didn't know what I was doing. She just wanted me to love her, but I couldn't handle the connection."

She was shaking all over. No warmth from the fire reached her. Isander had put his blade down somewhere and leaned forward with open palms. The beseeching look didn't fit him. Too vulnerable. Almost weak. As if he needed her to make things better. What could she do? The weight of the axe dragged her arm down.

She didn't need this man, this stranger, this monster. She neede d... Sucking in a breath, Farren flung open her mind. She stretched out to Delphi, still deep down in the Healing Caves.

*Please, help me!* She held nothing back from Delphi, entrusting her horror to the beast. Delphi would know what to do. She would come quickly. Maybe even quickly enough.

She closed her runebond with Delphi but kept her mind open. The space between the gryphon minds was empty, a void that Isander must have been able to feel because a moment later, he flinched.

"I need you to calm down, Farren. Or close your mind, please. It's getting to be too much, and I don't want to hurt you."

Was this the space where Camilla screamed during her nightmares? Farren gripped the axe, wondering if she had the gumption to lift it and bring it down on him. Her limbs didn't seem to be obeying, or perhaps it was that the very air had become a crushing weight on her shoulders.

Isander clutched his head. "Farren! Please, just close your mind!" He grabbed her arm and squeezed. "Calm yourself down."

"I can't calm down!" Farren's heart hammered in her chest. "You lied to me. You hurt Camilla and countless others. And I can't..." She shook her head numbly. The shattered pieces of her existence cut into her, impossible to make sense of, never again to be put back together.

"I was trying to help her." His mouth twisted, and his glistening eyes turned on her like a hailstorm. "Why can't you understand?"

And then he delved into her mind, forcing memories on her. A Runeless man bringing Camilla to Isander. Camilla's confusion and tears, the way her mind bent toward the memories of abuse that festered inside her, the night terrors that fed on her each night. Her longing for escape, to be free of her past. Isander's knowing that she could never be free from her past as long she lived.

Before Camilla, there had been others, so many others. Humans and animals and plants, all perfectly preserved. Most emptied of runes in that very room, except the one scarlet flower in the mountains—he hadn't been able to resist its beauty, the thought of it fading one day and rotting back into dirt. He had gotten good at it, emptying things quickly so the pain was brief.

But that wasn't how things had started. He had discovered his ability some years ago, when he had found out he could read from the book. Words that shifted the very nature of runes, bending them to his will. A miracle he had inherited from the Enchanters, his ancestors, but discovered the hard way with his first victim, Persepha.

A simple kiss had smoldered into something far more potent, and he had lost himself in her, only realizing what his body was doing when her terror surged into him. Instinct had taken over, and the words from the book broke open in his mind. He had used them as a tool to quiet her screaming, to relieve the way it clashed through his mind. Sensing her runes had made it so easy, and the words from the book had bent the runes to his will. He had pulled and pulled at them until they broke away from her completely, shredding as they did so. Instead of shining runes, blackness had filled the void, and with it, silence. Her physical body had remained as if frozen in time. Lifeless, yet full of beauty.

In his memories, Farren reeled. As it had been with Naronimus, her own feelings were smothered, but Isander was more twisted than Naronimus ever would be. She couldn't let him pull her in, twist her to his thinking. She had to protect herself, to protect Camilla.

In the void of her mind, Farren unleashed a scream. It erupted into the spaces between the gryphon minds and seethed down their runebond, singeing the place where Isander's mind touched hers.

Isander rocked back in his chair. "Please, Farren, you can't do this! It's too much, and I'll lose myself and—" He cut himself off, and his jaw set suddenly as he grabbed her hands. His shoulders heaved as he breathed. "I can't drown again, Farren. I can't lose myself like I did with Persepha. I'm so sorry."

Tears pearled in his spring mountain eyes, and Farren shrieked as fire swept into her.

# FORTY-THREE

PAIN ATE INTO SKIN, skewered deep into muscle and bone. Farren doubled over, unable to think.

Isander's iron arms caged her as strange words spiraled around her and tugged. The fire crept faster, hungry and yearning and seeking the deepest part of herself: the very rune-made core of her soul.

Her ears rang with the noise of her scream, with the furious pump of her blood as she struggled to resist. Something deep down in her stirred. It twitched out a talon and—

Isander yelped and jerked away. The agony fled, and Farren took a shuddering breath, her body going slack in the sudden absence of pain.

He looked at her, perplexed. "What—"

A gryphon's cry split the air.

The garden door ripped off its hinges. Splinters of wood pelted into the room as Delphi's massive talons cleared an opening. Isander scrambled back, then cast Farren a longing, reluctant look before he darted out the opposite door into the corridor Farren knew she would get lost in.

Delphi surged inside, head craning as she searched for danger, and Cato ran in behind her, his face tight with worry.

*Where is he?* Delphi asked, her words like lightning.

Farren panted as she struggled to clear her mind. *He ran into the keep. But the halls are Enchanted—*

*Cato will lead the way.*

*We need to help Camilla,* Farren told her.

"You found her, thank the Enchanters," Cato breathed. "Delphi heard your call, and we came as fast as we could." His gaze rested on Camilla long enough to see that she was still alive, but his stride took him straight through the room. "I'm going to look for him."

Farren lurched and grabbed his arm as he stalked by. "Cato, you'll get lost—"

He tugged away from her. "I won't. Despite hating this keep, I do know my way around a little."

"At least take Delphi," she said as he made his way to the door. "Where's Torch?"

"She left him at the Healing Caves with Elya. Delphi will do a sweep around the perimeter of the fortress," he said just before diving through the doorway where Isander had disappeared.

Delphi trotted back out into the gardens, and Farren's throat cinched tight.

*Don't touch anything in the garden*, she told Delphi. *Keep to the center stone path. Avoid anything that looks frozen.*

*Frozen?* She saw Delphi peer down at the plants around her massive talons.

*Please, be careful. There's a disease that kills at a touch.*

The information didn't seem to dissuade Delphi as she leapt to the wall, giving a great beat of her wings for lift. *Focus on Camilla*, Delphi said.

Right. Camilla. Farren shook out her frigid, useless hands. She sank down next to the girl and checked on her breathing. When Farren touched her cheek, Camilla's eyes slid open.

"Mother?" Camilla whispered, her eyes growing wide and wistful.

Something squeezed in Farren's chest. "No, love. It's Farren."

Camilla closed her eyes, her lips wobbling before tilting up to a smile. "Farren." When her eyes opened again, they seemed clearer. Camilla tried to sit up—nearly toppling over as she went to support herself with the arm that was no longer there—and Farren dove in to brace her.

"My arm..." As Camilla stared at it, her body turned rigid.

"I know. But I had to do it to stop the burning..." Camilla pressed her face into Farren's chest. Hesitantly, she pulled the girl closer.

"I remember," the girl said, her tight voice muffled by Farren's leather vest. A light trembling worked its way over Camilla's body, and Farren held her as she might a fragile egg. "I was certain I was going to die, Farren. I've never felt so much pain, like fire eating away at me—" A sob racked her, and Farren waited until the girl's tears and shivering subsided. Camilla sniffed, then spoke in a voice that quavered like a downy plume in a draft. "If you hadn't come, it would have eaten me. Everything. All of me. I'd be dead now."

"It's over," Farren said. "Isander's gone." She wished she could tell Camilla he couldn't hurt her anymore, but that would be a lie. "Camilla, how did you find Isander? After you fell from the balcony?"

Camilla stared at the fire, eyes distant over her damp cheeks. "I was able to swim with the current until I reached the shore. A man was there. He helped me out of the water. He had a basket—fish, he said—and told me he knew a shortcut into the city so that I could see a healer. I followed him up the bank until we reached a stairway..." Camilla blinked, her pale brows drawing down. "It's a bit fuzzy, but I remember climbing up a second stair, one made of stone."

"On the cliff?" Farren asked.

"You've seen it?"

"It leads to the Runeless Quarter," Farren explained.

"I didn't know that. He just told me it was the city. I was dizzy, and the climb hadn't helped. I just remember seeing all the people, and I haven't seen the city streets since I was with my father. It brought back all the memories, everything I've tried desperately to forget since coming to the fortress. But I've never been able to forget because they force me to remember them every night, and I can't sleep, and I haven't slept, and I just wanted them to be gone—"

Camilla's words cut off as a shiver swept over her again, and Farren began rocking the girl's slender form—stiffly at first, but the movement became fluid as instinct took over. Had Camilla grown thinner in the last weeks? Purple shadows carved crescents beneath her eyes.

The fire before them was dwindling, and the cold air coming through the shattered door blew against Farren's back.

Camilla pressed more deeply against Farren, cradling her wounded arm against her stomach. "And then the man brought me to a building, and that's where we found Isander."

Farren paused her rocking. "Isander was in the city? Was this in the Runeless Quarter?"

"I...I can't remember. But he was surprised to see me, and I was so happy to see someone I knew, and it was like he understood everything I was feeling. It was all a mess, but he said he could help me." Camilla's voice rose. "He told me that...he was the voice who stopped my night terrors. He was always there when they were at their worst, and I don't know how he did it. He said he could take the pain away, and the memories, too. I just wanted to get rid of them." Camilla looked down at her fingers, and Farren cringed at the scars littering the tips of them. "He said he could get rid of the night terrors forever."

Farren held her close, wishing she could protect her from Isander's darkness. The girl must've been confused from her fall and maybe also from her sleeplessness.

Cato burst back into the room, his copper cheeks flushed. An ink-stained hand shoved hair off temples sheening with sweat. "He's gone. There must be another way out at the back of the keep."

"What about Delphi?" Farren asked. "Did she see anything?"

"No, but she's circling one more time."

His eyes fell to Camilla, and he went immediately to them. "Camilla, what—" His mouth fell open at seeing Camilla's wounded arm, where the cut was sealed by the Enchanted axe. He reached for the detached arm.

"Don't touch it," Farren snapped.

The prince inhaled and gave her a sharp look. "Why did he cut off her arm?"

"He didn't. He...froze it. He did something to the runes. I cut it off to keep it from spreading."

Delphi swept into the room. Her wings knocked ceramic figurines off the mantle, and when her back paw stepped on one of them, she didn't seem to mind the way it crushed to pieces beneath her weight. She lay close to Farren, carefully avoiding the detached arm as her body sprawled over most of the floor.

Farren told Cato what had happened with herself and Camilla and how Isander's fire had felt—the burning, the reaching, being on the verge of losing her rune-made soul. And what it did afterward, making a statue of things that once lived and moved.

"The Emptiness," Cato muttered, his eyes wide as he looked at Delphi.

Delphi bobbed her head at whatever he told her, and Farren glanced between them. "I don't understand. I thought the Emptiness was just a myth?"

Cato gripped Camilla's hand. "It's an old legend, one about when the Enchanters formed the world. Before the Enchanters existed, the Emptiness reigned. Somehow, they were able to defeat it, and they used runes to fill the world with life."

"Isander could create the Emptiness with words he spoke," Farren said. "Something about Enchanter blood."

"The book," Camilla whispered, peering around Farren's arm into the room.

Cato jumped up and searched the cluttered space until he found what he was looking for. The small leather-bound book he held was the same one from Isander's room that Torch had nearly ripped apart. The one Isander had been reading as he sent fire down Camilla's arm.

Cato flipped it open and scowled down at the pages. "It's blank," he said and slammed the cover shut.

Camilla shook her head. "He can read it. He tried to show me, but I couldn't see what he could." Camilla's trembling had picked up once more, and Farren rubbed her back, urging warmth into the girl's body.

"He thinks it's the Tongue of Runes," Farren said quietly.

Cato cursed as he looked at the book's cover. "Mother always told us that the Tongue had died ages ago, when the Enchanters disappeared. I always assumed it was part of the myth but..." He shook his head. "It still doesn't explain how he can do it. Or why."

"He said he wanted to change his runes." Farren's head was beginning to hurt, but Cato was looking at her as if what she said made everything else fall into place.

"If he was trying to figure out how to change his runes, maybe he was trying to change other people's runes as well? He could've kidnapped those people out in the garden to experiment on them."

"It was more than that," Farren said. How could she explain to Cato all the twisted paths that Isander's mind had taken?

"Farren?" Camilla looked up at her, fine brows creasing. "I think he was sick. More than anybody realized."

Farren felt herself nodding, blinking back the tears that burned her eyelids. "Yes, you're right Camilla."

"That's why I've always told you to stay away from him," Cato told the girl as he tucked the book into the folds of his chiton and crouched beside them. "What happened before this? We searched everywhere for you after you fell."

Camilla frowned and struggled to sit up straighter. Farren helped her, and the girl turned toward the fire and stared at it mournfully. "I don't remember it very well. One moment, I was falling, and the next, the river was carrying me away, but I was able to swim to shore. I was dizzy and confused, and I remember thinking I had hit my head." She reached a hand up and winced as Farren's fingers examined the back of her head. Dried blood clung close to her scalp, and Farren found a large cut damp with blood.

"I think Elya saved you," Farren said. "She saw you falling. She tried to help with her magic."

"I remember, I think. I was falling, and things seemed to slow. I slowed. The air pushed hard at me from below." Camilla swallowed, but her lips tilted up at the corners. "I'll have to thank her when I see her."

"I'm sure she would've done more if she could've," Cato said. "We'll have the healer take a look at your head." Cato hesitated, glancing at Farren as he did so. "I have too many questions to ask, but the one thing I understand the least is who found you down at the river? And what was he doing down there?"

"Fishing, she thinks," Farren answered for Camilla. "And I can tell you what she told me, Cato, but right now she needs rest."

"Fishing? In the middle of the Festival of the Forging, with a gryphon mating display going on above him?"

"Wait," Camilla said, eyes squinting as she tried to remember. "He just had his basket. There wasn't a fishing rod."

They sat silently for a moment, perplexed by this information.

Cato sucked in a breath through his teeth. "Did he have a rune-mark?"

Camilla's brow scrunched. "I don't remember..." Her eyes widened. "Wait, I do. He had no markings, and I asked him about it. He said he was a free man, and he asked if I wanted to be free, too. My mind was all muddled." Her lips started trembling again.

Farren's heart ached for her. It wasn't fair that she had had a terrible father. It wasn't right that she still suffered after all these years, that she felt trapped by a childhood that should've been full of warm, sweet memories. Farren couldn't imagine such a stolen childhood, and a slow anger churned in her at the hand Camilla had been dealt.

"No, don't blame yourself," Cato chided, bending over the girl once more. "You're exhausted. We can talk more after you've rested."

"You didn't deserve this," Farren added. "No one does. It shouldn't have happened to you."

Farren couldn't help thinking of the missing children in the city. Of the people who might be taken by Isander or the Runeless Sect, if Cato's suggestion was correct. No one was there to help them, to find them and make things right.

Except Cato.

Farren watched him for a moment as he inspected the girl's wound, her heart so full that she couldn't speak. He had listened when she had first mentioned the missing people of Malodai, and he had tried to find them. Farren knew, without a doubt, that it was something the queen and king would never care to do.

He was different from them. Better. She had to believe that.

"What are we going to do about Isander?" Farren asked. "And this...Emptiness?"

"Well, if a Runeless man took Camilla into the city to meet with Isander, I would say that's proof that they are working together, no? I'm not sure if he's trying to find out how to remove runes... Perhaps the Runeless are convinced he can make them truly unbound from animals? Whatever the truth of it, it's clear that he's dangerous. I saw the people out in his garden, and I bet some of them were the missing—"

"They are," Farren said. "I found Persepha."

Cato went very still, his breath hitching as he studied her. "She's out there?"

Hurt shone in his eyes, and perhaps something else. A possible future, lost. A maybe-love, taken. But it seemed to Farren an old loss, not sharp and keen but rather an aged grief that Cato had mulled over and over.

A moment later, he ran a hand over his face. "He has killed people, but the Emptiness goes far beyond that. From the stories I've heard, it's a festering disease, affecting every living thing it touches."

"It spreads," Farren said, peering toward the door to the garden full of not-statues. People. Dead people. Worse than dead, with their runes destroyed and unable to bless another, their frozen bodies spreading the fiery scourge with a mere touch. Would it escape the stone walls surrounding it? If it did, it would keep spreading until it froze everything in the fortress.

"There's something else," Farren said. "When Isander was visiting the mountains near my village, he did the same thing to a flower to preserve its beauty. It's what killed my hawk. I'm afraid it's already outside the fortress, and I don't know how far it has spread." There was no telling how quickly the Emptiness would move through the Outskirts to her village. If it had gotten there—

Cato was squeezing her shoulder, and she expelled a breath. "Cato, this could mean that far more is at stake than the people of Malodai. If it spreads quickly..."

Cato's eyes glittered in the firelight, dark with understanding.

"The entire realm is in danger." They flinched at Camilla's words, spoken softly above the crackle of wood from the fireplace.

Cato stood and pushed dark locks of hair from his face. "We need to find out more about it. But first, we have to tell the queen." He met Farren's questioning gaze. "Both of us."

And just like that, the weight of everything lightened. She had to trust him, *needed* to trust him, because she didn't think she could carry everything on her own, not after failing to free all the gryphons, after nearly losing Camilla...

"I'm coming, too," Camilla said.

"No," Cato and Farren said in unison, and a strand of warmth uncoiled in Farren's chest.

Once they had gotten Camilla settled in her room in the mews, Cato went to the kitchens to secure her a bite to eat.

As Farren tucked the blankets around her, the girl's hand snagged her arm. "It's not your fault," Camilla said. "What happened to me, I mean."

Farren opened her mouth, hesitating. The girl didn't know that Farren had been linked to Naronimus and spurred his fury.

Camilla spoke first. "When I runebonded with Naronimus, I felt you there. I knew you would be trying to restrain him, to prevent him from hurting anyone else."

Farren's eyes burned, and she stared at the bedsheets. "It is, Camilla. I was the reason why he was angry in the first place. Anger was the only thing that kept him from drowning."

A long silence filled the room, and Farren's chest ached, knowing Camilla might never forgive her.

"You saved him," Camilla remarked, her voice rising like sunsparrow wings after a long storm. "You saved him, even though you hate him." She wriggled up in bed, and Farren met her eager gaze, wanting to deny the sudden lightness there. "I mean, do you still hate him?"

"Yes." Her voice sounded resolute, and her heart did too, thank the Enchanters.

Camilla looked breathless. "But not enough to want him dead."

"If I wanted him dead, I would've told the queen to execute him. I wouldn't have wasted my time working with him."

Camilla pursed her lips. "Not true. You did all that for Torch, and out of fear for the other gryphons."

Farren gazed at Camilla, who was starting to *smile* of all things. Once, Farren might've told her that she was uncertain, or rebuff with a joke, or, more likely, ignore the comment altogether. But Camilla deserved more.

Farren sank into the bed and rubbed her runemark. "I just want him freed. It's what I've wanted for all the gryphons."

There. She had said it aloud. Everything she had been planning since she had first gotten Naronimus to agree to train with her. Everything she had failed to do.

Silence stretched between them, and Farren risked glancing at the girl, startled to find that her blue eyes blazed with something fierce.

"You're the one who did it," Camilla said, her voice rising once more. "You're the one who tried to free them!"

"Shhh, please lower your—"

"That's why they were flying overhead during the mating display," Camilla urgently whispered. "You were the only recruit who didn't come."

"Scipio poisoned me. But I was still able to carry out some of the plan."

The color faded from Camilla's cheeks. "That awful guard. I'm glad he didn't hurt you more. Why didn't all the gryphons leave?"

"They wanted to help Elya. I think Eralius wanted to defend Naronimus. And Delphi—"

"Her young," Camilla said. "I sensed them in the mews on our way here. She won't leave until they are safe with her." The girl's eyes glistened. "Farren, I want to help."

"No. You were nearly killed by Isander already—"

"Do you think he'll be in the mews?"

The question caught her off guard. "I don't know. And it's too dangerous for you to go anywhere until we've found him and brought him to the queen."

Camilla pursed her lips and said nothing.

"Well," Cato said as he came in with a steaming tray. "I hope you're hungry, Camilla. They just made some fish soup and honeyed rolls."

Farren looked at Camilla imploringly. The girl's eyes snapped to Cato. "I'm ravenous," she said, unconvincingly. A flush spread over her cheeks, and she looked far too thoughtful.

"You need to rest now," Farren said, tucking her in firmly while Cato arranged the tray on her lap. "The healer should be in to see you any moment, just to check your wound."

"Thank you," was all Camilla said, and Farren pulled Cato away.

Grey clouds trundled across the sky as they made their way to the keep. Beyond the vast walls of the fortress, the distant rays of the setting sun submerged into billowing blue-grey, leaching the air of the last hint of autumnal warmth. Rain spat down as a chill wind snapped at their clothes.

Farren braced herself as the keep guards let them inside. She had to clear her mind, focus on what needed to be done with Isander, not on who he was or what he had said to her. She couldn't let herself get pulled into the tangled memories of their bodies in the bedsheets, into the mess of things that had happened before she had finally seen Isander for who he really was.

She glanced at Cato, reassured by the set of his jaw.

They walked down the entryway toward the front atrium that held the glass wall abutting the gryphon yard. Quietude steeped in the vaulted hall. A moment later, she became aware of the spherical presence of a gryphon mind close by, and ice hardened in her belly. She touched Cato's elbow.

"It's Naronimus," she whispered.

"I can feel him, too," Cato said with a frown. He strode forward and they rounded the corner at the end of the short entryway that opened to the atrium.

Grey light pooled over the rectangular cistern, falling in from the opening in the ceiling, where the spitting rain had already begun to drip inside. Beyond it, the queen sat in her throne, eyes latching onto Cato and Farren as they pressed into the atrium. Potted plants hung from chains overhead, thick tendrils of vines cutting between rows of armed guards standing at attention.

Farren's gaze swept over the guards, a chill spilling down her spine. There had to be at least two dozen of them.

Cato froze for a moment, then surged forward.

"Mother, what is the meaning of this?"

Queen Aurelia's finger stabbed like a sword through the room, pointing directly at Farren. "Seize her!"

# FORTY-FOUR

FARREN TENSED AS THE guards closed in. Scipio must've told the queen what happened, and now Farren was caught in the queen's trap. There were far too many guards to fight, and no escape routes beyond the wall of guards that moved to block the atrium entrance.

Cato stepped in front of Farren, but a guard shoved him aside. His face reddened and he cursed as he regained his balance.

"Bring her here!" the queen ordered once the guards had hold of Farren's arms.

They dragged her toward the dais. Cato rushed ahead of them but faltered as he reached the steps.

A moment later, Farren saw why.

Naronimus slumped near the glass wall. Tattered ashen feathers protruded from his chest and shoulders, a sign that he had been battered or that he had struggled, perhaps locked inside of the metal box. Shackles caged each leg, chafing bare skin already scarred from years of the same abuse. Short chains fettered him to the stone floor. When she reached out to him, his mind was lost in a cloud of misery.

"Oh yes," the queen said, as if they had been in a casual conversation. "I had him installed here permanently. He is a nice fixture, even if his magic is...dulled."

*What happened to you*, Farren asked him. Patches of his fur appeared blackened. Charred. When Naronimus didn't answer, she prodded him. *Did they break you?*

Naronimus lifted his head incrementally, his yolk eyes simmering. *They couldn't break what was already broken.*

Farren marveled at how he could still manage to feel anger—to feel anything at all—after what they had done to him. His haunches tensed, talons scratching deep, careless grooves into the stone.

Some other creature might've given up and died by now, but gryphons fought on. Or perhaps it was just Naronimus's endless need for a fight—a hunger she understood deeply.

The guards pulled Farren to the foot of the dais stair, and she glanced at Cato. The prince's face warred between horror and outrage.

"He doesn't belong in this room," Cato said, his voice like brittle sticks. "And what have you done to him? He looks like he's been beaten—"

Scipio moved from behind the thrones and stood in front of the gryphon, just out of reach of Naronimus' beak. His orange cloak twitched to the side, revealing the coil of a whip gripped in one hand.

Cato scoffed at his cousin. "I thought you were better than Anaxis. Now I see I'm wrong. You know how things ended for him. How Naronimus tore him to shreds."

Scipio gave a languid sneer. "And you still want me to believe you had nothing to do with it?"

"I'm not like you, cousin. I wouldn't want a gryphon to hurt someone, and I certainly would never do something like push an old king down a flight of stairs."

A sharp gasp resounded across the atrium.

Scipio's mouth twisted into a snarl. "Those are just rumors—"

"Quit your squabbling," the queen cut in. "Scipio is acting under my orders, Cat. Just as you should be doing. Now tell me. Where have you been hiding?"

Queen Aurelia wore a gown of silver, and the strange clear gem of her necklace glinted as it rested in the hollow notch at the base of her throat.

"We haven't been hiding," Cato said, straightening his back. "We've come to tell you that we've discovered a threat to the city."

"Oh?" The queen didn't sound very amused. "You found whoever released the gryphons?"

"No, we've discovered a much larger threat. Isander has been doing something to harm people—innocent people—and he had Camilla—"

"The girl, again? Really, Cato." The queen tisked, and Cato's cheeks darkened. "You are a bigger fool than I thought. Let me guess, this servant here helped you? Did you know that she is the one who released the gryphons? She led the attack on the keep. My guard informed me of her whereabouts during the attack. She was the only one, it seems, left in the mews when it all happened."

Farren caught Horat's eye. The Lord Falconer stood behind the throne like a haggard, reluctant boulder. Farren glared daggers at him. Even if Horat hadn't helped Scipio, he was still here, which meant he had been involved with Naronimus' poor treatment. He looked away from her.

"I know it's hard to understand," the queen continued. "You always have been soft-hearted toward the servants, never wanting to see them for who they really are. Well, they can be cruel. Heartless. And they will betray you eventually. Some of them, at least," the queen amended, casting a glance around guards gathered in the room. Along the atrium's perimeter, six coyotes slunk in the shadows, awaiting instruction from their guards.

Cato was being far too quiet. Farren stared at his profile, willing him to speak. But it was as if he had been frozen by Isander's Emptiness, a face chiseled by betrayal and hands curled into fists. He wouldn't look away from Naronimus.

Farren tore her gaze from him and lifted her eyes to the queen's. "The prince is right. I have seen what Isander can do, and he is a threat. Perhaps the biggest threat Malodai has seen in ages."

The queen's smile didn't reach her eyes. "Did my eldest son spurn your little heart, girl? These are wicked lies that I will not hear—"

"Isander has escaped," Cato burst out. "He needs to be found. He can take away runes, and I think he has b-brought back the Emptiness."

Queen Aurelia's laugh shattered along the walls. "The Emptiness? Don't be ridiculous, Cat. Why do you always go to such extreme lengths to accuse your brother of things? First, that he did something to poor Persepha, then that he took your little ward, and now that he has somehow brought to life something that exists only in children's stories. It's pathetic, Cat."

"It's the truth!" Cato said.

The queen's gaze flicked between them, irritated. "Perhaps you didn't hear when I accused this servant of treason. Or maybe you don't realize just how personal the treason is, son." The queen leaned forward sharply, her silver necklace swinging from her neck. "This servant brought down the gryphons after she released them. Do you not think, perhaps, that it was *she* who caused your child ward to go missing? My guard tells me that Farren appeared moments after Naronimus began killing my men. Just after Naronimus pushed the girl over the balcony."

Cato glanced at Farren, his eyes desperate as he searched her face for answers.

"It wasn't like that," Farren told him. "Naronimus was angry. He would've torn right through her. I calmed him enough that—"

"You'd be wise not to listen to anything she says, Cat. She's a deceiver."

"—I calmed him enough that he only grazed her. But it was still too much as he rushed past."

Cato's mouth pressed into a thin line as he considered her words. When he said nothing, she spoke to the queen.

"We can prove that Isander has brought back the Emptiness. And that he killed Persepha. There's a garden where the prince has hidden his...victims. It's deep in the keep, but we can take you there—"

"You aren't going anywhere other than the tallest tower of the keep," the queen said. "There, you will think about every treasonous thing you have done, until I have decided what to do with you."

The queen waved a hand, and the guards began pulling her away.

"Wait!" Farren dug heels into the flagstone floor, something simmering in her belly.

Cato pressed forward. "You must reconsider!" Guards held him back from the dais.

Naronimus' magic stirred, whispering down to her from the dais. It prodded her anger, bit into her vulnerability like a nip of a hawk testing its handler. *Will you be afraid*, it whispered, *or will you be strong and brave?*

Farren couldn't give in, because fighting would only lead to slaughter. But the more she pushed it away, the more the anger rose in her, and the more Farren was certain that blood was the only way. The fighter in her knew the stance of her captors, estimated their weight and height and how much force it would take to get them off their feet. The fighter knew, too, that she wouldn't be able to escape by running, but only by cutting down.

There had to be a different way, one that didn't end in blood or her probable death. Farren dragged her feet, causing her captors to stumble.

"Wait!" She wrenched away from the guards to face the queen once more. Potted vines framed the feet of the thrones, and scarlet irises rose from their depths, as delicate and bold as the queen herself, but ultimately fragile. Was that why the queen lusted for gryphon power? Queen Aurelia would never have a gryphon's strength or magic...unless someone gave it to her.

Naronimus' magic was too important for the queen to ever let him go. She hadn't realized it when she first struck her bargain with Naronimus and regretted doing so now. How could she ever hope to free him while he remained in chains, too weak to fly or fight?

Four other gryphons were still held captive. Without them, the queen's gryphon program would be temporary, and no other gryphons would have to suffer the way Naronimus had been forced to. If the queen had Naronimus, would she be willing to let the others go? The queen might never agree to it. But she had to try.

"You wanted me," Farren said, breathless in the silence of the atrium, "to work with Naronimus, and I did. I'm the only recruit who has worked with him successfully." Naronimus's anger pushed at her, threatening to slip inside. But the queen seemed to be listening, so she forced her body not to show the heat rising in her. "I will work with Naronimus on your behalf," Farren offered. "And go to your prison if you like. But only if you release the other gryphons."

Close to her still, Cato had managed to step away from the guards. Farren could feel his gaze moving between her and his mother.

A sly smile pulled at the queen's delicate features as if she could read Farren's thoughts. She swung a hand up in triumph, and declared, "She has admitted her treason!"

The guards' hands tightened around her arms, expecting her to try to escape.

"I do," Farren said, hearing some gasps from the guards throughout the room. Fingers pressed into her skin, bruising her arms. "And I am willing to accept your punishment, to work with Naronimus in whatever way you please, as long as you release the remaining gryphons."

Her belly tightened as the queen's laugh rolled through the room. When her laugh quieted, her fingers tapped thoughtfully on the armrests of her throne, wide eyes latching onto Farren as if she were an interesting pest she wasn't sure if she should squash or observe.

"I should have you executed," the queen mused, her smile still lingering on her lips but not touching her eyes. "But there's too much opportunity here. The problem is that you think you can negotiate with *me* about what you want."

The queen stood from her throne, and as she did, the gem of her necklace glinted yellow in the candlelight. Remarkable how so much protection could be had from a tiny stone. With it around her neck, Naronimus couldn't touch the queen with his magic.

One step after the other, the queen made her way down, her size seeming to grow as she came closer to Farren. "You should know that I have something precious of yours, and that I can use it against you at any time, if I wish."

The queen motioned toward Horat, and the Lord Falconer went to a door set to the side of the dais.

"You see," the queen said after he had stepped out. "I considered having my guards journey back to the Wildlands to bring your family here, but then my most trusted guard happened to run into a little something. Something that would motivate you...given your intimate runebond."

Talons and claws skittered on the stone floor of the dais as Horat returned, a chain in hand. On the other end of it was Torch.

Farren's heart dropped.

She snapped open a runebond with Torch. He felt her fear and froze. Rapidly, she sent him a soothing wave—or as much as she could muster beneath the painful grip of the guards on her arms. Visually scanning Torch, she found no signs of abuse. His ears flicked uncertainly around the room.

Horat pulled on the chain leash, forcing him to continue walking.

*Why am I here?* Torch asked. *Who are all these people?*

*I thought you were with Delphi?*

*I was...b-but she went to help you, and I just wanted to help, too. There were so many paths in the courtyard, and then a guard found me—*

"You two have bonded quite well," the queen said, pleased at whatever she saw on Farren's face.

Farren shuttered closed, pulling her eyes and mind from Torch after she sent him another quick pulse of reassurance. Torch should've been in the Healing Caves with Delphi and Elya. Farren stretched her mind out and out, and she located Delphi in the caves.

The moment she runebonded with Delphi, the gryphon's worry whipped into her.

*He is unharmed,* Farren reassured her.

*For now*, Delphi said. *Are you able to keep him safe? Or is the prince?*

*I will do what I can*, Farren said. It took all of her effort not to rip from the guards' arms and vault to the dais. But a league of guards lay between herself and the little gryphon. Delphi wasn't there and had no magic to help her. Farren had no weapons of her own, and Cato...

The prince was as still and tense as a cougar watching prey. His eyes pinned on Scipio as the guard moved to follow Horat and Torch up to the dais. Farren's palms sweat. The queen stood only a few arm-lengths from her, confident in her armed guard to protect her.

"So you see, girl?" the queen said. "You will have to do as I say with Naronimus. I think it best to keep you in the tower by yourself. You'll find it fitting as a dungeon. My late brother, Anaxis, enjoyed using it for his gryphons. I'm having some chains installed, and I'll give you a bit of time to acquiesce before we start our work with Naronimus."

Farren glanced at Naronimus, wondering if he was part of the reason why her blood had begun to boil. He stared back at her as if in challenge, and she knew he could feel her anger. But this wasn't Naronimus's doing. It was something within herself, a sprout breaking through the hard crust of fear, beckoned by the fiery voice of the Commander.

*Protect him.*

*Keep him safe.*

*Do whatever you must.*

# FORTY-FIVE

THE COMMANDER'S WORDS BREATHED fire into every rune of her soul.

It pointed her mind to the swords on the guards' hips. To the way they had loosened their grips as the queen approached. It focused her attention on the sound of the queen's breathing—soft and quick through her delicate nose—and the glint of her silvery necklace at the base of her throat. It calculated the distance it was to Torch's side, and how long it would take for her to sprint and leap up to the dais. How much force she might have to use to knock Scipio to the ground. To kill him.

Thunder pounded in her ears. This was the only way. *The only way.*

Farren jerked free from the guards and leapt at the queen's neck. The delicate necklace came free with a quick tug. The queen screamed as Farren turned and flung the jewels into one of the guard's faces, startling him. Farren grabbed the other guard and brought her knee into his groin as he swiveled, then gripped the pommel of his sword when he fell to his knee. His sword slid smooth as a feather from its scabbard. Twisting her body, she rammed the fat pommel into the other guard's belly, and he stumbled into the guard behind him.

A cry erupted around the room, and the queen darted up the steps as Farren spun around one guard and then another, swinging the sword wide. She had no intention of killing the guards—only to put them down for long enough that she could reach Torch, try to free them—

"Farren, duck!" Cato's shout punctuated the air, and Farren dropped to the floor. A throwing knife whistled overhead, narrowly missing her scalp.

Boots stomped as guards raced to protect their queen, and Farren's skin prickled at the scrabble of canine claws on the atrium tiles.

Her body contorted around a man who jumped in front of her. She cut her sword down on his blade as she moved and swore as she glimpsed four coyotes diving toward her. The sword was too heavy to lift quickly, so she threw it at their feet. One of the coyotes yipped as the blade bit into its leg, and another tripped over the handle. The other two came just behind, mouths lathering with spittle.

A sword flashed, and blood sprayed on the tiles. Another slice of sword, and both the coyotes were down.

"Farren!" Prince Cato leapt to her side, his bloodied sword in hand. Crimson flecked his face. "We have to free Naronimus!"

Farren's gaze flashed to the dais. Torch quivered at Horat's feet but seemed unharmed. Far on the other side of the dais, Naronimus still slumped against the glass wall, his eyes on her. She owed him this. They had made a bargain, after all.

"But Torch—"

"Horat has him. He's safe."

Cato grunted as he swung the sword, clashing it against a guard's. She parried a blow from another guard, then struck the guard in the side, sending him staggering back.

"Tell him to use his magic!" she shouted at Cato.

With hands free, Farren became a darting hawk through dense forest, using the oncoming guards to outmaneuver the coyotes. Swirling under flashing blades, lashing out at tender joints and necks, her body and mind sang a vicious harmony. Elbows and fists found their targets, and she twirled between two guards, parrying a blow from one while kicking the legs out from the other.

It was an intricate dance and one she relished.

Mid-step, something cinched around her ankles. She cursed. Green tendrils had wended down the dais steps and clamped onto her like little vices. She barreled into another guard as she tumbled over the steps.

Hands clamped on her arms and legs, and the tendrils tightened more. Low growls rumbled as the guards' coyotes surrounded her with bared canines and bristling fur.

Gritting her teeth, she reached out to Naronimus. She flashed him an image of when she had saved him from drowning. Just in case he had forgotten. He didn't answer, but she saw movement on the dais as he stood.

Then she felt the tug of his magic, spurring her body to move faster, lighter, more efficiently. The burn of it coursed through her veins, and she used it. She kicked at one of the guards, then rolled, swinging up a fist as she did so. The skin on her knuckles split as they met the bones of a man's face. She used his stunned moment to grab the dagger at his hip and tug it free.

The blade ripped clean through the vines tangling her limbs, and sliced deep ribbons along reaching hands. No one would take her. No one would touch Naronimus again. No harm would come to Torch.

But then a body fell across her, and another, crushing the breath from her lungs. Her vision narrowed, and the only thing holding her to the surface was Naronimus's magic. Her mind widened into his, seeking his energy and anger.

*Help me!* The last of her breath was leaving her body. She began succumbing to the dark, to the fold of silence webbing into her mind.

*Not like this*, a voice whispered. *I know you can do better.*

Farren fought to focus as her mind fuzzed. She needed to do more, but she couldn't move. She needed something else; she needed—

Naronimus's cry pierced into the fog, and the weight lifted immediately from her body.

"Unchain the beast at once!" Queen Aurelia's voice rose above the noise of pounding boots.

A moment later, Scipio's voice reverberated in the space. "Do not release the gryphon! The queen is compromised!"

Farren sucked in air, her body trembling as life fired once more in her veins, and she pulled herself up. The guards and coyotes had abandoned Farren to form a barrier between the queen and Naronimus. The beast thrashed toward the throne, his howling screech cutting across the atrium, and Farren urged him on, wanting him to break his chains. Behind Naronimus, Cato swung savagely at a chain with his sword, but they held fast.

Waves of fury crashed through their runebond. Guards had bent to his fetters to obey the queen, but with Scipio's words, they fell back, looking from the queen to Scipio.

"How dare you defy my order!" the queen yelled at Scipio, her face as sharp as an arrowhead.

"The gryphon is using the queen!" Scipio leapt across the dais—distancing himself from Torch—and shook the first guard he saw. "Find her necklace!"

Farren stumbled up the steps and nearly reeled back as a *crack!* split the air—Scipio's whip tumbling up to nip Naronimus's neck.

Chains and the poison slugging in his veins made Naronimus too slow as he tried to rear. The next crack of the whip sliced into his shoulder, and Farren felt Naronimus's magic fall away from the queen.

Cato shouted, and in the next moment, a piercing cry resounded beyond them. On the other side of the glass wall, the sky between the wall and the great iron dome filled with Delphi's massive form. Talons and claws outstretched as she dove straight at them.

Glass exploded into the atrium. Shards of it cut Farren's skin as she turned away. Delphi crashed into the thrones, scattering them like toys, and crushed one of the potted plants with the whip of her tail. The queen spilled down the steps and guards rushed to her side.

Farren closed her connection with Naronimus and flashed one open with Delphi.

*Avoid Scipio! He may have his poison darts.*

Delphi didn't seem to hear her. She used her head to knock three guards to the side and grabbed the sword from a fourth with her beak to toss it lightly through the air.

The queen lifted her hands, and the potted vines from the ceiling sprouted thicker and longer tendrils that grew and twisted together to form a wall around her. Farren scrambled up the last of the steps, knowing Delphi would do what she could to free Torch. The ring of metal on metal resounded in the air as Cato beat at Naronimus's chains.

Most of the guards had retreated to the queen's wall of plants, holding their swords out in case Delphi decided to attack her. Only one guard had chosen a different path, and he headed straight for the prince. Cato wedged his sword into the base of the chain anchor, oblivious to Scipio.

Farren's breath fired into her belly. *Naronimus, the prince!*

Somewhere in the gryphon's hazy mind, he heard her. He swung his head out toward Scipio, sharp beak snapping. But Scipio ducked and unleashed the whip once more, sending it flying at Naronimus' eye. Luckily, Scipio's aim was off and the whip cracked the air.

Too late, he seemed to notice Farren running full-tilt at him. They tumbled across the dais floor, flagstones bruising her body as they rolled. His sword skidded away, but she held her dagger fast.

Scipio wasted no time on the ground. As soon as they slowed, he popped up and pulled a long dagger from beneath the folds of his cloak. Farren grit her teeth as she stood, falling into the knife-fighting stance that Scipio himself had taught her: arms tucked, belly in, shoulders hunched with her hands in front of her, blocking her heart and throat.

She tried not to show fear as Scipio grinned at her.

"Just like our sparring practices, eh, bumpkin? Hopefully, you'll be better than usual now that your life is in my hands."

Farren forced a smile. "It should be easier now that I have no reason not to kill you."

Behind her, a low growl rumbled. Enchanter's cursed coyotes. She flicked a glance back. It would take a small lunge for the foam-lipped coyote to rip into her.

"You can certainly try, though my queen won't like it. Graydog, on the other hand, might enjoy himself quite a bit..." He nodded to where the coyote snarled.

Graydog, really? What a creative name.

Farren was finished waiting. She slashed her blade toward his arm, but he was as quick as one of his dogs. He clenched her wrist and thrust his knee into her stomach.

"Come now, that was a weak start," Scipio drawled as she doubled over. "I could've ended you right then."

"Then why didn't you?"

"Unfortunately, I'm under orders not to kill you. Silly, I know, but I'll have to restrain myself. Lucky for me, she never said anything about not hurting you."

Farren started to rise, but not before the hilt of his knife hit her on the back of the head. Pain and dizziness jolted through her skull, and she stumbled. Was that blood she tasted? The world spun. His coyote crouched closer, practically salivating on her sandals.

She regained her stance and eased to the left of the coyote. Eying the tilt of Scipio's shoulders, she caught the moment he decided to strike. She grabbed his arm as he slashed and went to jab him with her dagger, but he caught her wrist before the knife touched his skin. He held her tight, trapping her.

He huffed a laugh. "So close, little bumpkin—"

Farren used his weight and balance as she threw her leg out, kicking the coyote in the face. The coyote yipped and Scipio's hands went slack. In a moment, she wedged her dagger deep into his belly and turned the blade.

Then the coyote was on her, its canines sinking into her skin like little knives. As it pulled her down, she slashed toward her leg with her blood-slicked knife, gritting her teeth as the coyote twisted its hold and tugged.

Close by, Naronimus screamed and sent her a surge of fury. Farren grabbed the coyote's scruff and dug her knife into its neck. A fountain of red sprayed over her, and she pried the coyote's teeth from her leg, shoving the beast away as it collapsed.

"Graydog..." Scipio's words rang with disbelief. Even with blood staining his torso, he walked toward her, the wicked point of his dagger aiming straight at her. She shoved to a standing position, her leg screaming with the effort. If she didn't move quickly enough, if she stumbled...

Her knife was too slippery in her hand. She didn't have time to regain her knife stance. Scipio seized her knife hand and drew his arm back to pierce her with the blade.

A sword blade blossomed from Scipio's chest. Shock swam over his face just before he crumpled, lying prone next to his coyote.

"Farren!"

She swayed, blinking up at the figure with the sword. Cato. "I think you killed him," she said.

"He nearly killed you. We must hurry. I—"

He paused to slice his sword at another guard. Farren turned to see more guards leaving the queen's side—the woman was completely barricaded by a thicket of thorns and woody vines now, invisible and safe beneath the green and brown armor. A dozen guards that had surrounded her began to pair off, heading up the dais steps in short bursts.

Trembling and bloodied, Farren watched them come. She could hardly put weight on her wounded leg without pain spearing through her. Cato would be able to do more damage, but they would never be able to get Naronimus free with so many guards trying to stop them.

"I was able to get two of the fetters free," Cato said, breath coming fast as he readied his sword for the next guard. "But I need more time."

"I'm not sure how much I can do," she said, clutching her slick knife. She should've wiped it dry, but there was no time now. She reached out to Naronimus.

*We need to free your last two fetters.*

*There isn't time*, Naronimus replied, his words coming clearer now. *And there are too many guards. And Cato—*

*I will help him,* Farren said.

The prince put down another guard and held his sword up once more. His arm trembled. Farren grabbed a sword from a fallen guard, wishing she had practiced more with the heavy weapon. She'd be of little use to the prince with her lack of sword skills—

Farren's mouth went dry as a fresh wave of guards poured into the atrium. A dozen—no, two. They spotted the queen's barricade and then saw Farren and Cato on the dais, surrounded by injured guards. They shouted and moved as one, washing across the atrium and rising like a tide over the dais steps.

# FORTY-SIX

FARREN'S SWORD DRAGGED AT her arms. Pain lanced up her leg as she put weight on it. A tall, broad-shouldered guard came at her, face full of rage. Farren longed for the Commander to rise once more, to give her the courage she needed. But as the guard leapt over the last few steps, Farren's last hope faded.

It was Iana heading straight at her.

Farren lifted her sword, and her vision swam as dizziness rocked into her. Out of the corner of her eye, Prince Cato grunted and swore as he fought two other guards. Iana bore down on her, swatting her sword away as if it were little more than a stick.

Guards flocked onto the dais behind her, and Iana pressed her sword tip against Farren's breastbone hard enough to bruise.

"You're done, Farren Blackburn. Lay down your weapon and—"

A great silver serpent of water burst between them. It scattered Iana and her guards, and brushed against Farren's skin, cold and smelling of rain.

The water beast slid through the air and barreled into the writhing guards and coyotes surrounding the prince, coiling them within its translucent-grey embrace. Some of the guards jerked, a sporadic dance as their bodies begged for breath, and then they gently spun in the belly of the water beast before plummeting back to the stone floor. Others screamed and leapt away, diving back to the queen's side to protect her.

Farren stared as the water beast slithered down the steps. The metallic tang of rainwater scented the air. On the other side of the dais, Delphi stood guard in front of Torch as he worked his terrifying, brutal magic. The little gryphon stood with wings spread wide on the dais, beak gaping with effort. His chain was gone—Horat must have given into Delphi's threats and freed him—and he had tapped the cistern, molding water into a weapon to save Farren. To save Cato. Maybe even to save Naronimus.

Farren flung open a runebond with Delphi.

*Get out of here before you are captured!*

Delphi turned bright gold eyes on her. *I will keep him safe. He refused to leave you behind. You're his family.*

As if that explained everything. As if that justified risking his own precious life.

*He cannot be here. Please, just—*

Cato tugged on her arm. "Farren! Help me get these off Naronimus!"

He pulled her to the last two fetters, freshly-welded iron rings bolted to the floor.

Screams punctuated the air as the water beast moved across the dais. Naronimus thrashed against his chains, and when she reopened their runebond, fury spiraled down it. Scipio's poison was fading. The gryphon was done with the shackles slicing into his legs, done with being chained and lashed. His talons gouged the stone, threatening to do the same to anyone who came too close.

Farren, too, was shackled. Trapped by the fortress, by this vicious queen who wanted too much and never listened to reason. And so, too, were those other gryphons who had been captured: Delphi's other children and Eralius. She needed to do more, and this was her chance. Another weapon she—the Commander—could wield.

Farren closed her eyes and brought forth the Commander's image, the voice that sung into the deepest parts of her rune-made soul. She breathed into the chaos around her, the trembling in her body subsiding as the Commander rose into her.

Mind sharp as a talon. Body as quick as a hawk's. Gryphons her allies. Her weapons.

*Naronimus, can you use your magic again while you try to free yourself?*

His old, familiar contempt poured into her, and she smiled. Yes, that was the Naronimus she knew. She considered having him control the queen again, but the remaining guards would be on alert for the gryphon's manipulation. Far easier and more efficient to use the guards themselves.

*Choose a few guards closest to the doors*, she told him. *Send them to the mews. They are following the queen's orders to free the last gryphons. Can you do that?*

Her bones shuddered with Naronimus's ferocious scream.

*They will be her most loyal subjects*, he told Farren snidely, and she could feel his magic stretch and burn as it came alive in the minds of his chosen guards.

With Torch handling the remaining guards, Farren bent to the fetter and rammed her sword into the stone around the anchor, making it crumble. Naronimus tugged at the chains, causing the stone to fracture more. Out in the atrium, Farren sensed the water beast writhing. Sandals tromped and shouts turned to sputtering.

Something crunched on the broken shards of glass.

"Here," a voice shouted, and Farren looked up in time to see Horat—sickly pale and gasping—toss her something small. The keys. The *keys*.

But there was no lock at the floor. She gripped the chain, willing Naronimus to calm.

*Naronimus, you'll have to lay down.*

*I'm not a dog*, he spat.

No, *but if you don't want to drag chains, you'll have to lie down* so *I can unlock them.*

He simmered with disgust as he lay on the floor. Glass cracked and crumbled beneath him. Even lying down, the beast's head was well over hers.

*I'll have to climb to reach*, she said. *But we need to hurry.*

Already, the guards who hadn't been touched by Torch's serpent barreled up to the dais. Cato swore and went back to fighting, his sword swinging clumsily as he did so. His strength was fading.

Be *quick about it then*, Naronimus said.

*Just focus on the guards at the mews*, Farren said, *on your magic.*

The gryphon didn't reply as she climbed up his shoulder, clinging to feathers until she found the ring of scarred, featherless skin around his neck. There, on the heavy iron collar, she found a lock. The key slid in and turned. The collar opened, and Farren tossed it off. She leapt down and found the locks on the shackles at his legs and released those too.

*You're free*, she told Naronimus, hardly believing the words herself.

Her hands tingled as Naronimus stood. His thick limbs quivered, and his wings stretched.

*I won't forget that you helped me, small though you are*, he said. *You're not so useless after all.* Then he gave one last rebellious cry and lunged toward the opening in the glass wall.

Farren closed her runebond with him and opened one with Torch, racing after Naronimus as he ran across the dais to gain speed.

*We are finished*, she told Torch. *You must go with your mother!*

Love and worry collided into her. *I won't leave you!*

*We will see each other again someday. I promise.*

She raced toward them, past the queen's potted iris, which twitched oddly along the periphery of Farren's attention. Something pricked her torso, but she barreled on. Delphi was pushing Torch with her beak, urging him up.

*How will you get away*? Torch asked her, resisting.

She sent her urgency for him to leave spiraling down the runebond. *Don't worry about me!*

With great wing beats that blasted air across the dais, Delphi rose to the opening in the glass wall, and Torch followed, looking back at her one last time. And then they were winging through the space where the glass wall had been and arcing high over the iron dome of the gryphon yard. Delphi must've been speaking with Thella as they disappeared from sight a moment later. Farren held onto Torch's mind, savoring the bond they shared, wishing she had been able to hug him one last time before he was separated from her forever.

Naronimus's claws slipped on the stone as he ran. A gust belted over the dais as his wings pumped furiously, gaining height little by little. He was weak, but that wouldn't stop him. Not after all the years he had been held in chains.

The entire atrium gleamed wetly in weak candlelight. Bodies were strewn around the floor and steps, and creeping over them with rapid, unnatural pace were dozens of vines. They stretched out from the queen's thick barricade, from the potted vines overhead, and from the potted iris that stood yet where the thrones had been, fingers stretching and twitching with voracious life.

As Naronimus moved up to the opening in the glass wall, three vines snapped out, entangling his legs.

Naronimus and Farren screamed as he plunged to the floor.

Blazing, Farren's mind stretched between Torch and Naronimus, reaching and reaching until her mind rent in two. She cried out at the searing sensation of it—of her mind splitting to connect with both of them at once. A throbbing wound gaped—unnatural and impossible—and yet her mind still worked, like two hands fumbling in the dark. She found Naronimus and the other part of her mind grasped at Torch. Their runebonds brought fury and pain and fear—a great sweeping storm that threatened to carry them all away.

But Farren had practiced navigating the chaos of emotions with Naronimus. She knew what to do. Take hold of the runebonds. Focus them. Direct them as only the Commander could do.

As only she, Farren, could do.

*Torch, can you stop the queen from afar?*

Without a word, the water serpent reformed, puddles of water rising and coalescing into a great coiling mass. Farren used her eyes to show him where to direct it. It tried to snake into the queen's barricade, but thick wide leaves thrust over each opening while vines twined tighter, sealing the queen inside.

*Naronimus, can you get free?* she asked.

*My wing!* Naronimus flapped on the floor, his talons slicing through some of the vines. *It hurts.*

"Naronimus!" Cato rushed to his side with sword swinging and hacked at the vines.

Farren grabbed the nearest dagger and helped him, but with each swipe of her blade, the ones she cut were replaced by others, thickening and speeding their way across the dais and over Naronimus's body. The other guards had recovered from their shock enough to barrel toward them, and the slap of their boots beat a steady rhythm beneath Naronimus's keening.

A numbness was spreading quickly from where something had pricked her side. A green needle-like piece stuck fast in her leather armor. She pulled it out, wincing as a barb caught on her skin. Numbness washed up her torso, stretched into her arms, and slid down her legs.

A moment later, her legs gave out. She heard Naronimus groan, felt the pricks in his skin—too many to count—and they both knew that they were falling, that this was a different kind of poison.

The queen's poison.

Farren stared at the iris blossom in the pot, which opened toward her, its petals layered with rows of green needles.

"Farren?"

She looked up and met Cato's confused gaze. His arms had gone slack, and his sword clattered to the floor.

"The queen—"

Guards fell on her once more and pushed her onto the floor. Cato swore and went silent as guards did the same to him. Farren dragged her gaze back to Naronimus. Blood seeped from a wound on his wing from the fall, and Farren tried to crawl toward him, but the poison—and the guards—trapped her.

*Hold on, Naronimus. Don't give up...* Her vision blurred, and she blinked rapidly, intent on keeping him in her vision.

*Should we return?* Torch asked, sending waves of worry and fear into her.

*No! Stay with Delphi. You must get away from here, no matter what you do. If you love me, you will do this. Promise me.*

*I promise*, he replied. She could sense Torch, Delphi, and Thella circling high overhead, and knew they were invisible, but not yet out of reach of danger.

*And you can let the water serpent go*, she added, knowing it was no longer helping them. That nothing could help them now.

*The guards?* Farren asked Naronimus, widening her runebond so she could see the ones directed by his magic. She didn't have to look to know that he couldn't stand anymore, that he could barely lift his head. Her mind remained split, aching from the oddity of it, and she ground her teeth against the pain.

Naronimus's guards were in the mews, following their orders as obediently as ever, believing the queen wanted every gryphon released. One of the guards had even threatened a recruit in order to get to the doors.

For a moment, Naronimus's magic wavered, and she willed her focus into him.

*Fight it, Naronimus*, she told him, hating how she was losing feeling all the way down to her toes. She tried to wiggle her fingers, but nothing happened. Somewhere on the dais, she heard the rasp of vines along the stone floor, and she waited for one to wrap her neck.

It never came.

*My wing feels shattered*, Naronimus said, and Farren and Torch sent him waves of calm. Feelings flowed between and through them like water, warm and liquid and boundless. She might drown in that current, if she couldn't stay on the surface. And yet...she had never been closer to Naronimus, and she could sense that Torch hadn't, either.

In the distance of Naronimus's mind, she thought she sensed Cato. The prince kept him company, comforted him even while the guards bound him.

*I will never fly again*, Naronimus said. Despair seeped through the runebond. He had lost all hope of freedom, all dreams of flying once more. And if his wing were broken, it would be true. He would be bound here, forever.

Torch refused to believe it. He sent them a vision of the thundering falls: the white billowing mist and the pale pool below, mistfish glistening as they flew around curtains of water. The sensation of cool wind blowing him upward was like nothing he had ever experienced before. Sweet, pure freedom. And a slight sense of terror at the wide open space before him.

Bitterness twined with amusement. And a little...pride? The feelings trickled from Naronimus, and she longed to look into his eyes.

She loved Torch so much that it hurt. Their bond fettered them to one another, and she knew that connection would never leave, no matter how far he was from her. Like a blossom, she let the warmth of her love grow inside of her, widening until it embraced the little gryphon far away, expanding until it encompassed Naronimus, too. Torch responded, his glow cascading down their shared runebond.

Together, they folded Naronimus into their love.

Naronimus's despair dwindled in the light. His keening softened to a different sort—one of deep and harrowing grief. Only Cato had loved him like this before. And his parents. So long ago now, and they were lost from him. He had only ever gotten hardness from others—gryphons and humans alike. He had only ever hated. But this...this was strange, so forgotten and soft that it was hard to stay in it. Hard not to push against it.

*We are all a family*, Farren told him. *You, Torch, me, and Cato*. She stretched out her mind so that she could feel closer to the other human who dwelled in Naronimus's mind.

For a few more precious moments, their hearts and minds clung together, beating and moving as one.

But then the guards rolled her body to tie her wrists together. Her gaze landed on the opening in the wall behind Naronimus.

Naronimus's magic continued flowing to the guards. The queen's poison had weakened her and Naronimus's bodies, but not their minds.

"Well, girl?" Queen Aurelia hovered above her. "Do you see now why you can't go against me? You will lose, every time. Even to protect those you care most about. It's better for you to give in."

*Never*, she wanted to say. Her mouth wouldn't move.

The queen sighed. "The paralysis will wear off by tomorrow. Until I decide what to do with you—and your treasonous behavior—you will live as a prisoner. I'll have Cato stay with you for a while. You can suffer in misery together for your twin ambitions."

Through the broken glass wall, Farren sensed movement.

Beyond the gryphon yard, outside the mews, the brilliant spheres of gryphon minds lifted into the air. Eralius and the rest of Delphi's children...even Elya had joined them, well enough to fly now after a short time in the Healing Caves. Torch's exultation washed through her and Naronimus, and Torch sent her one last kiss of love. Her throat tightened as they soared over the fortress wall, hidden from sight by Thella's magic, and her runebond with Torch slid closed.

He was safe. The others were all safe.

Naronimus felt the tension leave her, and gave a great, bellowing sigh. Something warm and wet slid down her cheek.

"Take them to the tower," the queen barked.

The guards dragged Farren and the prince up with rough hands. Beneath the numbness of her skin, Farren nearly glowed, and she didn't care as the guards hauled her out of the atrium and up the winding stairwell to her prison.

They were free. At last.

# FORTY-SEVEN

Pain washed over Farren from a thousand different places when she woke. The guards had dropped her on the prison floor the night before, cursing her a few dozen times while their fists pummeled her to the black of unconsciousness. Cato had shouted and thrashed against his chain until his voice had gone hoarse.

She cracked open puffy, sore eyes. Her prison appeared to be a circular room, the wall around it rising halfway to the ceiling. Above the wall, autumn sun lent a bare breath of warmth to the misty air that trembled from the pound of the Alidonian Falls. Stark claw marks twisted into the damp gray stone of the round wall, and holes pocked the stone where it had crumbled and given way to gouging. Rusted metal stakes drove into the stone floor every six feet, anchoring serpentine chains. Along the edges of the room, feathers scattered among petrified feces and clumps of fur, and Farren caught the putrid whiff of decay.

She could move, a little, and the chain from her shackle rattled as she did. Her skin tingled from the remnants of poison, but she found sitting to be tolerable.

"You're alive," a voice said in relief. Another chain scraped on the stone as someone near her moved.

Farren turned, grimacing as pain burned along her abdomen. Cato sat ten feet from her, his ankle shackled to the floor, and his chain stretched to its fullest length from where it was anchored across the room.

"I thought you might be dead," he added, his voice scratchy. A bruise purpled his cheek, and dried blood smeared over split knuckles.

"No such luck," Farren said, or tried to say, but her mouth was swollen. One of her teeth wobbled as her tongue moved.

"I've asked for a healer to come. And some water. Your leg doesn't look good."

Farren eyed it. The back of her calf was a mess of lacerated meat. Skin hung in tatters, and blood covered it all. The pain of it was a steady roar above all the other pains.

"It needs to be sewn," she said.

"It needs more than a bit of thread and a needle." He gestured to her. "Come closer. I can wrap it for now."

With great care, she repositioned herself to face him and scooched closer while he tore a long strip off his chiton. By the time she reached him, she had a bit of chain to spare.

A shaft of light fell over Cato as he worked, the skin painting on his arms gleaming as he wrapped the cloth around and around her leg. Despite the wreck of skin and muscle, his hands were deft and careful, though his expression was pale. She clenched her jaw and closed her eyes, willing the light from the wall opening to lend heat to her body.

"You think they will do it?" she asked. "Send a healer? Water?" If not, they might get enough water from the walls, if they spent all day licking them. Perhaps they could chew the moss growing in between the stones for sustenance.

The thought almost made her laugh, but a sob hitched in her throat.

"They won't let us die up here," Cato said, his voice grave. "They would've killed us by now if they wished."

"Will they feed us? We can survive weeks without food."

Cato knotted the fabric. "It's better not to think about hunger. It'll only make it worse."

He was right. She shouldn't think about her thirst or her empty stomach. Nor should she think too closely about the blood on her hands, the blood crusting her nose and mouth, or on whether or not she regretted what she did. The slaughter. The prison. The fact that she would never see Torch again or her family.

Her family. She had to get them a message, warn them of the coming Emptiness.

Without moving, Farren stretched her mind, which ached as her muscles did after sparring for too long. She found the nearest free-flying hawk out in the city and called it to her. Within a few moments, the hawk landed gracefully on the wall ledge.

*Can you fly north to Capai?* Farren sent the hawk an image of her village, then an image of her father. *Find him, and tell him the Emptiness is coming. That they must flee east or south.*

*The Emptiness?*

She sent him an image of Mellion, precious Mellion who had been caught by the Emptiness, by the deadly flower Isander had left in the mountains.

The hawk flapped its wings, realizing that the word meant a sort of death. *The Emptiness is coming*, the bird repeated, bobbing its head. *They must flee. South. East.*

*Very good*, Farren said. *He will give you a fat mouse when you arrive.*

To bolster her impression, she sent an image of her father once more, their house and mews, and a big juicy mouse.

The hawk flew off immediately, and Farren closed the runebond. She trusted her father to tell Keira. He would believe her words, and would tell the others in the village the news.

"What were you doing?" Cato asked, a mere murmur that reminded her of how close he sat.

"Sending a message to my family."

Cato gave her a long look. "Where will they go?"

"Hopefully toward the Blades. Or south to Lidellia."

They would be safe in those places. At least for a time. Assuming that the Emptiness wouldn't reach her family before her message did.

"We should send a message to Camilla," Cato said.

Taking a shuddering breath, Farren reached her mind out to Naronimus.

His body ached much like hers. Muta had drugged him heavily to treat his wounds.

*Did he look at your wing?* Farren asked.

*Broken*, Naronimus replied, dizzy.

She didn't wish for him to dwell on the fact that he might not be able to fly again.

*I am in the tower*, Farren said. *Cato is with me.*

*I know*, the gryphon said. *It gets cold up there at nights, even with fur and feather.*

*Are you worried about me?*

Something akin to amusement twirled into their runebond. *Hardly. If I survived up there, so can you.*

His belief in her was touching. *Tell Camilla we are alive. Tell her not to worry.*

*She is here now*, he said. *Tending my fire. Chattering and chattering. She doesn't like the guards.*

*The guards?*

*Four inside with me. Four outside my doors. An irony,* Naronimus said, *since it would take little effort to move them away.*

*Even while poisoned?* Farren asked.

*They can't keep me like this forever.*

Farren pursed her lips. *Tell Camilla I said to close your mind and get some rest.*

*I'll be forced to rest for the remainder of my miserable life,* he said, his snide tone still clinging on through his drugged haze.

*At least we will be miserable together,* she said.

He didn't have anything nasty to say to that, which seemed like a good thing. She closed their runebond so he could rest.

Hadn't it been strange before, when she had been able to send a single impression to him and Torch simultaneously? It felt so different and stretched her mind to the point of pain...but something about it had been right. Fitting. As if that is what she was meant to do.

The hair on her arms rose as she recalled it. She had been one with them, completely trusting them as they trusted her. Was that what Cato meant when he said gryphons and humans were meant to be together?

"Cato?"

"Hm?"

"What if Naronimus can't fly again?"

The prince frowned and looked at his bloodied knuckles. "I don't know. But whatever happens...I'll be here with him."

"*We'll* be here with him," Farren corrected. "And if there's ever another chance at freeing him, I will take it."

"I think you had a hard knock to your head."

"I'm serious, Cato."

He gave her a perplexed look. "I see that. I'm just wondering how it would all work with us being in chains."

Farren sighed. "Something strange happened earlier."

"The whole thing was strange and awful, Farren—"

She touched his arm, stopping him. "This wasn't awful. It w as...different. When the queen brought Naronimus down, I was runebonded with Torch. And then, my mind split. I could connect with both of them at the same time."

The prince's mouth fell open. "What?"

"I-I thought maybe it was normal, just my runeskill getting stronger. I was hoping you might know more about it... Maybe you read about it in your books?"

He studied her for a long, silent moment, and she could tell his mind worked furiously at something.

"That's what I felt," he finally said. "After we fell, I was with Naronimus. I thought I could feel you with him, but I could somehow feel Torch too, through Naronimus's mind. There was this incredible feeling of warmth and—" He paused, his cheeks darkening, but a light shone in his eyes. "And a healing sort of love. How did you do it?"

"I don't know. It happened when I needed to be with them both at once."

"I need to write this down," Cato said, fidgeting with his chiton. "I've never heard of this happening to someone, except—" He shook his head. "It's just impossible."

"It happened, Cato."

Now he looked at her as if she were a puzzle to solve. And there was another mystery she couldn't figure out: why Isander's Emptiness hadn't affected her the way it did every other living thing. But she wasn't yet ready to tell Cato, to unravel the mess of all that had happened between her and the elder prince.

A sudden scraping at the wall caused them both to jolt. A wind gusted across the tower room, musty with the scent of gryphon.

"Thella?" Cato said, and in a flash, Thella appeared at the wall, her talons gouging the ledge as she leapt from it to the floor. Compared to Naronimus, Thella was small and lithe, easily fitting into the opening over the half-wall.

Cato went to the gryphon and put a hand on her chest, grinning wildly as he looked up at her.

*Thella, you're still here*? Farren asked the gryphon.

The young gryphon, as composed as ever, folded her wings before sitting. *I am glad you are still alive, Farren, although I hate to see you trapped up here. I chose to stay in the Healing Caves, hidden.*

*You're hiding from the queen? Does anyone else know you're here*?

Farren could tell the gryphon also spoke to Cato, so each impression took a few moments to come through. *Only you, Cato, and Camilla know.*

*And the others are all safely away*?

Thella sent her a trickle of reassurance. *They left the city safely. I went with them for miles before heading back. They fly for the Blades.*

*How did you know to wait for the others to be released*? Farren asked, recalling that Thella, Delphi, and Torch had circled overhead before the last gryphons were freed.

*Camilla told us what was happening. She was letting the last of them out, but a few recruits tried to stop her. Then the guards came and helped her. They told everyone it was the queen's orders.*

*Naronimus's magic*, Farren explained. *She really was trying to help.*

*She wanted me to tell you that she understands why you released us. She knows what it is like to be trapped.*

Farren rubbed her chest, which had begun to ache.

Thella's calm thoughts continued coming through their runebond. *She said thank you for showing her how strong she had to be to change things.*

*I'm glad she didn't suffer for her choice*, Farren said, thinking of all the choices she had made. The choice to leave her brother unattended at a festival. The choice to leave him once more after his accident, to hide away in the Kithyrian Mountains, punishing herself instead of mending the rift between herself and her family.

*Just don't regret this that you have done*, Thella said. *You have given us the option of freedom, and I never realized how important it was.*

A vibrant impression streaked through the runebond. The last of the queen's gryphons bounded out the door of the mews and splayed eager wings, running in short bursts of speed until their feathers caught the air. The gryphons had never been as close to one another as they were at that moment, urging each other on, dreaming of a new place where they could be safe and happy. No more chains, stone walls, or doors. No more being forced to mate with other gryphons, urged to use magic for others, or being trapped inside the yard cage. They would travel to the Blades and sleep in caves as their parents and grandparents had, drink from fresh springs, and hunt along the steep cliffs of the mountains. They would find other gryphons, and learn to live as they had before being captured by humans.

Life had never felt more vital or so full of possibility.

*Thank you for that*, Farren told Thella. *I needed it.*

*Anytime*, Thella responded. *I will bide my time in the caves.*

*Stay safe. Do not let yourself be seen or scented. The coyotes are keen.*

*There are far fewer of them, thanks to you.*

*Prince Cato helped me. And Torch.*

Yes, Thella said. *Delphi is very proud of him.*

*For...killing?*

*For staying loyal and protecting his family. Just as you would for him.*

Farren rubbed at her eyes, forgetting the blood on her hands. The runebond closed, and Cato brushed his palm along Thella's beak as he said goodbye. The gryphon vanished, and she only heard the scrape of talons on stone and the whisper of wings against wind as she flew away.

# FORTY-EIGHT

A HEALER CAME LATER that day and tended to their wounds. Farren tried not to cry out as the healer flushed her wounded leg and sutured it.

"Do you have something to give her for the pain?" Cato asked, crouching close while the healer worked.

The healer, starkly pale against the rich scarlet robe, gave the prince a firm look. "I'm afraid not, Your Highness."

Cato glared, but Farren spoke up before he could argue with the woman. "It's fine, Cato. I can handle the pain."

The prince shook his head. "You could at least give her a sleeping draught."

The healer's lips flattened. "I have two dozen wounded soldiers to tend to already, thanks to you two and those wretched gryphons. Some of them may not make it. There's hardly enough medicine to spare as it is. You should be glad I brought the poultice. Without it, her wound would rot and fester, which some might say she deserved."

With that, the healer whisked out of the chamber and the door slammed behind her. Cato muttered an oath.

The wound on her leg burned despite the fresh wrappings. Still, it looked a sight better than before.

"Help me up," she said to Cato.

He pulled her up easily and offered a shoulder for her to lean on. They walked to the wall ledge together, their chains clinking as they snaked along the floor.

Farren planted her hands on the mist-dampened ledge. Looking out at the wide-open space was like opening her eyes after a long, shadowy sleep. She swayed, breath puffing in the high brisk air, and curled her fingers around the stone, digging into it as a hawk would while surveying its home.

Brown-gold land and crystal water stretched in every direction, and the sky expanded in an upward sweep of cerulean. To the east and west of the River Kithyria lay Malodai, ringed by a great wall that glinted in the morning sun. Southward, the falls plummeted to the pool far below.

"Do you think he's out there?" she asked.

"I don't think he would come back to the fortress after we found out what he did."

"Would he care, with us imprisoned?"

Cato ran a hand over his face. He smelled of sweat and ink and gryphon musk. "I will speak to my mother, if I ever get out of here. She has to understand what he did. That he might be working with the Runeless Sect. If I can just get solid proof of it..."

Farren didn't voice her doubt. The queen was stubborn and blind. Would Isander learn how to remove the runeskills from the Runeless? How many more Emptied statues would be made while he tried?

It was sickening to think of all the things she had done with him—all the moments when they had felt connected, intimate—and to know what he truly was. Worse yet, that he had been the one to reveal the Commander to her. Something that was a part of her, and he had somehow seen it. He had believed in her.

She stared at the dried, tacky blood on her hands, remembering how confident she had felt while fighting the guards. How powerful and desperate. Those feelings hadn't left entirely. The more she focused on them, the more they sparked to life once more.

And yet... Two dozen guards wounded. She wasn't sure she wanted to know how many were dead, how many had died by her hands or by Torch's magic. The gryphons had to be freed. She only wished it could've been done with less sacrifice.

She pressed her hands into her chest. Cato gazed at the river as he leaned on the ledge, his brows drawn. The healer had tended to a few of his cuts and a nasty bruise around his shackled ankle, as if he had tugged and yanked against the chain.

"Why did you try to stop the guards from hurting me?" she asked.

He gave her a puzzled glance. "They were pummeling you like a sack of hay, Farren."

"I wouldn't have thought you'd mind them punishing me after everything I've done."

His jaw flexed and he gripped the stone ledge. "I was just as much to blame for killing guards as you were. Yet they didn't touch me once we were put up here."

"I'm not certain if I would've made it through without you," Farren said. "And even though we weren't able to help Naronimus, I think we did a good deal just by trying. You changed your mind and..." Farren groped for the words to explain some of the swirling mess inside of her. "I'm grateful for it."

"I was wrong, Farren. I never thought my mother would be like that...just like Uncle Anaxis. When I saw the way Naronimus had been treated... Something in me just snapped. I realized that I had it all wrong, that I was living a delusion. A hopeful child wishing his mother was another person entirely." He huffed and dug a hand through his dark locks. "I... I owe you an apology for..."

"For being a pain in the rump?" She crooked a brow at him.

He smiled lightly and looked down. "For being blind. And not listening very well."

Farren licked her lips and tasted blood. "I only hope you listened when I told you that all of Malodai needs you."

"I did," he said quietly, looking out toward the city.

"Then you know what we need to do now?"

"Find Isander," Cato said, squinting in the light.

"Find Isander," Farren repeated. "And stop him from hurting anyone else." She would do whatever she could to make it happen—even groveling before the queen and playing puppet to her master.

"There's only one problem. We're chained up here."

Farren grinned and clasped the wet wall, leaning out farther so she could see more of the vine-covered city. "Lucky for you, we have many feathered friends."

"Thella? But I wouldn't want to risk her being found, or worse, shot out of the sky—"

"Look." Farren pointed to a swath of grey birds dancing over Malodai.

"Are those pigeons?"

"They can help us. And maybe Thella can, too. Safely," she added. "And Naronimus, if we can convince him."

Cato scratched his stubbled cheek. "I'm not sure how I can help with any of it."

Farren studied his profile, so similar to Isander's, and yet different. More pensive, more worried, and far less confident. But what lay beneath that was a loyalty and strength she had only glimpsed these past weeks. She wouldn't forget how he had fought to free Naronimus, no matter how difficult his sword had been to lift.

She turned her gaze away. "I'm sure you will think of a way."

And then she called out to the flock of pigeons and sent them one after another down to the streets, each with an impression of Isander's face.

*Find him. Follow him. Then come back to me.*

Thank you for reading Of Gryphons and Runes (Book 1 of Enchantress Rising Trilogy)! If you enjoyed it, I would love if you left a review on your favorite bookish site. While I'm working on Book 2, turn the page for a sneak peek of the prequel novella, The Gryphon Key, which is a story of how Anaxis' wife, Immenia, takes charge of her own life.

# SNEAK PEEK: THE GRYPHON KEY

## ONE

IMMENIA'S HEART SLOWED AS the thrumming call of pond peepers filled the vast ceiling of her open bedchamber. Three pools of water surrounded Immenia's bed, separated by narrow walkways limned in the golden light of beeswax candles. Her frogs perched on dozens of white-flowered lilies, sentinels of the night. It was a comfort knowing they were just a mind-touch away, that they looked into the dark to sense things that she could not in the throes of her nightmares.

Beyond the fluted columns of her chamber, Immenia peered into the prickly gardens of her family's villa, where the moonlight fell cool and quiet. No walls stood between the gardens and the raised stone platform of her chamber. As a child, Immenia had preferred the openness of it, where she could live close to her rune animals, with only a ceiling to keep out the rain and a wall against the back of her bed holding the door that led into her parent's home. It hadn't felt much like Immenia's home since she had been married off, and her aging parents never ceased to remind her of the fact that she was a *guest* living there, despite the fact that it had been her childhood home.

Immenia touched her inner wrist, where a frog runemark was imprinted into her skin with ink—a symbol written there at her birth that declared her runeskill with frogs. It wasn't the strongest of runeskills to be blessed with by the Enchanters who had made their world, but it was one she had grown to embrace.

She focused on an arrow frog that clung to one of the pillars framing her room, sensing its mind like a door. Opening the door with her mind, their telepathic runebond strung between them, and the frog's warm wash of contentment spilled into Immenia.

*Anything?* Immenia asked him with a short inquiring impression.

The long, low thrum of its croaks grew bolder, pressing at the quiet.

*He has not come*, he said, sending her an image of the empty gardens.

The tension in her belly unspooled. She thanked the frog and closed her eyes, trying to think of beautiful things to lull her into a dream. When her mind went to dark places—the ones where her husband touched her, used her, hurt her—she pulled back, so far that her mind went numbly into the chorus of frogs reverberating through the chamber. She nestled in it. She could breathe. Be safe. And just...be.

But he hadn't visited in weeks, and she knew that he would be coming soon. Her heart beat a familiar rhythm of dread, a painful thump-thump, thump-thump that made her ache to escape further than her family's villa.

At least she had broken free of the fortress. He had allowed her that one small thing, if nothing else. The openness of her villa chamber, the cherished memories of her childhood in every sun-washed nook and cranny, were a far cry from the tomb-like walls of Alidonia.

A small part of her hoped fervently that perhaps he had finally given up. Perhaps he'd accepted that she no longer loved him, that even if he owned her body, he could never own her rune-made soul. She wanted desperately for it to end; she dreamed of the days she could laugh freely, of the nights she could sleep deeply, without fear. Enchanters, but she had tried so many times to make those dreams a reality.

A splash resounded nearby. Probably one of the green-speckled frogs going for a midnight dip. They liked to feel the water against their skin, and to stretch their long legs hard against it as they dove through the feathery reeds at the bottom.

Immenia, unable to sleep, turned onto her side, wincing at the familiar pain that lanced through her shoulder—an old wound from when she had tried to protect her son from harm and her husband had wrenched it. She closed her eyes and reached out to the frog, longing to feel what it felt.

As their minds runebonded, panic surged into her. Immenia gasped and lurched forward as something wrapped her torso and squeezed. She clutched at her body, realizing that the feeling was coming from her frog and there was no way to stop it but to close her runebond, abandoning the frog to a death without comfort. She sucked in a breath, and her mind cleared for a moment as air filled her lungs.

The water in the pool to her right thrashed. The frogs around it fell quiet, and Immenia could see nothing beneath the surface. Her runebond with the frightened frog lay open, bare. Something squeezed the life from him, and his heart slowed, slowed, until it thudded like a fatal drum. Bum. Bum. Bum. A pause. With his stunned and fading mind, the frog could do nothing to stop its encroaching death.

Immenia dropped out of her bed, knees clapping painfully onto the stone floor. She reached a hand into the pool and grappled wildly among the slippery tendrils of plants.

*Where are you*, she cried out to her frog, willing her desperation to keep the frog from death's grip.

Nothing answered, and the coldness that severed her runebond to the frog was final. There was no going back to him.

Her hand touched something cool and ridged. Scales. Without thinking, she yanked it out and tossed it onto the flagstones. A blue-black snake writhed in apparent surprise, dropping the frog before it slithered away. Immenia followed it with her eyes, wishing, not for the first time, that she had a knife. Knowing that if she didn't kill it, it would keep coming back to hunt her frogs. To hunt her.

Just like *he* did.

Immenia pulled away from the water and crawled to the edge of her chamber, where the raised stone floor dropped away into the endless gardens. She vomited into the nearest rose hedge and lay back against a hard column, her pulse racing.

Tomorrow. Tomorrow, she would buy a new knife. It would have to be a different knife than all those before, so Anaxis and his spies would never find it.

**FIND OUT WHAT IMMENIA DOES IN THE GRYPHON KEY, A NOVELLA EXCLUSIVE TO E.A. BURNETT'S NEWSLETTER. SIGN UP AT WWW.EABURNETT.COM.**

## ACKNOWLEDGEMENTS

I have so many people to thank for this work, which took three and a half years to get into reader hands. I was afraid to endeavor on a series, but I'm glad I forced myself to do it. I learned an amazing amount about my process and craft along this arduous journey.

I owe a huge thank you to my developmental editor, Fiona McLaren. Farren Blackburn's story was in a much different place then, and she helped me see major revisions the story needed. Thank you to my many beta readers, Mary McCracken, Allie Burnett, Christina Davis, and Isabelle Felix. Even though most of you didn't enjoy Farren's story, you all provided invaluable feedback. Also thanks to Sharon from Devil in the Details, my line editor, who sorted my (probably insane) issue with commas. Many thanks and love to Christina Davis, fellow fantasy author. I have learned a lot from her, and loved our writing sessions together.

Great thanks to the indie author community. The support and value I glean from the community every day is truly remarkable—you all are a strong, empathetic, and intelligent group.

To my family and friends—thank you for being there. Thank you for asking about my work and encouraging me when I most needed it.

Lastly—and most importantly—I owe an enormous thanks to my readers. You are why I write. Thank you for your patience and belief in me.

## About E.A. Burnett

E.A. Burnett is an epic fantasy author who writes evocative tales set in lush worlds full of magic, animals, and strong female protagonists. She began her first novel in middle school, with her youngest sister as her primary audience, and hasn't stopped writing since. Today, Burnett lives in the beautiful forests of Ohio with her husband, two little people, two corn snakes, and two rambunctious Labradors.

Visit her at eaburnett.com, on Instagram (eaburnett_author) or Facebook (eaburnett.author)

www.ingramcontent.com/pod-product-compliance
Lightning Source LLC
Chambersburg PA
CBHW020307030826
48979CB00029B/2285/J
* 9 7 9 8 9 8 9 9 7 1 6 3 3 *